ANNO
DRACULA
1999
DAIKAIJU

KIM NEWMAN

TITAN BOOKS

KIM NEWMAN
ANNO DRACULA 1999 DAIKAIJU

Print edition ISBN: 9781785658860
E-book edition ISBN: 9781785658877

Published by Titan Books
A division of Titan Publishing Group Ltd
144 Southwark Street, London SE1 0UP

First edition: October 2019
1 2 3 4 5 6 7 8 9 10

This is a work of fiction. Names, characters, places, and incidents either are the product of the author's imagination or are used fictitiously, and any resemblance to actual persons, living or dead, business establishments, events, or locales is entirely coincidental. The publisher does not have any control over and does not assume any responsibility for author or third-party websites or their content.

A CIP catalogue record for this title is available from the British Library.

Printed and bound by CPI Group (UK) Ltd, Croydon CR0 4YY

What did you think of this book? We love to hear from our readers.
Please email us at: readerfeedback@titanemail.com,
or write to us at the above address.

To receive advance information, news, competitions, and exclusive Titan offers online, please register as a member by clicking the 'sign up' button on our website
www.titanbooks.com

For Sean Hogan

Rekishi wa nandomonandomo shizen ga ningen
no oroka-sa o shiteki suru hōhō o shimeshite imasu.

Blue Öyster Cult

MR RICHARD JEPERSON... PLUS ONE
THE DIOGENES CLUB,
LONDON SW1Y 5AH
UNITED KINGDOM

MISS CHRISTINA LIGHT REQUESTS THE PLEASURE
OF YOUR COMPANY TO SEE IN THE NEW MILLENNIUM.

AT DAIKAIJU PLAZA, CASAMASSIMA BAY,
TOKYO, JAPAN.

DECEMBER 31ST, 1999 – DUSK TILL DAWN.

SIGNIFICANT ANNOUNCEMENTS WILL BE MADE.
DRESS CODE: CYBERFORMAL.
INVITATION NOT TRANSFERABLE.

RSVP.

Miss Mouse, this means you...

DECEMBER 31, 1999

UNKNOWN MALE – RICHARD JEPERSON (GEIST 97)

The sky above the city was the colour of arterial blood splashed across a shower curtain.

Nightfall in the Land of the Rising Sun.

Richard was in downtown Tokyo.

One song shrilled from every speaker. A remix of Prince's '1999' by the girl group Cham-Cham. The single might as well have been pressed on tissue paper. Its zeitgeist window was an arrow-slit. The multi-tracked rinky-dink organ riff made his fillings throb.

Lu lu too sousand zeiro zeiro Pātī wa owari – oops! – jikan ga nai…

Holograms of the flounce-sleeved bubblegum trio wavered above mini projectors concealed in the oddest places. Drinking fountains, food stall hotplates, rubbish bins. Two phantom soprani and a vampire contralto. Miniature dancing ghosts.

Kon'ya wa pātī siyou 1999 fuu ni…

Mima, the vam in Cham-Cham, was a crossover artist. Her pearly fangs were *kawaii* – cute. Many warm girls (and not a few boys) wore plastic choppers and purple wigs to copy her. She started underground in the bloodletting bars of the Bund, then mainstreamed into the warm wide world. The pretty, unthreatening face of Asian vampirism. Poster child for the handover. In peppy public service ads underwritten by Red Label Sprünt, Mima ran through FAQs with a funky *anime* bat. 'Give you strawberry kisses when the Wall comes down,' she sang. That sawtooth smile wasn't wholly reassuring.

The song would get heavy play at Christina Light's party. Blatant was 'in' this season. Every season, really. Cham-Cham '1999' was as inevitable as 'Auld Lang Syne'. Should Richard have Nezumi commandeer the

3

karaoke mike and warble 'Three Wheels on My Wagon' till dawn? It would not be worth the diplomatic fallout. The Diogenes Club didn't want to have to explain itself to Peter Mandelson. The Prime Minion could turn into fog and seep through keyholes.

A velvet rope hung across the footpath to the checkpoint. Security measures were in place until midnight.

A *yōkai* steward waddled over to inspect invitations.

'Richard Jeperson,' he declared. 'I'm on the list. I'm on a lot of lists. Best Dressed, Most Eligible, Most Likely To...'

Extra eyes glinted in the gatekeeper's cheek-folds, like threepenny bits stuck in a fleshy pudding. The sexless goblin wore an English/Japanese nametag. Hyakume/百目. It shook a glitchy electronic clipboard. *Kanji* scrolled across greenscreen, fast as the credits of an overrunning live soap.

The back of Richard's mind tickled.

One of those! A brain peeper.

More reliable than a photoelectric reader.

The steward accepted his *verites*.

Nezumi, his plus one, also passed muster.

The rope was lifted and they joined the next queue for the Gate. Though they didn't need to show passports, they were leaving Japan. The Bund, as any fule kno, was vampire territory. Until the handover.

Here be *monsters*.

Of course, *everywhere* be monsters. That was the twentieth century for you.

The Wall encircled the enclave, a relic of less tolerant times. Sniper towers repurposed as snooper towers. Swivelling cameras scanned the crowd for mischief.

Decapitated triffids guarded the Gate. *Kadomatsu*. Strawbound bamboo sheaves. Temporary homes for harvest spirits, to be burned on January 7 freeing the appeased gremlins. A more uplifting end to the festive season than leaving a needle-shedding fir tree on the pavement for the Chelsea bin men.

The Bund was a temporary home for less airy creatures.

At midnight, the hundred years were up. The Treaty of Light expired. Christina Light – formally, the Princess Casamassima – was an exponent of the grand gesture. Her first idea was to blow up the Wall as the chimes sounded, but advisors suggested she *not* set off explosives at the height of a city-wide party. Demolition was due to begin next Tuesday, handled by professionals more concerned with job safety than staging spectacle for TV news.

Richard saw stencilled human blast-shadows at the base of the Wall, a fools' dance amid a swarm of dayglo graffiti.

One shadowman moved, detached from his conga line, and scaled the brickwork. He was not ominous street art, but a two-dimensional vampire.

Only in Japan…

The Wall was in poor shape. Funds for maintenance must have been hard to justify these last few years. Christina Light had already arranged a promotional tie-up with Sprünt GmbH to sell souvenir bricks. The energy drink came in blue and red cartons, with different additives for warm and vampire palates. All over the world, Blue Label Sprünt was a gold-mine and Red Label a loss-leader. Richard doubted gumming chunks of brick to Red Label cartons would change that, but the one-time socialist firebrand had a gift for turning a profit from every little thing.

Handy right now.

This bash must be costing Light Industries a packet. The millimetre-thick invitations had gilt edging and an inset microchip. They doubled as phone cards and trebled as tracer bugs. Disabling the chip voided the invite. His was going into the nearest flush toilet as soon as he was accredited at the bar.

Before the Gate, they had to submit to a pat-down.

Nezumi unslung her portable poster tube and handed it over. A security flathead popped the stopper to peep inside. The tube was returned without comment. Nezumi shouldered it like a rifle. It wouldn't be the strangest bit of kit waved through tonight.

The flathead assessed the white-haired girl. Him: wide-shouldered, sharkskin suit. Armpit bulge, curly wire earplug. Her: slight, school uniform. Skirt, blazer, boater, knee-socks.

Richard knew who his money was on in a scrap.

A long shadow fell across the rope.

'Voltan,' declared a one-eyed elder. 'Aside, vassal. I've urgent business within.'

He sounded as if he'd smoked fifty gaspers a day since Mr Benson copped off with Miss Hedges.

Hyakume waved its e-board. Flatheads scratched holsters.

From under his cloak, Voltan fished out a laminate on a lanyard.

The goblin's face-folds stretched tight. Voltan's eye roamed.

Forged invitations to the Light Industries *mireniamu* party were circulating. Bootleg chips held up for twenty minutes before burning out. A thousand yen in the Chatsubo Bar.

No wonder the Princess had a mindworm on the Gate.

Hyakume farted contemptuously around its lesser eyes. The official didn't care if Voltan was Count Chocula or the Duke of Earl. It knew a chancer with a snide invite when he brainscanned one.

The elder drew up to his full height – eighteen inches of the tally were stack heels and tall hat – and boomed, 'Don't you know who I am?'

Hyakume was unimpressed. Its wattle sacs inflated.

'That question has two possible answers, chum,' Richard interpreted. 'You wouldn't like either of 'em.'

Voltan's mouth gaped. He had top and bottom fangs but no other teeth.

He fixed his cold eyes on Richard.

Nezumi angled her poster tube, declaring that he was under her protection.

Venturing into v-territory, it made sense to bring a vampire of his own – or at least, one sponsored by the Diogenes Club. Nezumi embodied school spirit. Big on not letting the side down. If provoked, his *yojimba* was a lovely little mover. Mistress of the Six Painless But Fatal Cuts.

'I have been vilely insulted,' said Voltan. 'The Hunchback shall hear of this!'

Richard was with British Intelligence. His calling was to be well-informed. He could rattle off the dirt on most of the world's rascals. He knew Voltan's record. 1945: arrested by Occupation Authorities in

Bucharest for selling adulterated blood products. 1973: cashiered from the Mexican National Guard for malfeasance. But he had no clue who this Hunchback was when he was at home.

Nezumi's thumb squeezed the top of the tube.

Voltan's face darkened. Stiff hair crept across his cheeks.

He was holding up a queue. Intolerable in Japan. Shaven-headed, saffron-sashed functionaries with fighting poles chivvied him off the red carpet.

'You've not heard the last of this,' Voltan ranted.

Nezumi solemnly waved a bye-bye at the elder she hadn't had to kill.

Voltan was wrong. This *was* the last they'd hear of him.

Tomorrow would be a shiny new millennium. Relics like Mr Tall and Shouty – and his bloody Hunchback – would get stuffed head-first into Trotsky's Dustbin of History. On top of Comrade Trotsky, come to think of it. And skiffle. That was never coming back. Or little blue bags of salt in potato crisps.

Richard had a sympathy twinge for Voltan, stuck behind the rope while the Space Ark lifted off without him. The elder hobbled away.

Sometimes, Richard felt close to the Trotsky Bin himself.

Never more so than tonight, with the century's expiration stamp flashing everywhere. Digital displays counted down. Retro clocks ticked on.

At midnight, *hana-bi* – fireworks!

UNKNOWN FEMALE – NEZUMI (MOUSE)

'Going home for the holidays?'

An innocent enough question, asked by dorm-mates when they saw her packing.

Nezumi replied – honestly – that she couldn't say. Girls giggled at her spaciness then remembered she was a thousand years old and stopped.

Her warm friends were a tiny bit afraid of her.

Sad, but she was used to it.

This was the holidays and she was in Japan, where – *more* than a thousand years ago – she was born.

Was she home?

Words lost meaning over time. Faded *kanji* looked like splotches.

Home.

Country.

Nezumi was last here just after the War.

Another splotch word.

War.

Now, that meant the Second World War.

You'd think one world war would be enough, but no, people had to have another. Maybe world wars were like sweets. You can't have only one. Even if they're bad for you.

Vampires knew the lure of things that were bad for you.

Still, 'the War' had meant the Second World War for over twice as long as it had meant the First World War. That had to be progress.

Then again, Mr Jeperson said 'the double Ws' weren't the wars that counted.

There had been others, which few who didn't fight in even noticed.

She still served.

Her principal in 1945 was Mr Edwin Winthrop, another Man From the Diogenes Club. A British agent had disappeared while looking for Dr Jogoro Komoda, code-named the Key Man. In Europe, Russia and America competed to net the 'best' Nazi mad scientists. The Western Allies had a freer run at Japan's von Brauns and Merkwerdichliebes.

Tracts of the city were burned ruins. GIs swarmed through bathhouses and gaming parlours. Japanese who'd only heard about Hiroshima and Nagasaki didn't fully understand why their indomitable fortress nation had surrendered to barbarians. Tokyo had been bombed and the Emperor didn't give in. Why was this different? Only first-hand witnesses knew the world had changed.

A defeated people saw Nezumi as a traitor before they saw her as a vampire.

The agent was found folded into a cupboard, eye sockets empty, mouth open wide enough to fit in a coconut. Dr Komoda, a surgeon who turned mutilated soldiers and captive vampires into living weapons, surrendered to the Americans. Nezumi supposed he continued his programme under new sponsorship. The War was over, so his operations couldn't be war crimes any more.

While in Tokyo, Mr Winthrop sent a note to the Princess Casamassima 'to check in after the fuss and bother'. She came to the Gate to thank him for the courtesy but did not invite him into the Bund. A famous beauty of the 1890s, the Princess seemed paper-thin to Nezumi, so pale as to be almost transparent. It hurt to look at her. One of her eyes was a red blood marble. She'd fought for her ground.

Professing loyalty to vampirekind rather than any nation, the Princess kept her head – in two meanings of the English phrase – throughout the War. It helped that she could claim to be more Italian than American. She was piqued that the Allies had incidentally fire-bombed her domain by scattering incendiaries over Tokyo.

Nezumi had heard many stories about the Princess. Few flattering, some amusing.

In 1895, Kate Reed – her sometime downstairs neighbour in the Holloway Road – shoved the incorporeal Princess into a wall of the Tower of London. It took ages to detach Princess from stone. Geneviève Dieudonné – another Associate Member – filed a report to the Diogenes Club, detailing how the Princess came to Tokyo on the cursed ship *Macedonia* and founded a refuge for persecuted vampires. Nezumi read Miss Dieudonné's hundred-year-old journal on the plane instead of watching the new *Star Wars* film on a seat-back screen.

It was telling that Geneviève chose to be an ocean away from Daikaiju Plaza tonight.

Would Nezumi meet the Princess? Probably not. She was a schoolgirl disguised as staff. Princesses seldom noticed staff. Or schoolgirls.

The Bund – a village inside a city – was strange, but she was used to strange.

She'd got into scrapes in England, but never felt particularly persecuted. Not for being a vampire, at least. When Britons insulted her, they more often called her 'Jap' than 'viper'. During the War, she carried papers to explain why she wasn't interned. Hitler said vampires were sub-humans. If the Bund were in Berlin, the Princess would definitely have lost her head. The Allies were obliged to stick up for the undead.

Romantic stories painted the Bund as a wartime nest of spies. That went back to *Casamassima*, a Hollywood film with Alan Ladd in a grubby mackintosh and Veronica Lake in a silver sheath dress. The Paramount backlot Bund offered slatted shadows, character actors with fake fangs, dry ice fog, patriotic musical numbers, and Chinese actors forced to play shrieking Japanese baddies.

In 1945, standing outside as Mr Winthrop met the Princess, Nezumi was not tempted to seek sanctuary within.

Now it was too late.

The Bund was nearly done with.

Most countries had established vampire communities. Transylvania was an undead state. Dracula's domain – even if the King of the Cats mostly lived in California. Not all *nosferatu* accepted John Alucard as Dracula Redivivus. Many refused to hail him as their liege. In Asia, natural subjects of the sleeping ice witch Yuki-Onna mostly acknowledged Christina Light as their effective regent.

Nezumi was *ronin* – a masterless samurai.

She served her own standard. Mr Jeperson understood that.

She could be asked but not told. She could be persuaded but not ordered.

She didn't care about politics, only about who got hurt.

RICHARD JEPERSON

There was little motor traffic in the Bund.

Road security couldn't have been more rigorous (and time-consuming) if engineers dismantled vehicles outside the Wall and carried the components between checkpoints for reassembly. Richard did not regret leaving the legation's tricked-out limo in Tokyo Proper.

A two-car cortège was held up at the Gate. A stretch hearse followed by a people mover. Transylvanian diplomatic pennants hung limp. A lantern-jawed chauffeur loomed over an intimidated non-*yōkai* steward. The people mover carried pallbearers in mourning clothes and white grieving masks. An elder vampire must be exhaling angry smoke on his bier.

Hyakume, senior to the warm woman, waddled over.

Would cars and bikes roar through the district after tonight? Dozens of shortcuts would suddenly be viable. Skirmishes were inevitable. Some on both sides of the Wall must nurture grudges. Riot was a risk. Such things happened, even in Britain. Highgate 1981. Whitby 1997. Wounds still bled.

The slow procession led to Casamassima Bay. The Princess had slapped her upscale name on the formerly low-rent Yōkai Town waterfront. Red carpet on the pavement marked the route. Wraiths in evening clothes drifted along. *Dress Code – cyberformal.*

For once, Richard felt underdressed. His outfit: rust-coloured frock coat with burnished gold frogging, crimson highwayman britches, oxblood elastic-sided knee-boots, shocking pink dress shirt, metallic finish waistcoat that'd set off an airport scanner, lilac gloves, black butterfly bow tie. No hat. No cane. No man-bag.

All around he saw posh frocks and silver antennae. Mirrorshades and fractal moiré cummerbunds. Robogauntlets – mailed fists with jewel knucks for the gent who wants to punch through steel plate. Serpentine elbow-length tinfoil sheaths with talons for the lady who knows how to scratch any itch.

Human billboards sported variant configurations of skull plugjack. Gummed-on mock-ups of implants liable to be painfully permanent when neural interfaces hit the civilian market. He wouldn't put it past the Princess to talk Apple, Samsung and Sunway Systems into subsidising her New Year ball as a promo showcase. All those eyes on Christina were valuable, justifying the buy-in. She had gone from anarchist to corporate figurehead in only a hundred years. The Light Channel commanded a global audience.

Nezumi flicked her fringe, indicating he should look over his shoulder. Richard glanced casually. A tall thin vampire woman walked behind them, stunning from the neck down in a white sleeveless Eiko Ishioka. She wore expensive digishades, probably following the stock market on one screen, watching a pre-release cut of next year's Best Picture on the other, with the real world in front of her reduced to a tiny inset image so she wouldn't bump into a lamp-post. The effect was finished by a bathing cap fissured like a swollen brain. A veiny ruby eye served as turban jewel, pinned to the puffy cerebellum.

The Orb was an Aum Draht symbol. The new-ish belief system had started in Japan and caught on in Silicon Valley and Points Cuckoo.

He was surprised the cult had recruited this adept.

Syrie Van Epp, the Iranian billionairess. An international *eminence mauve*. Wealthy and nuts enough to have her own space programme, an island hunting preserve stocked with athletic donors, and a seat at the long table when Vampire Masters of the Universe convened to carve up the next five hundred years of history. Her primary fortune, built on late Mr Van Epp's shipping line, was in freight transport, though her empire encompassed many, many other businesses. Strange to see her on foot. She owned fleets of vehicles.

She was a prime mover of Wings Over the World. The controversial charity organisation deployed prototype wondercraft to drought-, famine- or war-torn regions. Aid packages with strings attached might turn out as deleterious in the long run as any disaster. When Syrie's whirling saucers or swing-wing dropships showed up, populations learned to 'beware a Persian bearing gifts'.

In 1969, when Syrie was technically still warm, she'd had sex with Richard in the gondola of a hot-air balloon. He hadn't taken her post-coital murder attempt personally. Other fellows might have been miffed. Syrie hadn't acknowledged him the last few times they'd run into each other at Groover's or Guildhall. Mistresses of the Universe could be petty.

It was not his place to tell the eighth richest woman in the world her brain-bonnet looked ridiculous. Or that her pet church epitomised a poisonous crackpottery that crept out whenever centuries wore thin.

Aum Draht extremists committed crimes – assault, theft, murder – against victims they said weren't real. They saw the world as a computer simulacrum. Adepts were the only actuals. Everyone else was virtual. They were playing a game.

The Wire is watching went the mantra.

Other Aum Draht activities involved too-clever-by-half japery. Worms, bugs, and the like. Adepts weird-scienced the Millarca e-mail virus which infected one million computers worldwide, causing an estimated eighty million dollars' worth of damage. The cult's weedy keyboard interventions had muscular names like 'Project Madbomb' or 'the Shitzkrieg'. Richard had more respect for yobs who smashed up phone boxes. At least they got some exercise.

Syrie advanced with imperious dignity but tripped on a fold in the carpet. Richard offered a supportive shoulder. She wordlessly evaded his touch and regained her balance, focused on whatever her shades beamed into her brain.

Nezumi repressed a schoolgirl smirk at his rebuffed gallantry. She was up on club gossip.

Was Syrie glaring daggers through her gadget glasses? She swept off on five-inch heels.

Nezumi whistled 'Up, Up and Away in My Beautiful Balloon'. She was an imp sometimes.

Either Syrie was a new Aum Draht convert or making a calculated fashion statement in support of a dubious cause. Richard made a mental note to update her file. The Wire might be watching, but its database had nothing on the Club's cabinet full of scribbled-on envelopes, shirt-cuffs and beermats.

Tonight, Aum Draht promised e-pòcalypse. They probably hadn't been invited to the good parties. Adepts would ascend to a higher plane of the simulacrum. *Mlecchas* would be scrubbed, never to be retrieved from the junk folder.

Tomorrow, if mundane life went on as per usual, excuses would be trotted out. No, we meant the *true* millennium. The end of the year 2000. When 2001 was rung in, a fresh revelation would establish another near-off date of direness. 2012, most likely, when the (disputed) Aztec calendar ran out. Followed by another and another until (appropriately) the last syllable of recorded time.

In the end, some sandwich board-wearing doom-crier would be right. However, the pisshead in the Hand and Racket who always said tomorrow was Wednesday was a more reliable prophet. One night in seven, he was on the money.

UNKNOWN MALE – HAROLD TAKAHAMA

Hal's left hand *hurt* like a monumental motherfucker.

… as if gloved with honey and stuck in a nest of fire ants.

… as if white-hot pins were shoved under each fingernail.

… as if Thor were taking out an aeon of pent-up wrath, pounding on Hal's second-favourite jerking-off paw with Mighty Mjolnir!

… as if it just fucking *hurt*, okay!

… but when Hal looked, he didn't *have* a left hand.

Uh-oh, Spaghetti-Os!

Sticking out of his sleeve was a hand-shaped machine.

He held it up, feeling unexpected strain in his shoulder. Though no great weight, the gizmo was heavier than a regular hand. The skin sheath looked glassy, but might equally be clear plastic, carved crystal or fucking kryptonite. A rigid transparent shell enclosed a sealed drive. A microprocessor.

He might, at some point in the far future, appreciate the compact design.

Immediately, the prosthesis gave him too much grief to rate stars out of ten.

Flashing lights synchronised with pain waves.

He skinned back his shirt-cuff and found the join. A shiny chrome rim bolted to his wrist. His nerve endings were wired to live current.

In the smooth palm was a round metal grille.

The pain stopped. Thanks be to Christian Slater!

'You should be alert,' said a neutral voice.

His hand talked! When it spoke, the grille vibrated. Works flashed and clicked.

'What was that for, Cornholio?' Hal asked.

'Intense stimulation was necessary.'

'Next time, ask before turning the agonizer up to eleven.'

'Your instructions were implemented, Mr Zero.'

Hal had no idea who Mr Zero was or why the hand thought he was him.

'This unit is to be designated "Cornholio"? Confirm if so.'

Hal was tempted but held back. It might not do to piss off a 'unit' that could turn on the zap-juice any time.

Thinking back, he remembered only pain. 'Intense stimulation' was his robot hand's idea of an alarm clock – the cyberfiend's way of waking him up.

It worked. A jolt of Blue Label would do as well, though. If he ran into Mr Zero, Hal would impress that on his ass in no uncertain terms.

Mr Zero.

Sounded like the bad guy in a Japanese cartoon. A hundred-chapter *anime*, dubbed and distribbed to Saturday morning TV… not OAV *hentai* with penis tentacles and vagina dentata.

Hal was up on geek pop culture.

Coolio.

That'd set him up for a battle with Mr Zero. He had the tool.

One thing he knew about was breaking things with robot hands.

Some things he didn't know about were what he was doing and where he was.

Or, beyond his name, much of anything else. He was Hal. He knew that, or thought he did.

But who was Hal?

Nada.

He would have to get back to himself on that one.

He had zero recall of losing his flesh and blood hand. A circumstance that should have stuck in the mind.

The hand had called him 'Mr Zero'.

Was it right and Hal mistaken? He was Mr Zero, not Hal… uh, Hal Last-Name-on-the-Tip-of-His-Mind's-Tongue. Harold To-Be-Determined.

No, he was Mr Zero *and* Hal… Harold Takahama.

He was Japanese?

So why did he think of *anime* dubbed in English?

Oh, he was Japanese-*American*. From Ojai, California. As they said in his parents' house… *Ohayu*, California.

Maybe 'Mr Zero' was his username.

It was the kind of ident Hal Takahama would choose if he wanted to sound like an arch-nemesis.

Mr Zero. No, 3-2-Jun… Zero! Jun'ichi Zero.

'Operator is set as, ah, Jun Zero,' he told his hand. 'Confirm?'

'This unit can confirm,' it responded. 'Good evening, Jun Zero.'

That was settled.

He was at a workstation, sitting on a big rubber ball. Magazine ads said space hoppers on steroids were better for the spine than regular chairs. He couldn't get comfortable. He was in a large, windowless, low-ceilinged room with panel lighting. Cooling fans whirred. The air was dustless. Server banks hummed, cabinets bulky as 1950s refrigerators. The configuration was library-like. Narrow paths between stacks.

'Where am I?' he asked his hand.

Basic Question # 1.

'The Processor Room, Floor 44 of the Daikaiju Building, Casamassima Bay. A self-governing district within the Tokyo Metropolis.'

'Japan?'

'Legally, no. Geographically, yes.'

On the desktop were items of flair, the strictly controlled junk corporations allowed – nay, insisted – drones deploy to personalise workspace. Porcelain eggs in china lattice nests. A super-deformed Adam West Monk. A dish of plastic hair grips. A Hello Kitty mousepad hinted this was a *girl's* terminal. An under-desk waste-bin was full of squeezed-out plasma packs. A *vampire* girl's terminal.

So, he was trespassing.

Up to no good?

The terminal was partially dismantled, housing removed, wires pulled out. A spycam fixed to the monitor was disabled. The screen was live. Vertical lines of code came down like rain. An illicit program was running. Hal guessed he was responsible for that.

Or maybe his hand was.

It could interface with any system. He didn't trust the sinister fucker.

Basic Question # 2. Who was he? Who was Jun Zero *really*?

He ran his tongue over his teeth. They weren't fangs.

He was not a vampire.

Good to know.

He wiped his damp forehead. Scum came off on his flesh fingers. He seemed to be sweating red-threaded grey slime.

He had a flash memory of something worse than pain.

Jesus Fucksticks!

He was terrified, sweating through his shirt, copper taste in his mouth.

The Processor Room was as much labyrinth as library. In this maze was a minotaur.

'You may wish to take evasive measures,' said his hand.

Hal knew – remembered! – he was in immediate danger.

'Something's in here?'

'Correct-a-mundo.'

'Something other than you?'

'Yes.'

'Reassuring… *not!*'

Speaking out loud was blood in the water.

He stood up, unsquelching the ball. His back ached, so the magazine ads lied. He steadied himself, denting the partition board with robot fingers. He had horrible pins and needles. He checked to see if his legs were real. So far as he could tell, they were. He was not an android imprinted with the approximate consciousness of Harold Takahama. His only external cybermod was the hand.

The ball rolled to the end of the row.

A running man collided with it and fell to the floor.

He was terrified too. A fresh scratch on his cheek.

He wore a white shirt with pocket protector and pens. His glasses had little lights in the frame. One lens was cracked. He was Asian. Stereotype coder.

He tried to get up but couldn't. Slapstick comedy.

Then something pounced on him. Graphic horror.

The fallen man screamed and flapped ineffectually.

The minotaur was too wide to pass easily between stacks. So tall it had to arch its backbone and hang its head not to scrape ceiling tiles. Ripped purple Hulk pants identified it as a shapeshifted human. Its elongated feet and hands were knotty and clawed. Its torso was a barrel of muscle, support for fleshy folded wings. A bulbous bald cranium. Tufts of fur around the earholes. Beady, malicious eyes. Obscene anteater proboscis – a leathery tube ending in a tooth-ringed hole.

The lamprey mouth stuck into the coder's forehead and *sucked*.

The screaming stopped and the fallen man went limp.

Not dead, but the fight gone out of him. And everything else.

'You will want to evade the chiropterid,' said his hand. 'It will come after you again once it has finished with Taguchi.'

'Again?'

'The chiropterid caught you first but abandoned its feeding. Ishikawa and Taguchi were higher-priority targets…'

Hal felt insulted.

He knew where the slime came from. He cringed at the idea of that horror trunk gummed to his forehead.

That had happened to him. He was glad the memory of pain blotted it out.

The minotaur – a chiropterid, apparently – lifted Taguchi from the floor, wrapping him in its wings. Taguchi's expression was blank. His eyes were poached. Whoever he'd been – no matter how high priority a target – he wasn't that person any more.

'Ishikawa?' he asked his hand.

'Reformatted.'

Instinctively, Hal understood reformatting. The chiropterid did to people what a hard-erase did to a drive. A complete wipe.

It was a vampire, of course. A mind vampire.

RICHARD JEPERSON

The Bund – once Yōkai Town, now Casamassima Bay – was known, of course, for nightlife. At sunset, neon signs buzzed and shop front shutters rolled up. Guests kept to the carpet. Stewards waved luminous table tennis bats to discourage strays.

Richard didn't like being herded.

Quiet, curious spectres appeared to gape at incomers. Smiling, bowing salarymen and demure kimono ladies. Japanese murgatroyds in Regency peacock finery, cerulean make-up bars across their eyes. Other creatures were little more than skin-rags with top-knots and teeth. Christina's people, the vampires of the Bund.

The Transylvanian cortège was finally through security. It cruised past the procession of guests. Presuming the unknown Very Important Vampire capable of walking – even flying – unaided, the flash motors and platoon of masked coffin-hefters were for show.

The long car glided by. He saw a red-on-black gothic 'D' on its doors. The escutcheon of Dracula. This VIV was super-well-connected. An apex predator among Big Beasts.

Every landless margrave in Europe claimed kinship with the King of the Cats and declared his (or her) high position in the Order of the Dragon. Syrie Van Epp, a new-born, was your actual vampire royalty. She'd blow her nose on Dracula's cloak if she felt like it. She slept not on her native soil – she'd been born on a dirigible in-flight between Teheran and Washington, so that was out of the question – but on pallets of large denomination bank-notes.

Beside the tall chauffeur sat a young – or young-*appearing* – Japanese girl in a crimson sailor suit. The nob's secretary or catspaw. Not a VIV herself, or she wouldn't be up front with the help.

Nezumi strayed off the carpet and road-hogged in front of the hearse. She strolled, zigging and zagging deliberately, not getting out of the damn way. She dared the driver to toot his horn. Or nudge her with the razor prow.

Instead, the front passenger window slid down. The v-girl stuck out her head. Her hair was teased into a dandelion clock of watch-spring spirals. She was Asian but with big, round fish-eyes. A slight cosmetic shapeshift or a characteristic of bloodline?

She stuck her little fingers in her mouth and puffed her cheeks.

Richard's fillings hurt again. Sailor Crimson had whistled – at too high a pitch for human ears.

Somewhere off the main thoroughfare, dogs – or dog-like things – set to howling.

Nezumi eyed the whistling mariner, who simpered. After a pause, she gave a Girl Guide salute and stepped aside, tube held back like a courtier's cloak.

The hearse passed. Fifteen small skulls were scratched over its rear-wheel housing – like the little victory tally swastikas on a Spitfire. The rear lamps were chandeliers with tinkling ruby quartz pendants around a tube of flame.

More bloodline than taste, obviously.

'*Gotta make way for the homo vampyria,*' John Blaylock had once sung.

'Eat my native dirt, peasant scum,' the tinkling chandeliers implied.

Mycroft Holmes, founder of the Diogenes Club, had known Dracula for a monster straight off. But the Ruling Cabal did not entirely resist the Vampire Ascendancy. While followers of Van Helsing hung garlic in their windows to ward off bloodsuckers, Britain's most secret servants began to recruit the *right type* of vampire.

As a warm man, Richard was now in a minority at the Club. During the Thatcher Years, when Caleb Croft was Grand High Pooh-Bah of the Secret Services, the Diogenes Club was nearly shut down. Croft was back in Civvy Street with his column in the *Daily Mail* and Lord Ruthven, Home

Secretary in the Blair Government, proved an unlikely champion of an institution which once blackballed him for biting someone's sister. Richard was kept on like an old armchair no one could agree to throw out.

He had a literal blood connection with his pale agents, maintaining his network through pinprick communion. In the 1960s, they started calling his vampires the Lovelies – and that stuck. Not all of them liked the name. But they took regular drops of his blood on extended tongues. They could feel what he felt. The psychic bods labelled him an empath. He was a feeling man. His instincts were, on the whole, good.

Nezumi was not quite a Lovely. The Club brought her in for odd jobs, but she was deniable and disavowable. That gave her time for school. She'd been at Drearcliff Grange, off and on, for three-quarters of a century, earning ticks, playing the game. Lessons faded from her goldfish memory, so she learned them over and over.

Miss Mouse – that was what 'nezumi' meant, and she had no retrievable real name – was one of fewer than five hundred people on the planet who'd been around the last time the odometer turned over all the numbers.

Of course, the European calendar was all but unknown in Japan in 999 CE.

He'd looked it up. In a book, not online. 999 was the end of the Chōtoku Era and the beginning of the Chōhō Era, which lasted until the Kankō Era began in 1004. Barely four years counted as an era in mediaeval Japan.

He had asked Nezumi if she remembered that particular New Year festival.

The vampire schoolgirl shrugged.

He had an idea nothing in particular stuck in her mind from all those Erae. Would tonight be any different?

His birthdays blurred and blended, after barely sixty of them. A war orphan with no memory of his early childhood, he didn't know his birth date or even his age. He had no retrievable real name, either – and archives had been scoured. Captain Jeperson, who adopted the stateless boy, hadn't wanted Richard to miss out on cards, parties and presents. He picked June 25, six months either direction from Christmas, as the lad's birthday. It seemed only a few summers since Richard was excited to unwrap a Gene

Autry cap pistol and a Tiger Tim annual... though he might be getting that mixed up with last June's haul, an antique fowling piece and a first edition Aubrey Beardsley.

Now, around significant dates, he was targeted with offers of Caribbean jaunts for sexy OAPs and affordable interment plans for the unturned. Fewer birthday cards and more spam e-mails. Cyber-boosters hadn't mentioned that miracle pestilence in the pitch meetings.

That was his own short warm life. A mayfly moment, like Cham-Cham's Jane Grey reign at the top of the Hit Parade. He tried to conceive of Nezumi's thousand birthdays... a thousand *thirteenth* birthdays – too old for dollies, too young for make-up, just right for pop records... a thousand New Years... a thousand Christmases... a thousand Hallowe'ens... *four thousand* bank holidays.

Thinking about Nezumi's past gave him an ice-cream head.

He was an empath, though. And connected to her by a drop of blood. He understood how the v-girl coped. By not worrying too much.

She could appear distracted, but she was in the moment. Any moment.

As the warm learned not to stare into the sun, the long-lived learned not to peer into time's abyss.

At present, he didn't feel particularly warm.

He wished he'd worn a scarf. None of the ones he'd brought to Japan matched his outfit.

Getting too old to change – in any sense – meant becoming susceptible to the chill. In the Bund, the temperature dropped. It wasn't just night. Fewer warm bodies. Far fewer heat sources. Locals didn't feel the cold. Ice sculptures formed in the park where the Temple of One Thousand Monsters had once stood. Beneath the snowdrifts was the tomb of Yuki-Onna, sleeping vampire queen of the East.

Richard had read the reports and talked with Geneviève Dieudonné, who had been in Yōkai Town when the treaty was struck. Geneviève had an invitation to tonight's do. So had her business partners, Katharine Reed and Penelope Churchward. They were in Los Angeles, keeping well away. Richard inherited history with Geneviève from his predecessors. She took his call and dutifully retold the story for one more member of the Ruling Cabal of the Diogenes Nuisance. She insisted Yuki-Onna was the source of Christina's icy glamour and warned him not to get too near either of them. Light and Snow both burned.

An *oni*-masked, shock-wigged apparition shriek-laughed at a pretty police boy. The copper's hand went to his baton. The hag flapped up from the street and perched on a street-lamp. Richard suspected invisible monofilament.

A vampire policeman – in ill-fitting mufti, but unmistakably a plod from his boots to his whistle – rebuked the young officer for letting the trickster cheek him. The warm copper, face stippled with shaving cuts, nodded and backed away. The detective slouched like a fighter about to punch. One of his eyes swivelled independent of the other. Richard got an impression of sad kindness and a furnace of inner rage. He would not like to be a criminal on this man's beat. That vulture eye would not miss much.

The masked hag – perhaps a *kabuki* drag act – leaped from lamp to a wall and clung like a gecko, head turning with a *crick-crick-crick*. A livid tongue stuck out between wooden teeth and licked stiff demon lips. With shoulder and hip moves that would dislocate a living person's joints, she scuttled up the wall.

The vampire detective shouted in Japanese.

'... and *stay* fucked off!' Or words to that effect.

DETECTIVE YOSHITAKA AZUMA

He scratched his knuckles. His scrapes healed fast, but the itch was constant. Telling him something. Nearby, a perp needed his face punched. In this district, he might well need his head slammed into a concrete pillar too. And his ribs could definitely do with kicking-in.

Most vampires felt red thirst in their teeth. Azuma had fangs in his knuckles. Little extra nubs of bone shifted under the skin, poking through when he punched a perp. He got more blood on his hands than in his mouth. That kept him going. The punching was more important than the bleeding. That's what kept his *kyuketsuki* fed. Righteous violence. He needed to dish out justice.

Ghoul Town on New Year's Eve was a punishment detail.

Last week, Azuma bit off Jiiji the Pimp's ear and spat it in his face. This was not conduct Captain Takeda approved of. Jiiji ran a nasty racket. His needle-fingered mermaid lured pervs into alleys. He peeled watches and rings off shrivelled raisin corpses and filched cash and cards. Azuma tossed the mermaid in the bay. Embarrassingly, she couldn't swim and had to be netted by a patrol boat. She was mindlessly hungry. The thievery was Jiiji's idea.

The parasite's injury would heal, but his cellblock pals would make fun of the pink curly baby ear flowering from his scab.

Azuma wasn't nicknamed 'Beat' because he liked beat music.

Though he did. He played the Stray Cats full volume while he thumped perps in the interrogation room. When the knuckle-teeth came out, he got results. Catches squealed. His clear-up rate made complaints go away. If perps got bent out of shape, they'd been asking for it. Lowlifes who hurt other people absented themselves from the courtesy of not being thumped. Or bitten. Or stabbed. Or shot. No matter what their shysters said. Or their relatives. Or his boss.

Captain Takeda kept finding punishment details.

Tonight, Azuma might as well be in uniform.

'Hah,' said Takeda, 'this should suit you. You'll be a real "beat" cop.'

Azuma kept his rolling eye on Tenjo Kudari, who was taunting Officer Kamikura. Still showing off for the crowd, the masked he-hag ziplined along overhead wires and stuck to walls. His neck twisted like a wrung-out towel. His burglary/assault sheet said he liked to slither into spaces above hotel ceilings, then crawl down light fittings to bleed sleeping drunks. He also lifted wallets from bedside tables. The Festival brought him into the open air.

Kamikura should watch himself if Tenjo Kudari had taken a liking to him.

Every scumball in Tokyo was celebrating the New Year with aggravated scumballery.

All around were petty crims and pilot fish. The thing was to protect guests, though Azuma's gut told him most of them deserved a thumping too. Few got to wear a tux or furs without stealing something or hurting someone.

If he saw a perp, he'd drag them off the red carpet.

Go for a gun, and *pow!* between the eyes.

A flash of fang and *silver-stiletto-stab!* in the heart.

He liked elder vampires. They crumbled to dust and could be swept off the dock. Warm perps stuck around inconveniently, dead or alive. Some, of course, came back.

As he had.

He'd turned after being shot in the head. The metamorphosis was offered by his union medical plan. He'd checked a box on a form years earlier without thinking. A Type V transfusion was administered in the ambulance. He wasn't dropped off at the morgue but a resurrection clinic. Azuma sat up, blood in his mouth, and got back on the case.

What cop wouldn't want to solve his own murder?

The shooter was no longer in a position to boast about his kill. Others would have reinforced the message by stamping the shooter's dog's head flat, but Azuma didn't extend grudges to animals. It wasn't any mutt's fault its owner was a lowlife. He took the dog home and looked after it for a while, but it ran off.

Azuma felt little changed in himself. In bars, he drank ounces of blood rather than sake. And he had fangs in his hands. He'd always worked at night. Seeing better in the dark was a new advantage. Perps were more afraid of him now. Solid citizens were no less wary. Meeting a cop was seldom good news. Meeting a vampire cop always meant having a bad night. He didn't brood and got on with the job. Takeda, a warm man concerned not to appear prejudiced, eased off on reprimands when Azuma became a vampire – if not punishment details.

Guests flowed along the red carpet.

Three cosplay cops joined Kamikura. Their hydraulic-assisted armour hissed at the joints as they stamped across the street in arrow formation. Saki-A, senior rank signalled by flashing blue epaulettes, lowered a cyber-monocle from a wire pyramid fixed to her wig. A laserlight tagged Tenjo Kudari. The ceiling spectre flinched, but it wasn't a cutting beam.

He twisted to present scrawny, mocking buttocks.

Saki-K, the shortest cop, flicked a razor yo-yo on a thirty-foot string with deadly butt-stinging accuracy. Tail salted, the shrieking Tenjo Kudari made himself scarce. Saki-K reeled in her yo-yo with a wrist-snap and held up her hand for a high-five. Kamikura sissy-slapped her palm. The vampire cops giggled like four-year olds.

Kamikura would have been better off with the trapdoor demon.

For now, the Bund had its own police force. Urufu Inugami, the watchdog who ran the yo-yo girls, wouldn't stay in post after the handover. His department swallowed by Takeda's command, Inugami would lope off unthanked. Azuma felt for the hairy bastard. Inugami's policing was not to the Captain's taste. The Wolfman wouldn't take to a choke collar.

Azuma had been in and out of the Bund for years. Perps stupidly thought that because it wasn't strictly Tokyo they could claim sanctuary here. Survivors learned a hard lesson. Beyond the Wall, crims had no right to draw breath. Predators smelled the difference between a tourist protected by diktat of the Wolfman and a scumball who was anybody's for the taking. Some hard nuts begged Azuma to haul them back to a district with interrogations and beatings and lawyers and courts.

Even as a vampire, this wasn't his patch. He'd locked horns with Inugami, fighting over scraps. Takeda dropped hints he'd sponsor Azuma for the command if he straightened his tie and became the department's tame blood fiend. Azuma wasn't interested in promotion. He didn't want to live in Ghoul Town. If anything, he wanted to move out of the city. He idly fancied a house on the beach.

Azuma had been warm most of his life. He was still wary of vampires.

RICHARD JEPERSON

H e was never more aware of the beating of his heart – of his neck and wrist pulses – than in places like this.

In cities where vampires clustered in roosts and catacombs – or were penned in run-down warrens by warm-majority governments – the undead retained a mystique long since worn off in London, Toronto or New Orleans. No reason why Tokyo shouldn't integrate. According to the latest census, four-fifths of the city's *yōkai* had addresses outside the Bund. The Principality of Light was an anachronism.

A couple of *bakeneko* in frilly bikinis mewed at Nezumi, brushing the furry backs of their hands against her blazer. Their ears pricked and whiskers quivered. The catgirls were taken by her straight white hair. They might copy her frostilocks. Nezumi didn't tell them how she came by the look. It was not a fashion choice, but a scar. It went back to her first involvement with the Diogenes Club, nearly eighty years ago.

Did Nezumi ever mistake Richard for Edwin Winthrop or Charles Beauregard? They had sat in his chair before him and set her extra-curricular assignments. She treated missions as homework. She was diligent, prompt and neat – if often whimsical.

Vampires weren't supposed to be so imaginative.

Richard sensed friendliness in the *bakeneko* but also prickly territoriality. A newcomer excited curiosity. They admired Nezumi for holding up the ostentatious hearse. Bund residents must be bored with the same old fangfaces. A fresh playmate was welcome but also potentially a rival... or a snack.

Nezumi was polite but reserved. Her Japanese was formal. She wasn't up on the latest slanguange, fashions and crazes. Her school socks were tight, when cool girls were wearing them wrinkled. And she was a professional. A mouse cats couldn't play with.

The *bakeneko* got bored and abandoned Nezumi to tease a passing Japanese fellow about his peculiar pompadour. This guest was a better prospect for affectionate pestering. They slunk towards their target, tails up, furry midriffs taut.

Richard had the shivers – not just fear (though fear never went away completely), but anticipation, excitement. A thrill. Threat was there. And promise.

He glanced at his Seiko digital.

31/12/99, 09:44 44, London time.

He fingernail-pressed a rim button.

31/12/99, 17:44 45, local time.

Halfway round the world, eight hours into the future.

Like everyone who owned a gadget with a timer, he'd experimented with a temporary reset to see what might happen at 01/01/00, 00:00 01. His watch didn't explode, but it was only a dry run. Video recorders and microwave ovens knew when they were only being tested and saved the surprise until midnight. No matter what whizz-for-atoms boys said, Richard had a sneaking suspicion contraptions could think and feel and plot and plan. And did not have the best interests of their makers at heart.

He remembered when computers filled rooms, chattering yards of needle-scratched butcher's paper from letterbox slits. Wise old heads reckoned Britain needed no more than five of the things. A Big Thinks apiece for Oxford and Cambridge, WOTAN on top of the Post Office Tower, the General at the MoD, and REMAK at GCHQ. The rest of the country could get by with adding machines or sums done on fingers.

Now you could take a mini-HAL 9000 home from Radio Rentals. Computers sat on desks. In kids' bedrooms. In portable phones. Disguised as tools and toys. A connective tangle of shrill modems, dedicated telephone lines, and international exchanges. Cybernets were built to answer questions. What happened when they started asking them? From his Sri Lankan veranda, Arthur C. Clarke cheerfully floated the idea that a million, million binary bits might add up to a new-born intelligence. A neural net around the world.

What vampires were to the late nineteenth century, computers were now.

Agents of sudden change. Contributors to a quickening of *everything*. Untameable tigers, sat meekly in the kitchen, pretending not to be ravenous. Dreaded by the hidebound, embraced by futurists. Here and not going away, no matter who grumbled or waved a crucifix.

HAROLD TAKAHAMA

With a last slurp, the chiropterid's sucker unstuck from Taguchi's forehead. The reformatted man slipped out of its wing-grip and hugged the big rubber ball.

The chiropterid looked around, nastily alert.

Its hunting dog proboscis pointed at Hal. Spiteful eyes fixed on him.

It had tasted his mind. That was why so much was missing.

The thing was back to finish him off.

'What date is it?' he asked his hand.

Basic Question # 3.

'December 31, 1999. 17:02, Japan Standard Time.'

The last date he was sure of was 1992. The cops who ass-whupped Rodney King got off. Riots in L.A. and a quake in Mendocino. Governor Clinton was headed for either the White House or the Jail House. Michelle Pfeiffer was smokin' as Bat-Woman in *The Monk Returns*. That 'Achy Staky Heart' song got way too much airplay.

Hal definitely didn't remember being on Japan Standard Time.

He was in a Silicon Valley garage with scavenged kit and seed cash from his parents, cranking out killdroid templates. *Gargantuabots* was catching fire. Players bought schema and customised them for console combat. Leagues were forming, with rankings and tables. Ace gamers and bots had fandoms. An e-cash betting culture was springing up. Jacked street kids in Tijuana or Cluj put in the hours accumulating scar tokens and power points in prelim bouts, then sold mettled avatars to dilettante botjocks who wanted to crash the board with a sure-win mecha.

Cyberspace was a Wild West and there was gold in them thar hills. Hal was resisting pressure to go back to college. Making connections online. Imaginary robots rolled off his production line. In his mind, they were vast, clanking, *oily* real things… not bits and bytes and near-plagiarisms, existing only in constantly upgraded graphics.

Hal understood what all these memories and half memories were.

The chiropterid had erased his drive, but his last back-up installed automatically.

Overwritten so often it was mostly sludge. But him. Harold Takahama. Him as he was.

He made decisions. He'd not been good at that, but was now.

Jun Zero 1999 was a million degrees cooler than Hal Takahama 1992. That's who he was now.

It irked him not to have as high a target-value as Taguchi or Ishikawa. Whoever they were. They didn't matter any more. Taguchi had no '92 back-up. His brain was a walnut.

The chiropterid still looked at Hal, fascinated by his hand.

It *was* an unusual feature.

'Might I make an observation?' chirped the bot-bit.

'Permission granted. All input is welcome.'

'I have advised evasion. Why are you asking questions?'

'Information is power.'

The hand clicked and flashed. Calculating.

'That is correct.'

The chiropterid stepped away from Taguchi, drawing in its shoulders to sidle between cabinets. Hal backed off, maintaining distance between them. The flying viper was stronger, faster and meaner. But the Processor Room was not its natural habitat. Wings were a handicap here.

He raised the hand and aimed its grille at the chiropterid.

'Can you zap it?'

The clicking and flashing represented mocking laughter.

'This unit does not have that capability.'

'If I built you, I'd put in a plasma cannon.'

'This unit *was* designed by Jun Zero.'

'Hal Takahama would have done a better job, then. He was aces on inbuilt weapons systems.'

From designing cyberspace killdroids.

'Jun Zero outgrew Harold Takahama.'

Heavy philosophising for a perspex prosthesis.

Why would Jun Zero build an add-on that could hurt him but not anyone else? Had Hal turned into a cyber-masochist?

'We won't grow much more unless you have smart ideas.'

'This unit cannot initiate. This unit can only respond. I have all the stored knowledge of the world…'

'… at your fingertips?'

That didn't get a machine chortle.

'I can advise and suggest. Only you can *do*.'

The chiropterid took another step forward. Hal took another step back.

He checked his pockets. He dressed like Taguchi, except without the birth control glasses. He didn't feel at home in black pants, white shirt, off-brand sneakers, and blood-red tie. He saw no way to MacGuyver a fistful of pens into a grenade but flung them anyway.

This wasn't how Jun Zero dressed. The drone threads were a disguise. Taguchi, Ishikawa and Jun Zero were up to sneaky shit. They were in the Processor Room to affect backdoor access to a closed system.

And run into serious real-world security?

The chiropterid made a deadly combination night watchman and guard dog.

No, that wasn't the picture.

Another two-step. The chiropterid was by the workstation now. Wing-barbs trailed over the unknown operator's flair. The porcelain eggs rattled as if hatching. Adam West's squashed head bobbled.

'What did we do here?'

'This unit does not have that information.'

'So much for all the knowledge of the world.'

'Information was not archived, Jun Zero. It was a condition imposed by the client that no mission parameters be input or record kept.'

'Who is the client?'

'This unit does not have that information.'

When pissy, his hand reverted to calling itself 'this unit'. If so disposed, it could be informal. Inconsistency made it more like a person than a machine.

Hal supposed he could be proud of that. It was his programming.

His kung fu was best.

'How many in our team?'

'Four.'

'Taguchi, Ishikawa, me… and… you?'

'This unit does not count itself separate from Jun Zero.'

'*That's* the fourth member,' he said, nodding at the chiropterid.

'Verbal specification required to process.'

'The chiropterid. It's on our side.'

'Of course not. But it came here with you.'

'It represents the client?'

'Affirmative.'

'Does it have a name?'

'It self-designates as Karl.'

Was Karl ready to pounce? It couldn't fly in the room, but could jump. It could latch onto the ceiling and crawl upside-down.

Hal had the picture in focus now. The gang – the Zero Boys? Team Taguchi? – were hired to hack into this system. Upload an alien process or download illicit data. That mission accomplished, the client had its rep initiate a Dead Don't Tell protocol. The outcome must be so desirable it was worth burning high-skills operators for. Not to save cash, but to keep the caper quiet.

The only crimes Hal ever committed were to do with pirated software. The outlaw Jun Zero had forgotten the thing even Hal knew about crooks.

You couldn't trust them not to screw you over too.

Hal wondered whether he hadn't turned into a bit of a dick.

A dick with a glass hand.

NEZUMI

Clouds of fogged breath rose. Everyone here, on the red carpet and off, felt the cold. Even vampires.

But Nezumi didn't.

Her long-ago childhood was a landscape seen through a blizzard.

She recalled little. Only a memory of a memory of a memory. Portraits in frost on thick glass, which melted if she tried to concentrate.

She concentrated on now, mostly.

Woods, mountains, ice in streams. Animals?

Mother called her Nezumi. 'Mouse'.

Affectionately. But her frost picture of Mother had cats' eyes.

Slit pupils, like the girls who admired her hair and chattered so fast she couldn't keep up.

Were the *bakeneko* distant cousins?

Japan had snow vampires and cat vampires.

And schoolgirl vampires.

Like the brat in the hearse. With the wire-curl ringlets and dolls' eyes.

At Drearcliff Grange, she'd be tagged a bad penny.

Nezumi had seen generations pass through school. She could always tell a bad penny from a sound shilling.

This year, her dorm-mates were sound shillings. Fields, Bronze and the Trenchcoat Twosome.

Clara Fields was taping *The Bowmans* and *The Vampyre of Dibley* for Nezumi while she was out of the country. Erzulie Bronze was the only warm girl quick enough to kendo-spar with her on a trampoline.

The mystery-solving noses of the Twosome twitched for U-certificate crimes. Nezumi hadn't the heart to tell them whodunit solutions were rarely as innocuous as the Case of the Missing Make-Up Case (confiscated and in the Prefects' Hut), or the Riddle of the Smugglers' Cave Beast (the rubber tentacles were what was left of a monster Doug McClure fought in a film made on location in North Somerset in the 1970s). The Twosome didn't open cupboards to find screaming eyeless contortionist corpses.

Nezumi's friends were interested in what she'd been like as a warm child.

'Cold,' she always said.

Again, not trying to be funny.

She couldn't even imagine what it was like to be warm. She might have been born the way she was.

She had been a baby, she thought – and a little girl. Then, at the age she appeared to be, an ice wind blew and she froze.

Sometime later, she came down from the mountains.

Many, many years passed.

Plains, lakes, bamboo. Battles. Lords. Enemies.

She had been at schools most of her life. Not English public schools. Monasteries, convents, training camps.

She'd been married – or pledged to marry. To cement an alliance. She fancied she'd never met her husband. In the 'marital status' box on forms she wrote 'widow'.

Her name was lost. She was given others.

Along the way, she picked up a sword. Good Night Kiss.

She took lessons from masters.

She passed exams. She was good at that. Especially practical exams.

Nosferatu all seemed rich, rolling fortunes from century to century, piling up treasure in European castles.

She had to earn a living. With her sword.

It wasn't the seconds of violence she was paid for.

It was the years of peace and quiet.

She wouldn't hurt anyone unless they hurt others. But she wouldn't let such a person profit from cruelty.

She didn't tolerate bandits or bullies.

She offered no loyalty to tyrants. She believed in fair play.

She was resolved to be a sound shilling not a bad penny.

That scruple made her less employable than other *ronin*.

Most of her class – samurai, whether warm or *yōkai* – scorned those weaker than themselves. If told to by a lord, they would hurt indiscriminately…

and not taste the ash in their mouths when they described themselves as honourable.

The Diogenes Club took the trouble to understand Nezumi before hiring her.

Mr Winthrop saw she was wilful about fair play. Mr Beauregard encouraged him to see that as her strength rather than a weakness.

Her current principal was more like Mr Beauregard than Mr Winthrop. Mr Jeperson knew what was and what was not cricket.

Which was more than many cricket players did.

DETECTIVE AZUMA

The crowds got thick. Carpet-walkers acted as if this were a premiere and stopped to be admired. That held up the flow. Opportunities arose for assault and theft. Fujifilm had given away a hundred disposable cameras, promoting a stock fast enough to catch the image of an elder vampire. Guests and onlookers snapped away to see what might develop. The plastic cameras had a distinctive snapping-turtle click. If any bigwigs misbehaved – and it was a dead cert most would – there'd be photographic evidence.

More work for the Vice and Blackmail Squads.

Something blue crunched underfoot. A Sprünt empty.

Azuma's fist-fangs pricked. Even litterers were perps.

He scanned for faces.

Perps all had a look. Before turning, he had cop instincts. Now, guilty foreheads might as well be marked with red flame. Some perps he could put names to. Others he just knew for what they were.

Small-timers, exclusively.

He would point out the most likely troublemakers to the Sakis. Slicing off a few sticky fingers would save later hassle.

A pickpocket was working the crowd. The dip's long coat flapped weirdly around a spindly but functional extra arm rooted in the small of his back. Azuma put on a burst of speed and grabbed the crook's third wrist, snapping the arm up against his shoulder blades. Out of curiosity, he nipped the prominent vein. Thin, tangy *yōkai* blood sloshed around his mouth, sharpening his teeth. He gulped with a covering cough.

The pickpocket was surprised by the sharp pain of the bite.

Buzzing from blood, he should drag the dip to the holding pens set up for the night's catch.

But something bothered him. Something he'd missed.

Blue Label Sprünt. Wrong for this district.

He scanned again – not looking for faces, but for blanks.

Masks. Festivals were always an excuse. This whole district liked dress-up too much. Tenjo Kudari was one of many habitual mask-wearers.

He saw them on the far side of the street, the other side of the carpet. Two of the breed. Flared black vinyl coats. Towels wrapped around their heads. Faces covered by a long-lashed open eye motif. Orb bobbles on epaulettes. Aum Draht. The cultists who thought life was a video game. Often a first-person shooter.

He let the surprised dip go with a shove. He stumbled off, third arm flapping like a broken tail.

The eyeheads moved like handicapped racehorses, weights clanking. Barrelled torsos on thin legs. Something nasty under their coats.

His knuckles dribbled blood as his fangs cut skin.

RICHARD JEPERSON

Richard and Nezumi stepped into Daikaiju Plaza.

A rearing dragon loomed over the square, serrated silhouette stark against red sky, searchlights playing across its rough concrete hide. A building shaped like a giant pot-bellied avocado was propped on two thick slanting leg-columns, balanced by a tail that curled around to meet plush carpet. Above the avocado rose a sturdy tower.

Atop the Ruff – a revolving restaurant floor – was the Head of the Dragon. Lights burned in twin windows. One red, one white.

The eyes of Christina, in the face of a monster.

Dai = Bloody Huge.

Kaiju = Fucking Monster.

Daikaiju.

Welcome to the future, Mr Jeperson. Kneel in the shadow of a Colossal (Bloody Huge) Gargantua Gigantis (Fucking Monster). Smell its sulphur breath. Hear its thunder roar.

The world had given the Princess a hundred years to erect her inhabitable idol. In the 1930s, after decades of stress tests, she constructed an iron armature of quake-proof girders. That stick figure survived the War, though flame-clouds blackened its cavities. Since then, Christina Light had clad the skeleton with concrete flesh. Its nerves were thousands of miles of wire – copper in the 1960s, fibre-optic cable now. Its hide was stone inset with glass facets. Its temperature had to be regulated. In its legs, furnaces and turbines generated power independent of the Tokyo grid. In its belly, freezing coils – a Yuki-Onna of freon tubes – kept cathedral-sized computer arrays from raising the building's internal temperature to a point when even vampire blood boiled.

Cities around the world where Light Industries operated could boast smaller-scale landmarks. Mere *kaiju* for San Francisco, Birmingham and Copenhagen. A six-tentacled octopus by the Golden Gate Bridge, a giant ape above the Bullring, a flimsy-winged reptile tethered in the Tivoli Gardens.

This, though, was the original Beastie.

The Daikaiju Building opened in 1970, but construction continued. He suspected the monster wasn't finished yet. Like its High Priestess of Light, it evolved towards a final, higher form.

Richard couldn't help himself. He whistled.

What a whopper! What a blooming walloping whopper!

HAROLD TAKAHAMA

'What are the weaknesses of chiropterids?' Hal asked. His hand pondered for unreasonable seconds.

'Exposure to sunlight causes degradation of cells,' it said. 'They petrify and crumble, with an appealing, ice-cracking tinkle.'

'No use here. And thanks for the poetic frill. Next?'

'A stake through the—'

'Next?'

'Silver bullets or edged weapons.'

'Ne… uh, is there any silver about?'

'Not in appreciable quantities.'

'Next?'

'Lightning strikes have been known to—'

He was getting impatient with the machine. 'Lightning! Wait, that's electrical discharge. Is high-voltage current effective against chiropterids?'

Whirring.

He was almost impatient with the shapeshifter too.

What was it – Self-Designation Karl – waiting for? It had dealt with Taguchi – and, presumably, Ishikawa – with merciless swiftness. Was it stuffed to the gills after two big feeds? Did the mulch of victims' minds slosh around its oval rat-skull, threatening to squirt through cilia-frilled nostrils? Or was it simply confident, taking the time to enjoy torturing a lower-priority target?

It still didn't seem right that Jun Zero was Number Three.

He was the one with the computer hand.

'Electric current has proved fatal to some bloodlines of vampire. In 1951, in the Arctic Circle, an arc of—'

'Discontinue,' he snapped. 'No need for a history lesson, Lefty.'

'This unit is to be designated "Lefty"? Confirm, if so.'

'Confirm.'

Whirring and processing. 'Designation set and filed. Renaming is possible within thirty-six hours. Then designation is permanent. Does user Jun Zero wish to rename?'

'No, Lefty. User Jun Zero wishes to know if high-voltage cable is immediately accessible.'

The chiropterid looked at him askance.

Could it understand English?

Lefty talked to Jun Zero in English. Both were also fluent in Japanese. That was a revelation. A shortcut around the blanks.

It was as if he'd checked a filing system. Two languages were there. He only had to think of Japanese and he could think *in* Japanese. The partial reformat hadn't affected that function. His memories of the last eight years were gone – and those of the years before hazy – but skills learned in that time were available to him.

At home in 1992, his parents spoke only English. He had enough Japanese to hold a two- or three-minute conversation with Gramma – who was still pissed at FDR for clapping her in a camp during the Second World War – but not enough to follow unsubbed *Overfiend* bootleg videos. Since then, Jun Zero had become fluent in the tongue of his ancestors.

He had a stab of panic grief – was Gramma still alive? She'd been *ancient*.

What did his parents think of his career choices? Dad was a notary public and Lodge Master of the Ojai Sons of the Desert. He took pride in contributing to the community and voted for law and order candidates.

'You're nothing to me,' Joji Takahama would say to a criminal son. 'A *Zero*!'

Was that where the username came from?

The chiropterid had stripped Hal of years, kicked him back in time. It was still fixated on him.

Self-Designation Karl might know more about Jun Zero than he did.

Was that why it was cautious? Not attacking yet.

Was it *afraid*?

Did Jun Zero know more than computer fu?

He made a fist and thumped his chest. Then felt his stomach and sides. Unfamiliar cords of muscle under his shirt. No flab handles above his belt.

Hal Takahama's little wobbly gut was gone.

Jun Zero had racked up serious gym time. Maybe with steroids and surgery. He obviously wasn't against scientific augmentation.

So he might be up to a fight – if not with an eight-foot-tall bat monster.

Hal had a sudden little thrill in his water. He might not be a virgin!

He tried to check the filing system for sex skills – highly inappropriate at this moment – but they weren't hardwired like knowing Japanese or designing robots. An outlaw hacker like Jun Zero was a probable babe magnet, though.

Hal Takahama got flustered when a check-out girl at Vons smiled at him.

Jun Zero slept with tattooed Asian women who had switchblade fingernails.

Fuck Hal Takahama, then! He was Jun Zero now.

Was Winona Ryder still hot? She'd dig the Zero.

Had she become a vampire? Was she friends with Ally Sheedy?

This was *not* the time to think about celebrity threesomes.

'The cable ahead of you carries sufficient voltage,' said Lefty.

He looked down.

He had nearly tripped over the python-thick rope. Now he knelt and reached for it.

Part of his disguise was rubber-soled shoes.

Good planning or happenstance?

He took hold of the cable with both hands.

Lefty's fingers bent. As they curved, steel points slid out from the tips. Lefty had claws – and a USB plug in its thumb.

Hal had more questions for his hand. They could keep.

The chiropterid cautiously advanced.

Hal banked on Self-Designation Karl being cunning, not clever. Thirsty brute, not calculating creature. An *Alien* alien, not a *Predator* alien. It wouldn't start talking to him with Taguchi's voice. It would stick its mouth into his forehead and bore into his brain.

As the shapeshifter pounced, Hal's perceptions adjusted.

His thoughts sped up, goosed by his electric hand. His reactions kicked in.

In that serious gym time, he had worked on his reflexes. Hal could control a virtual robot. Jun Zero could trash monster ass.

He yanked up the cable and rammed it against the chiropterid's spear-tipped proboscis.

Tiny teeth ground through rubber and bit into live current.

Hal was thrown backwards by the shock.

He slammed against a folding wooden chair that came apart.

The spasming, fallen chiropterid couldn't detach its mouth from the cable. It had relatively puny human arms. A branching network of string-thick veins inflated around its neck. Its ears caught fire. Its eyes burst like squeezed grapes.

An electrical arc played around its head. It fell forward.

To be sure, Hal took a snapped-off chair leg and used Lefty to hammer it through Self-Designation Karl's ribcage. Lefty did not appreciate the abuse.

'It is not advisable to mistreat this unit. Warranty may be invalidated.'

'How expensive are you?'

'Unit cost four million dollars. Surgical attachment procedure and neural implants two million dollars. Research and development—'

'Discontinue,' he said. 'Who paid for this?'

'You did.'

Jun Zero was fucking loaded. *He knew it!*

Hal had *told* his parents there was a fortune in fighting robots.

Though he reckoned Jun Zero had come by his money by diversifying. The road from G-bot designer to outlaw hacker must have serious kinks.

The chiropterid's death-mask flaked off its elongated skull. Fissures spread across its chest, with – as Lefty had promised – a sound like ice breaking. It wasn't 'pleasing'. Karl crystallised, then turned to white and red clinker.

'A security sweep of Floor 44 is due in seven minutes,' said Lefty. 'It may be advanced ahead of schedule because of power interruption in the Processor Room. Evasive action is advised.'

Frying Karl hadn't blacked out the building. Fail safes and redundancies kept the system live and online.

He found a vampire crouched by the frosted glass door.

Ishikawa.

The third member of Team Taguchi was dressed as a security guard and had a slime-rimmed hole in his forehead. He had centre-parted grey hair.

A key card was discarded nearby.

'Aggressive action is recommended,' said Lefty.

Ishikawa snarled through fangs. As a mind-wiped, new-made being, he only had urges and appetites.

Hal should have brought another chair-leg stake.

Ishikawa scented blood and looked around, snorting.

His eyes were big and red.

Had Jun Zero worked for this viper? That didn't feel right.

Jun Zero was his own man. He must have had a wary alliance with Ishikawa. Mutual respect for unique skills. Precautions taken against betrayal – though not, unfortunately, against the client who was definitely on Jun Zero's shit-list. What Bat Bod Karl had got was a taste of what Unknown Douchecanoe had coming.

Someone would pay for this – for Ishikawa and Taguchi.

And the partial rewrite of Jun Zero.

To get out of the room, he had to shift the vampire from the doorway. He also had to keep it off his neck.

Vampires were mostly civilised these days. Their urges and appetites were different from those of warm people, but kept on a leash. The undead wanted to continue to enjoy the benefits of living in a complex society where abducting a virgin every night and biting her neck had immediate legal consequences. Strip all that code and what did you get?

Ishikawa.

A bloodthirsty blank slate. Learning fast.

He'd need serious training to adjust. If no one staked him before he grew back a personality, a conscience, and a sense of self-preservation.

He held up Lefty, mentally kicking himself again for not fitting a repulsor ray.

Wet hair flopped over Ishikawa's fractal screensaver eyes.

Then, the vampire caught another scent and his head snapped up.

Lurching down a row between server cabinets, hands out like a sleepwalker, was Taguchi. Another blank slate, but warm.

Taguchi shouldered Hal aside. Moving on instinct, towards the light.

Ishikawa leaped like a cat and sank fangs into Taguchi's shoulder, well away from the jugular. He had vampire instincts, but no skills. Taguchi screeched and flapped his hands at Ishikawa's head.

Hal had a moment of concern.

This had been his gang. His friends?

The men he might have known were gone. These meat-sacks were what were left on the plate after the chiropterid feast.

They were lost. He only had Lefty.

Jun Zero would avenge his comrades.

Locked in their clumsy clinch, vampire and victim slammed into a cabinet.

An alarm sounded.

Hal didn't need Lefty's advice.

He picked up the key card and let himself out of the Processor Room.

NEZUMI

A mime troupe dressed as robots performed in the square, slowing the procession towards the Daikaiju Building. Their display was sponsored by Sprünt. To Nezumi, both flavours tasted like something that could eat through a spaceship hull.

A fat American senator dressed in a silver toga and a laurel of Christmas lights held things up to make drunken *haii-yü* gestures she supposed he thought typical Asian greeting. Just the politician to send to a diplomatic bunfest. She hoped the Japanese Diet sent a farting sumo in a cowboy hat to Washington D.C. in return.

Teenage-appearing *kyuketsuki* cops broke up the guerrilla marketing show. They accepted free cartons of Red Label but moved the spray-painted mimes on.

Bund police officers wore stiff blue wigs and form-fitting body armour. They used yo-yos instead of truncheons. Some piloted brightly coloured one-person tanks. The gear looked like toys.

'Hey,' said the Senator, 'my Dad bombed this block!'

The cops took his tactlessness lightly and frog-marched him back onto the red carpet. They'd be glad when the night was over.

This city was barely recognisable from 1945.

This Japan was by no means the land she had wandered for a thousand years. She had outlived tyrant lords and their retainers.

There were new tyrants. Billionaires, CEOs, Presidents.

Some wore the same faces as their predecessors.

London had changed too. 'Cool Britannia' was the thing.

Even Drearcliff Grange was changing.

Cells were now called dorms because parents stopped wanting daughters packed off to prisons or convents. Exams were called assessments. Whips were prefects and no longer used whips. They were up on social sciences and expected to understand the problems of juniors and have long cosy chats with them when they got into scrapes. Punishments were called anything but that.

Girls stopped calling them scrapes for a while, but did again. They picked it up from Nezumi. She was slow to change, of course – and influential, if generally quiet. Every year, she was a novelty.

The only vampire in the Third Form.

A few Sixths turned, picking eighteen as an age they wanted to stay. They often asked for her advice. Desperate to be told they hadn't made a huge mistake. Confused by appetites their bodies interpreted as a mutant form of eating disorder. Hoping for tips on biting people who didn't want to be bitten and getting away with it.

Those chats weren't long or cosy.

She had little to share with new-borns.

So far as she knew, she hadn't turned. She'd *stuck*.

Only yesterday, by her lights, her cell-mate and best chum 'Inchworm'

Inchfawn was mooning over a film magazine, trying to decide the swooniest – Rudolf Valentino or Antonio Moreno. Now, 'Strawberry' Fields pestered her to pick a favourite Spice Girl.

Sporty, of course.

'Not Scary?'

Nezumi had made herself smile at that.

Fields gulped and changed the subject.

If Nezumi wore mask, tights and cloak to become a superheroine – given her kendoline skills, she'd be a good one – she'd pick 'Cool Britannia' as her name.

Cool. She understood that. Cool, not cold.

It was how she felt.

It was what girls said she was.

It was a word she used often.

Mr Jeperson said it too. It was from his teenage years.

Cool, like a jazz musician. Straight from the fridge.

Mr Jeperson wasn't thrown by running into his old flame, Mrs Van Epp. From what the Lovelies said, he had enough old flames to burn a forest.

He remembered their names and what they did and how they were doing. He sent small, thoughtful presents on birthdays.

Like Nezumi, Mr Jeperson couldn't remember his early life.

The first Mr Jeperson – Captain Geoffrey Jeperson – had found him as a child in a camp and brought him to England to be his son.

He'd been given a birthday to go with his name, and shared it with her.

Every year since they first worked together – tracking down the Great Brain Robbers in 1963 – he sent her a thoughtful present for June 25. And a card.

Nezumi once asked him if he had frost picture memories of his family.

He shook his head, then rolled up his green puffy sleeve to show her a tattoo.

GEIST 97

'Nazis did that,' he said.

He had a gift. He felt when anyone else was sad. Or happy.

He could spot bad pennies too.

She made a point of sending him a thoughtful present on his birthday. Surprisingly few others did. Mrs Van Epp, who could afford to buy Harrods and hire someone thoughtful to pick presents even if she was busy herself, never bothered. Nezumi thought less of her for that. She wasn't a bad penny, exactly – but she was no sound shilling either. A crooked sixpence, perhaps. Mrs In-Between.

The Persian vampire was wearing the *silliest* headgear.

Even that lady who wore hats shaped like Blenheim Palace or the Starship *Protector* to Ascot wouldn't be seen dead in Syrie Van Epp's veiny spongebag.

In the crowd, Nezumi saw a man in an over-the-head hood that made his head look like a naked swollen brain with one big cyclops eye. Then she spotted another shifty bloke with the same look.

In an ideal world, the duo would be Japanese superheroes. They wore long black dusters, as if they didn't know the Trenchcoat Twosome copyrighted the name.

Nezumi had always known this was not an ideal world.

They were Aum Draht too. Not just for dress-up-and-play.

As if alerted by buzzing in their brainhats, the two adepts strode towards each other – and Nezumi realised she'd be caught between them.

Suddenly swift, one grasped her from behind. The other rushed at her.

She heard clockwork turning inside their coats.

They had suicide waistcoats on.

RICHARD JEPERSON

A man in a long black coat held Nezumi, gripping her upper arms. His head was the size and shape of a football. His face was covered by an Aum Draht Orb.

Was this anything to do with Syrie?

Richard saw her, huddled on the pavement with other panicky guests, crouching wonkily in high heels, handbag held over her eye-turbanned head. Not the attitude of an involved party.

So, a rogue Aum Draht faction. Mr Mystery Eye was dangerous.

Of course, so was everyone else in the street – including the schoolgirl the adept thought was his hostage. If this kicked off, it would make a bloody mess.

Richard had seen too many of those.

The vampire detective assumed a shooting stance. His gun aimed at the big eyeball.

If Aum Draht wanted to graduate from cyber-nuisance to streetfighting, they might reconsider wearing targets on their heads.

Mr Eye was the second of a two-man team.

The other eyehead was shorter, but with a coat the same length. Handily for identification purposes, Mr One wore a metallic numeral on his lapel.

As Mr One walked towards Nezumi and Mr Eye, he kept his right arm up as if his wristwatch were a raygun. He unbelted and unbuttoned his coat with his left hand. Under his off-brand black mac, Mr One wore a less fashionable drab canvas waistcoat. Not this season at all. Glass phials, wires and wind-up mechanisms were sewn into the lumpy thing. Works whirred. Vile liquids boiled.

The Diogenes Club had given Richard a report on Recent Unusual Activity in Japan as light plane reading. A break-in/murder at Unwin-Fujikawa Chemical's Osaka laboratories was flagged. A transparently bogus press release mentioned stolen narcotics. Intel was that U-F did R&D with hallucinogens, but their unconventional warfare programme involved fungus hybrids and spore derivatives.

The Aum Draht clowns were wearing Bug Bombs.

The detective fired a warning shot. He couldn't plug Mr One in his bullseye iris, for fear of detonating his deadly waistcoat.

Mr One didn't flinch. He was intent on reaching Mr Eye.

Nezumi didn't struggle but used her pennyweight to stagger her captor backwards a few feet. That frustrated him. He was supposed to have the upper hand.

Not using a switch. So – proximity fuses!

'Keep them apart,' Richard shouted. 'Or they'll go off.'

Only now did the eyeheads notice him.

Mr One twisted his whole head round – seeing through that mask must be a bugger – and his big pupil narrowed. The head-wrap wasn't just painted cloth. There was a lens in there. Richard imagined Mr One could pick up FM. He hoped Cham-Cham were chirruping the wax out of his ears.

The terrorist stepped grimly onto the carpet.

Nezumi planted her feet on his chest – soft-soled school shoes against the bandolier of deadly phials – and straightened her back. The adepts couldn't clash with her between them.

The cop didn't have a shot.

The crowd formed a circle. Sensible folk scarpered, but many – perhaps thinking this was Christina Light's idea of chiliast street theatre – stayed to watch. Spectators made it hard for the security to get through. Syrie tapped her temple with her forefinger. Her glasses could take pictures. A lovely end-of-the-world souvenir.

Mr Eye tried to let Nezumi go, but she wouldn't be dropped. She had a grip on his greasy coat-sleeves.

Mr One tried to get around her, but she swivelled with him. He stepped back so she couldn't stay a living bridge and came at the problem from a different angle. Nezumi pushed firmly against Mr Eye, let his arms go, did a mid-air somersault that drew applause, and landed with gymnastic perfection, knees bent, well-balanced, arms outstretched. A second later, the popped top of her poster tube landed nearby. She held the tube, which now contained only a scabbard, with her left hand, aiming it at Mr Eye. In her right hand was a sword. It was directed at Mr One.

He was the more determined of the two, readier for death in his cause.

Which Richard would be sure to get Syrie to explain so it made approximate sense. The doctrine of the Wire was some fortune cookie *koan* about life being a game and everyone being pieces on a three-dimensional board.

Mr One stepped back. Retreating? No, getting ready for a run-up.

He was going to charge the little girl.

Nezumi whirled around in a complete circle. Mr One could not see what she had done. Red marked her blade.

Mr Eye was done. Blood sprayed from a necklet wound and his big eyeball head rolled off. His body stood still for a few moments, then his knees went and he crumpled in a heap.

Mr One paused.

The proximity fuse should work even if the waistcoat-wearer was down a noggin.

But the adept might not think that through. To his mind-set, the bomb might have died with its wearer. No telling what these fruit and nut cases believed.

He held his open hands apart – to give Nezumi mocking applause?

No. He'd have secondary detonators in his glove-palms.

Richard didn't have to tell her that.

Nezumi had trouble keeping principal exports of South American countries in her head from term to term, but paid attention in practical lessons. Richard shouldn't have been surprised Drearcliff Grange had BioTerror Response on the curriculum. The school offered young ladies a thorough education.

If Richard were her, he'd chop the adept's hands off now – which would trigger another failsafe, he instantly realised.

A good thing he wasn't her then.

She advanced on Mr One, sword above her head and angled slightly down, tube-scabbard held behind her back like a baton.

The big pupil fixed on the sharp point of the sword – which is what she wanted.

She whipped the tube round and smashed his right knee, which brought him down to her level. He knelt under her blade, as if before the Queen to be knighted. She was close to his chest, so he couldn't clap without reaching around her body. The iris narrowed.

Deftly, almost gently, Nezumi pricked his neck – a stretch of bare Caucasian skin between coat-collar and the rim of his mask. The sharp of her *katana* wasn't a pointy tip, but a honed end. She eased six inches or so of steel down into his torso, then pulled it out.

Mr One clapped a hand over the blood-bubbling wound. Nezumi broke his other with a quarterstaff jab from the blunt end of the tube-scabbard. The Wire taught that pain was illusory. Judging from this adept's high-pitched yell, it must be a convincing illusion.

Richard knelt to one side of them and the detective on the other. Neither wanted to get in the way. Most other spectators were well back. Of course, thanks to the brainboxes at U-F Chemical, keeping well back in, say, Tierra del Fuego might not be far enough from this ground zero. La di da, the wonders of science.

'Slide his coat off his shoulders,' Nezumi told Richard.

Then she said the same to the detective in Japanese.

'Gently,' she specified, needlessly.

The big eye managed to look furious.

Richard didn't need unusual empathy to understand the terrorist's rage.

He'd expected to be dead by now and ushered into the digital winners' circle.

The Wire is watching – and, most likely, frowning.

Failed suicide bombers found that God stopped taking their calls.

Together, Richard and the detective lifted the plasticky coat away from Mr One's shoulders. Wires looped around, cutting into a plain white shirt. He wore a skinny black vinyl tie. The phials were hooked up to a Heath Robinson contraption of wheels and cogs and acid-smelling batteries.

Whatever deadly germ boiled inside the containers made pretty colours.

The phials were like little lava lamps. Blobs in liquid, breaking apart, coming together. Mandrake-tendril knots formed in each glass ovum.

A six-pack of apocalypse.

Only in 1999…

Nezumi sheathed her sword and shoulderslung the tube.

She took a Girl Guide penknife from her blazer pocket. Eighteen blades and doodads, including the thing for prising pebbles out of horses' hooves and, thanks to the foresight of the manufacturers, the exact set of little scissors required to disable a Bug Bomb detonator.

She kissed the chunky knife and snipped five times.

Richard, Nezumi and the detective stood up. The waistcoat came away from Mr One's torso. Nezumi carefully laid it on the carpeted pavement, trusting someone qualified would secure it.

Mr One still held his leaking collar-wound. Nezumi had left him alive.

She didn't use lethal force when it could be avoided. She thought it wasted effort. Distasteful to her way of thinking – which was as much school spirit as *bushido*.

The detective kicked the defanged terrorist.

If the vulture-eye cop made the arrest, Mr One might envy his late partner. The adept was not going to have an easy time of it. Especially if this crowd tumbled to what would have happened if he'd pulled off his 'spectacular'.

'Detective Azuma,' said someone, repressing panic.

They looked at the speaker, the uniformed officer Richard had seen earlier.

He stood over Mr Eye. His shoe was stained yellowish-green and bulging at the seams. Spatter had got on him and was spreading up his leg.

A snail-trail of slime from the beheaded terrorist's waistcoat mingled with the blood-gush from his neck-stub. Once free, the stuff sought out a host.

Nezumi drew her sword again and hacked off the policeman's foot – below the knee, above the line of infection.

He screamed and fell over backwards.

The detective – Azuma – aimed at Nezumi now.

Richard laid a hand on his taut forearm.

'He'll thank her for it,' he said. 'If he gets help, quickly.'

Azuma – who must understand some English – holstered his weapon and unclipped a walkie-talkie from his jacket.

Nezumi, stepping well away from the slime, sheathed her sword and tried to help the copper, improvising a tourniquet from his belt. She might have a Girl Guide knife attachment to tie off and suture snipped veins. The patient was too shocked to resist her battlefield nursing. A sue-for-malpractice mood might come later.

Other security staff had to be told to stay back from the dead adept and his deadly leakage. A curious eye – Syrie's jewel monitor – peeped from between the shoulders of a couple of flatheads. The hearse driver was with them. Sent by his unknown master to check on the hold-up? The vampire chauffeur had iron fangs – a rusty beartrap crammed into his red-stained mouth. Richard had heard of a Gorbals hardnut with that trademark. A Mr Horowitz who earned the name Mr Horror on the terraces at Ibrox Park. His reputation as a nutter carried over from football hooliganism into the club bouncer scene. Now he'd gone international.

But where was Mr Horror when a tiny schoolgirl was saving everyone?

Azuma made the same report to several people over his walkie-talkie. The bad news was relayed to superiors up the chain of command, and along side-kinks to authorities other than the police.

Azuma did his best to convince whoever he talked to that this was Most Serious.

Richard looked at the policeman's chopped-off foot. The swelling, dribbling, bright yellow puffball was no longer recognisable as part of a human being.

DR KIYOKAZU AKIBA

In 1988, twenty-seven-year-old Kiyokazu Akiba – then interning at the Self-Defence Forces Central Hospital in Setagaya – was recruited into EarthGuard. He was told not to reveal to anyone outside the organisation that it existed. He told his fiancée Reiko, an investigative journalist, that his induction course was a conference on the mathematical mapping of infection vectors.

He was given the rank of First Lieutenant. Accepting a generous retainer obliged him to carry a beeper. EarthGuard were liable to call on him in unthinkable emergencies, which were more common than anyone wanted to believe. Without resolute, well-funded action there wouldn't be an Earth to guard. Based in Japan, EarthGuard drew on personnel from across Australasia.

Akiba only knew what the alarm sounded like because he had to send a message every month that was answered by a test beep. He received new, more compact beepers every year until 1995, when EarthGuard phased them out in favour of cellular phones. His first phone was a plastic brick with a shaped rubber aerial. The gadget looked like an electric sex toy and was a nuisance to carry. Sleeker, smaller models made things easier, especially when he needed to lug two around. Reiko, now his wife, made a fuss about him having a cell she couldn't call.

Under the alarming command of General Gokemidoro, EarthGuard had a military structure. Its reservists included policemen, scientists, bureaucrats, reformed (and active) criminals, science fiction writers, and a famous television comedian. Akiba attended crisis seminars that felt like fantasy role-playing games. With various degrees of seriousness, the think tanks formulated response plans for unlikely eventualities. Overt and covert alien invasion, another nuclear attack, climatic or geologic cataclysm, sudden sentience of hostile fauna or flora.

'One hundred and twenty years ago, few believed in vampires,' said the General – himself a bloodsucker, with a fanged, vertical extra mouth in his forehead. 'Fewer still were prepared for the Dracula Declaration. We must not be taken by surprise again.'

For most of the year, Akiba worked at the Tokyo Medical Centre. He published papers on zoonosis – the phenomenon of animal, bird or insect viruses mutating into forms communicable to human beings, with particular emphasis on the susceptibility of vampires or related *yōkai*. An untaxed ghost salary augmented his declared income. EarthGuard service was undemanding, though exercises were always scheduled at inconvenient times. When Reiko gave birth to their son, he was absent – coping with an imaginary epidemic of suicidal mania.

His beepers never beeped and his phones never rang, but he carried an EarthGuard contact device at all times. Failure to do so was punishable by a ten-year stretch in military prison. The honorarium meant a bigger apartment, a newer model Toyota, and a house by the sea for his wife's parents. Strictly, he shouldn't have told Reiko about the money. After the collapse of the bubble economy he had to explain their liquidity. He implied, not inaccurately, that he benefited from a government grant for epidemiological studies.

The 1997 outbreak of A/H17Nx ('bat flu') in Guatemala was a fillip to the field of pandemic preparedness. A new strain of an old disease jumped the species barrier from a fruitbat to a vampire (immune but a carrier), then to the wider human population. The next year, EarthGuard sent Akiba to Malaysia, where the *pontianak* community was decimated by the bat-borne Nipah virus. He was requested by Wings Over the World, who needed all the epidemiologists they could get, to staff their aid station.

The question of whether vampirism was a disease or a condition remained unsettled after more than a century of study. Diseases didn't care either way. Vampires tended to take immunities for granted while bugs evolved all the time. If Nipah spread beyond relatively remote climes, it could be as devastating to haemovores as AIDS was for haemophiliacs in the 1980s.

Like most folk, Akiba considered turning vampire. He weighed a low-level addiction against theoretical immortality. His specialism convinced him the risk wasn't worth it. One bad bat could cough up a superbug and render the undead extinct within a warm generation. His position might be a symptom of a catastrophist mind-set. Years of considering worst-case scenarios must have an effect.

After the divorce, Reiko kept the apartment, the Toyota and their son, but her parents quit the beach house.

Promoted every few years, he now held the rank of Major.

His phone did not ring. The Earth was – he presumed – relatively safe.

He had New Year's Eve plans. His girlfriend Tokiko, deputy manager of the five-star Uchoten Hotel, was troubleshooting a party in the Garbo Suite. He was to be a living prop, to show she had a life outside work – which she was willing to sacrifice for the hotel. He was to stand around making light conversation while she put out fires. No unthinkable scenario was as terrifying as Tokiko's vision of celebrities amok. The combustible guest list included an alcoholic *enka* star with a history of farcical public suicide attempts, a fashion model famous as an ex-call girl (terrified gossip columnists would find out she'd invented a scandalous past to make herself interesting), and a blind vampire jazz pianist with a reputation for nipping the waitresses.

If it were his choice, Akiba would have observed ōmisoka – staying home in the flat, tidying up, performing ritual exorcism, throwing away unread medical journals, finishing leftovers from the fridge, and watching *Kōhaku Uta Gassen* (*Red and White Song Battle*) on NHK. When Japan took the Gregorian calendar, the New Year festival shifted from the last day of the twelfth lunar month to December 31. That was no reason to turn Tokyo into Times Square and surrender to this millennium mania. However, when her job came into it, Tokiko suspended democracy in their household.

As the sun went down, Akiba – in dinner jacket, starched shirt and bow tie – was in the hotel kitchen, a witness to potential violence. Tokiko held a cake-knife to the throat of the caterer. She was not satisfied with the sushi.

The sample tasted fine to Akiba – who was, on the sly, something of a foodie.

His EarthGuard code-name was 'the Gourmet'.

But Tokiko had mutant taste buds.

The fish was supposed to have been swimming three hours ago – still flapping as the first guests arrived. Tokiko said it was four hours out of the water. At least.

Akiba would have to intervene.

It wouldn't do to murder anyone before midnight.

The wafer-thin object in his inside breast pocket vibrated for three seconds. Then a ringtone sounded.

A wag in the communications centre had decided 'Return the Sun!', an anti-pollution protest song from 1971, was the EarthGuard anthem. Akiba's cell blared out a sample of the rousing chorus.

'*Kaese! Taiyô Wo! Kaese! Taiyô Wo!*'

Tokiko and the caterer looked at him.

'I have to take this,' Akiba said.

Tokiko shrugged angrily, eyes popping.

He hadn't told her about his ghost job. She wouldn't pay attention anyway. She once let slip that she assumed he was a plastic surgeon. Her main girlfriend plus point was not being an investigative journalist.

The ringtone persisted.

This was not a test. He took out the phone and flipped it open.

'Gourmet,' he said.

'Golgotha,' was the response.

He didn't know who went with that code-name.

'I'm at the Uchoten—'

'We know,' interrupted the voice. 'RV-1 will be outside the main entrance in a minute and a half.'

The call cut off and Akiba began walking.

'Where are you going?' said Tokiko.

'To save the Earth,' he said, not expecting her to believe him.

NEZUMI

The policeman whose foot she'd chopped off was still unhappy about it. 'That's a good sign,' said Mr Jeperson.

Nezumi understood, but reckoned Officer Kamikura didn't.

In the gutter was a mushroom-spouting puddle with a shoe in it. Not being a man-sized mess of yellow mulch was a good sign.

Being conscious enough to look unhappy was a good sign.

Breathing and having a pulse – overrated, but good signs.

Her shocked patient was surrounded by cooing vampires. Police girls offered support and succour, but might also want a crafty lick of his stump. That might even help. Vampire saliva contained a numbing agent and an anti-coagulant. Some *nosferatu* really could 'kiss it better'. Then, all at once, the yo-yos tumbled that cosying up to the victim of a bio-terror attack was risky and abandoned Kamikura. Nezumi had a pang. She wanted to like them but the callous streak disappointed her. Were the badges just costume jewellery?

Kamikura sat on the pavement, stump elevated and seeping only a little. Nezumi had done a proper job with the tourniquet. Worth a gold star from Nurse Wretched. At Drearcliff Grange, practice dummies bled rhubarb purée – used in first-aid lessons because the canteen ordered vats of the gunk only to find no girl would eat it. That purple splurge didn't prickle Nezumi's fangs. Spilled blood did. She kept her mouth closed. A smile of encouragement might be taken the wrong way.

A departing yo-yo dabbed her finger in the splash on the carpet and touched her long tongue with it. One of her comrades made a 'yeurgh' face. The bloodlicker showed no shame.

'That better have come from the leg not the foot,' said Mr Jeperson.

Horrorstruck, the girl cop spat into the gutter.

If Nezumi hadn't acted swiftly, the taint would be in Kamikura's blood. She'd saved his life.

She preferred to think of him than the man she'd killed.

Him, she'd diagnosed as a decapitation case and acted accordingly.

It ought to be a comfort that the dead man woke up this morning fully committed to being a suicide bomber.

His friend, she'd just immobilised.

Now she'd done what she could for Kamikura, she was obliged to look at the man she'd stuck with her sword. He was handcuffed to the front bumper of the stretch hearse. Since she'd put him out of the fight, he'd sustained extra injuries. Detective Azuma had given him an unsportsmanlike kicking.

The Bad Penny peered hungrily through the front passenger window, snub nose pressed to glass. Her unusual eyes burned electric blue as her brain buzzed with red thirst. Her mouth stretched like the cat's in *Alice*. Extra teeth crowded out of her gums.

Her chauffeur – a big-chinned plug-ugly – stood over the prisoner.

He wore polished boots with steel toecaps. Azuma wasn't the only rib-kicker at the scene of this crime.

The Aum Draht looney was in a sorry state. She didn't feel very sorry for him.

If he'd had his way, everyone in sight – which was a *lot* of people –

would be fungus heaps. The Plaza would be a sprouting pool of noxious man-mushrooms.

The prisoner's brainwhorl-patterned hood was stained with leakage. His cyclops-eye visor was stoved in.

She gave him a once-over. Cracked ribs. Broken arm. Not her doing. That collar-wound. Bingo.

One of the yo-yos had a medical kit. Nezumi asked for a big plaster, which was reluctantly handed over. Unpeeling it was a fiddle, but she managed. She slapped the plaster on the neat slit she'd made under the prisoner's collarbone. A carton of Blue Label Sprünt fitted into his shirt-front pocket with an attached straw. Gamers practically lived off the brew, she knew.

His head moved. He was awake and trying to look at her.

The cloth over his mouth was torn. He gave a snarly smile.

'What *were* you thinking?' she asked, fitting the straw into his mouth.

He sucked, ungratefully.

He couldn't be more than eighteen. A boy.

With great effort, he raised his hand and made a finger-gun then flicked up his thumb as if shooting her in the heart, and collapsed in pained exhaustion.

The chauffeur stuck a boot-cap into his side again.

'No call for that,' said Nezumi.

The chauffeur smiled. His false choppers were rusty, staining his gums.

The terrorist groaned.

DR AKIBA

Early arrivals dawdled in the lobby of the Uchoten Hotel. Zenbu, the *enka* star, gestured to a thin crowd, re-enacting his moderately well-known attempt to throttle himself with a scarf. He was politely ignored by a group of middle-aged men who wore matching furry balaclavas topped with deer ears and antlers.

Akiba pushed through a set of double doors into a bank of cold air. He'd not retrieved his topcoat from the cloakroom. Staff were aghast as a blue-grey armoured personnel carrier rolled into a prime drop-off spot. A commissionaire tried to shoo away the urban tank. An amplified voice ordered him not to approach.

Rolling Vehicle One was an EarthGuard transport, nicknamed 'the Armourdillo' for its thick shell of overlapping plates and outthrusting ram-raider snout. The logo on its steel flank was supposed to confer instant authority. It was assumed panic and puzzlement would be problems. The EarthGuard symbol was a burning pyramid with a human female smile. Akiba wondered whether the design team read the brief backwards, and devised an image to foment panic and puzzlement.

The front passenger window rolled down. A lean, crop-haired man looked out. He had hawk eyes and sharp cheekbones.

'Gourmet,' said Akiba.

'Golgotha,' responded the man.

His black jump-suit had a Colonel's bars and stars on the sleeve. An EarthGuard insignia badge was pinned to his beret. Tinted spectacles shielded glinting eyes. He was in obvious command.

An intense young guy sat in the driver's seat, gloved hands on the wheel. All haircut and attitude. *Hashiriya* – a street racer. Not military.

Golgotha thumbed towards the rear compartment. A hatch opened with a purr of motors.

Akiba walked round and looked in.

Two rows of EarthGuard personnel in off-white HazMat suits sat opposite each other, helmets on laps. Nine spots were occupied. Akiba was tenth man on the team. This crew looked more like combat-ready troops than the multi-disciplinary kooks he'd met on war games. Not the sorts to pick a silly song as an official ringtone.

'Make your jokes in training,' General Gokemidoro said. 'Sense of humour will not survive deployment.'

Two and a half minutes after the phone that never rings rang, Akiba was starting to be terrified. He'd thought anything would be better than Tokiko's party. Now he had his wish and wanted to take it back.

The sky was red but not on fire. Crowds weren't streaming past, shrieking and pointing behind them. Decapitated corpses did not litter the streets. No giant mother-ship hovered over the Diet Building. Akiba ruled out any of the scenarios EarthGuard had role-played.

If he was on the first response team, it must be infectious or contagious.

Tokyo was the *Titanic* after the iceberg hit but before the passengers realised what that bump, scrape and rip meant.

Only a handful of people knew the ship was sinking.

He climbed into the 'dillo and found a space ready for him.

Neighbours helped him into his HazMat. The loose suit went over his clothes and sealed with a press-shut Y seam in the configuration of autopsy sutures. Condom-thin, rip-resistant plasticised fabric would shield him from contaminants – but not, he now realised, the cold. He banged his unhelmeted head on the roof as the Armourdillo moved out, and sat down, bumping his coccyx. A floppy-haired youth who looked to be high-school age showed him how to strap up and buckle in.

An intercom screen came on and Golgotha reported to the team.

'Less than ten minutes ago, a terrorist affiliated to the Aum Draht sect let loose a fungal agent in Casamassima Bay.'

Akiba knew the bio-capabilities of Aum Draht. They were beyond sarin in the subway. The cult appealed to D&D obsessives, cybernet hackers, manga *otaku* and garage band Frankensteins. Adepts had tech-savvy, disposable income, laboratory access, and the free time that comes with not having girlfriends. Who knew what they'd cooked up?

Weaponised athlete's foot? Murdering mushrooms?

A culinary countermeasure might be garlic – which, joking aside, had proven immunosupportive properties. Garlic would be scarce in a vampire district.

'Does EarthGuard have authority in the Bund?' asked a woman.

'The Bund is on Earth,' said the Colonel. 'We are EarthGuard. Our remit is to guard the planet.'

'And the moon,' chipped in a bearded New Zealander. 'Hi, I'm Derek. Code-Name, uh, Derek... didn't have time to think of a better one. I'm a xenobiologist. Bugs and such.'

'Gourmet,' said Akiba, 'infectious diseases and contagions. Smaller bugs. We met at the Mu symposium.'

'Oh yeah, rayguns and sea-horse chariots. And sharks with legs. Good times.'

EarthGuard had gamed an attack on Japan from a hitherto-isolated, technologically superior civilisation. In a huddle with an attractive archaeologist and a *bosozoku* gang leader, Akiba and Derek brainstormed guerrilla resistance to an advance of barnacle-encrusted hover-tanks.

The New Zealander was one of only two persons here Akiba recognised.

Akiba looked at the others, expecting self-introductions.

'Cottonmouth,' said the woman, who was Asian but had freckles, 'expedited solutions.'

As she spoke, Akiba saw fangs. A vampire.

Other code-names were volunteered. Hunter (an American), Killer (the high-schooler), Furīman, Panty-Mask (!), the Butler, Caterpillar, Astro-Man ('infiltration'). Akiba and Derek were the only whitecoats. The rest seemed olive-drab: military or security. The Butler and Astro-Man were vampires. The cat-eared Butler wore dress gloves over his HazMat, with *saimin* sigils sewn in red thread into the palms. That made him the squad's spiritual advisor. Caterpillar was encased in armour – his plastic overalls were stretched thin over rivets and plate – and had mechanical limbs wired to a control helmet. One arm ended in what looked like the spout of a flamethrower. The other had a grapple-claw attachment.

Astro-Man was vague in outline, as if permanently on the point of shapeshifting – or dissipating – into mist. He was the other person Akiba had met before. It was the only time an active EarthGuard mission had intruded on his civilian life. Astro-Man was brought to TCM in semi-vapour form, in need of multiple transfusions of warm and vampire blood to achieve solidity. He had been injured during a bank raid Akiba was assured served the cause of defending the planet. Something other than money was kept in the vault. Team leader Hanjuro, 'the Black Ninja', had scores across his face, as if he'd been clawed by a tiger with the handspan of Rachmaninov. Even for *kyuketsuki*, Astro-Man's physiology was unusual. Akiba trusted he was fully recovered and fit for the field.

Golgotha stayed on the intercom, face grim. Other screens showed the streets, busy with festival crowds, people on their way to parties.

Akiba took it as read that he was no longer in a relationship.

A map image showed a blip. RV-1 was nearing the Yōkai Town Gate.

Panty-Mask, a muscular fellow, bulked out his HazMat suit so much that he looked like the Michelin Mascot. It was easy to see how he came by his code-name. A filter over his nose and mouth looked like women's underwear. He didn't see anything funny in that and gave the impression no one else should either.

In charge of equipment, Panty-Mask handed out small arms. Everyone but Akiba, Derek and Caterpillar got Minebea 9mm pistols and oily PM-9s. Against JSDF regulations (and Japan's Post-War Constitution), the submachine guns were modified for combat use with folding stocks, detachable suppressors and mounted reflex sights. Weapons-proficient personnel set about clicking, sliding, sighting and generally fiddling with their new toys.

As party favours, Furīman and Cottonmouth got blades that slipped into pouches on their thighs. Cottonmouth smiled and patted the handle as she pocketed her extra fangs. She was a sparkle-eyed flirt.

Caterpillar, armed already, received only a thumbs-up from the weapons master.

Derek and Akiba lacked lethal ordnance.

'Oi, mate, do I get a shooter?' asked Derek.

Panty-Mask gave him a briefcase, which he opened. He drew a pistol-grip syringe and pointed it around, going 'pow pow pow' like a kid playing war.

Hunter and Killer pointed their real guns back at him.

'I surrender,' said Derek, smiling. 'It's not even loaded.'

The briefcase contained vials with different labels.

Akiba was issued with a large medical bag and checked inside. Standard stuff – even a stethoscope – with a few extras. Serums, blood-packs, vaccines and anti-venoms. Black phials of fast-acting poison. A firebreak protocol was in effect.

'I hope you've all had your shots,' he said.

'We're all dead,' said Furīman, who had colourful tendrils of tattoo curling around his neck. 'We were dead as soon as we signed up.'

'I was dead once,' said Cottonmouth. 'I got better.'

Furīman, a gloomy soul, shrugged. The tats suggested he was *yakuza*. Organised crime had a stake in the survival of civilisation the way vampires needed the warm. Parasites don't want a host to die just yet.

On the map screen, the RV-1 blip passed through the Gate and into the Bund without stopping for anything like a security inspection. Calls had been made and channels opened. General Gokemidoro must have cancelled holiday plans to be at post in the command centre, which was disguised as a film studio.

Cottonmouth smiled sharply. She, at least, was home.

NEZUMI

A siren sounded. Crowds shifted in the Plaza. People went on to the party. The Senator led the way with tales of an open bar and specialty dancers. Most guests had no idea what the disturbance was. It was over quickly. Her special talent was ending things quickly.

An armoured car the length of a London bus drove up. Its wraparound windshield was tinted so even vampire eyes couldn't see inside. The vehicle parked without running anyone over. It didn't even dent the fancy hearse with the big prod that stuck out of its cow-catcher.

A door unsealed. Steps unfolded like landing gear. A tall, dark-haired man emerged, pistol in hand. Nezumi couldn't identify his beret insignia but could tell he thought a lot of himself and expected people to agree with him. This was a big cheese. His stance was supposed to make her feel like saluting.

The rear doors opened. Operatives filed out like a pop group deplaning in front of a fan club crowd. One or two stumbled. They wore baggy white coveralls and space helmets. Someone with an approximate Australian accent apologised. He made her feel better. People who said sorry for things they couldn't help were usually sound.

The Big Cheese looked down from his step. He spotted the goo shoe and gestured with his gun.

A spaceman clanked over to the puddle. He had machine arms and legs. One of his arms terminated in a nozzle. He hitched his shoulder, ratcheting an internal mechanism, and poured flame onto the foot. The burning shoe and its contents ponged worse than the fungus. The mess blazed for seconds and was consumed, leaving only a smear of sulphurous soot. The cyborg gave another squirt for luck.

'We should have taken a sample,' said one of the crew.

The Big Cheese didn't bother to answer.

Nezumi had seen through him.

The commander had been wrong about something that was his fault and *hadn't* apologised. She'd not rely on him in a crisis.

Which this was.

'Everyone, stay where you are,' said the Big Cheese. 'Surrender yourselves to be examined for signs of contamination.'

'No need to panic,' said the quasi-Aussie, which, of course, was not reassuring.

DON SIMÒN DE MOLINAR Y VAZQUEZ

As Head of Security for Light Industries, Molinar commanded a small army from an office suite on Floor 88 of the Daikaiju Building. He benefited from a healthy bonus package, a near-unlimited supply of donor blood, and stock options. It said 'Executive Vice-President' on his business cards.

The Fairy Princess graciously included him in decision-making – partially because, as he could admit when she wasn't there, disagreeing with her gave him a grinding pain behind the eyes. Christina Light ensorcelled him in 1895 and he'd been in her thrall ever since. She was practical enough to know an echo chamber of yes-men overfed her vanity and made an effort to dampen her glamour. Zombie minions couldn't run a megacorp. There was enough play in the line for him to do his job, but the hook was in him. All the Princess had to do was lift the veil and he'd tear out his own heart and give it to her on a gold tray.

Molinar still thought of himself as Captain of the Guard. Armour and weaponry changed but the duties were the same. His breastplate: a $17,000 Leonard Logsdail three-piece, tailored to accommodate shoulder holster. His sword: a Beretta M9 semi-automatic pistol, modified for silver rounds. His helm: Walker and Blinde mirrorshades. He didn't need a page to run messages to men-at-arms. A Brilliant-Smith Digital Solutions two-way radio looped him into the corporation's dedicated communications network. Designed to look like an expensive wristwatch, it even told the time – which reminded him he was too busy to see Dr Pretorius.

Not tonight. When the Princess was due to Ascend.

Nevertheless, he headed down to the alchemist's lair. Ignoring a summons was impossible. Sending a Junior Vice-President or a Senior Secretary wouldn't do. Only Molinar's personal presence satisfied the quack.

He had a key, card or code for every lock in the Daikaiju Building. Including the sectors LI left out of brochures. The Donor Pens. The Suicide Gardens. The Crypt of Correction.

The sole exception was the domain of Septimus Pretorius.

Molinar stepped from the elevator into the fusty foyer. A door dead ahead was ornamented with a cluster-rut of cherubs, gargoyles, nymphs and stags. No card-reader to swipe. No lock to pick. Not even a handle. It only opened from the other side. Pretorius had been known to issue summonses then leave people waiting for days.

Molinar considered dynamite.

The Mad Gnome, as he rather liked to be called, adored finding excuses to remind the Executive Vice-President of this one limit to his omnipotence. Pretorius always twisted the screw when a hundred and one other things had to be done. The Genius Without Portfolio hid under the Princess's skirts like a jester sheltering behind royal patronage. Nose-tweaked courtiers must laugh or be thought to have too high an opinion of their own dignity.

Molinar anticipated Dr Pretorius's fall from favour – to be followed immediately by a fall from Floor 88. He imagined diving off the balcony alongside the alchemist. Sprouting wings through tailored vents in his Logsdail, he'd keep pace with the plummeting jackanapes. Then, after explosive impact, he'd thrust his face into a man-shaped carpet spread across flagstones and feed. He hadn't washed with the blood of an enemy in a hundred and fifty years.

Until that glorious night came – and, after the Ascension, who knew what plane the doctor's Princess and Protector would occupy? – he was required to report, salute and pay attention. Pretorius never had good news.

Molinar pulled a Victorian bell-rope that set off chimes, then had to stand on a ratty mat and look at a camera to be recognised. The bell-pull was a relic filched from the London home of the well-remembered researcher Henry Jekyll. Dr Pretorius prized ugly oddments with evil associations.

Antique foyer mirrors reminded vampire callers that they weren't really alive.

Molinar didn't care that he had no reflection. A valet trimmed his beard.

The Princess's guests were arriving, already causing headaches and ulcers. Senator Blutarski was drunk and pestering the prettier staff, asking where the real shindig was. The hospitality was too stuffy for his liking. He was sure an A-list orgy was getting started elsewhere in the building.

A buzz came in on the wrist radio from Officer Saki-A in the Plaza. Some Aum Draht altercation. Saki-A worked for LI but also Bund PD. Molinar had wanted to bar all eyeheads, but Chief Inugami nixed that. The Treaty of Light was expiring and the Bund was supposed to be welcoming. After the handover, things would run smoothly. As a major employer, LI could demand whatever policing they paid for. The old dog would be let go.

For the next few hours, he'd put up with it.

From a security point of view, the evening would run more to his liking if no one showed up. Christina could do her party piece in an empty ballroom, debut her new gown, pirouette in sparkles, make a speech, and ascend to her mysterious higher plane. The staff would clap and cheer. The Light Channel had a global reach so the world would know how wise she was within minutes of midnight.

Why did she need an in-person audience?

Molinar knew the answer. The Fairy Princess was a vampire.

Mostly too insubstantial to take blood, she drank admiration, excitement, emotion, applause. She was a *draining* woman. Everyone noticed that. Christina needed warm – or *not*-warm – bodies in the room.

Going by traditional undead rankings, Simòn de Molinar y Vazquez was an elder and Christina Light a new-born. He was the offspring of Don Sebastian de Villanueva, turned vampire in 1521. She was one of the multitude who rushed to rebirth during the chaos that followed the Dracula Declaration of 1885. But she had her hook in him. She was the Fairy Princess and he the Coachman Rat. Not even a courtier. Staff, with a gun.

Adventuring with Cortés in Mexico, Molinar had the Dark Kiss forced on him. He happened to be in the tent when Villanueva needed a mine canary to test a rumour. Xochitl, high priestess of Tezcatlipoca, was said to have a sorcerous knack of turning a vampire heart to dead stone with a look. She didn't. When Molinar survived the Evil Eye of True Death, Villanueva – another blasted alchemist! – lost interest. Neglecting his obligation as father-in-darkness, he left Molinar to fend for himself – admittedly in a land where human blood was easy to come by. Bowls of fresh gore adorned every altar and pyramid.

Like many soldier-vampires, Molinar spent centuries marching under whatever flag paid in gold rather than silver. Before Dracula, armies had a don't ask/don't tell policy about *nosferatu* berserkers. So long as they bit enemy throats, they found a billet. He ranged up and down the Americas, a continent never short of wars. He only slunk back to Europe with the French when Maximilian was shot. After the Declaration, he went to

London and joined the Carpathian Guard. The wearisome company of brutal, puffed-up Slavs prompted him to petition Dracula's Prime Minister, Lord Ruthven. Molinar became Captain of the Guard for 10, Downing Street.

He met Christina when arresting her after a botched terrorist outrage. That was early in her career, before she embarked on her quest to establish a safe haven for vampires who didn't recognise Dracula as King of Anything. The disembodied Princess was embedded in the stone of the Tower of London. Getting silver cuffs on her was a problem. While he puzzled it out, she glittered at him. He'd been warned of her effect on the male animal. Katharine Reed, the reporter who blew the whistle on the plot, kept insisting the Princess should be detained and guarded only by women. She should have been listened to.

Molinar had been under the spell so long he couldn't even say if it had worn off. He'd prospered under her patronage. Cashiered when Dracula was finally dragged off the English throne, he sought sanctuary in the Bund and was promoted swiftly through the ranks of the Princess's socialist utopia. Christina needed her back watched while she busied herself with good works.

The Fairy Princess didn't want a castle, but a palace. From experience, Molinar knew a palace was a castle with fancier curtains. But Christina *must* shine. It was the dominant trait of her bloodline. But did she have to shine out of a towering lamp shaped like a prickly dinosaur? She reminded him of that Xochitl. Not just a priestess, but the earthly shell of a god.

He would have liked to lock all doors, batten hatches, and do a headcount every eight hours. Even then, there'd be security issues. The Daikaiju Building showed the folly of putting all available eggs in the biggest possible basket. Its roaring stance seemed to invite ground fire – and Molinar kept imagining rocket attacks, shells bursting against windows, missiles streaking at the dragon's eyes.

Molinar made do with a stretched, but reliable staff. Vampires he could count on. Marit Verlaine, his *Segundo*, and Mitsuru Fujiwara, who ran the surveillance/communication systems. Knowing everything was the same as being everywhere, Fujiwara said. He'd tried to get a feed from Pretorius's laboratory using robot insects, but the alchemist caught them and fed the crushed remains to his plants.

He'd never ranked above Captain in anyone's army. Now, he was a general. That was what Executive Vice-President meant. Kings put about that they only submitted to the burden of a crown because their subjects loved and needed them, but hired the best generals they could find. They all actually ruled by fear, the sword and the boot.

Molinar had the keys and kept the enemies lists. From Floor 88, he could reach across the world. Light Industries was everywhere. He could have Don Sebastian dirked in Malibu tonight and be using his brain-pan as office spittoon tomorrow.

But he still had to stand on Dr Pretorius's mat and look in the camera.

A screen above the lens filled with a staring eye and feathery brow.

The door opened with a recorded creak.

RICHARD JEPERSON

Men with guns telling crowds to be calm seldom got what they asked for.

With no secure perimeter around the incident, onlookers found other places to be. Few chose to linger where there was a likelihood of incineration, amputation, or having their going-out clothes splattered with a bio-terror agent. Outsiders hurried towards the Daikaiju Building. Locals scarpered to regular haunts. No one volunteered to be examined 'for signs of contagion'.

The CO of the Emergency Response Team wasn't that fussed to lose the crowd.

A casual attitude. Not what Richard expected.

He noticed Syrie Van Epp – shoes off – smartly heading back to the Gate. He followed her thinking. If there *was* to be a secure perimeter, the logical move would be to seal the Bund – trapping the entire population and a host of invited guests in a potential hot zone. Was that the terrorist plan? A strike against a predominantly vampire community? To keep the Wall up beyond midnight?

It took a lot to make Syrie miss a party.

Did she know something he didn't? She was Aum Draht, like the pair of deuces who'd tried to kill everyone. She wasn't in on it, since she'd been in harm's way. Still, she might have a fair idea of the mischief capabilities of the radical wing of her fruitcake church.

'Detective Azuma,' he said, and pointed at Syrie.

The cop's vulture eye swivelled and he picked up Richard's meaning.

Azuma spoke, loudly.

Without knowing much Japanese, Richard caught the drift from a universal copper's tone of voice when addressing a shifty member of the public, 'Stop right there, missy, my girl, and prepare to assist the constabulary with their enquiries.'

Syrie froze, shoulders hitched.

She looked like a Christian Crusade activist caught shoplifting dodgy videos in Mary Millington's Sex Supermarket.

One of the v-girl cops laid the traditional hand on Syrie's bare shoulder, a symbolic 'got you' tag.

Richard hadn't acted gallantly but, even if the vampire socialite wasn't going to spread Terror Fungus, she was a witness worth interviewing. A possible person of interest.

He earned a sticker for being helpful to the boys in blue.

On instinct, he trusted Azuma more than the blokes in the battletruck. Gussied-up sten guns didn't go well with decontamination suits. They acted as if they were here to clean up not help out.

His hunches were usually worth paying attention to.

Nurse Nezumi surrendered her patients – the passed-out plod and the defanged suicide bomber – to the newcomers. The squad ran at a ratio of five gun-pointing goons to every one medical bag-toting clinician.

So far, this wasn't an outbreak – just a nasty trickle.

He looked at his hands, which weren't sprouting colourful fungus.

He felt his face, which was not sliding off his skull.

His layman's self-diagnosis was 'all clear'.

He'd been close enough to breathe in a lungful of pathogen. So had Nezumi, Syrie, and a dozen others who weren't screaming mushroom patches. Some extra factor was involved in the young officer being stricken. One for the labcoats to grapple with.

Conscious of his hypocrisy, he pulled the manoeuvre he'd blown the whistle on Syrie for trying. Taking a few steps back from the kerb, he slipped into the mainstream of the procession. He nodded to Nezumi to come along. He had a sense the real action wasn't down in the Plaza.

More than ever, he needed to be at the party in the Head of the Dragon.

All roads lead to Christina Light. She was up there, shining down.

He shoulder-bumped someone broad, standing still amid human flow.

Mr Horror.

Thin lips parted to show iron fangs.

'You should get those choppers seen to,' said Richard. 'You may have grounds to sue your dentist for malpractice.'

Nezumi's thumb went to the stopper of her poster tube.

Several guns were raised.

Richard was petard-hoisted. Mr Horror peached him out the way he'd grassed up Syrie.

He opted to de-escalate the situation.

'Everybody be a polar bear,' he said, hands open and out but not stuck up. 'Polar bears are cool, right? I'll turn myself over to whoever is in charge of the medical side of things.'

Translation: I'll talk to a doctor, not a gunman.

Nezumi rendered what he'd said into diplomatic Japanese.

The guns held steady. Eyes fixed on him, glaring through helmet windows. Pigsnout breathing filters wheezed.

The pukka ruler-of-all-he'd-conquered type ignored the developing stand-off, but one of the doctor johnnies perked up. The surviving culprit would most likely prove intransigent and/or incoherent, so Richard was the response unit's best bet for a sitrep. Guns wavered as the doc signalled, then pointed down at the asphalt.

A little-noted corollary to Chekhov's First Rule of Drama is that if you give a man a rifle in Act One, he'll immediately want to shoot someone. Towards the end of Act Two, the itch becomes too strong to resist. Act Three is guest-scripted by Quentin Tarantino.

A wasp-waisted vampire slid throwing knives back into thigh-sheaths. Her coverall was cinched with a utility belt. Not an inherently fetching outfit, but worn well.

Nezumi comfortably backslung her poster tube. Good girl.

Mr Horror barred Richard's escape until the sawbones took custody.

Odd. Richard would not have pegged Rusty Puss as particularly civic-minded.

He must be following orders from inside the hearse. Given half a chance, anyone who flew the Dracula standard would put one over on the Diogenes Club. The long-lived have long memories.

Or it could be that Horowitz took it into his tiny nut to be a prick this evening. Some folk were like that.

The doctor johnny escorted Richard to his bus.

Only then did he clock the burning pyramid logo. He knew who these people were, or at least who they were from: EarthGuard. Most countries had similar departments. In a roundabout way, they imitated the Diogenes Club – though the French liked to point out their Opera Ghost Agency was founded earlier. Someone had to deal with affairs too terrifying for the regular police, armed forces and intelligence services. Preferably hush-hush and on the QT.

America's Unnameables – *a* Federal Bureau of Investigation, as distinct from *the* Federal Bureau of Investigation – were tasked with keeping a lid on paraphenomena. They'd been cooking up cover stories since the *Mary Celeste* and were behind a generations-long ad campaign selling the myth of unidentified flying objects. They preferred Americans watch the skies rather than worry about spooks under their noses. Germany's Lohmann

Branch and Russia's Night Watch policed similar shadowlands. Even Wings Over the World had a Ghost Division.

In the 1920s, the private eye Kogorō Akechi founded Japan's Boy Detectives Club. An admirer of Mycroft Holmes, he appropriated the Diogenes Club methodology, rallying investigators against the Fiend With Twenty Faces, the Black Lizard and other threats that now seemed almost quaint. After the War, technocrats took over. The Boy Detectives lost amateur status and evolved into EarthGuard, an unpublicised branch of the JSDF.

EarthGuard's best remembered exploit was saving Expo 70 in Osaka – held to celebrate 'progress and harmony for mankind' – from an attack by a huge *kappa*, a grudge-holding vampire turtle.

So, soldiers, not mercs.

But these EarthGuard personnel weren't *acting* like soldiers.

Still, as someone said while reviewing *On the Beach*, whatever constituted normal behaviour in these circumstances was anybody's guess. Most of Richard's life had been spent 'in these circumstances' and he was none the wiser.

Under General Gokemidoro, EarthGuard deployed maser tanks, soldiers in exo-skeletons, and all manner of murder-tech. For obvious reasons, Japan cooled on militarism after 1945. EarthGuard hadn't got that memo. A faction – Kaname Kuran, Subaru Sumiyagi, Kyoichi Kagenuma – stubbornly preferred the plod of investigation to firing bigger and bigger weapons. Admittedly, they had advantages. Kuran was Christina's chief rival – the vampire Lord of Tokyo (excluding the Bund). Sumiyagi was an *onmyōji*, a sorcerer who could command demons. Kagenuma was a psychic detective who solved cases by waltzing through people's dreams. None of them were here. This Gokemidoro-sanctioned unit brought firepower not skills. Shooting at the problem had worked against the big turtle. The tactic was always high up on EarthGuard's list of preferred options.

The doctor helped Richard up inside the armoured dustcart.

'You speak English,' he said, voice tinny through an amplifier in his helmet.

'I *am* English,' Richard responded.

'Princess Diana, crumpets, *Merry Christmas Mr Bean*,' the doctor said. 'Brown Windsor soup.'

'Yes,' said Richard. 'That England.'

He hoped the doctor hadn't used up all his vocabulary in one burst.

'I am Dr Akiba. You have been exposed to weaponised fungus with a fatality rate of one hundred percent. Do you understand?'

'Yes, I understand.'

'Good. So why aren't you dead?'

SI MOLINAR

'Come in, come in,' said Dr Pretorius from a tennis umpire's chair perched on fifteen-foot stilts. 'The Gods despair of dawdlers.'

The alchemist wore a starched white tunic and elbow-length black rubber gloves. Goggles with a dozen adjustable lenses held back his explosion of hair. He sat in the middle of a circle of keyboards and control panels.

Not a vampire, he was alive beyond his allotted years. He said he was pickled in spirits but made no effort to quash rumours that he'd traded his soul to the Devil. Molinar wondered if the Mad Gnome dyed his nostril hair. He had birdnest nose-plugs. His chin got pointier every time he stroked it.

A saluting automaton – a toy soldier's helmeted, moustached head bobbing on a spring stuck out of a vacuum cleaner – ushered Molinar into the laboratory, bleeping and burbling in robot language. Its spherical form was dented. Visitors couldn't resist kicking it.

The door shut behind Molinar and multiple locks engaged.

Dr Pretorius had taken over a cathedral space in the core of the building. The name of his laboratory changed from week to week, but it was currently called the Integratron. With no exterior windows, the sanctum was cut off from direct contact with the outside world. The walls and ceiling – even support columns and sections of the floor – were hung with screens. Half emitted the bluish white glow of the Light Channel. The rest were live feeds, abstract art pieces, graphs and lifelines, disco lamps, old movies, www.porn, pirate videos, spycam views from around the building and the city, Indian cricket matches, and Transylvanian *Big Brother*. The wiring was a nightmare. Short circuits were part of the system. Cascades of sparks fell from the eaves. Spider-limbed mobile extinguishers crawled the walls, puffing squidgy white foam to douse fires.

If Pretorius wasn't crazy before he moved into his Integratron, ten minutes of sensory bombardment would have done the trick. He said he was swimming in the zeitgeist. Anyone else would drown.

A clanking cart approached in the shape of a black swan. It was stocked with bottles.

'Have some gin, Molinar,' said Pretorius. 'It's my only weakness.'

'You always say that. It's a lie. You have many weaknesses. Being half-mad is one of them.'

'I never do anything by half-measures,' he responded, pretending to be affronted. 'I am *completely* mad. *Perfectly* mad. *Gloriously* mad. How else can one stay attuned to this crazy-paved continuum? Look at the evidence of the maelstreams. Count Dracula gets the Jean Hersholt Humanitarian Award. The President of the United States fills a thousand pages with testimony about a stained dress. Do you really think that's how the universe is supposed to be?'

'Gin isn't even a weakness,' Molinar continued, ignoring the speech. 'It's a vice. You have many of those too.'

'Who among us cannot say the same?'

'Her,' said Molinar, pointing at an arched, curtain-framed section of the Integratron devoted to Christina Light. A calming presence in Pretorius's maelstream. Mostly portraits and photographs of her as a warm woman. Even film stills and posters. Veronica Lake, Meryl Streep and Madonna in *Casamassima*, *Voyage of the 'Macedonia'* and *Miss Christina*. The Princess's image couldn't be captured or recorded. She only manifested live, if not in the flesh. She *was* the glow of the Light

Channel. It was all she could transmit.

'Ah,' said Pretorius. 'I would never include *her* in any generality. She is her own entire uncommon category.'

'We agree on that then.'

'Once, she was light. Now, she is *electric*.'

Dr Pretorius was old-womanish. Molinar suspected he was immune to the effect the Princess had on men, and threw in with her project for his own reasons. That meant he must be watched. Mitsuru Fujiwara had the latest equipment and Pretorius lived amid a junkyard of obsolete television sets. There must be ways to turn the alchemist's own screens into spies.

'What is this intrusion? I'm very busy, you know.'

'You asked me to come,' said Molinar, wearily.

'Oh yes, dear dear, yes… silly me.'

'I'm reasonably busy myself.'

Dr Pretorius fiddled with knobs and switches.

'Just a mo… need to get a fellow patched in. Watch that wall there.'

Molinar looked at a cliff-face of moving images.

The screens blinked, then came on again. A pattern of light and dark, sixty feet high, formed a *trompe l'œil* pixel portrait. A bald man with a moustache.

'Am I supposed to recognise him?'

'This is my late colleague Brian O'Blivion – the first human to transcend. He left the flesh behind and did not turn vampire, but re-formed as a virtual person. The synthesis of all his teachings and thoughts and quirks and annoying little habits are now on hundreds and hundreds of Betamax videotapes. A wild prophet of the airwaves and a dedicated shockwave surfer, he picked the losing side in the format wars of the '80s. He'd be obsolete now, trapped in dead plastic boxes. I made it a project to transfer his information to our servers. We have him in our machine. Not a soul, if such things there be, but a process. A digital daemon. Brian in a Box. We can talk with him. I find his company refreshing. He foresaw the coming of Our Lady of Light, and his prophecies and cryptic warnings have been crucial. Without Professor O'Blivion, we would not be where we are.'

Cortés once charged Molinar with hanging a Jesuit who'd murdered a sacred monkey. High on psychedelic mould, the condemned man jabbered in different tongues as if possessed by five squabbling demons. Molinar had understood the priest better than he did Dr Pretorius.

'Don't look so glum. It's basic. O'Blivion is an O'Racle. Dead and gone from the realm of the flesh, he survives in a sphere of pure information. His bits and bytes make a kaleidoscope. Often, he issues helpful hints.'

Molinar was dubious.

The mosaic portrait moved like a film clip. The ghost professor shifted in his seat. The back of his jacket rucked up.

'A message from the beyond, just for you?'

'No, my dear Molinar, for you.'

A huge voice filled the screen-studded cavern. Molinar pressed his palms over his ears. Dr Pretorius wobbled in his precarious chair. His hair flew back as if he were caught in a wind tunnel.

'*Beware*,' boomed Brian O'Blivion. '*Beware Jun Zero!*'

All the facets of O'Blivion as if every blood vessel in the Professor's face exploded at once. The picture froze into photo-negative silver-on-grey afterimage, then degraded to static snow, except for eyes which hung there in space, composed of a dozen screen-savers, and looked straight at Molinar.

'There,' said Pretorius. 'Now you've been told.'

'What, exactly? That we should beware of a criminal who's on the watch-lists of every police agency in the world?'

The Mad Gnome tugged his lip and said, 'I may have exaggerated when I claimed we could talk *with* Professor O'Blivion. It's more a matter of him talking *to* – well, let's not beat about anyone's bush, *shouting at* – us. Oracles, as a rule, discourage follow-up questions. Takes the edge off the mystique. It is up to we lesser mortals to interpret and decode.'

NEZUMI

She was concerned Mr Jeperson might not be safe inside the big bus, but he wanted her not to pick fights with the cleaners. Her first duty was to protect her principal. Her second was to do what he asked. She sized up the newcomers and roughed out the order they'd need to be killed or disabled if they forced her to fight.

The vampire woman with the knives first.

The cyborg second. She didn't like fire.

The Big Cheese third. Nobbling a commanding officer always threw the enemy into a tizzy.

Then, the schoolboy and the larger of the two vampire men. The lingering smell of old blood was on them. They were the most practised killers.

The four remaining *ronin* – space-age samurai – in no particular order. The smaller vampire man was a wispy reed who'd shift to mist, a trick of limited use inside a sealed space suit.

Maybe the driver, to be on the safe side. She could tell least about him. Surprises weren't welcome.

The doctor who was talking with Mr Jeperson she could leave. If he snuck a poison needle out of his bag, Mr Jeperson could take care of himself. He had a fussy dislike of guns and knives – in Britain, he usually carried an umbrella shooting stick instead – but could go a round or two with the biggest bruiser in any given pub. Years of Sergeant Dravot's refresher courses in 'holds and throws and breakfalls' kept him fighting fit.

She'd not kill the semi-Aussie. Someone had to be alive to surrender.

And tell the tale.

'You do that?' the vampire woman asked her. She stood over the boy Nezumi had killed. Someone had fetched his eyeball-hooded head and put it back in place. It rolled over.

'Yes, miss,' Nezumi admitted.

'Nice work. What iron are you playing?'

Nezumi partially slid her sword from its sheath.

The woman whistled, which rattled through her helmet speaker.

Nezumi would have to thrust through her heart – the steel rim of her helmet was too thick for a head-chopping slice.

'Silvered steel,' the woman observed. 'Classy.'

Nezumi had taken her *katana* – crafted in the fourteenth century by Bizen Kanemitsu, the swordsmith known as *sai-jo o-wazamono*, which translated to Grand Master of Great Sharpness – to a Hatton Garden silversmith for plating. She was reluctant to subject the Kanemitsu to such treatment, but many famous blades had broken against vampire necks.

'Does it have a name?' the woman asked.

'"Good Night Kiss",' Nezumi admitted, resheathing the sword.

The woman patted the knives on her thighs. 'I call these "the Captain" and "Tennille". They're new.' She tapped her holstered pistol and shoulderslung machine gun. '"Simon Smith" and "Amazing Dancing Bear".'

'Good names,' said Nezumi.

'I think so. The naming of weapons is an art. Men give their guns and knives names like the ones they give cars and speedboats. As if they were naming their willies. Bragging and compensating.'

Nezumi giggled.

'Women name weapons as they name their babies. To nurture and protect and wish them well in the world. "Good Night Kiss". It's not a boastful name. It's a promise.'

'I am Nezumi. Mouse.'

'I'm "Cottonmouth". It's what a man decided to call me. Men like reptile names. It's better than "Viper". I'd have preferred "Garter Snake". My real name is O-Ren Blake.'

The semi-Aussie knelt by the dead boy.

'This is Derek,' said Cottonmouth.

'Hya,' croaked Derek.

'Nezumi took down the eyehead.'

'Choice,' said Derek.

He examined the suicide waistcoat, spotted the cracked canister, and took a small aerosol can out of his bag. He sprayed fast-setting sealant on the crack, then emptied the can coating most of the other phials. Airfix glue smell stung Nezumi's nostrils. The suspect goop was sealed in.

Cottonmouth gingerly picked up the waistcoat Nezumi had taken from the boy she hadn't had to kill and called for a lock-box.

'It's gonna be a mare to get this cluster bomb off Johnny No Head and into the chilly bin,' said Derek, holding up gauntleted hands. 'Can't undo the bloody knots with the glovies on, eh? Could one of you chop off his arms? Then I could wriggle the bang-bang vest off him and no worries.'

'Think of the optics, gorehound,' said an American.

'Aw, c'mon, Hunter. He's totally munted already. Double armodectormy's not gonna piss him off any more than losing his bloody coconut.'

'"The Wire is watching", remember,' said Hunter. 'We're on candid camera. All the time. Golgotha will do worse than rip your arms off if you start a riot by mutilating a corpse in public. At least drag him into an alley first.'

Nezumi took out her Girl Guide knife again.

'Careful there, Missy,' said Derek.

Disarming the charges was easier when the wearer was dead.

She stood back and let Cottonmouth strip the clinking waistcoat off the corpse. Hunter had another lock-box ready.

'You might want to take a shower,' Derek told her. 'Scrub with bleach, if you can. To be on the safe side. We're EarthGuard, by the way. Here to, ah, do what it says on the packet… guard Earth. From extranormal threats and suchlike. If Evil Squid from Mars were flopping about, we'd nut 'em. More of a calling than a grind. You can put in a chit for helping out.'

Derek picked up the severed head.

'So, matey, learned your lesson? Never bloody threaten Earth, because it's bloody guarded. And don't go spoiling a nice party with a bio-terror attack, 'cause no one likes that.'

'Derek is from New Zealand,' said Cottonmouth, solving one mystery. There were others. Like what EarthGuard were really up to.

A skill Nezumi picked up at school was sitting in a new classroom during the larking-about period before the register was called and mapping the invisible web of friendships and enmities. With careful observation and intuition, she could work out who was shamming, or stuck in the wrong group, or harbouring feelings that would bubble over eventually. Girls secretly liked as often as they secretly disliked. The history of Drearcliff Grange's shifting alliances and flare-up hostilities over any term was more complicated than Japan's Sengoku Era (the 'Warring States' period). Nezumi was used to living in a house of cards built on top of an apple cart.

She liked Cottonmouth, but didn't trust her. Friendly before the match, she'd smash your face with a stick as soon as the ref looked the other way.

Another cleaner – 'This is Panty-Mask, if you can believe it,' said Derek – brought over a body bag. Clear polythene, with a seal rather than a zip for use in cases of infectious disease. Derek handed over the head to stuff in with the rest of the corpse.

Panty-Mask hoisted the bag over his shoulder and walked back to the bus.

Only now did Golgotha step down to the street.

The Big Cheese came over to inspect the burned stain.

His crew stood to attention. Even Derek.

Nezumi was invisible to him. She didn't even need vampire powers or ninja stealth. He was used to ignoring children, girls, civilians.

It was odd, then, that he *did* notice the chauffeur. Their eyes didn't meet, but there was an awareness. The vampire with iron teeth was *expected*.

Mr Horror – not a friendly name.

A webstrand, the merest filament, stretched between the Colonel and the chauffeur.

Golgotha – also not a friendly name – was worse than a bad penny.

He was a bully, and self-righteous about it. To his way of thinking, he was born in charge.

Even Cottonmouth threw him a salute.

Bullies didn't have friends – only minions. They had wary alliances. Bullies never picked on each other. They marked out territory, then were beastly to whoever they could get away with picking on.

Golgotha had his gang about him, but there was another web. Some of the EarthGuard team were Inner Circle. Others were camouflage or cannon fodder.

Derek didn't know his principal had another gang that he wasn't in.

Sometimes, girls pretended not to be as close as they were. For advantage later in the day.

Golgotha knew Mr Horror not as an equal, but a minion. Someone else's. Bad Penny was most likely another. The sleek hearse's big cheese – most likely a fat bat – hadn't popped out of the coffin yet.

EarthGuard were doing more than tidying up. They were taking over.

Their bus was called the Armourdillo. She suspected it ought to be called the Trojan Horse.

The Aum Draht terrorists hadn't launched a random attack.

This was more cunning and much worse. A plan was side-tracked – the fungus dispersal she'd prevented would have needed more than aeroplane glue and a flamethrower arm to suppress – but not derailed.

Golgotha was through the gates.

SI MOLINAR

The Integratron was off the grid. It could pull signals from the Andromeda Galaxy but was not on the internal phone network. Dr Pretorius bothered people with scrawls stuffed into tubes and delivered by compressed air. When the Princess first commissioned visioneers to sketch plans for a futuristic skyscraper, they proudly included a state-of-the-art *pneumatique*. Decades later, when the Daikaiju Building was under construction, no one thought to amend the blueprints and install FAX machines instead. Only the Mad Gnome used the antiquated system. A fangs-on-edge-making *brring* sounded whenever a scroll plopped out onto a botheree's desk.

Inside the Integratron, Molinar's wrist radio didn't buzz. When he left, it practically electrocuted him. Ninety-seven urgent alerts from a dozen users.

In the elevator, he clicked through the gadget's greenscreen.

Multiple messages from Officer Saki-A, demanding response. Several from Saki-K, who wanted to know why her colleague's calls were ignored. Code signals for a terrorist incident. A report on the nature of the attack that corrupted into a hash of symbols because the Bund PD's beepers weren't compatible with LI Security's next-gen communi-tech. The terror code alert could mean anything from a Tatenokai nutjob beaning people with a kendo stick at the Shrine of Higo Yanagi to a tactical nuclear weapon set off in Mermaid Ancestor Place Market.

Hyakume wanted to know when the Gate would be open again.

The Gate was shut!

Highly Urgent voicemail from his *Segundo*, Marit Verlaine.

Rolling updates from staff about annoying guests. Senator Blutarski was charging around the kitchens waving a sushi knife. Waitresses wanted to know if they were cleared for a wet job on the fat fool.

Code signals for a fatality or fatalities. In some instances, that wouldn't be bad news – but Molinar's kill-list remained in a contingency folder. He had issued no hunting licences. People with no business dying had got clipped on his watch.

As Executive Vice-President, his watch was All The Time.

The express elevator wasn't express enough.

How long had he been with Pretorius? Twenty minutes, at most. How could so much go so wrong so quickly?

Was this what the oracle foretold? Was this Jun Zero?

He stepped out of the elevator into the Security offices. Emergency lights alternately bathed Floor 88 in blood-red and ultraviolet. Vampire eyes glowed like the heated points of torture pokers in the crimson. Fangs and shirt collars radiated eye-searing white in the UV. The accompanying siren was loud enough to scramble the Four Horsemen of the Poxyclypse.

A case in the reception area displayed his conquistador morion. He was tempted to break the glass and put the helmet on again. Cortés swore by his Toledo steel skid-lid. This is your best friend in a *tormenta de mierda*.

Verlaine was on the phone.

She was already in her black party minidress. A bow at the small of the back hid her hold-out gun. Her scarlet lipstick matched her bobbed hair.

In a hundred years, Molinar was the Bund's fifth Captain of the Guard/ Head of Security. Marit Verlaine, who came over on the *Macedonia* with the Princess, was its first and only *Segundo*. She refused promotion to the top spot and had literally buried two of her former bosses. She stood in her stockinged feet. High-heeled pumps, just out of the box, were on her desk. She'd taken off one earring to answer the phone.

Only a few of his people were still in the office.

A swivelling chair indicated that Suzan Arashi, the invisible geisha, was at her desk. Her job was monitoring who was in the building at any time.

Watson and Kuchisake were faffing around with the alarm. Kuchisake translated aloud from instructions printed in Japanese and German (giving away the period during which the equipment was purchased). Watson followed instructions, thumping buttons like a toddler who can't yet understand why a square peg doesn't fit a round hole. Against the odds, the smiling lovers – who usually wore matching anti-pollution masks over *sardonicus* grins – succeeded. Lights and siren shut off. Several panic phones rang and flashed, but could more easily be ignored.

The rest of Molinar's Guard would be at posts around the building, with a particular concentration in the ballroom.

Mitsuru Fujiwara's terminal was shut down, hooded with a dust cover. He was not on site. Damn. Molinar wanted to toss the Jun Zero thing at the cyberguy.

'… We will extend all cooperation,' said Verlaine, scowling.

She saw Molinar and held the phone to her chest.

'It's Gokemidoro of EarthGuard,' she said. 'He's sent in the Armourdillo. All holy hell is let loose. Where have you been?'

'With the Mad Gnome.'

Verlaine looked at the ceiling and shook her head.

'I know,' he said. 'Waste of time at the best of times.'

'This isn't those. This is the other ones. The worst of times.'

She put the phone to her ear again.

'Vice-President Molinar is here now. I can put him on… oh.'

She replaced the receiver and unwound herself from the long curly cord. 'He's hung up. General Vag-Face. We learned not to trust him in 1899.'

'Which mouth was talking?' he asked.

'The deeper, gruff one,' she said, pointing to her forehead.

Molinar hadn't often heard that voice. When the cranial jelly spoke through the cleft, the General nodded off. The higher brain was in charge. The rest of the body was someone else's – a suit the vampire wore. He was another relic of the days when the Treaty of Light was being drawn up. Macedonians didn't like him. Neither did anyone else, much – except successive Japanese governments who gave him plum jobs.

Verlaine put her earring back in, drawing a bead of blood. Licking her finger, she grimaced. Few loved the taste of their own blood. Most vampire women – unable to get piercings thanks to the healing ability – used clip-ons. Sliding fresh steel through the earlobes every night showed Verlaine's commitment. Mostly ascetic, she splashed out on earrings.

She gave him a recap. Aum Draht. Two eyeheads. A bio-bomb. Fungal plague. The terrorists got taken down quickly.

'The Sakis?'

Verlaine shook her head.

'Civilian security. One of the guests' bodyguards.'

'What have Gokemidoro's toy soldiers done?'

'Ordered the Gate shut.'

'I heard. Hyakume's goggling.'

'Only a few latecomers are stuck outside and no one will want to go home till after midnight. So that's breathing time before the shrieking starts. But no one complains as loud as rich people who have to stand in a queue for twenty minutes.'

'So, we have another deadline. Get back to EarthGuard and insist they open the Gate by twelve. Who's their team leader? The Black Ninja? Rider Kuuga?'

'Golgotha.'

'Don't know him. Don't want to know him.'

'He's not responded to my messages. It'd be professional courtesy. And he could use the manpower. Though all our ops are busy busy, manning the Gate or standing upstairs. I've talked with Inugami. He's in the dark and growling. Tokyo police have a presence inside the Wall. Detective Azuma.'

'A beat in the Bund is a step down from being suspended. What did he do?'

Verlaine smirked.

'Bit off a pimp's ear.'

'But what did he do *wrong*?'

'Spat it out again. Azuma's a v-and-v cop, by the way. Vampire and *violent*.'

Molinar suspected another free-range headache.

'Where's Fujiwara? Kicking loose at the party already?'

'He headed out with a sack of New Year presents. He's visiting his girlfriends in the police box. The Sakis will be delighted, though they'll hardly have time for a snack and a cuddle what with the terror alert and all.'

The thing Christina Light did to men Mitsuru Fujiwara did to women. Even Verlaine got catty when mentioning Fujiwara's *femme* fans. She couldn't mention the IT guy without blushing – and she was a death-white *nosferatu* with skin stretched *memento mori* taut over her cheekbones. When he wanted his apartment cleaned or his laundry done, Fujiwara went out on the street and put the glam on the first skirt he saw.

'What did Pretorius want?' Verlaine asked.

'To drop a name in the most annoying and overcomplicated way imaginable. Jun Zero.'

Verlaine thought a moment.

'Suzan,' she shouted. 'Can you shoot me over something from Fujiwara's system?'

A souvenir fan lifted from Suzan Arashi's desk and flapped. She often used the prop to prove her presence. She less often revealed that she didn't need to use her hands to do it. With limited telekinesis, she could pick things up from twenty yards away. She could swivel the chair too. Shooting at where you thought she was wouldn't do any good. Besides being invisible, she had a quiet voice – often mistaken for an echo or a ghost. Of the Bund's old-school *yōkai*, she was strangely best adapted to the modern world. She held down a job. Most of her peers, here before the Princess made her Treaty, sat about like museum exhibits. Watson and Kuchisake were on his team because they filled an employment quota. Suzan earned her badge. Her talents had practical uses in Security, Surveillance and Infiltration.

'Thank you,' said Verlaine as a document pinged on her screen.

She typed an access code – scarlet nails clicking on her ergonomic keyboard – and aha-hahed.

'Here we go. Jun Zero's dating profile on the FBI's Most Wanted list. He's a super-hacker. Providing he is a he, which isn't certain. A cyberspace terrorist. Deadly prankster. Brings down a government before breakfast. Transfers corporate slush funds to random citizens. Leaked a workprint of *Monk & Bat-Boy* online, before the nipples could be CGI'd off Clooney's habit. Fujiwara's triple-highlighted him as a threat.'

'We should beware of Jun Zero, according to Pretorius – or, rather, according to a ghost the Mad Gnome has trapped in his machine. Professor Brian O'Blivion, if you can believe it.'

'That can't be right.'

'It's his television name, Pretorius says. Not what he was born with.'

'No, not the name. Brian O'Blivion can't be telling us to beware Jun Zero.'

'Why not?'

'The FBI list known aliases. Brian O'Blivion *is* Jun Zero.'

DR AKIBA

The Englishman's pulse, temperature and blood pressure were normal. No pupil dilation. No external liquefication. Was Richard Jeperson randomly immune to Aum Draht's bespoke bio-weapon? Akiba didn't think so. The world, in his experience, was seldom as merciful.

So far, only Officer Kamikura was infected. Akiba had yet to determine whether the sedated policeman had been treated in time. It made sense to start with the patient who could answer direct questions.

Jeperson was calm and cooperative. It was peculiar that his BP and heart rate *weren't* elevated. Akiba was inside a HazMat suit and sweating bullets. Though he knew he'd been exposed to a deadly airborne agent, the dandyish gent was cool as iced cucumber. Not all Englishmen were as phlegmatic – or fatalist. With his dark skin, hawk features and fierce (dyed?) moustache, Jeperson could be taken for Berber or Cossack. When he spoke, he was as British as a BBC Shakespeare.

It was fortunate EarthGuard rallied so swiftly.

None of the others on this scratch team acted as if they'd been dragged out of New Year parties.

A vampire girl had taken off the policeman's infected foot.

Quick thinking. And a decent job. Nearly a professional, surgical amputation.

Akiba ripped the velcro blood pressure cuff loose. On Jeperson's forearm – over the extensor digitorum muscle – was a tattoo.

GEIST 97.

The Englishman saw him notice.

'I know it's an oddity,' said Jeperson. 'Auschwitz tattoos were strings of numbers. I wasn't in a concentration camp. It was some other ghastly thing. Still Nazis, though.'

Akiba was of a generation obliged to apologise repeatedly for Japan's conduct in the War. He accepted responsibility though his own family were victims of the Tojo regime. His father's father, an army doctor in occupied China, was executed in 1938 for refusing to assist Dr Komoda in a programme of inhumane experiments. The Key Man wanted to graft the legs of *jiangshi* – the 'hopping vampires' of Manchuria – onto the stumps of loyal soldiers mutilated in battle. When that didn't work, Komoda shifted to research that eventually lead to the Caterpillar's mechanical limbs.

Akiba's father was understandably a committed anti-militarist and fervent advocate of *demokrassi*. That Akiba was required not to tell family members he was in the armed forces was a relief.

To honour his grandfather, Akiba took an interest in crimes of science. The Black Ocean Society, the Kempeitai, industrial concerns, and all branches of the imperial armed forces had taken part in shameful activities.

Before the Treaty of Light, the Bund was Yōkai Town, where Japan put its monsters. The nation kept back sufficient monsters for its own use. Not all fiends had fangs. Blood debts were still outstanding. Even fifty-five years on, culprits might yet be brought to justice. The Key Man was unpunished and possibly still active.

He looked at Jeperson's tattoo a few seconds longer than he should have.

'Have you seen one like this before?' Jeperson couldn't hide his eagerness. This was a lifelong mystery for him.

Now, Akiba would guess, Jeperson's heart was racing.

'Not precisely the same,' Akiba admitted. 'But similar. Equivalent. "Geist" is German for "ghost"?'

Jeperson nodded.

'I have twice seen a tattoo with "Yurei", Japanese for "ghost", and a prime number. Once on a corpse…'

In Malaysia – a *pontianak* elder, dead of bat flu. 幽霊 23. YUREI 23. Performing a rush autopsy in a tent surrounded by soldiers with cans of gasoline and lit torches, Akiba had pressing concerns but noted the tattoo as a distinguishing feature – only for his supervisor to strike the detail from the record.

'… and once on a living man – well, a vampire.'

Astro-Man had 幽霊 139 on his forearm. YUREI 139.

When the EarthGuard agent was in his care, Akiba had asked where he got his mark.

'In the War.'

Of course.

Tojo's Japan and Hitler's Germany exchanged secrets shyly, like couples who killed together, relieved and stimulated to find partners not utterly repulsed by their predilections. The YUREI/GEIST programme was an Axis operation.

That *pontianak* wore an Imperial Army officer's cap, shorn of insignia. The Black Ocean Society had a presence in occupied Malaysia. They took as much interest in Malay vampire variants as in *jiangshi*.

'97 is a prime number,' said Jeperson. 'You think that's significant?'

With only his tattoo to go on, Jeperson hadn't considered its prime status. Even with only three examples, it was unlikely to be happenstance.

'Primes are not usual,' said Akiba. 'They get scarcer as you count upwards.'

'I'm not usual either,' Jeperson said.

'Neither were the individuals I mentioned. The Yurei Primes.'

'The living vampire? Do you know his name?'

'I know a name he uses.'

Jeperson smiled, understanding Akiba's caution.

'I apologise,' he said. 'Shouldn't dig for state secrets on such brief acquaintance. We've barely been introduced. I'm a damned foreign devil too.'

Jeperson handed over an oblong card.

RICHARD JEPERSON

MOST VALUED MEMBER

THE DIOGENES CLUB

LONDON SW1Y 5AH

UNITED KINGDOM

Akiba knew what the Diogenes Club was. Representatives from equivalent agencies attended EarthGuard seminars. Some years ago, the Diogenes Club sent a vampire specialist called Hamish Bond. He claimed to have a double first in oriental languages from Oxford but could barely manage enough Japanese to ask a geisha for a rub-down. Commander Bond had no interest in spitballing solutions to theoretical problems. He hared around Tokyo, biting local girls. He crashed nightclubs, bathhouses, gambling hells, and expensive vehicle prototypes. Everyone supposed the British sent him on overseas missions to keep him away from the secretaries in home office and stop him blowing up half the London subway on his morning commute.

'I see you've heard of us,' said Jeperson.

Akiba hoped his frown hadn't given him away then wondered how Jeperson had read his face. The helmet obscured most of it. He'd spotted his interest in the tattoo as well.

He must be slightly psychic.

The YUREI/GEIST Primes could have qualities in common.

Two vampires and a warm man. All unusual – gifted? Cursed? And branded in the War.

'We are colleagues,' Akiba said. 'In the Bund, we are both damned foreign devils.'

'Until midnight.'

Akiba nodded, bumping forehead against faceplate.

HAROLD TAKAHAMA

Floor 44 of the Daikaiju Building was a closed system. Narrow windowless corridors. Locked frosted glass doors. Exposed ducts. Steam belching from wonky joints. Scuffed last-walk-to-the-electric-chair linoleum.

Vending machines offered squeaking live vampire snacks and shrink-wrapped porno on CD-sized laserdiscs. He recognised none of the stars and understood only about half the kinks. Throat sprockets? Trampire tanlines? Tailstub upskirt? Eight years brought exciting, perplexing changes in adult entertainment. Was Rac Loring still on top – or underneath, or in between? Hal's fang fantasy wouldn't have aged since 1992.

A sour, behind-the-scenes smell permeated the recycled air. Floor 44 was invisible to higher-ups who took an overloaded system for granted. Processor rooms were the basement boilers of the twenty-first century. He'd seen that coming.

Lefty told him the Daikaiju Building was HQ of Light Industries, a world-spanning corporation. Their highest-profile biz was the Light Channel, which broadcast a soothing off-white glow around the clock. People tuned in and zoned out. Hours and hours of nothing were prized by an information-saturated society. Carried on basic cable in the US, its greater reach was on the World Wide Web. LI owned virtual continents of cyberspace.

Widescreen monitors at every junction were set to the Light Channel. Hal first took them for light fittings. The icy glow had a pulse. It vibed like a Zen Trojan Horse. Pumping subliminals into the backbrains of a million screen junkies?

Go out and buy. Reproduce and consume. Blame the poor.

Humpty-humpty humpty-humpty. Six more hours to Y2K, Y2K, Y2K. Six more hours to Y2K. *Silver Shamrock!*

So Jun Zero's posse had broken into a *zaibatsu* lair.

Hal tried to remember what he'd done when he had system access. Searching for overwritten memories was like probing a tooth abscess with a thumbtack. Light Industries must have high-grade firewalls. Jun Zero would have to be a hotshot to crack the system. Getting into the building can't have been easy, either. The client had laid out serious coin to set this up. Even Hal's murder would be expensive.

He must have completed the job, to flip Chiropterid Karl from Muscle to Assassin. The building could be counting down to conflagration. This was the last day of the century. Hal doubted the op was a freak-prank, like rigging the Light Channel to transmit a laxative thrumm to millions of loose-bowelled couch potatoes. Could be the client wanted to ring in the New Year by taking out the competition with an almighty Ker-Blammo.

Hal had invented a pulsar which hijacked an opposing G-bot's OS and set off all its bang-bangs in their silo-sheaths. A virtual v-weapon. Jun Zero might have ironed the bugs and developed a real-world version.

In this future, Harold Takahama was a terrorist!

If he was the digibomber, Dad would commit *seppuku* from shame.

Radical college girls would pin up his wanted poster in their dorms and write poems about his killer ops.

And the CIA-FBI-NSA would send kill-ninjas after him.

But right now, here on Friendly Floor 44, he was going to be slicer-diced by the ninjas before he got to make out with any rad chicks.

If he had to mind-jaunt into the future, why couldn't it have been to the good parts?

He recognised landmarks. A crescent-shaped bleach stain in the lino. A sign-up sheet for the Daikaiju Dodgers Battlefield Baseball team.

Coming back to where he started after a complete circuit of Floor 44, he still jumped at the shadow on the frosted glass.

Ishikawa walked into the translucent door over and over, like a bird flapping against a window. Blood smeared the other side of the glass. Vampires were strong. When Ishikawa redeveloped coordination skills, he'd get out of the Processor Room.

An alarm still sounded. Not a blare, but something like amplified wind chimes. As strangely soothing as the Light Channel. A coded signal beamed at intruders? Sit in the designated area and await qualified executioners to clip your lanyard.

The security sweep was overdue. Ishikawa was wearing a night guard uniform. Had the team replaced the regular security detail as part of their infiltration strategy?

'Lefty, can you access plans for this building?'

'Affirmative.'

'Share them with User Jun Zero.'

The appliance shot an unnecessary pain-jolt up his arm, which jerked out and aimed its palm at a blank stretch of wall, glass fingers splayed. A three-dimensional frame hung in the air. But not the plans he'd requested. Lefty was on the fritz! And far too free with the agonizer.

'That's not a building,' said Hal. 'That's a page from a D&D manual.'

The hologram was an anatomical model of a bipedal saurian. A big-bellied dragon with overdeveloped thighs and an Elizabethan ruff. It would make a righteous mecha. Hal saw where to implant weapons. Eyes, mouth, crest, chest, claws, tail. A warbeast of the wasteland.

'This *is* the Daikaiju Building,' said Lefty.

Daikaiju – Oversized Monster.

Conceptual breakthrough!

He was in an office block in the shape of a dinodroid. An actual G-bot, built life-size.

Way cool!

He had wished he were outside the building so he'd be safe. Now he wished he were outside so he could get a proper look at the edifice of awesome.

Hal Takahama thought that outstanding. And outrageous.

Jun Zero wanted to slay the beastoid, bring it down with a spear thrust to its heart. That was megachill too.

If Hal were in charge, he'd commission smaller-scale robo-versions of the building to patrol corridors and breathe fire on intruders. Maybe Jun Zero had been consulted and suggested just that.

Being totalled by his own idea would be the bring-down of all time.

'I give up,' he said. 'Lefty, where are the elevators?'

'Floor 44 is not accessible by public elevator or stairwell. In Japan, the number 44 is considered ill-omened. The Processor Room is located in a part of the building many assume not to exist.'

'Terrific. So this is a *cursed* floor!'

'The only points of entry or egress are the transporter circles marked on the plan.'

The framework blew up, giving a cross-section of the guts of the dragon – Floor 44 was the cloacal region, natch – with a scattering of flashing emerald lights.

'Transporter circles? Is *teleportation* a thing in 1999?'

Eight years could have seen all sorts of advances. Faster than light travel. Peace in Central Europe. Harold Takahama having a girlfriend.

'Transporter circles are hatches. With ladders.'

A disappointment. Still, less chance of getting his atoms scrambled.

Three emerald lights blinked red.

'What does that mean?'

'These circles are activated.'

'"Activated" means "open"?'

'Affirma— yes.'

The hologram shut off. A skeleton afterimage danced in his vision.

'Let's get this off the table,' he said. 'We're not being rescued, right?'

'The combination of tenses, double negative cut-outs and ambiguous interrogative inflexion renders your statement-stroke-question a non sequitur. The individuals who have gained access to Floor 44 do not share desired outcomes with Jun Zero. A ninety-two percent likelihood exists that their actions will be inimical to your survival.'

Figured. Killbastards incoming.

'This way,' said someone shrill. 'The nitwit's talking to himself.'

Thank you very much, Lefty – he thought.

Did his hand want to quit the partnership? Maybe it had an urge to take Vegas as a solo act. Or find another wrist to clamp.

He smelled old lady smell. Lavender water.

A child-sized head peeped around a corner. She had a lot of frizzy hair. Did electric filaments grow out of her scalp?

'Peek-a-boo, I see you,' she said.

A vampire kid. They were the worst.

He remembered what a horror Cousin Helen had been as a kid. Hellish wasn't even a bloodsucking fiend with hundreds of years of practice.

A little Japanese girl stepped shyly around the corner. The skirt of her red sailor suit was two sizes too small to cover frothy petticoats. A jaunty cap was pinned to her curls. She licked a glistening red lollipop. Not cherry flavour.

'Want to play tag, Mr Zero?'

She knew who he was. Maybe everybody did!

The girl's eyes were big and strange as those horrible orphan paintings old people in Ojai hung above hearths they never lit fires in. Her lolli-lipsticked mouth was a pushed-out rosebud. She'd grown an adult vampire dentition without losing her baby teeth. Sixty-four fangs! Not a biter – a shredder. Patsy Piranha, with Shirley Temple pumps and a pom-pom hat.

Li'l Orphan Alucard was prepped to take on Jun Zero.

Jun Zero – aka Hal from 1992 – knew she'd have no trouble killing him.

And she had friends with her. Also bent on actions inimical to his survival.

'Lefty, input would be appreciated.'

The girl looked around for the phantom he was talking to, then shrugged. She figured him for bonkers in the nut.

'Talking to yourself is a bad habit,' said the vampire girl.

Lefty whirred, clicked and flashed.

'Evasive action advised,' said Lefty.

That song again. One of Lefty's standards.

The girl's eyebrows flared archly. She peeped he was talking to his hand.

'My name is Tsunako Shiki and I'm eight years old.'

'Maybe you *were* eight,' he said, hoping he sounded tough. 'When you *died*.'

Tsunako tutted and made an exaggerated sad face.

Shielding her maw with her hand, she whispered, 'It's *rude* to say the d-word.'

Her eyes grew bigger, rounder, with red whirls in the irises.

He knew she was putting a glamour on him – to *hack* his brain!

No, in this room, he was the hacker. Tsunako was… a peril, an obstacle.

Without needing a prompt, he improvised. A thing had worked before – with another monster – and he didn't mind the repetition. Flash-pan gamers who didn't deign to reuse plays crashed out of their level. Botjocks in it for the duration hit rinse and repeat until the battlefield was a litter of broken mechas and mangled pilots.

Hal sliced his cardkey down the reader-slide. The Processor Room door unlocked.

Ishikawa stumbled out, eyes red. More ghoul than vampire. He'd bitten through his lips and dribbled a gore goatee. He lurched at Hal, then sniffed the dust-free air and turned his red gaze on Tsunako.

She giggled.

'I was wrong, Jun Zero,' she said. 'You're *fun*!'

YOSHIO MIZUNO – ASTRO-MAN (YUREI 139)

The plan was a tri-pronged pincer movement. Shiki, the speartip, would drop down from above. Mizuno (Astro-Man) and Kurokawa (Caterpillar), the prongs, would come up from below.

The objective was to put down a stray.

They didn't need to know the dog's name, but Shiki told them anyway. Jun Zero. Not a vampire. A code cowboy.

Eesi-peesi, she said. A minor piece to knock off the board. This was tidying up before getting on with the rest of the evening.

Nothing was ever simple outside a briefing room. After more than half a century as a ghost soldier, Mizuno should have drummed that into his skull. Especially after the unholy catastrophe of the 'Cthulhu in Shinjuku Caper'.

Whenever he went to mist, Mizuno lost his train of thought.

Each coalescence was a new start. He had to reassemble memories. Trying to recall specifics was as frustrating as singing one song while a different tune played on the radio.

Like his mother-in-darkness, he was condemned to re-enact his death for eternity. She had done it for terrified audiences. He did it mostly in fog.

According to characters on his arm, he was a ghost.

YUREI 139

As mist, he was a ghost of a vampire. As meat and bone, he was *yurei* turned *yōkai*.

Colonel Golgotha gave orders, not explanations. Shiki, from the private sector, shared information. They were mopping up someone else's mess. A chiropterid was supposed to blankslate the hackers after the breach. It hadn't finished the job.

Tonight, they weren't soldiers, but janitors. The turd Jun Zero refused to be flushed. A big smelly dump on a clean floor.

His lowly station always came back to Mizuno when he pulled his droplets together. He was janitor, minion, stage-hand. In the mud, not on a horse. Even as a vampire, he was a renfield.

Mikaeris (the Butler), the elder on the Golgotha Squad, wore pride like armour. Despite self-identifying as a servant, he was lordly and resolute. A true vampire. He wore European Victorian clothes. He didn't turn to fog. He marched up to front doors and demanded an invitation. He fought enemies face to face. People he killed admired him.

Mizuno seeped through drains, cracks in walls, gaps around doors and windows, chimney flues. No draught excluder could keep him out. He was *Johatsu Ningen* – the Evaporated Man. He swirled into nostrils and mouths, drew breath from lungs. He got into veins, forced blood through the skin. He could suck the life out of a room. People he killed often didn't even know he was there.

He offered to snuff Jun Zero like that.

Shiki said no. She wanted to *play*.

An old child, she hadn't outgrown whimsical cruelty. She was high-born, like Mizuno's maker. Some vampires treated get like children or lovers. Lady Asaji turned retainers.

In the seventeenth century, the warm Asaji Washizu was a radical. When the Noh theatre was forbidden to women, she posed as male in life to play female parts on stage. The double imposture was remarkable enough to draw audiences even after her secret was out. By the 1930s, the vampire Lady Asaji was a traditionalist relic, perpetuating a production draped in frosted cobweb. Every night, she acted to the same music, in the same mask, with the same gestures. Like a ghost walking. Or a record stuck in a groove. Strictly, *The Demon and the Lady* should have been part of a whole evening's programme. She pared the *jo-ha-kyū* ritual down to her star turn. Ten stylised minutes, repeated forever.

Kiri – the Demon Play. *Kyū* – repeated rapidly.

Kiri-kyū... kiri-kyū... kiri-kyū...

Mizuno found the access hatch. A hollow column sheathed a ladder. The internal architecture of the Daikaiju Building mimicked anatomical forms. Corridors and ducts were veins, threaded through meat and around muscle. Rooms throbbed like organs. The Astro-Man knew the insides of bodies.

As mist, he had different senses.

He *felt* the spaces he filled. He could rise as a cloud, floating to the next floor without opening the hatch. But the EarthGuard issue HazMat suit didn't dissipate. Without properly willing it, his limbs went gaseous. His coverall sleeves flopped like used condoms. His boots dragged. He was contained, trapped. He had to focus to solidify his hands enough to grip the ladder rungs.

He found the hatch hanging open. While he climbed, his lighter-than-air substance rose inside the HazMat suit. The chest and arms swelled, leaving him shrivelled below the belt. He had to drag himself through the hatch, making an unmistlike clatter with the helmet. He tried to stand but his ankles crumpled and his boots tipped. The hampering garment was camouflage, a stage costume – but getting it off was a two-man job. Seals that kept out contaminants kept in the Astro-Man. The sooner this charade was over, the better.

He concentrated and solidified.

Why was he here again?

For Jun Zero.

Who? A stray dog. Hacker trash. Survivor of a trio. The Third Turd.

Mizuno couldn't see far down the corridor. The inside of his faceplate was fogged with his own mist. His feelers extended only to the man-shape of the suit. Four tubes, a barrel and a nubbin. Was this what it was like for the warm, trapped in single shapes, unable to feel anything beyond their skins? He couldn't remember being so limited.

He tried to think back. Ancient history was in focus. The present blurred. In 1935, Mizuno – a student librarian obsessed with Noh – sought out Lady Asaji's small theatre, a former chapel in the Bund. Japan had turned away from Hollywood musicals and Western dress to revive its own traditions. Mizuno saw *The Demon and the Lady* so often he could shut his eyes and replay it in his mind. He couldn't remember his family home or what he'd done last week, but knew every nuance of the damned play.

The Chapel Theatre was one of the attractions of the vampire enclave. Connoisseurs sought out a performer of Lady Asaji's vintage, though they would rather a male master had preserved the purest form of Noh. The star ignored carping traditionalists, except on the rare occasions she had them brought to her dressing room with knives at their throats. She lifted her horned, snarling demon mask to show her blank-white, unpowdered face as she lapped their blood from a lacquered bowl. It pleased her if they died as she took a last swallow.

Mizuno's first duty as a serf was to get rid of the bodies.

The Princess Casamassima disapproved of such things in the Bund but understood their inevitability. Some warm fools were born to be bled. Vampires could no more abstain from hunting humans than cats could observe fast days. Lady Christina valued her realm above any of its residents. She must abide by her Treaty with Japan. Penalties for murder, if the charge was proven, were severe. Therefore, charges must not be proven. If Mizuno didn't get rid of corpses, his duty was to confess to the crimes – no matter that he was (then) a warm man and the dead were exsanguinated. He was even guilty. He stuck knives into throats. Lady Asaji, at worst, received stolen goods – in a bowl. She did not give orders. She did not need to. She accepted offerings.

In life, Lady Asaji played the *onnagata* part – reserved for an actor who specialised in female roles – of the Lady in *The Demon and the Lady*. Fray Sebastian, a vampire who disapproved of her unwomanly behaviour in taking to the stage in the first place, thought it a great joke to replace her co-star one night. At the climax of the play, he unmasked and bit through her jugular. The barbarous Christian dripped his blood into her mouth as she died. Thrown off her stage like a discarded rag-doll, she turned. Her loyal company rallied to their new-risen vampire mistress. For disrupting the Lady's performance, Sebastian was bound in chains and thrown into Kagami Pond. He survived but never came near his daughter-in-darkness again. Lady Asaji was no one's minion. She would not be the passive acolyte of a red-headed *gaijin* leech.

The Lady bore the European *nosferatu* taint, but conducted herself as *yōkai* – as if the get of Yuki-Onna herself. Long hair, white face, white robes. As a vampire, she switched roles and played the Demon. Over hundreds of years, she enacted her tragedy thousands of times. Never varying a jot.

Lady Asaji enslaved her troupe. Her play had only two characters.

Shite and *waki*. Star and Support. Diva and Stooge. She was the Demon *shite*. There was a turnover of Lady *waki*, female and male. Typically, she selected a smitten supporting actor and bled them till they could bleed no more. Most, she got rid of. Some – like Mizuno – she turned, not for solace but because theatre needed jobbers to do the scut-work.

As a new-born vampire, with his mistress whispering in his head, he was still flesh and blood.

The misting came later.

Lady Asaji turned him from warm to vampire. The Key Man turned him from vampire to wraith. Circumstance made him a ghost soldier.

Mizuno's mother-in-darkness was truly dead. Her old haunt was a *pachinko* parlour. The din of pinball replaced the chords of a *samisen*. Even the longest-lived residents walked by without remembering the Chapel Theatre.

In March 1945, an American air raid seeded incendiaries throughout Tokyo. One hundred thousand died. High winds spread blazes across sixteen square miles. Industrial and military targets were sited in residential and commercial prefectures, so the bombing was indiscriminate. Even the Wall was no barrier. Fire – deadly to many bloodlines – caught in the crowded, overbuilt Bund. Ironically, the spirit O-Same – who razed the same area, with about the same death toll, in 1657 – was heroine of the hour, absorbing so much flame into herself that she expanded into a phantom fire giant and exploded warplanes above the reach of anti-aircraft guns. Few noticed that Lady Asaji's theatre burned down with her inside. Mizuno was out on the bay in a small boat, tipping a weighted corpse into the water. That made him sole survivor of the company.

At first, he professed not to believe the Lady was gone.

But she no longer whispered in his head. He faced the truth. His obligation as loyal retainer was to avenge her.

As a vampire of the Bund, he was exempt from conscription. A week after the raid, he renounced stateless status and volunteered for the Imperial Army. He expected to be shipped out to kill GIs. He looked forward to tearing into greasy barbarians with teeth and claws. Instead, he – along with other patriotic *yōkai* – was sent to Higanjima Island, where the Black

Ocean Society maintained an underground facility. He was entrusted to Dr Komoda, who augmented his natural abilities with transfusions and operations. That's where things got misty.

He had few memories of the rest of the War, but was awarded a China Incident Medal for meritorious service. He wasn't sure if he surrendered in 1945 or was ever mustered out. He had only foggy impressions of the immediate post-war era.

Besides the medal, he'd picked up the tattoo. YUREI 139. That made him a ghost, vanished from official records.

In 1960 or so, he came to his senses long enough to seek Lady Asaji's birthplace and make a shrine to her. He spread ashes from the Chapel. The peaceful spot was long since abandoned. The Lady had returned with her troupe a hundred years after her final performance as a living woman and killed every man, woman and child in her village, then burned down their homes and dismantled the castle where her descendants cowered and bled their last. Mizuno thought to sit by the shrine and shapeshift permanently, becoming a low-lying reddish fog travellers would do well to avoid.

But his country called again. His mind came together, if imperfectly.

Major Golgotha recruited him. He knew Mizuno's war record, which was more than Mizuno did. Golgotha browbeat him into signing up again. He wasn't necessarily serving his (or any) country, but he hadn't truly fought for the Emperor last time. His obligation to Lady Asaji was discharged. He kept going over his and her story, the demon and the lady, whenever he came back from the mist... and, though he believed it, he no longer felt it. The Lady was ashes and he was the Demon now.

Golgotha took him back to the Key Man. Multiple blood transfusions partially cleared his head and helped him keep his body together. Mizuno was with EarthGuard when Big Man Turtle attacked Expo 70. He took part in other actions. Gokemidoro's upper voice sent him on missions that had little to do with defence of the planet. Most of the time, Mizuno held down a sinecure. He was a university librarian, in charge of a wing with no books. At night, he sat in his office and remembered *The Demon and the Lady*. He hoped that eventually the play would not be there when he thought of it.

As for what he did under Golgotha's command – he didn't care what it was, just that it was done properly. He followed orders.

His fogged brain could manage that.

Tsunako Shiki reminded him of Lady Asaji. They might have been cousins-in-darkness, recipients of a tainted Portuguese-Carpathian bloodline. Different in manner – the Lady distant where Shiki was forward, Shiki frivolous where the Lady was grave – but alike in *attitude*. Their worlds were toy theatres. They were *stars*. Everyone else was a marionette. Or a boy with a mop and a bucket.

Shiki was around the corner, flirting with her victim.

Lords and ladies did that. Minions crept up and struck.

Shiki said Mizuno and Caterpillar were poor playmates. They had no imagination. If she had her first picks, Cottonmouth and the Butler would be with her. Golgotha wanted to hold them back, for his own purposes. Officers often squabbled like that, childish but stuffy. Still, Mizuno knew no one wasted a stiletto or a knight on a blocked toilet. That was a job for the Astro-Man.

Caterpillar was on the other side of the building. He was surprisingly stealthy. When he lost his arms and legs, he learned to creep, undulating forward on belly muscles and with his chin. Now he was a Human Swiss Army Knife, he didn't clank.

He listened, waiting for Shiki's signal.

When she whistled, Mizuno and Caterpillar were to pounce on Jun Zero and hold him down. Then, she would play with him. Only when she was bored would she let them finish him off.

Golgotha wouldn't approve, but he also took orders. Chain of command did that to the highest-ranking. There was always someone senior. The Colonel answered to Gokemidoro, or at least to the voice which came from his upper mouth when he nodded off. The General had a puppet master inside his head. He wasn't the vampire. The sponge that wound tendrils around his brain was. When Gokemidoro died, the red jelly would ooze out of its fissure and seek a new host.

Shiki was privileged. Her master's favourite. A pet to be indulged.

Caterpillar must be in place now.

Lady Asaji would not have cared for Shiki. Similarity bred rivalry.

He heard a commotion. The pincer plan was scotched.

Without waiting for the whistle, he stepped round the corner. Caterpillar had the same instinct.

Jun Zero, as was the way of cornered dogs, had done something unexpected. Opened a door and let loose a mad vampire.

Shiki was delighted. Mizuno less so.

Jun Zero was dressed as a salaryman but stood like a karate master.

The mad vampire was dressed as a security guard.

'Hello, friends,' said Shiki. 'This is Jun Zero. He's a hoot and a half.'

Mizuno tried to keep flesh solid on his bones.

He knew what was wrong with the vampire. The chiropterid had got to him. It ought to have wiped Jun Zero too.

The vampire was acting on instinct. Mizuno had been like that for long stretches of his service, unleashed rather than deployed, coralled between missions, fed like an animal.

He looked at the unflushable Jun Zero. The hacker held a fighting stance, eyes on Shiki. His strange hand was raised, lit from inside like a *pachinko* machine. That would have to come off and be broken to bits.

The mad vampire was in the way. Mizuno saw how he could be useful.

He dashed at the vampire. It turned and scratched Mizuno's chest. Horny, new-grown talons dented and stretched plasticised fabric, then punctured it. Puzzled by the lack of blood-gush, the mindless viper tore rents in Mizuno's HazMat suit.

Mizuno heard a hiss of escaping gas.

That was him. He was free.

He filled the corridor, then concentrated. No point in tackling the vampire, who didn't need to breathe.

He aimed himself at Jun Zero's head and made himself into a thick cloud.

HAROLD TAKAHAMA

Ishikawa attacked the decontamination suit with claws and fangs, a dog savaging a plastic scarecrow. Something intangible and invisible flew at Hal – *fast*.

Lethality Points – Bonus Ultra! Threat Level – fucking off the charts!

A ghost constellation embraced him.

Too late, Hal held his breath. His eyes watered.

Weights pressed on his chest. Tiny hooks scraped his skin.

'Red and orange and pink and green,' sang Tsunako Shiki, in accented English, 'yellow and violet and blue...'

Hal wanted to cough but couldn't.

'They're the colours your face will go when he strangles you!'

She laughed, taking pleasure in his upcoming death.

Tsunako was *worse* than Cousin Hellish.

Ishikawa held the tattered suit. The bull-necked, shaven-headed warm man Hal took for a back-up goon extended concertina arms with a mechanical rasp. Barbs clicked out of the knuckles of his mace-fist. He began hitting Ishikawa's head as if it were a punching ball. A nozzle appendage squirted fire into the vampire's face.

'Evasive action is advised,' repeated Lefty.

Maybe Lefty was dumb. Not a mindless tool but stupid. Ill-programmed. Glitchy. Inconsistent. No help. Evil Stretch Armstrong's robot arms were at least weapons. Hal could have done with a blowtorch hand just now, though he'd most likely set fire to his own head to free himself from the Intangible Asphyxiator.

He felt pressure in his ears and against his eyes.

His head was wrapped in invisible wet leather.

He saw spots. Angry glitter.

Mouth firmly shut, he couldn't ask Lefty to elaborate.

As if he needed more grief, the hand agonised his arm, lighting up pain circuits to the shoulder. Was he betrayed by his own add-on? He'd never trusted the wonky widget.

Lefty struck an oddly-cricked forefinger – with an extruded rind of flint like a bitten-down nail – against a metal pad set in its thumb. It made sparks. Usually vampires were afraid of fire. Not this time.

How long could Hal stay conscious? Or alive?

His arm spasmed and convulsed like an electro-stimulated dead frog's leg.

Lefty punched in the direction of the open door of the Processor Room. Hal was yanked after it.

The Moppet of Menace clapped, head turning like a tennis spectator's. Which was the most delicious? Ishikawa being turbo-pummelled and skull-barbequed or Hal struggling with a rebel limb and an unseen smotherer?

She didn't want to miss a hilarious second of either treat.

Hal slammed against the door-jamb and couldn't hold his breath any longer. He gulped air and was *invaded*. The thing enveloping him could wreak damage inside and out. A horribly intimate violation.

He blundered into the Processor Room, still fighting something he couldn't touch. The door shut and sealed behind them. A disappointment for the Little Horror. She'd have to make do with just one entertaining death.

Did Lefty have a plan? That door-closing flail couldn't be an accident. Come on, Mr Hand. Save the day!

As much as was possible, Hal went limp. He tried not to resist Lefty and not to inhale more viper vapour. He was worried the Gas Man could force past his sphincter and solidify inside his rectum as a venom-barbed porcupine. His mind junkfiled eight years of valuable life experience that turned him into an outlaw cyberwarrior but retained the process that could imagine ass-infiltrating metamorphs with poison spines. That was a concern.

Databanks thrummed. Screens beamed the arctic luminescence of the Light Channel. Fans whirred.

He'd noticed the dustlessness of the room. The odd, distilled water taste of the air.

The fans weren't only for cooling. They maintained atmospheric purity.

Tech wonks called dust 'the slow EMP'. Using a mini-vacuum on the guts of a computer was the fix-it's second resort after turning it off and on again. Mr Clean and Bill Gates agreed on one thing – dust was an enemy of progress.

The thing killing him was intangible (except to hurt you), invisible (except with the Light Channel behind it), and non-flammable (as Lefty's tinderbox proved) – but not truly insubstantial. The shapeshifter transformed from solid to vapour by redistributing molecules or whatever. It still had a body, though its matter was thinned. It couldn't be knocked out by, say, landing a roundhouse right on its chin. It had no coherent heart to drive a stake through.

But it was particulate matter – even if measured in microns. Now, thanks to Lefty, the Gas Man was locked in a room set up to rid itself of grit, grime, droplets and ash.

Lefty used minor pains – not even stings, just jabs – to direct Hal to a panel labelled 'Atmospheric Control' in English and Japanese. A big red button begged to be thumped, like a prop on a kids' TV show.

The pressure in his ears grew. He felt a warm liquid gush.

Blood. That made the vampire cloud simple-minded. It withdrew from his body, tearing through his nostrils, to gather around his ears, molecules absorbing leakage. Jun Zero's blood was an intoxicant.

Lefty thumb-flicked a side-switch and an airline emergency mask fell from a ceiling hatch and dangled at the end of a clear tube. Contra-intuitively Hal forced as much air as he could out of his lungs, then clamped the mask over his mouth and nose. He willed his inner ears shut and clenched his butt-cheeks as if cracking a walnut at a frat party. Fuck off, Mr Poisonpine!

Lefty extended all five digits, producing extra knuckles from inside its works, and jammed them into ports.

'Extreme Atmosphere Flush Imminent,' it announced.

Now, Hal breathed bottled air.

Vent grilles clicked to open. Extractor fans revved like jet engines. A reverse tornado whipped through the room.

It was like a spaceship being breached.

Lefty anchored Hal to the control panel, but his feet were off the floor. The pull of air being drawn out of the room was enormous. Maximum suckage, but in a good way.

Items of flair – stowed when this process was executed routinely – flew off desks and slammed against vents, clattering through to gum up works or be lost forever. Maintenance would find ground-up fidget toys in the filtration system for years. Taguchi's drained corpse was dragged along a path, then hauled upright to stick over a vent. His head lolled.

How well had Jun Zero known his dead comrades?

It would be a bummer if those were his best friends.

Bits and pieces of chiropterid were vacuumed, mixed with the struggling invisible monster. Truly dead, Karl had no bodily integrity. All that was left was friable crystal.

Breathing through the mask, Hal looked up at the shape trying to form. The gaseous vampire was straining to shift back to solidity, but too much matter whirled through its body. Regular grime, leaves of scribble-pad, chiropterid smuts, paperclips, staples, items of flair.

Hal saw that face again. Metres across and transparent.

Angry fangs. Violent eyes.

Sayonara, Super Gas Giant!

The vampire had coherence for an instant.

The big black rubber sphere – that fucking waste of space pseudo-chair – bounced between cabinets. It cannoned smack into that shimmering face, which came apart, spiralled and was funnelled through the largest vent towards the whirling blades of the deadliest fans.

There's always a bigger sucker to get you.

The extraction burst lasted only ten seconds. Then the fans shut and the grilles closed.

The chairball careened off again. Taguchi slid to the floor.

Hal, choking and coughing, landed on his feet. Lefty detached from the control panel.

Beyond the frosted door the vampire girl pressed her face to the glass.

Hal wasn't foolish enough to think he'd won. But he'd beaten this level.

He couldn't remember being Jun Zero – *becoming* Jun Zero – but the hacker outlaw was burned into his DNA. He had skills. He had instincts. His survival so far wasn't just down to Lefty's smarts – which the mechamitt only had because Jun Zero coded them into its core.

Jun Zero was an individual who got away with crimes, then walked into the sunset with Rac Loring on one arm and Winona Ryder on the other.

Tsunako Shiki knuckle-rapped the door.

'Come out and play, Mr Zero,' she said. 'Come out and play.'

RICHARD JEPERSON

He scratched his sleeve as if his tattoo were an itch.

GEIST 97

In the last fifty-five years, whole days must have passed when he hadn't consciously noticed it. But not many.

Whenever he took his shirt off in company, he had to explain. Not that he could say much. It was his unsolved mystery.

After the War, Captain Jeperson found him in Aussenlager Richard, a displaced persons camp on the outskirts of Litoměřice in what was now the Czech Republic. His age was presumed to be five or six. Seemingly mute, he learned English as if it were his first language. Speakers of Czech, Romany, Hebrew and other tongues couldn't unlock his mind. Shouted or purred at in German, he didn't flinch – unusual in the circumstances. Hypnotism didn't work on him. Later, he tried many forms of meditation and past regression techniques with no useful results.

As a teenager, he sometimes told people he wasn't sure whether his distinguishing feature was a tattoo or a birthmark. His adoptive father said tests had been done. It was ink not melanin. Nazis had written on his arm.

The DP camp which gave him his name was successor to underground forced labour factories code-named Richard I and Richard II. The state of his hands indicated he hadn't worked in them. The neo-gothic Villa Pfaffenhof, in the nearby woods, had been used during the War by the Ariosophist Institute. At her trial, Dr Heike Ziss, director of the Nazi Occult Sciences division, presented documentation establishing she had not been within two hundred miles of Litoměřice in her life. Which was suspicious. Richard had never been to Arbroath, but couldn't have proved that in court.

Richard was uncircumcised, so almost certainly not Jewish. A best guess was that his biological parents were Roma. Probably from far to the southeast of where he was found. At school, his Young Heathcliff looks got him nicknamed 'Gypo'. For all his dandyism, he'd never had his ears pierced. Seven years of 'cross my palm with silver' jokes were enough for him.

The obvious inference of GEIST 97 was that he was marked for death – scheduled to become the 97th ghost. It wasn't as if Nazis even needed a reason to kill him. The tattoo was a puzzle. At Auschwitz, only prisoners fit for work were numbered. Time and ink weren't wasted on those to be exterminated. 'Geist' hinted he wasn't to be murdered, but forgotten – rendered invisible and unknown. A ghost.

If so, the project was successful.

In 1978, Richard sat across a table from Heike Ziss in an East German 'high-security retirement home'. He read only boredom and weariness from her. The plain, elderly *hausfrau* had a number of her own, stitched on her blouse. He was supposed to believe she'd been in prison since 1947, but knew she'd worked for the GDR satellite of the Night Watch. When he showed her his arm, she remarked the tattoo was off centre. It seemed to mean nothing to her, though she was interested. She recognised it as unusual. His inbuilt lie detector didn't register a flicker.

Silently, he was relieved.

In his worst imaginings, the Dreadful Dr Ziss would turn out to be his mother.

He celebrated not finding out anything useful by sleeping with Charlotte, the friendly guide who was (of course) spying on him for the Stasi. She offered to chew off the tattoo to help him forget and did sink her fangs into it. He learned more about her than she did about him – or any long-range plans the Diogenes Club might have to undermine the Warsaw Pact. When the scab came off, the tattoo was still there.

After Reunification, Charlotte spent a few months as a resident of the cosy prison they'd visited. Two-thirds of the country were suddenly terrified records of spying on their neighbours would be made public. Examples were made of the relatively few Stasi officers who did real intelligence work – keeping tabs on foreigners. Charlotte was let out after Richard recommended clemency. She transferred to Berlin and was now an Inspector in the Lohmann Branch. She made a better detective than she had a spy.

Dr Ziss died peacefully in her bath a few years later. Her secrets gurgled down the drain.

Unable to let it go, Richard visited the ruins of the Villa Pfaffenhof. At the time, a film company was using the abandoned estate as a location for a horror movie. The empty house triggered no suppressed memories. Well before the Nazis set up shop, the villa had ghost stories. But he sensed no presences, auras or ethereal miasmas – as if the stone tape were erased by blood ritual around the time paper files went into the fire. For Richard, another dead-end.

To make up for the disappointment, he slept with Callie, the leading lady's stand-in. Despite his extra sensitivities, he wasn't a hundred percent certain Callie wasn't Jennifer Jolie, the star of *The Hobbs End Horror*, de-squeaking her voice and brushing her hair a different way. That experience with a warm woman or women was more draining than his bloody nights with the vampire Charlotte.

He swore off the habit of ending any investigation by sleeping with the nearest attractive eccentric. But he'd said that before.

The vampires of the Diogenes Club made fun of him.

Nezumi – over a thousand years old! – clicked an 'at your age, too' tchah in his direction whenever he so much as nodded politely to a woman.

He looked at his own face, reflected darkly in a puddle.

He couldn't see the child, whoever he had been – whatever his birth name or ethnicity or culture.

He saw an Englishman named Richard Jeperson. An *old* Englishman.

He felt for people, which meant he felt for the person he had once been, the person he might have grown up to be.

When lines of inquiry stalled, he let it rest. He had many mysteries to solve. There were many attractive eccentrics in the world.

Still, when he rolled up his sleeves to wash his hands, there it was.

GEIST 97

Now, after he'd almost given up, a clue was handed to him on a platter by this Dr Akiba. He intuited no deception from the man.

He'd never considered the 97 as anything but a number. Now, its indivisibility might be significant. Or was that another false trail? British Intelligence hadn't turned up answers since 1945. He knew this to be true. He'd risen so high in the Diogenes Club he had access to secrets withheld from his father. Sometimes, he wondered whether that privilege – more than duty or aptitude – was what had kept him at his post all these years.

This trip, undertaken at the end of the century, had seemed an honourable finis to his front-line career. It might be time to step back, take a consulting position. Advise the Ruling Cabal. The Lovelies could look after the mysteries. Now, apparently, Jeperson's Last Case reopened Jeperson's First Case – the mystery of himself.

That made him suspicious.

Standing outside the Armourdillo, he looked up beyond the vehicle's ridged back at the Daikaiju Building. Eyelights burned in the sky.

He had to concentrate to stop scratching his sleeve. His whole skin prickled.

Something didn't fit properly. No, something fit *too* properly.

The Ghost/Yurei connection was convenient – a nice, juicy, *personal* distraction.

Who wouldn't want to solve their own mystery first and last of all? And would drop anything else to hound after that hare.

But he was in the Bund for something else. He was to look up, not in. Think forward, not back.

Did he detect the subtle touch of Christina Light?

Or any of the other Big Beasts in the Rogues' Gallery. John Alucard. Derek Leech. Jun Zero. The Broken Doll.

He must focus. See what was in front of him.

Which was Syrie Van Epp. Dr Akiba had given her a once-over too. She was clear of the frightful fungus. So far as could be told. But she was still coldly furious.

Syrie was a Big Beast too.

Before Wings Over the World moved in, there had to be a disaster.

An epidemic would count. Were there WOtW wondercraft above the clouds? A high-priced antidote ready to roll, provided the Princess signed over half her realm?

Nezumi stood unobtrusively nearby, eyes on him.

Mr Horror was gone and the funeral cars nowhere to be seen. Who'd given them a clean bill of health? It couldn't just be bribery. In any situation where money and position could open a door, Syrie had unmatched power.

Who *was* in the back of the hearse?

It couldn't be Alucard – the Man Who Was or Might As Well Be Dracula. He had his own New Year's Eve party to host. Geneviève said Mr A planned to bungee jump off the Hollywood sign at midnight, before the premiere of *Vladiator*, the new Ridley Scott historical epic.

But it was someone close to the King of the Cats.

The ranking EarthGuard officer – who wasn't in a decontamination suit – strode over and barked at Dr Akiba.

Richard tried to read Colonel Golgotha, but got only static. Richard's trick didn't work on stone-cold sociopaths. Monomaniacs threw him off too – the devout and dutiful, vampires with counting fixations or overwhelming red thirst, the deeply dry and boring, and run-of-the-mill addicts. Whatever they thought or felt was blotted out by *idées fixes*.

Golgotha was a tall, hard man. Tight cheek muscles. The sort of flat belly you'd break your knuckles on if you tried to sucker punch. Tinted aviator glasses. Male model haircut.

'You can go,' he said, in English to Richard and Syrie.

That was a surprise to both of them. Welcome, but worrying.

Neither wanted to query his decision with 'Are you sure?' – but, really, *was* he sure? Golgotha acted more like a fighter than an epidemiologist. Richard looked to the doctor for a qualified second opinion.

Dr Akiba shrugged inside his suit.

'Enjoy the party,' said Golgotha, with an unmistakeable shooing motion.

Richard wished Syrie would take off her digishades. He'd like to see her eyes.

She'd been annoyed to be detained. Now she was irritated to be let go.

A man was dead. Another mutilated – for his own good, admittedly. A dangerous disease was possibly loose.

And EarthGuard's response was 'Happy New Year'?

That couldn't be right.

SI MOLINAR

The phones stopped ringing and flashing. Molinar wasn't relieved. Verlaine speed-dialled from her desk.

'Who are you calling?' he asked.

'Inugami,' she said, 'but it doesn't matter. It rings, but no one picks up. Not even a machine.'

'Busy night,' he suggested, knowing that wasn't the issue.

Verlaine cut off the call and speed-dialled again.

'Hyakume has had some woman who can speak leave a dozen messages,' she said. '… and the same, her number just rings.'

Molinar tried to raise Hyakume's interlocutor on his wrist radio. No response. He clicked on a couple of random contacts. No one answered. Which was improbable.

Verlaine gave it a last shot. 'Nope – nothing from EarthGuard. An emergency service. We've been deliberately cut off. The lines don't seem dead but we're not getting through.'

'Arashi,' Molinar said, raising his voice – which everyone did with Suzan, though they knew she was invisible not deaf. 'See if you can reach *anyone*. Use Fujiwara's line. He has every woman in the Bund on auto-dial. He always bangs on about how *his* system can't be hacked.'

He followed what he assumed was Suzan walking across the room. She took care to shift chairs, brush the leaves of potted plants, and tread heavily – so far as bare feet on plush carpet could tread heavily – so people knew she was coming. She had a phobia about being bumped into. Something to do with walking around naked most of the time.

Mitsuru Fujiwara's cordless phone – sleeker, blacker and with more functions than anyone else's – lifted from its cradle. It beeped as buttons were pressed.

Verlaine looked at her screen.

'The system is telling me it's running. I've got position markers all over the building, pinging locations. Our ops are reporting in. All normal – except they're getting responses from us, which we aren't sending.'

'How?'

'I don't know. Fujiwara would, but—'

'He's chasing *bakeneko* tails.'

'Well, yes. Could this be…?'

Verlaine pointed at the ceiling.

Molinar looked up. The Princess?

'The thing that's to happen. The Ascent?'

So long awaited, so little explained. Christina Light thought it would be a nice surprise that way. So Molinar did too. He tried to explore, theoretically, the possibility that the Ascent was a dangerous jaunt into the unknown with potentially catastrophic side effects. That went against the glamour. Needles burned in his eyes.

'Can't see it. Fujiwara said not to worry about the Bug Thing. This is something else. An attack. Aum Draht?'

'What have they got against us?'

'They're terrorists, Verlaine. They don't hurt who they want to, they hurt who they can.'

'That's just it. They can't hurt *us*. We're not a soft touch.'

She gestured at the office. Computer terminals, racks of equipment, weapon lockers. Framed commendations. Charts and plans. The Princess wouldn't rely on this department if it wasn't fit for purpose. They'd been on a war-preparedness footing for a hundred years.

Even Watson and Kuchisake were formidable. Devoted to each other and terrifying to everyone else. Albert 'Smiler' Watson had taken a razor to his own cheeks to match the scarification that gave Kuchisake her nine-inch open mouth. Unlike Verlaine's, their bloodlines did not automatically heal self-inflicted wounds. They sliced their faces like paper sculpture to suit *muy loco* ideals of beauty. Watson wore a red regimental tunic with medals and sabre. Kuchisake's party outfit was a formal kimono with layers and lattices. Instead of Verlaine's hold-out gun, she carried a fan with dart spines. Open and held over the lower half of her face, it displayed a demure painted simper. A considerably less elegant weapon was concealed in the folds of her dress: a pair of old pruning shears.

'Listen up,' he told them. 'You too, Arashi.'

Watson's and Kuchisake's eyes swivelled at him. Fujiwara's phone held still in the air.

'Until midnight, the Bund is a country. We are its army. We can only rely on ourselves. Outsiders are to be considered enemy combatants unless they prove themselves otherwise. We urgently need intel on the situation in the Plaza and in the rest of this building. We need to know how our comms have been disabled, and we need – dammit, we need *Fujiwara* – to get back online.'

The elevator arrived. Someone coming down from above.

Others must have noticed the shut-down. Security was the logical place to come.

Who would the Princess send?

Or was this an enemy incursion? Floor 88 might be the last ditch.

He pulled his gun.

The elevator doors opened. For a long second, no one moved.

Then a fat man erupted from the elevator. He was wrapped in a metallic sheet and wore a twisted silver foil tiara. He held a stone bottle of *sake* in one fist and a sheaf of hundred-dollar bills in the other.

NEZUMI

As Derek aimed a blacklight gun at her, he made a *zhzhzhzh* with his mouth. The gadget looked like a prop from a science fiction TV programme.

'Ex-ter-min-ate,' he croaked.

She smiled that he'd had the same thought she did.

He passed the UV over her hands and feet where spatter would most likely be found. No suspect spots were lit.

Then, to finish up, he told her to shut her eyes and flashed the projector in her face.

When she could look again, Derek was concerned. He pointed at the corner of his mouth.

'You've got some specks, ah…'

The blacklight wouldn't only reveal the fungal agent. It was used at crime scenes to find where splashed blood had been cleaned up. .

'I fed, earlier,' she admitted.

He looked at her as if she were a monster.

'A rabbit, at the legation house where we're staying,' she explained.

'Ah, poor bunny.'

The unctuous liaison official had offered to source human blood. That would have upset Derek less.

'It's all right,' she said. 'I didn't finish it off.'

That was true. The rabbit would be good for a few more feeds. She didn't reckon it had much of a future, though. She'd tasted imminent death in its blood, like mould in jam.

The smudges weren't visible without the blacklight. But she still licked the back of her hand and wiped her mouth with it.

'You look like a little kitty,' said Derek, cheerful again.

Nezumi remembered the *bakeneko* girls. Cat vampires were as common in Japan as bat vampires in Europe. Her bloodline was unlike either. She couldn't shift shape. She was a winter witch, like Yuki-Onna. A girl of the snow. Warmer than the Ice Queen, though. Her body temperature was 93.4 degrees – higher than the undead average. Still cool enough to tick off the 98.6, the hate group which professed to take pride in their 'normal' warmth. Other people – she thought of them as butterfly collectors – were more interested in classifying her than she was herself.

'You're good to go,' said Derek, giving her the thumbs-up. 'No flies on you. Or necrotising fungus.'

She thanked him.

'Give us a toggle, would you,' he asked, half-turning and shaking his head inside his helmet. He pointed to a release catch just out of his reach.

She pressed, and seals unstuck.

Musk escaped and her fangs prickled. Fortunately he was looking the other way. She kept her lips pressed over her teeth.

He twisted his helmet as if releasing a bayonet-cap light bulb and lifted it off its ridged rim.

He vigorously scratched his nose.

'Been wanting to do that since about ten seconds after I put it on,' he said. 'Imagine poor old Neil Armstrong having an itchy hooter from the Earth to the Moon. No wonder NASA wanted to shoot off one of your mob in a coffin. No complaints to Ground Control, then. Still, good on Neil. Inspiration to the warm world.'

Olof Carlsen, the seventh astronaut to walk on the moon, was a vampire. Sunlight, unfiltered by Earth's atmosphere, blinded him. The warm mission commander – played by Tom Hanks in the film – had to donate blood to save his life. Since then, only the Russians sent *nosferatu* into space.

'It's safe, then,' she said.

Derek confidently breathed in lungfuls of air.

'Can't be sure without fiddly tests back at the lab,' he said, 'but the likely scenario is that your nasty has mutated on contact with the environment. Turned harmless. At the worst, nothing a tin of foot powder won't shift. Terrorists generally don't know jack about microbiology. Word's come down we shouldn't make too big a brouhaha. No one likes a party-spoiler, eh?'

Nezumi remembered the policeman's foot melting in his shoe.

Nothing harmless about that.

Derek scratched his scraggy beard.

'I always have this reaction,' he said. 'I reckon these nuke-bio-chem jim-jams keep in as much dreaded lurgy as they keep out.'

'What will you do now?' she asked.

'Too much to hope we can pack up and go home. We'll be here all night at this rate. Colonel G-Force wants to have a shout at chummy the mad bomber. The bloke you pigstuck. Reckon he'll be wishing you'd stabbed deeper.'

Nezumi agreed. She hadn't left the boy alive as a mercy.

Kill only when necessary to save life. A wounded enemy is often more use than a dead one.

Derek dug a fat, swollen paperback out of his kit-bag. *The Lord of the Rings*.

'Before the balloon went up, I was getting to a good bit… the Siege of Minas Tirith. Have you read Tolkien? He's my absolute favourite. Rather read a page of names by him than a bloody shelf of Jeffrey bloody Archer.'

'Tolkien? The man who wrote the very long book?'

Derek was mock-offended.

'Long?! Nah, mate, it's not long *enough*. Whenever I get near the end, I wish there were more of it, you know. Pages and pages more. Extra chapters, fit in between the ones that are there. More endings. Longer farewells. I suppose that's why when I turn over the last page I always take a breath, chug a couple of weeks' worth of *Shortland Street* on video, then start again at the beginning. Well, before the beginning… with *The Hobbit*.'

'I like *The Hobbit*,' she admitted. 'But I prefer stories without dragons, swords and wizards.'

'Get enough of that at home, do you?'

'I like books about girls at school.'

'You certainly ought to get enough of *that* at home.'

She admitted he was right.

Being at Drearcliff Grange wasn't like reading books about school. Nezumi had tried not to be disappointed. The difference between real school and Louise Teazle's books about school was nowhere near as tragic as the shortfall between the honourable code of *bushido* and the scurvy conduct of most samurai. She had school spirit in her heart and strived to live by it.

Just, kind, fair.

Only decapitate when absolutely necessary.

'I think your Dad wants you,' said Derek, waving his helmet.

Nezumi looked. Mr Jeperson stepped onto the red carpet a few paces behind Mrs Van Epp.

'That's not my father,' she said, wrinkling her nose. 'I'm looking after him.'

'Oh, I see,' said Derek. 'You're his minder.'

She nodded.

'Well, *mind* how you go,' he said. 'Don't drink anything that tastes rum. Or anyone either.'

'Good night, Derek,' she said, bowing. '*The Road Goes Ever On…*'

He grinned and waved his *Lord of the Rings* at her.

SI MOLINAR

The Senator did backflips and a cartwheel, showing the dress pants – rolled up to his chubby knees – he wore under his robe. In a mood to par-tay, he wasn't shy about letting everyone know it.

John Blutarski (R), Illinois.

Red-flagged on the 'annoying guest' list. But not someone Molinar could shoot.

The Senator slid his bottle-arm around Kuchisake and flapped dollar bills at the fan held over her mouth.

'How's about a little kissy-kissy, nursie?'

She folded her fan-mask and the Senator boggled. He wasn't too far gone to notice her cheek rifts.

Watson drew his sabre and was on the point of causing a diplomatic incident when the drunk American was pulled away from the Japanese vampire and waltzed across the room. His limbs jerked as if on strings. The foil sheet unwound from his blubbery, hairy torso.

'I can't see lips,' he said, in wonder, 'but I can feel them.'

Then an invisible pillow flattened his nose. He went cross-eyed. Panic momentarily cut through his drunk daze and he went to sleep. The sheet fell over his face and riffled with his snore.

'Thank you, Arashi,' said Molinar.

'I'd 'ave stuck 'im, the blighter,' said the Smiler.

The *sake* bottle rose. A bubble glugged out of the neck then disappeared.

'We can't be at war with America,' said Verlaine.

'Dunno,' said the Smiler. 'This is Japan-like and them Yanks 'as memories like blinkin' elephinks. Remember Pearl Bailey?'

A Victorian ranker – with a Victoria Cross to prove it – Albert Watson had a shaky grasp on the twentieth century. He was another one who came over on the *Macedonia*. He'd be even further out to sea tomorrow. Only his sweetheart with the matching horror-gob kept him compost mentist, he said.

'The Senator was on the razzle earlier,' said Molinar. 'We had complaints. He's a nuisance, not a threat. Tie him to a chair as a precaution. Put baby's bottle where he can reach it.'

'I'll piss in it first!'

'Smiler, play nice,' said Verlaine. 'We're in Public Relations. What we do reflects Light Industries.'

The Britisher grumbled. He smiled even wider when annoyed, and his eyes – which often didn't smile at all – got huge and shiny.

Verlaine's monitor issued shrill bleeps.

'Turn that egg-timer off, miss,' said the Smiler.

Verlaine paid attention to the screen.

'Alerts are coming in,' she said. 'Automated, not from actual people. I don't know whether they're real or a part of the hack. Unauthorised activity on the 44th.'

'There ain't no 44th,' said the Smiler. 'Kuchi-koo says it's an unlucky number. Like thirteen back 'ome. The floors go from 43 to 45 with nothin' in between.'

'That's what the building wants you to think,' said Verlaine.

Tired of standing about being told phones, screens and radios weren't doing their jobs, Molinar strode into the elevator, pistol first. He'd have to go down to the 45th and use the access hatch.

He stabbed buttons.

A recorded voice told him the elevator was out of order and apologised.

He shot the grille the voice came out of. It didn't make him feel better.

NEZUMI

Detained by the bio-terror incident, they arrived late at the Daikaiju Building. Mrs Van Epp was waiting in a reception area. She still pretended not to know Mr Jeperson, which didn't mean she wouldn't take advantage of the confusion to do him a bad turn. She was steamed that he'd told on her so she couldn't get out of the Bund earlier.

Strictly speaking, venomous ex-girlfriends weren't the scale of level-ultra threats the Diogenes Club expected Nezumi to protect their most valued member from. But there was no specific exclusion for grudge-holding, ill-advised cop-offs left over from the swinging sixties. Small, thoughtful presents hadn't drawn Mrs Van Epp's fangs.

The woman was dangerous. A feudal lord accustomed to commanding minions to deal with enemies, but capable of doing her own dirty deeds. She was wise enough to know turning vampire hadn't made her untouchable. She hired her own drill instructors and trained hard. Many giddy, blood-simple new-borns didn't bother. They thought they'd been bitten by a radioactive bat and got super-powers. They were dust before the end of their first week as a vampire. Mrs Van Epp worked at being formidable.

The latecomers were held up.

The dragon's sturdy tail curled around its clod-hopper feet and ended in a cavemouth.

After their invitations were passed through more scanners, the guests were escorted to a suspended, egg-shaped carriage that could be drawn up into the tail like a funfair ride – something between a lift and a cable-car.

An attendant opened a door for Mrs Van Epp. She got into the capsule and tried to close it behind her as if it were a private coach.

Smiling firmly and radiating an inability to understand any language but Japanese, an attendant held the door for Mr Jeperson and Nezumi.

'All aboard for the Tunnel of Love,' said Mr Jeperson.

Nezumi gripped her poster tube like a quarterstaff. Mrs Van Epp flung herself on an upholstered divan. She clicked the hornrim of her digishades as if it were a slide projector, adjusting the contraption the better to ignore the people she was sharing intimate space with.

Mr Jeperson shouldn't tease the vampire woman.

He wasn't the one who'd have to protect himself from her.

Mrs Van Epp was being silly too. Lords and ladies could be astonishingly petty. Nezumi learned that ages ago, standing to attention while a shave-pate *daimyo* threw a tantrum and ordered the beheading of a horse he'd fallen off. Just like an infants' school crybaby, except he could start a war against the horse-breeder in which a thousand loyal retainers would die and five villages would get rased.

Nezumi looked around the capsule. A 'no smoking' sign was bolted to a little doric column supporting a full ashtray. There were no windows, but curved screens at viewing height pulsed with gentle light. Chill-out musak played – a distant waterfall, a woman's wail, Philip Glass on the piano. It was so calming most people would want to scream after five minutes.

Nezumi didn't like it. They were in this small space, under the control of unknown others. It could be flooded with gas or simply sucked into the building and made to vanish. Trodden-in paper streamers on the carpet and abandoned bottles under the divans suggested the lift had seen recent heavy use.

The delay with Mrs Van Epp's extremist co-religionists had separated them from the mass of other guests. Mr Jeperson and Nezumi were in a perfect position to be picked off.

Or they could be on their way to a nice party. With games. And surprises. And presents.

'Hold up,' said someone to the attendant shutting the door.

A young-seeming vampire in top hat, white tie and narrow-waisted tails squeezed through the closing gap. He was Japanese, with an Elvis 'do and sideburns. An eyebrow pencil smear passed off stray hairs as a moustache.

'Room for one more inside,' said Mr Jeperson, cheerfully.

The vampire was comically stricken. His shoulder pads shivered.

'Don't say that,' he gasped. 'I've heard of a fellah who had a dream where someone said that. Ended with an awfully big catastrophe.'

'I know that story too,' said Mr Jeperson.

'I adore creepy stories,' enthused the newcomer. 'Hanako in the girls' toilet. The hairy-handed hitch-hiker. Isn't there a ghost story about four strangers in a lift? The lights go dim, they count heads, and the tally keeps coming to five.'

He was only pretending to be a nervous soul. As he was only pretending to bend and stretch and shiver. Nezumi sensed a steel core.

Mr Jeperson introduced himself.

'Anthony Peak,' said the vampire. Not a name that sounded Japanese.

'This is Nezumi,' said Mr Jeperson. 'We are not strangers.'

Nezumi nodded. This vampire did not rate a bow.

'I shall have to watch you, pretty thing,' said Peak. 'My heart flutters easily.'

He kissed her hand, leaving wet on her knuckles. His hair oil was pongy.

The door finally shut, a lever was thrown – the controls were on the *outside*, which she didn't like – and the capsule began a smooth ascent into the tail.

'This is Mrs Van Epp,' said Mr Jeperson.

'So much beauty, so little room,' said Peak, making butterfly motions with his hands.

'She is a stunner, though you can't tell with the x-ray spex and the brainbag hat. Sacrifices made in the name of faith. The Wire is watching, I understand. Or the Watch is wiring. Never can tell.'

Mr Jeperson was still ribbing Mrs Van Epp.

'Beauty shines through,' said Peak. 'I am perfectly dazzled.'

Nezumi knew exactly who this was and what he was here for. Anthony Peak – the name came from a *genus lupinus* she'd studied in botany – was a charmer and a cad, and not averse to nipping a fair maid or two. But he was mainly a thief. She bet he was on his way to the penthouse to rob everyone.

If she'd been wearing rings, he'd have had them in his mouth while he was smarming her hand. She'd better tell Mr Jeperson to check his wallet.

Mrs Van Epp was tense, as if she suspected she was trapped with assassins.

'We have no plans to harm you,' Nezumi said to her in Farsi.

That perked the woman up. Addressing a person in their own language was always a welcome courtesy and conveyed sincerity.

'But you should mind Mr Peak's fingers. He's a crook.'

'I resent that remark,' Peak said indignantly, in English. 'What, surprised I know Persian jaw-jaw? We're all cunning linguists in this tin egg. I'll have you know I'm no ordinary tea-leaf. Just as none of you are ordinary guests. I've come to steal nought but a lady's heart.'

'Yuck,' said Nezumi, meaning it.

'So young, so bereft of romance… 'tis tragedy,' said the creep.

Anthony Peak had no idea who she was. He took her for a new-born dolly biter. That suited her fine. He'd be surprised when she ran him through.

She'd already cut off someone's foot this evening.

Where Mrs Van Epp came from, they chopped off thieves' hands.

That rude joke about cunning linguists was second-hand. Nezumi had heard it yonks ago from a third-form filly who collected smutty postcards.

Naturally a thief would steal comedy material.

The capsule rose, at speed. Gimbals and giros kept the ride smooth. All very high-tech and frictionless.

Then, with a lurch, they stopped.

'Oh, dearie me,' said Peak. 'I shouldn't have tempted fate by mentioning that spook story. We appear to be stuck in the gorge of the dragon.'

DETECTIVE AZUMA

The surviving perp's passport and wallet were in his back pocket. More bad news: the Aum Draht pustule was American.

Thomason, Andrew A.
Date of Birth: 13 Sep 82
Place of Birth: Capital City, USA

Thomason had been in Japan three weeks. His visa paperwork declared his visit was for 'spiritual reasons'. At the airport, they'd assume that meant a tour of shrines. Maybe a few days sitting on a mat and humming. Not mass murder.

In the wallet was an organ donor card. That didn't square with a belief that the world was a simulation. If he'd been successful in blowing himself up, his bits and pieces wouldn't have been harvestable anyway.

The fanatic also carried a Chuck E. Cheese loyalty card and receipts for airport limo services. First class all the way. Suicide bombers didn't care about expenses.

The poacher's pocket of his trench coat was weighted with mini-cartons of Blue Label Sprünt. The clue Azuma had literally tripped over. The wrong flavour of fizz for the Bund. Perps were always undone by details.

So, Andy the A-Hole?

The US was unlikely to get – or want – him back. Aum Draht hired ace lawyers if adepts came to trial, but instructed them to read out garbage manifestos in court. The tactic irritated judges so much even accuseds with wriggle-room drew harsh sentences. Wolfman Inugami couldn't just eat the catch. The rudimentary justice system of the Bund wound up at midnight. It'd be a headache to sort out who got to do what to the almighty prick.

Azuma's fang-knuckles were knots of thirsty pain.

An alley off Daikaiju Plaza was a makeshift holding area. A canvas canopy stretched overhead. The drunks, pervs and dips busted since sunset were let loose so the prize public enemy could get proper attention. The scumballs weren't grateful. They took release without charge as vindication.

Andrew A. Thomason was trussed in a yo-yo cat's cradle. Saki-A, the senior officer, tugged. Her razor string cut into the perp's torso. Saki-K and Saki-G held fast, letting boss-girl have most of the fun. They all pulled at once and Thomason lifted on tiptoes. Without his eyeball hood, he looked like a student who hadn't slept for days. The Aum Draht regimen of staring at a screen all night while toggling a joystick was hell on the complexion. Blue Label and Chuck E. Cheese didn't help either. Thomason was pale, blotchy and bleary-eyed.

'This does not hurt,' he lied. 'There is no pain.'

Azuma walked around, sizing up the perp from all angles. They'd get less from him than from his headless boyfriend. He'd worked enough occult cases to know that. With the millennium looming, religious crimes spiked. Few new churches encouraged contemplation and non-violence. Many advocated murder and mutilation. Azuma filed robed cultists with cranks who could only achieve sexual arousal during earthquakes. Brainwashed Aum Draht dolts believed they were disembodied go masters and their flesh forms merely pieces to be shifted about a board. People they killed were only tokens. Points scored. Even their own deaths were illusory. By making sacrifice, they ascended to a higher level of play where their rewards were extra weapons and functionalities. Mass murder won them afterlife guns and rainbow glitter.

'This is a pause in the game,' said Thomason.

'A game which you lost,' Azuma pointed out. 'To a girl.'

The yo-yo cops giggled and tugged.

Thomason had no smart answer. He might not believe in pain, but felt it.

Kamikura was in the Niide Clinic on Pear Blossom Street. Azuma hoped he was getting good drugs. EarthGuard – who had called the fucking Dick Boy Club? – were all over the crime scene with a flamethrower. Inugami would be on the phone with Captain Takeda, sorting out how to blame Beat Azuma for the mess and get commended for the clean-up. Real credit should go to the little vampire with the sword, but she was in the wind.

This whole thing smelled like a dung-heap.

Who let bughouse bombers through the Gate? Who fitted out their vests? Thomason and his beheaded pal – a Japanese with no identifying papers – hadn't set this up alone.

According to EarthGuard, the hazardous material was stolen from an Unwin-Fujikawa facility in Osaka two days before Thomason entered the country. Why was U-F cooking up death fungus in the first place? Azuma bet that line of enquiry would not be pursued. No one wanted to know if Big Pharma were outsourcing deniable field trials of their murder products to Aum Draht.

One thing he'd learned from cult investigations was that doomsday churches were all for hire. Every psycho *sensei* had a numbered Swiss bank account.

Thomason wouldn't know who was paying for his killing spree. But someone sewed him into his suicide coat and pointed him at the Plaza.

Most perps would cough up their connection after being face-punched a few times. When Azuma got blood on his fangs, they spilled their guts. *Yakuza* hoods talked tough, but plead for a deal when their cheekbones broke.

Aum Draht weren't like that. Their brains were scrambled. They talked as readily as anyone else. Indeed, they never shut up. But their truth was shaky. Questioning brought out demented fancies. You got a lecture, not a confession.

Azuma took off his jacket and undid his shirt-cuffs. His knuckle-fangs jutted.

This beating would be retributive, not investigational.

He took boxer's shots at Thomason's torso, then jabbed to the throat.

His hands tingled as blood ran over his knuckle-fangs. Something was wrong with the kid's blood.

'Bored now,' grunted Thomason. 'You're cycling through the programme. NPCs. Bad cop, worse cop. Everything you say and do is scripted. You run your wheel. You do what you do. I'm just talking to myself.'

Azuma punched Thomason in the stomach.

'I knew you'd do that.'

He raked across the perp's face with the fanged back of his hand.

'... and that. Can we jump to the reset?'

Azuma boiled. Few things angered him more than homicidal pointlessness.

'If these officers waltzed off in different directions, how many slices would you fall into?'

'None,' said Thomason. 'Just pixellage. I go and you reset.'

RICHARD JEPERSON

If Syrie or the new boy started trouble, Nezumi was positioned to protect him. The stalled lift wasn't spacious enough to draw Good Night Kiss with the proper flourish. She'd bop someone's chin with the pommel before executing a twirly reverse and laying a slicing edge against their neck.

In a pickle like this, Sergeant Dravot might pre-emptively cripple Syrie and Anthony Peak to be on the safe side. To a hammer, everything looks like a stake. Richard brought Nezumi to Japan because she wasn't a hammer.

They were all in the same becalmed boat, stuck in the craw of the Daikaiju Building.

The enclosed capsule reminded him of a certain hot-air balloon.

Syrie must have the same thought.

Their gondola had been filled with pillows. It had useful leather loop hand-holds. He had soft focus memories of making love as they drifted from St Tropez to Monte Carlo. If he concentrated, he had to admit the route was Warrington to Runcorn. The picnic hamper was Riviera style. Champagne and oysters, not stout and chips. Though there was Kendal mint cake. A welcome restorative.

He saw Syrie smile. Then she saw him notice and set her mouth in a grim, annoyed line. A shame she took it like that.

You'd think he'd pushed *her* out of the balloon.

Richard looked at the other passenger.

Anthony Peak was perpetually amused but not disposed to share the joke, as if he genially thought everyone else slow-witted. Nezumi took against the fellow but Richard admired his style. The Diogenes Club kept a slim file on his antics. A fresh one. Someone pinched the original, fatter dossier and left a pressed flower in its place. A lupin. That showed a certain cheek.

'We should call for help, I suppose,' said Peak. 'I hadn't anticipated so intimate a New Year celebration, though it'd be churlish to complain of such charming company.'

The thief experimentally tipped his silk hat to the billionairess. He'd have to be wary of her morning-after routine. Mr Peak – become Mr Plunge.

A telephone was fixed between screens.

Richard picked it up and heard a recorded message in Japanese. He handed the receiver to Nezumi, who listened for a moment.

'It's an advertisement for an emergency phone system,' she said.

Peak knocked walls like a treasure seeker hoping to find the panel that hid the family diamonds. As he clanged, the lift swayed.

Richard saw Peak's act was for show. He had a way out, which he wasn't sharing. What could it be?

'Is it me or is it getting warm in here?' said Richard. His brow was damp.

The other three were vampires. They didn't register temperature variations.

If they were stuck here for weeks, he'd be the emergency rations.

The Princess had been working on this monster for nearly a hundred years, but there must still have been a last-minute scramble to completion. How much was unfinished? The failsafe installed next week would be state of the art. In the meantime, here's a message about its future spiffiness and try not to asphyxiate in your stalled lift.

Syrie walked from one side of the lift to the other. She took off her shades, which unplugged from her turban. An LED in her third eye jewel went out.

'That's better,' said Peak. 'Bellissima.'

She shot the thief an electric shut-up glance and undid the strings of her brain-pattern turban. The ugly hat popped off her head and she shook out her hair. She'd gone back to blonde when she turned vampire. The eye gadget was stuck to her forehead like a caste mark, the centrepiece of a platinum mesh tiara that matched her gadget glasses.

'Something is wrong with the screens,' she said.

Incandescence throbbed. Devotees tuned into the Light Channel for soothing vibes. Richard acknowledged that alpha waves and world music turned down low might well have therapeutic properties. He personally preferred to nod off of an afternoon with the racing on Channel 4. The glow was flecked with sparks.

Syrie felt around the edge of the screen.

'No off-switch?' Richard ventured.

She bared her fangs for presuming to know what she was doing. And being right.

'Can we prise one of the panels loose?' Richard asked.

Peak slid out of his tailcoat and laid it on a divan. Little custom-sewn pockets in the lining held an arsenal of implements. The tails accommodated flexible strips of metal useful for popping locks. Nezumi, mistress of the Girl Guide knife, disapproved but was interested.

'That's a very complete set of burglar tools,' she commented.

Peak took the dig with good humour.

'It's as well to be prepared for eventualities. Like this one, for instance.'

He selected a jeweller's loop with an inbuilt light and something that looked like a dental pick. He fit the loop into one eye and began probing around the screen with the pick.

'No accessible wires,' he said. 'A challenge!'

Syrie looked into another screen, haloed by a static fringe. She was reaching out but not touching the light.

This seemed less and less like an accident.

Peak gave up and put his gadgets back in his cracksman coat, then pulled it on again and wriggled until it settled properly. The well-tailored garment could not be comfortable. The rogue was wasp-waisted, with oddly cut clothes – tight above the belt, floppy below. The coat was for tools. The trousers were for swag.

So, a gentleman bandit. Knows the right order to steal the silverware. Knocks out guards but leaves a tip. Not who you expected to find at this end of the century, but archetypes were stubborn. The Diogenes Club often had a larcenous toff or two on the rolls. British specimens of the breed were mostly non-violent. French exemplars tended to the casually murderous.

'You'll think I'm pulling your leg,' said Peak, 'but have you done a headcount?'

The screens glowed brighter, but the lift was dimmer overall. The overhead lighting strips fizzed out.

One, two, three, four, he counted.

'Remember yourself,' said Peak.

Richard caught on.

He counted again, starting with himself… one.

Two, Nezumi. Three, Syrie. Four, Peak.

Five… ah, indistinct.

A column of black smoke rose at one end of the sealed lift. Roughly the shape of a person. It extended arms with trailing sleeves or batwings.

Nezumi demonstrated perfectly how to draw a long sword in the confined space. Without cutting herself or anyone else. She pointed at the dark shape.

It was womanly. Gathered at the waist, with a dress-like flare below. Long unbound hair or a veil. The smoke tried to come together. Shoulders appeared – bare, elegant, sparkly. Delicate disembodied hands. Eyes like far-off stars. One white, one red.

The spirit of the Daikaiju Building.

A muffled, indistinct voice sounded, impossible to make out.

'Trust me to hop into a haunted lift,' said Peak.

HAROLD TAKAHAMA

Hal was grateful to Jun Zero – his unknown self – for doing the crunches, sit-ups and reps. The chubbins from 1992 wouldn't have fit into this ventilation duct. He was less grateful, now, for Lefty. The smart prosthesis was awkward in a confined space.

With killer vampires at the door, he'd had to prise the grille off a duct and escape the Processor Room. Lefty issued calm instructions, telling him which turns to take and how far to crawl ahead. The robot hand switched on a light behind its palm-speaker that showed him the cramped tunnel's aluminium sides. He wriggled on elbows and knees, scraping sparks with Lefty's claw-thumb appendage.

In or out of shape, he got a pain in his back after twenty minutes or so.

Following Lefty's advice got him this far. Next, he should try to get out of this hole, this building, and this country. If Jun Zero proved as unpopular as Hal now suspected, he'd have Lefty explore options for leaving the planet. They must have space zones with no extradition treaties by now. On asteroids or the moons of Jupiter. He'd have enough credits stashed in off-world accounts to live like a rock god on a luxury outpost. If Winona Ryder was unavailable, Catherine Mary Stewart – Number Two on his Fantasy Movie Girlfriends List – would make a substitute space pilot. Or Ally Sheedy from *WarGames*, Number Three. Or—

But he had to live through the night first.

He figured the Gaseous Ghoul was a goner, though there was an offchance he could get his act back together and be mightily pissed. A vengeful viper vapour on his ass he didn't need. Tsunako Shiki was bad enough, plus her flame-projecting hench-borg.

Who knew who else wanted Jun Zero dead? Hal certainly didn't.

He decided against asking Lefty for a ranked list of arch-nemeses. He was close enough to wetting himself as it was.

His internal monologue sounded like a hysterical squeak in his head, and he knew he had to calm down, to talk to himself in the deep, confident voice of Jun Zero, not Hal, who got called 'Short Round' even by other Asian kids. Where were they now? Stacking shelves or donating blood for a living... while he was crawling through a ventilation shaft, pursued by monsters.

His own blood pounded in his ears. The slick tin under him squeaked as he crawled. He'd sweated through his salaryman shirt. It was getting hot in the tube.

To calm down, he recited his old list:

1: Winona Ryder, *Edward Scissorteeth*.

2: Catherine Mary Stewart, *The Last Starfighter*.

3: Ally Sheedy, *WarGames*.

4: Kelly LeBrock, *Weird Sorcery*. Man, *Kelly LeBrock*...

5: Karen Allen, *Raiders*... but fuck *Temple of Doom* – though Capshaw was hot – because of fucking Short Round. He hoped Jun Zero had tracked down that kid – who also ruined *The Goonies* – and siphoned his trust fund. Oh, and fuck *Karate Kid* too – and fuck *Karate Kid II*! – because kids only stopped calling him 'Short Round' so they could call him 'Mr Miyagi' and wave their arms in joke karate moves that *never* stopped short of his head.

6: Brigitte Nielsen, *Beverly Hills Corpuscle II*. He'd totally avoid tapping that... *not!*

7: Lea Thompson, *Howard the Bat*...

He heard a skittering – like rats' claws on corrugated iron, but with a giggle mixed in – and a few CC of pee squirted into his boxers. A scent of lavender wafted along the duct.

He should have known.

If he could squeeze into this maze, then so could Tsunako Shiki.

RICHARD JEPERSON

The smokeshape wasn't a ghost. Its effect was more thing than person. Looking at the Light Channel made him uncomfortable. Looking at this apparition piqued his interest. He wanted to solve the 'what's wrong with this picture?' puzzle. Not the obvious wrong thing – the scary ghost! The littler wrong thing – the nagging thing. The clue to spark the grey cells. The loose thread.

'Why put a "no smoking" sign on an ashtray?' he asked.

'Insurance,' said Syrie, who owned airlines and ocean liners. 'If you tell passengers not to do things you damn well know they'll do, you're indemnified against lawsuits if they do themselves injuries they deserve.'

'Close, but no Cuban,' said Richard.

'Pawky surrealist humour,' suggested Peak.

'Does that sound like Christina Light? The woman had her funny bones surgically removed.'

Nezumi thought about it longest, then sheathed her sword with a click.

'You wouldn't,' she said. 'That's not an ashtray.'

'A stuffed elephant or a dying goldfish for you, Miss Mouse,' said Richard. 'Madame Montgolfier, any chance of a lend of your surplus hat?'

Too annoyed to respond to the dig, she passed it over.

Her hand brushed his. Her skin was cool, but she *was* a vampire.

In his memory palace, champagne fizzed, loins stirred. Wind whistled through his hair as he plummeted towards a mill-pond. His ears had popped. Tinnitus troubled him whenever he was in Cheshire.

Back to the present and the impossible ashtray.

He picked up the fag ends and dropped them into the upturned hat.

'That's an original by Tetch,' she said.

'Seven hundred and fifty quid well spent and you'd never wear it twice. At least it's being useful.'

The tray was a glass indentation. Richard rubbed ash off it with his cuff.

The indentation was a lens. The column was a hologram projector.

'... lcome to Daikaiju Plaza, guests.'

The smoke ghost lightened and came into focus. Now, it was a three-quarter size woman in a Victorian ballgown. She wore her hair like Veronica Lake in *Casamassima*, a wing artfully over her red eye. Her arms waved as if providing simultaneous translation in sign language. Lattices of light made up her form.

'Our hostess,' said Richard.

'Ahhh, *principesa*,' said Peak, going down on one knee and trying to take hold of an insubstantial hand.

'It's not the real her,' said Richard. 'Though Christina *can* turn herself into light. It's a recorded message.'

'We've missed what she had to say,' said Syrie.

'I doubt it was much more than welcome waffle,' said Richard. 'This is what happens when you give a fortune to a design company. They make something wonderful which looks so much like an ugly ashtray they have to clap a notice on it. Then they underestimate the exhilaration of rule-breaking. We're in the Bund now. An exciting interzone. We didn't expect to be told to mind our Ps and Qs and not light up when we feel like it. The vibe is "go on, do as thou wilt". Nagging messages from nanny only add to the spice. Look at the divans. This isn't a lift, it's a whoopee wagon. It's a wonder it hasn't got "*Défense de Hanky-Panky*" signs.'

Peak's eyebrows went up and down and wobbled his hat. Syrie looked as if she wanted to hide behind her shades again.

Mini-Christina gave a little bow. The lift started moving again.

KIM NEWMAN

DETECTIVE AZUMA

The circus-tent flap lifted and Colonel Golgotha strode into the holding area. Two Dick Boys followed. Hunter and Killer. Their safety suits baggy. Machine guns slung over their shoulders. They carried plastic lock-boxes – high-security picnic coolers. Azuma did not expect EarthGuard to bring beer and snacks.

'Let the American drop,' ordered Golgotha.

The Sakis recognised authority. When the strings slacked, Thomason flopped to his knees. A puppet taking a bow.

The perp looked up, irritated. He'd expected to be dead by now and ascended to the next level.

Azuma would have been happy to kick him to where he wanted to go.

The yo-yo girls unwound the cat's cradle. Thomason pitched forward.

The Dick Boys swept aside paperwork and set their crates on a trestle table. Hunter – another American who shouldn't be here – punched a code into a digital lockpad, finger-stabbing in slow motion to compensate for bunch-of-bananas gloves. After two tries, his box opened. He lifted one of the confiscated suicide vests. The detonator was disabled but phials of lethal matter were still attached.

With a butterfly knife, Hunter carefully cut a jar free of the webbing and passed it on. Most boyish of the Dick Boys, Killer looked like an A student who dealt drugs at break. Mustard-yellow death-goo sloshed in the stoppered container, more swamp-mud than fungus. Killer tossed the deadly phial in the air – to shocked hisses from the yo-yo girls – and deftly caught it. No risk to the idiot in his safety suit. Possible peril to everyone else, including his bare-faced boss.

Thomason looked at Killer, spark of puzzlement in his eyes.

'If you know so much,' said Azuma, 'what's he going to do?'

'I... have... no... idea,' Thomason said.

Blood trickled down the perp's face. Azuma looked at his own knuckles. They were clean. Sores around his fangs sucked like little mouths. He had

Thomason's blood in him. It was as if he'd swallowed a hallucinogenic glowworm. Ghost images glitched. The Sakis were big-eyed poster girls. Golgotha was carved granite, with a yard-across mushroom for a beret. Hunter had porcupine quills and a goat beard.

A tall, wide phantom stood behind Killer, grinning like a cartoon bulldog. It bent to whisper into his ear. *Go on, open the bottle, let the kill-genie loose.* The *oni* was a God of Bad Influences.

Azuma did a thing he thought of as swallowing. Normal service resumed. He saw the world as it was, hard-edged and clear. Thomason's blood was saturated with something perception-altering. Blue Label space dust.

The veins in his arm tingled.

Killer squatted by Thomason and unstoppered the phial.

Saki-K squealed. The other Sakis would make fun of her.

'Mmm-mmm-mmm,' said Killer, pretending to sniff the open container held close to the visor of his sealed helmet. 'Mushroom milk. Auntie's tonic.'

Thomason's smugness drained away.

Azuma didn't feel as happy about that as he should.

The Dick Boy lifted the phial to Thomason's lips, a caring nephew helping an elderly relation take medicine.

Thomason blanked now. All programming gone.

Killer emptied goo into Thomason's mouth.

The perp glugged. Yellow poison dribbled on his chin.

Thomason's eyes swelled to the size of tangerines. Spongy ochre matter erupted from the scrapes on his cheeks.

Golgotha drew his side-arm.

Azuma stepped back, assuming he'd breathed airborne spores and would be dead inside a minute. The bio-bomb must be formulated to be lethal to him. It was supposed to be set off in a crowd of vampires.

He *didn't* choke.

Thomason expanded inside his clothes. Buttons popped and seams split. Blood-threaded pulp welled up through tears. The perp grew tubby. Sausage limbs stuck out like starfish arms. His throat closed and he couldn't speak.

Golgotha withdrew to the canvas flap-door. Hunter and Killer stepped back with him. Hunter aimed his machine gun at the swollen Thomason. Killer tossed the near-empty phial to Saki-G, who instinctively caught it – then shrieked and flung it away. A yellow smear dribbled on her bare wrist. Saki-A and Saki-K backed off from her.

Saki-G cut her scream short.

'It's not working,' she said. 'It's nothing.'

'The fungus is Part One of a compound weapon,' said Golgotha. 'It needs Part Two to be activated. Part Two is a human fuse, saturated with special accelerant. It's not easy to prepare. You have to persuade the fuse to drink seven or eight measures of accelerant a day for months.'

Azuma looked at Thomason's cast-aside coat. Blue cartons spilled from it.

Kamikura had been splashed with fungus but also the blood of the dead terrorist. That was why he – and no one else – had been affected in the Plaza. Thomason was full of the bloody secret ingredient of Sprünt when the fungus was poured down his gullet. What was happening to him is what would have happened to the crowd he'd planned to spatter with the toxin and his own shredded flesh.

The perp became a giant maggot-dumpling, face stretched, eyes a foot apart, starfish arms absorbed back into a doughy mass.

Human hands stuck out of the puffball, clenching and unclenching.

The Colonel gave a sign.

The Dick Boys opened up with their machine guns. Under the tarp, the juddering reports assaulted eardrums. Outside, they'd be taken for firecrackers. Witnesses always said they heard firecrackers. On New Year's Eve that was even more believable.

Bullet-rips appeared in Thomason's leathery hide.

Geysers of bright blood squirted at the yo-yo girls.

A splash on Saki-G's arm sizzled like acid. *Now*, she was infected.

Saki-A, legs soaked with deadly stuff, flicked her yo-yo and tore off Golgotha's beret. She'd been aiming for his dark glasses. The Colonel shot her in the thigh. The yo-yo *shuriken* clattered on the ground, fully unreeled.

Golgotha was a perp!

All three girls were drenched. Mushrooms sprouted on their faces. Fungus swelled in their mouths and around their eyes.

Saki-K opened like a giant flower, bursting through her armour.

Azuma looked down at himself. No splatter.

Killer advanced on the sprouting heap that had been Andrew A. Thomason. He dipped a gauntlet into the biggest gaping wound and pulled out a fistful of squirming animal-vegetable froth.

Even without blood-buzz, Azuma saw the Dick Boy's personal demon, draped over his shoulders like a cloak, mouth attached to the side of his head.

Killkillkillkill...

The Dick Boy grinned through his faceplate at Azuma.

He was going to chuck the poison like a deadly snowball.

The Sakis weren't down by accident. This was a pre-planned backstabbing.

Azuma reached into his jacket for his own gun. EarthGuard gear wasn't hardened against bullets. Hunter, Killer and Golgotha were warm. They could be shot.

Killer assumed a baseball pitcher stance, ridiculous in the clumsy suit.

Golgotha trained his pistol on Azuma.

Another bullet wouldn't kill him – unless it were sterling silver – but the fungoo would.

The Sakis were down. Melted off their bones.

With a final burst of strength, Saki-G flicked her yo-yo, which made Killer duck and hold off his throw for a second or two.

Hunter raked the dying cop with gunfire.

Her yo-yo sailed off its string and thunked against the wall, high up. Its blade severed a key rope.

The canvas canopy came down, flopping over the Dick Boys and the infectees.

Azuma was standing, suddenly in fresh air, looking at a big top collapsed on the pointy heads of struggling clowns. The canopy had missed him. A Dick Boy fired his machine gun with a wretched burp of noise and stink. Blackened holes stitched through the canvas. Spent bullets pattered like hail.

Cheers rose from drunk locals who didn't know what was going on.

Azuma ran across the Plaza, skirting the shadow of the Daikaiju Building. The canvas wouldn't hold the Dick Boys for long.

The yo-yo girls proved him wrong. They were good police. Not just security guards in sexy costumes. The good cops were truly dead. EarthGuard weren't here to help, but to make things much, much worse. Golgotha was part of the attack. No one called him in, because he'd known what was happening.

The evil plan was sideswiped, though.

The little vampire with the sword had stymied the original intention – to cause an outbreak among the crowd in Daikaiju Plaza.

Were the Dick Boys being vindictive now?

Or was the fungoo outrage Part One of a compound evil plan? A distraction from something worse?

Azuma's knuckle-fangs stuck out like saberteeth.

NEZUMI

She looked at the space where the ghost woman had projected.

She smelled sulphur. Holograms had no chemical presence so it must be cigarette residue. The lift whiffed of fag-ash.

Mrs Van Epp was talking to them now so that was one thing the hitch had sorted out. She wasn't their new best friend, but stopped pretending they were see-through.

Anthony Peak was still insufferable.

Mr Jeperson was enjoying himself. He mostly did. Nezumi liked him for that reason. Their blood connection was warming. She appreciated his positive attitude. He would make a good Girl Guide. Everyone else worried about what might happen at midnight. Mr Jeperson wanted to find out. Things he didn't know excited him. That was one reason he needed a bodyguard. He was too curious to be properly afraid so she had to be cautious for him.

Mr Jeperson knew how people felt. That was his talent. Had he noticed Mrs Van Epp still fancied him? Beautiful, rich and with powers of fascination, she could have all the young blood she wanted. Was Mr Jeperson a rare vintage to her? Aged in the cask, matured by experience. Impossible to buy and so more desirable than the priciest stock on the vein list.

With her funny hat off, Syrie Van Epp was pretty. Not smiling, cheery pretty, but moody, soulful pretty. Enviable cheekbones and long eyelashes. Lips too thin for a real pout, and fangpoints you almost didn't notice. The eye jewel was a *de trop*, but its gleam meant she didn't have to explain to everyone she met that she was very, very rich.

Nezumi bet Mr Peak was thinking up ways of snaffling the gem.

Given half a chance, he'd fill his turn-ups with jewels and run for it.

She must not get distracted by the obvious rotter in the room.

Larceny on legs he might be, but Mr Peak didn't pose an immediate threat to the Most Valued Member of the Diogenes Club. If he got in the way, he'd be a nuisance but he was a red herring.

Nezumi had proper fish to fry.

Above the fiftieth floor, the capsule emerged from its shaft and climbed the outside of the building like a funicular railway. A Plexiglas window afforded a panoramic view of Casamassima Bay. Party lights twinkled on boats. Blimps and helicopters kept out of Bund airspace.

The lift was drawn up the dragon's spine.

Mr Jeperson and Mrs Van Epp admired the sights.

Mr Peak admired their valuables and calculated how distracted they might be.

Nezumi waved her poster tube at him.

He shrugged a 'can't blame a chap for weighing options' shrug and stuck his hands in his pockets.

The view disappeared as the lift pulled back into the dark. The ninety-fifth floor was the Ruff, the revolving restaurant in the Gigantosaur's throat. They were going above that, into the apex structure of the Daikaiju Building. Doragon no Kuchi – the Dragon's Mouth. This door opened. Nezumi heard music and saw light.

DETECTIVE AZUMA

The Gate was shut and barred.

A middle-aged, sad-faced American actor Azuma recognised from commercials but couldn't name and a pretty younger woman with pink-tinged hair were getting no help from Hyakume, the doorkeeper. The many-eyed *yōkai* pretended not to understand, though it was a telepath. The tourists wanted to leave the Bund to get to a party. At the moment, they couldn't.

Azuma flashed his badge.

All Hyakume's eyes rolled.

The Gate was barred from the outside. Golgotha had sealed the Bund in anticipation of a fungoo outbreak. With a news blackout in force, the lockdown looked like another fuck-up. Probably the Millennium Bug. No need to holler for Wings Over the World.

This early in the evening, more people would want in than out. Later, that'd go the other way. Hyakume's staff – nightclub bouncers, not soldiers – would be under more pressure than they were prepared for. They couldn't open the Gate by themselves. Rioters with whatever they could find for a battering ram wouldn't put a dent in the iron-bound door. Over a hundred years ago, the Wall was built to keep residents in their place. Yōkai Town used to be a prison camp.

Azuma looked up. The guard posts were rarely manned. The Bund hadn't been a true ghetto for years. Had the Dick Boys posted snipers?

'Can you see anyone up there?' he asked.

Search me, Hyakume beamed into his mind. *I'm short-sighted.*

He asked if he could talk to his opposite on the other side of the Gate.

Phone's gone dead.

The pink-haired warm woman took a cell phone out of her bag.

'No signal,' she said. 'And the only number I've stored is my husband's.'

Azuma figured Golgotha shut down communications. His walkie-talkie wasn't working either.

The actor wasn't unhappy to be missing his party. There were parties right here. He wore silly cheap souvenir bat-wing glasses.

Hyakume's many eyes watered with worry.

From Azuma's mind, it gathered this was more than a routine fuck-up.

Danger! Warning! Ai-eeee!

Panic would spread faster than fungus.

One of the security staff – who must be getting side-pay as a tout – gave the actor and his date sucker coupons for a nearby karaoke club. The reduced rate on offer was three times normal cost. They recognised a scam but drifted off anyway.

Azuma suggested Hyakume keep trying to raise the outside world. That would give it something to do.

He didn't tell the *yōkai* not to worry.

RICHARD JEPERSON

Richard stood aside to let Syrie leave the capsule first. Pearls before swine, as it were.

He immediately regretted the gallant impulse.

Crack! Unmistakably a gun-shot.

Syrie was slammed back into the lift. This time, she didn't dodge his attempt to catch her.

Someone had shot her in the face. A neat round hole above one eyebrow.

Nezumi drew her sword. Anthony Peak hopped up on a divan.

Richard looked down at Syrie, who was wide-eyed and speechless. Her hand went not to her wound, but to her eye jewel. Reassured her bauble wasn't broken, she used her long nails to pluck a flattened bullet – a lead one – out of her wound, which scabbed over at once. Bruising radiated from dent. He presumed she had a star-shaped fracture.

She closed her eyes and concentrated. Blood leaked from her ears. The dent pushed out as her skull-plates reknit.

This wasn't the welcome she'd expected.

He helped Syrie stand and gave her a clean handkerchief to wipe the blood. She didn't give it back to him – paranoid that the Diogenes Club would use the DNA smear to transform a generation of secret agents into vampires who could piggyback on her psyche and sue for non-payment of get-maintenance.

The door shushed shut again. Everyone looked at each other, alert but mystified.

Nezumi had always thought this was a trap. Assuming that saved time and shielded against disillusion – though she enjoyed parties less than her friends by expecting assassins behind every curtain.

Peak wished he'd picked somewhere else to rob.

Syrie, white with fury, was on the point of blaming Richard.

He had, after all, let her walk into fire.

Nezumi held Good Night Kiss over her head, point scraping the ceiling, positioned to slice anyone who came into the capsule. Her shirt pulled out of her skirt-waist as she stood tense and ready.

Peak edged around the lift – not setting foot on the floor, as if worried it would flap open and drop them into the shaft. That wasn't an idea Richard was pleased to pick up.

The doors opened again.

'Welcome to my party,' said someone – contralto, but a man. Not Christina Light, then. 'Do please join the fun. There'll be no repetition of the foolishness. I've reprimanded Mr Quick-on-the-Trigger.'

No one made a move.

'Really,' continued the voice, in a harsher tone. 'I insist.'

The capsule shook. Richard suspected Peak wasn't far wrong about what might be done to shift them from it. Their mystery host was controlling the vertical – and could drop them at any moment.

This time, he stepped through the doors first.

'Age before beauty,' he said.

HAROLD TAKAHAMA

With those light-bulb eyes, Tsunako Shiki could see in the dark. Maybe flap on bat-wings. She could get about the duct system like a lab-rat dosed on brain pills – not hesitating at intersections, zooming like a blood-seeking missile towards the treat in the lever-opened box in the middle of the maze.

If she came from behind, she could sink her fangs into his ankle and he'd not be able to turn and thump her with Lefty. If she came from up ahead, she could open her mouth like a python and swallow his head before he could squirrel out of biting range. He was constantly escaping from one trap into a smaller one.

'Lefty,' he whispered, 'H-E-L-P…'

'User Jun Zero requests assistance or advice?' his hand responded, loud enough to rattle the sheet aluminium.

A few bends away, someone laughed.

'Is there any way to turn the volume down?' Hal asked. 'An alternate interface. Daisy-wheel printer or something?'

'User Jun Zero can reset communication options,' said Lefty.

'Yeah, that's right…'

'An alternative is pulsed sensor stimulation in Morse code.'

Hal knew Morse. He'd learned it in grade school and made his own home telegraph, patiently teaching his cousin Helen the code, though Hellish then only used it to send mean messages no one else in the family understood. Lefty's Morse function reminded him that, though he couldn't remember it, he was the hand's programmer.

'Contin—wait, query "pulsed sensor stimulation"?'

Pain jolted up his arm like a hotwire shoved into a vein.

His scream reverberated through miles and miles of ductage.

Hal should have seen that coming.

Was Jun Zero intent on overcomplicated suicide? He might be some sort of cyber-nihilist. Jun Zero 2.1 was not into that.

He must stop thinking of himself as the kid who'd grow up to be Jun Zero. He was who he was now – Jun Zero Plus, not Jun Zero Minus. He had Jun Zero's skills and instincts, plus Hal's smart-kid smarts. He'd made it this far.

An eerie whistle began – Tsunako, mocking him.

It was his cousin's favourite song. 'You're the One That I Want', from *Grease*.

He hated it on principle. Did the vampire know that?

'Okay, Lefty – give me the percentages on my options. Keep evading or stop and fight?'

'I can *hear* you,' sing-songed the poisonous poppet. Only two or three turns away.

Lefty clicked as its drive executed a query program.

'An evasion route is accessible twelve yards ahead.'

'What kind of route?'

'Information not available at this time.'

'Not helpful.'

The hand had nothing to say at that.

Tsunako whistled again. 'Never Smile at a Crocodile'.

Hal shuffled forward on bruised elbows and knees. He was slowed by a feeling that a cushion of belly-fat should be scraping under him. Amputees suffered pains in phantom limbs. Sprung to life in the toned bod of Jun Zero, he had a phantom stomach.

Incidentally, he *was* an amputee. That was a story he wanted to hear.

'Access is six yards ahead.'

'*Wa niwa… kesshite warawa-naiiii,*' warbled the pest, drawing it out.

Hal smelled the lavender Tsunako doused herself with.

He realised what it was for. To cover the whiff of rot.

'Three yards,' said Lefty.

The hand's light shone on a red-painted column that cut vertically through the vent. A relic of a previous era of construction – rigid cast-iron, not flimsy aluminium. Hal figured the column was fitted with love and respect by a proud craftsman whose cost-cutting grandsons ran the firm by the time the vents were knocked together.

The intersection was taller and wider than the vents that fed into it. Hal could stand up in it, though he banged his head when he did.

'Peek-a-boo, I see you!' said Tsunako, from behind.

He turned and couldn't tell which vent she'd spoken from.

'Pook-a-bee, you can't see me!'

A rushing and creaking came from inside the column, as if something were forced up from below. It was hollow, like a fat pipe. Fixed to its side was a lever, like the handle of a slot machine. Without a prompt from Lefty, Hal took a gamble and yanked.

The column split open on hinges. Cold air blasted him in the face. He was grateful it wasn't water at high pressure. He hadn't considered the possibility of drowning. Hal didn't take risks like that. Jun Zero's leap-in-the-dark philosophy had got them both – them singularly? – into this shituation.

A padded cylinder like a one-person elevator was snug inside the column. He turned and plumped his ass into it, squidging to fit the coffin space. His weight triggered a mechanism that snapped the doors shut, almost clipping his nose. In the instant before the cylinder sealed he saw Tsunako's big eyes in the dark.

Pools of fury.

Had he trapped himself again?

The cylinder had a leathery, brassy, old-timey smell.

When the doors closed, lights fizzed on. At a level with his hands was a panel with a keypad and ports. He scraped Lefty's thumb across the panel until it fit in a slot. His arm tingled with the memory of pain – a sensation he'd come to recognise. Lefty was interfacing with another system.

'*Pneumatique* overridden, User Jun Zero,' said Lefty. 'Instructions are required.'

'Let's go down and get out of the building.'

'Express to Floor 93 – confirmed.'

'That's *not* what I said.'

With a pressured *whoosh*, the cylinder shot up, up, up…

NEZUMI

Good Night Kiss raised in the *ko gasumi* defensive position, Nezumi stepped into the Doragon no Kuchi after Mr Jeperson. A sunken dance floor the size of a thousand *tatami* mats constituted the monster's tongue-bed. A fleshy, ribbed canopy allowed flow-through of night air. The ballroom was dotted with *kotatsu* heaters for the benefit of guests who would feel the chill breath of Yuki-Onna.

The canopy was hung with festival lanterns. From outside, it would look like the monster had fairy lights stuck in its teeth. Enormous, segmented television screens showed the Light Channel. One noughts-and-crosses array was scarred with bullet holes. A calming, chilling aurora still emanated from cracked glass. A splash of blood had gone tacky.

In a tangle near the lifts lay twenty or so vampire corpses.

Mostly big men in tight suits, with a few women in practical dresses mixed in. Wires fixed to ear-plugs. Lapel pins. Light Industries Security. From floor-scuffs and spatter, she saw they'd been surprised by a charge from the lifts. An enemy had come out, guns blazing. After the volley, a sweeper with a silver spike finished the wounded with heart-stabs. Several were elders. Truly dead, they decayed to salts and bone scraps, leaving the odd signet ring or glass eye after the wind blew the dust away. New-borns looked like everyone did when killed – surprised and empty.

Gunfire stench stung her nostrils. Spoiled vampire blood turned her stomach.

Tossed onto the pile were a few well-dressed dead without lapel pins. Plus ones, like her. Private Security for individual guests. The take-down was thorough.

She was almost offended not to be dropped by a head-shot. Mr Quick-on-the-Trigger might be sulking after being reprimanded for shooting Mrs Van Epp. Didn't the designated sniper take Nezumi seriously enough to waste the silver? Centuries of shouting sergeants should have rammed home the message that presuming a schoolgirl – or anyone! – harmless was a fatal mistake.

Good. The people she was up against made slips she wouldn't.

'What's she smiling about?' squeaked someone sharp-eyed.

She set her mouth in an inexpressive line and awarded herself a black demerit for unbecoming smugness. Three of those and she'd get a service detention. Picking up litter. Scraping 98.6 hate graffiti off the bus stop. Rolling pitches. Drearcliff Grange invented service detention after the last groundskeeper retired and no one local wanted the job.

Mr Jeperson held out empty hands to show he was unarmed.

If whoever shot Mrs Van Epp decided to kill him, Nezumi couldn't stop them.

No. She could stop them *once*. She could slice the first bullet out of the air. She was swift enough to do that. She could pinch a hummingbird's wing.

The trick wouldn't work with a machine gun.

'Missy Katana,' said the commanding voice who'd spoken earlier, 'should you wave that about? It looks dangerous. And valuable. Self-harm is a regrettable epidemic among Japanese teenagers. I read that in *Time Magazine*. We don't want to encourage sad habits. Best put the sword away, eh? Swap it for a breadstick. Or a pull on a piggie. The buffet is stocked with positively *delicious* treats. You can binge-suck and purge after if that's your kink. You look like a healthy portion of blood sausage would do you the world of good.'

Nezumi couldn't make out the person who was speaking.

Beyond the heap of bodies, an overturned *kotatsu* spilled burning charcoal on the polished floor. The flames imprinted images into her eyes. A spotlight aimed directly at the lifts was deliberately dazzling.

A lot of people were in the ballroom. Alive.

Hostages, she supposed.

And hostage-takers. She had no idea of enemy numbers yet.

'Nezumi,' said Mr Jeperson. 'Stand down.'

'Yes, do,' purred the Mystery Voice.

Against instinct, she sheathed her sword.

'There, *so* much friendlier,' said the Mystery Voice, mocking, but blithely in charge. 'Now, come join the party games, Mr Jeperson of the Diogenes Club, and… ah, Nezumi, wasn't it?'

Did he really not know who she was? Should she be insulted?

Mr Jeperson paused by the bodies. His instinct was to see if anyone was alive.

A lost cause but he always had hope. Nezumi saw his hesitation and took his arm. Convincing the Mystery Voice that he was a doddering codger might give them an advantage of surprise when they made their move.

Which they would have to. No doubt about that.

'You too, Madame Van Epp… if you're quite recovered from that, ah, nasty bump on the noggin. And, why, if it isn't our chum Tony Peak. Quick of wit, light of fingers. Watch your baubles, ladies and gentlemen. For — whisper it if you must — we have a *thief* in our midst. A desperate character.'

Nezumi glanced back.

Mrs Van Epp strode out of the lift, steady on her feet. Her bruise was already gone.

Peak snuck behind her, contorting his shoulders to fit into her silhouette so she was a perfect bullet-shield for him. Someone was not too fussed about the 'gentleman' part of the gentleman burglar routine.

Light Industries' security was wiped out. A decapitation strike. The Doragon no Kuchi was taken.

The Aum Draht incident wasn't an end in itself. It had been a starter pistol. For whatever this was.

The spotlight swivelled, keeping the glare in their eyes. Nezumi could see well in the dark. Not so well, it now transpired, in the light.

Could this be the Princess's doing?

The Mystery Voice was a man, but this was the Princess Casamassima's party, her building, her domain (till midnight), and her security, her people, her event in ruins. Like many respectable heads of state, the Princess used to be a terrorist. She might still blow herself up to make a point (if she had a way out). This didn't feel like her, though.

Someone else then?

Nezumi's instinct was to blame Dracula. She'd never met him, though she'd run into plenty who had – and could name dozens who'd jostle to be the next King of the Cats if the Son of the Dragon were ever really truly positively most sincerely dead.

The Diogenes Club had a mantra: 'Not everything is Dracula'. Any number of Awful People lived in the world. She'd met some prize pilchards before she ever heard the name Dracula. This could even be a new breed of horrid. A debutante Nogbad the Bad, making a splashy entrance at the start of a new century.

She made out the person working the spotlight.

A slender figure with a big belt on her hips. Long dark hair.

Drat. O-Ren Blake. Cottonmouth.

Nezumi had liked the vampire, though she'd known not to trust her.

Still, she was sorry. She took people for kind until they showed her otherwise.

She was close enough to see the woman's sweet smile. She didn't seem any different. She took her hand off the light and gave a chummy wave.

Nezumi acknowledged her with a nod. Not a nod of forgiveness or submission or anger – just recognition.

She knew Cottonmouth for what she was.

Golgotha's team were Trojan sneaks. Very disappointing.

She lamented the loss of the people she'd taken them to be – people they would have been happier as. Few villains were finally happy in themselves, no matter how much they bragged about advantage gained through bold wickedness. Bags of gold, buckets of blood, and good-looking lovers were passing distractions. Bad pennies were all sad, waiting to be put out of their misery.

Men in suits and women in party frocks – vampires and warm – grouped in a circle, some clinging together, all shocked and sober. A few had scrapes and slashes. Several were pale, skimpily dressed pretty people, with stents or spigots implanted – *hors d'oeuvres* on the hoof. Staff lumped in with guests. One vampire woman – an ebony lady in a leopard-skin jump-suit – sat cross-legged holding a messy stomach wound, gnashing tiger-tusk fangs. Three of Golgotha's gunmen – Furīman, the Butler and Panty-Mask – casually kept the hostages covered. They had taken off the helmets and space suits. Their real uniform was dark commando gear. They'd removed any EarthGuard insignia.

Not a rescue squad. Black *ronin*. Killers for hire.

Furīman stripped his shirt to show a lean, muscular illustrated torso. A three-headed dragon curled around his ribs, one claw raised over his heart with a rose in its paw. The beast was in apparent battle with an out-of-proportion moth on his hip, a demon-horned pterodactyl on his shoulder, and a fire breathing anteater whose eye was his pierced right nipple. An allegory of a *yakuza* feud dating back centuries? Or the poster for one of those children's science fiction films?

Backing up Golgotha's goons were armed vampires in matching funeral outfits – mourning suits, high hats, tragedy masks. They had come with the luxury hearse. Nezumi had known that crew were wrong 'uns to a man. The brat with the corkscrew curls and the chauffeur with the rusty grin would be in it too.

Ah-hah!

The Mystery Voice must be their principal, the man in the *haute couture* coffin. His cars flew the Transylvania pennant and bore the arms of Dracula. So, maybe – for once – the Diogenes mantra was off the mark. This time, it *was* Dracula.

A curved buffet table was set against a row of tooth-shaped slats that supported a safety rail. Guests could graze as they looked down on Tokyo. Standing there, sucking on a spigot stuck into a fat pig hoisted above his shoulders, was a tall vampire in a dark crimson new wave suit so roomy it looked like a padded envelope. He was immaculate, except for a splash of blood-froth and sick on one enormous shoulder-pad.

As if he'd arranged it, a shaft of light fell on his face.

A handsome devil. Flared ears, sensuous mouth, fang-grooved lips, hooded violet eyes. A pointed goatee and moustache arranged in individual curls. No wonder he needed his coffin time. That look took hours of immobility to set. Thick reddish-black hair oiled and shaped on his head. Bristles on the backs of his huge porker-hefting hands. White, diamond-shaped nails manicured to talon points.

He twitched a smirk at the crowd, as if unashamed to be caught being naughty, and casually tossed his empty over the rail.

As the pig soared before its plunge, she saw it was no animal – but a short-limbed, round person in a pig-mask, a row of taps stuck into its belly. A sumo bonsai, fattened to order as a VIV treat, drained and wasted by this grinning greedy-guts.

The donor squealed all the way down. Nezumi heard, or imagined she heard, it explode on impact hundreds of feet below.

By the time Piggy went Splat! their host had introduced himself.

'I… am… Dracula,' he said.

Though, to state the obvious, he wasn't.

DR AKIBA

Something slammed onto the prow of the Armourdillo and exploded. Akiba's ears popped.

'Are we under attack?' he asked.

The driver tried to keep his cool, but was rattled. With the Golgotha Squad deployed around the Plaza and inside the Daikaiju Building, the driver and Akiba were alone, holding the fort in RV-1.

The windshield was completely covered with red, viscid matter. Something organic. The bulletproof glass was cracked. A direct hit from an artillery shell might have done that, but shells weren't filled with meat.

The driver turned on the wipers, which squeaked against gristly matter.

'What *is* that?' he asked.

Red smears across the window.

Akiba worried that he knew what he was looking at.

'It came from up there,' said DK, pointing.

Not a trebuchet outside the Bund, then. An attack from above.

From the Daikaiju Building.

Akiba checked the med-kit he'd been issued. The emergency supplies included ampoules of morphine, phials of vampire blood, and a syringe-gun. He stepped out of the 'dillo, dress pants bunched in the crotch of his HazMat, and waddled around to the front of the vehicle.

He smelled blood.

All around, vampire fangs would prickle.

Whatever – whoever? – had fallen from the skies was mostly on the window and hood of the vehicle, though scraps spread twenty feet from point of impact. Nothing in the first-aid kit would help. A mop-cloth would be more immediate use.

He looked up at the jutting jaw of the monster. A hundred floors or so above the Plaza.

It was a balcony.

Lights glittered like saliva gleams on the dragon's gums.

Akiba trod on something non-organic. He bent to examine the object.

A spigot on a spike stuck into a chunk of pink flesh. The sort used to tap wine barrels. Bloodletting bars used these gadgets. Surgical steel, sterilised to prevent infection. As much sado-masochist accessory as aid to bleeding/feeding. Fancier than the hollow spikes used on animals.

Rules about the measures that could be drawn from any single tap-ee were strict. Consent could only go so far. Three pints down, and the law obliged whoever stuck in the tap and took the money (but not their bloodthirsty customer) to consider the health of any warm participant, no matter how willing. A mutually agreed-on act became assault and a donor became a victim. Edgier underground clubs recruited (or procured) teens from cutting listservs and had them fit their own vein-spigots. Management was off the hook if things went too far. Akiba didn't know why gloomy kids bothered with self-harm when so many others were eager to hurt them.

All safety regulations were out the window here. Or off the balcony.

Infection and exsanguination were not issues. Neither, apparently, was consent.

Akiba heard licking and slavering.

Derelict *yōkai* – frog-turtle *kappa*, psittacitic *tengu* – crawled from the shadows to lap the leftovers. The Bund residents they didn't show the tourists. Near-mindless alley-rats and sewer-dwellers.

The local police must be overstretched if these creatures were emboldened.

Where were the cops? Like EarthGuard – off somewhere else.

These bottom-feeders were more pathetic than monstrous, but Akiba felt – for the first time – threatened by the vampires of the Bund.

Someone had *died*. EarthGuard should pay attention.

A *tengu* raised her parrot beak from the mess and sang-chortled, 'It's raining men… *hareruya!*'

The *yōkai* was blood-mad.

DK was fiddling with his wipers, aggrieved by the state of his ride. Jets of water played, turning the curtain of gore to runny sludge.

The rest of the squad were nowhere around. Not even Derek.

Akiba had an itchy sense he'd been cut out of the loop – not overlooked in a fast-developing situation, but deliberately skipped over.

'Keep trying to raise Golgotha,' he told DK.

The youth gave a fish-sign 'OK' and coughed into a CB radio.

More bystanders gathered around the 'dillo, taking care not to step in the splat, looking up at the Daikaiju Building. From this vantage point, low and close, the skyscraping folly was unwieldy. Its main section swelled as if from middle-aged spread. The head was crowned with horns. Pylons and antennae. Light Industries was a communications giant, after all. Eyelights shone, red and white.

Had the monster spat out someone?

Most in the crowd looked up.

Tengu and *kappa* – historic rivals – tussled over scraps and bayed for another meal to fall from the heavens. A *noppera-bō* – traditional *ofuku* hairdo framing a smooth curve of powdered flesh – quietly rubbed her hands together. The faceless one's *hōmongi* was embroidered with multiples of the features she was missing – disembodied eyes, mouths and noses. Blooded lips slurped in her palms. Kneeling to dip her mouths into the feast, she'd got circular bloodstains on the front panel of her kimono.

If Golgotha was missing, Akiba should report back to EarthGuard Central. He could contact Gokemidoro.

The driver's door opened and DK leaned out. He held the receiver to his ear.

'Message for you, Doc,' he said. 'From the Colonel.'

Akiba was relieved. Chain of command held.

He gripped a handle and pulled himself up to the cab.

Something cold sliced across his chest, cutting through the plastic suit, his only tux and his dress shirt. Razor spikes attached to DK's glove ripped through his skin. A deep wound, not fatal – but a shock.

The driver pushed him and he fell onto concrete.

The fall was worse than the cut.

Worse than either was the rending and tearing as blood-hungry *kappa* and *tengu* gathered around to feed.

The pulsing little mouths in the *noppera-bō* lady's hands neared his eyes. The woman without a face wanted to tear his off.

'Over and out,' said DK, cradling the receiver.

RICHARD JEPERSON

'I... am... Dracula.'

That hung there.

The speaker paused, disappointed not to get an argument.

'Usually, people jump on that,' he said, 'tell me to my face that I'm pulling their piddler.'

Richard knew exactly who this was.

Not Dracula. But arguably entitled to the name.

'No harm in trying it on,' the fellow continued. 'It's more a title than a name, you know. Dracula.'

The vampire who'd brought killers to the party got to do the talking.

He could call himself what he liked.

'Very well,' he said. 'If Dracula doesn't fly, there are alternatives. I am Ejderhaoğlu Bey. In your English, that might be Lord FitzDragon.'

'The brother,' said Richard. 'Radu.'

The Bey smiled like a little boy. Not sweet, but sly. He liked to be known. Recognised.

Richard understood. An age of resentfulness as 'the other one', overshadowed and overlooked. A pinprick of pique, repeated endlessly. Canker festering in his heart till that was all there was to him.

A dangerous man.

'Radu the Handsome,' said Richard.

'If you say so, duckie. For the benefit of the slowcoaches at the back, "Radu the Handsome" is what people called me when I was warm. Radu cel Frumos. I'm not vain, just reporting the opinion of others. I am beautiful. I was a lovely baby, a pretty boy, a gorgeous man, and a *divine* vampire. It's what I am known for. I didn't choose the honorific. It was given me.'

'By the Turks.'

'By *everybody*, Mr Jeperson. It wasn't meant to flatter. In my day, a Prince would rather be known as "the Terrible" than "the Good". They smiled – all their teeth were rotten, from Turkish candies, you know – and called me "the Handsome". What they meant was "the Soft". It was "Radu the Handsome" to my face and "Radu the Pouffe" to my behind. I took a name spat as mockery and embraced it. I have transcended the slur.'

'You know, I believe that,' said Richard. 'I can tell you're over it by the way you never mention it any more.'

The Bey laughed. Now Richard knew from the way he wasn't hurled off the balcony that Radu still needed hostages. Doubtless, he'd relish killing him – but would defer the pleasure.

'In my English we have an expression,' Richard said. 'Perhaps you know it. "Handsome is…"'

'"… as Handsome does". Yes, very tiresome. Very British. And not *meant* at all. At bottom, you British are Turks with dreadful cuisine. Maltesers, rissoles, bread and dripping. And no Empire left, boo-hoo. No wonder *he* doesn't bother ruling you any more and has pitched his tents in California.'

'The *real* Dracula,' said Richard, prompting, needling.

He felt Syrie Van Epp thinking 'Are you *trying* to get him to kill you?'

In the circumstances, it was almost kind of her.

'Yes, *him*,' said the Bey, fangs gnashing. 'My brother. Know what the Turks called him?'

'Vlad the Impaler.'

'Precisely. Vlad Tepes. Vee the Eye. They meant *that* with respect. If you had a meeting with someone called "the Impaler", you trembled for days. He nailed turbans to heads. Stuck pointed poles up jacksies. Drank goblets of blood. This, by the way, was *before* he turned vampire. In contrast, nobody was too fussed about meeting a "cel Frumos". The less terrifying brother. Vlad Tepes fought the Turks to a standstill. Radu the Handsome came to an – air quotes – *accommodation* with them. The *stories* they told! Shameful, I tell you. History is written by those with blood on their hands. Especially those who linger for centuries to insist on it. I've given up penning letters to *The Times* complaining whenever I'm mentioned in a glancing, unfortunate light.'

Richard suspected Radu's recent clippings file was slim. He wasn't often mentioned in *any* light. Come tomorrow, that might change.

One way or another, the Bey would be famous.

If still 'the other one'.

Absent-mindedly, Radu scraped pointed nails through bloody foam on his shoulder shelf and flicked it away. Someone among the hostages whimpered.

Syrie gave a little disgusted cluck.

Radu stuck out his lower lip in a pantomime of offence.

Syrie turned on her basilisk stare. Salad shrivelled. Ice sculptures went liquid. Birds that picked at the dragon's teeth fell dead.

Radu tittered.

'We can play duelling side-eye all evening, Madame Van Epp,' he said. 'My Adonis against your Aphrodite; my powers of fascination against your enchanting glamour; my title and lineage against your pots and pots of cash.'

Syrie *could* kill with a glance. The Bey must have on a glance-proof vest under that big square sleeping bag he called a suit.

She turned away and Radu made an 'I thought so' click.

Cottonmouth, one of EarthGuard goons, had a gun casually pointed at Syrie's back. She was waiting for the nod – a prince's 'kill them all' nod.

Richard decided he definitely didn't fancy Cottonmouth.

Except he did, a bit. It was the freckles.

There he went again. No wonder he got thrown out of balloons.

'Dracula, as everyone knows, means "Son of the Dragon",' continued Radu, warming to a favourite subject. 'My father was Vlad Dracul, "the Dragon". King of Wallachia. My brother and I are *both* Sons of the Dragon. I – *am* – Dracula. Just not *that* Dracula. I'm the other one. The better-looking one. When I kicked Vlad the Bad out of his castle and took the throne – a thing that actually happened which you never hear about in those self-serving lectures about his blundering, blood-soaked reign – the coiners of Wallachia were relieved to stamp my perfect profile on the money instead of the Impaler's ugly beak.'

Self-serving lectures were evidently a Dracula family trait.

Richard looked at the Bey. He sounded English, though he'd seldom visited Britain.

His tone was National Theatre come to Hollywood. Dance, Irons or a Fiennes playing wicked non-specific foreign.

Richard looked about for an Action Hero. Willis in a ripped vest. Kilmer in the Monk's hood.

Nezumi was there, sword sheathed. Biding time.

Young Sigourney Weaver, Michelle Yeoh, Linda Hamilton.

In a movie, this would go well. Unless Radu had script approval and rewrote the ending.

From where Nezumi stood, Nezumi had Cottonmouth in check. Knowing where to stand was an undervalued martial skill.

Radu flattered himself with his affected manner. He was no BAFTA/ Oscar hopeful.

He was the Frank Stallone of Transylvania.

Was he really in control here? It seemed horribly likely.

Colonel Golgotha was his sword-arm. The sham – or bent? – EarthGuard crew and the pallbearers were his shock troops. The gun-bunnies had struck hard and fast to take out potential opposition. No Action Heroes left standing!

The Bey also had Mr Horror, the Vampire Dolly, and who knew how many others on the payroll. He had thrown Aum Draht into the fray first.

Radu showed up with force enough to take the party and hold it for a few hours.

Until midnight.

After that, well, other arrangements would be made.

The Princess must regret sending an invitation to the House of Dracula. Where was she, come to that? Not tossed out of the Dragon's Mouth.

Might Christina be off somewhere with a silver knife pressed to her eyeball, opening a vault or transferring electronic funds? There must be a literal prize in view. This was a lot of trouble to go to spoil an evening.

Or was the Princess hiding her literal light under a figurative bushel?

Also biding time.

Knowing all eyes would follow him, Richard walked to the buffet.

In comfortable individual pens sat human pigs. Chubby, near-nude cherubs, steel spigots stuck in their sides. One pen was empty. Fear tears dripped from the chin guards of porky masks. The pigs wore sashes with '2000' on, representing the New Year. When 'Auld Lang Syne' struck up, posh vampires would tuck in to these symbolic babes. They or their families were being rewarded – as it were – handsomely. Their blood would be of the rare degree of purity known as 'golden'. These fat lads wouldn't have had an impure thought in their lives.

The secret of 'golden', and the reason it was officially banned in most countries, was gelding and crating donors, keeping them artificially child-sized into their twenties. They were milked for no more than six months. A huge cash bonus went to those who survived. Ex Golden Boys owned islands, record labels and luxury yachts. Many turned vampire, grew back their balls, and set about taking revenge on the world.

Other fare was on offer. Blue and Red Label Sprünt in barrels of ice. Laboratory rats injected with absinthe. Raw steak snacks. Fish swimming in shallow tanks – the idea was to sliver live sushi off their flanks. Plenty of Champagne Krug, Vintage Brut 1988. The most expensive sparkling wine in the world, if only arguably the finest.

'I'm sure the Princess won't mind if I uncork one of these early,' said Richard.

A pallbearer stepped in as wine waiter. His white mask had a red diamond teardrop below the left eyehole.

At the pop, the pigs squealed and shivered.

The cork sailed over the balcony.

By the time it landed, it'd have enough impetus to crack pavement.

Brut frothed into a flute. Richard pricked his finger with a sushi scalpel and dripped blood into the fizz, which he handed to Syrie.

He took the second glass himself.

Nezumi, he decided, was too young to drink. If he treated her like a child, others might think she was one and be surprised later.

'Peak,' he called. 'Refreshments?'

The cracksman had slid into shadows, but popped out and hustled over.

He picked up a bottle of Millennium-branded Sprünt.

'"Limited edition",' said the thief, reading the label. 'Any century that extends the concept of "limited editions" to fizzy drinks deserves to be on the way out.'

Richard wouldn't argue with that.

He raised his glass to the Bey and clinked it against Syrie's. He sipped. Perfectly chilled.

No sense wasting the Princess's hospitality.

Peak twisted off the top of his bottle and chugged.

One or two guests muttered. Their early drinks were drunk and they suddenly realised how thirsty, hungry or sober they were. When the first fearwave receded, physical needs became insistent. At the best of times, vampires wanted blood. Rounded up by goons with guns, VIVs felt red thirst like a lash. They wanted to rip veins and quaff gallons. A natural response. Christina's guests weren't used to being threatened. They were princes and princesses too. Rich, famous, notorious, handsome.

As Radu had said, 'the Soft'.

Richard sipped, didn't gulp.

Syrie knocked it back. Her eyes went red.

The blood droplets in her champagne sparked in her.

Richard knew what she wanted to do to Radu. And, flatteringly, to Richard.

He had promised. No more eccentric women. Or was that no more *new* eccentric women? Were return engagements ruled out?

Richard summoned the pallbearer to refresh his glass.

'Help yourself, Mr Jeperson,' said Radu. 'We all deserve to be sated.'

Golden Boys shifted and squeaked in suppressed terror.

Connoisseurs reckoned the finest 'golden' came from Eton schoolboys, Mormon missionaries, and African orphans adopted by American celebrities.

Radu wiped his mouth with the back of his hand.

Why had a minor royal turned up at the Princess's party dressed like the front man of Talking Heads? With a paramilitary retinue.

Richard saw Nezumi had her eye on the Bey. She was tempted to cut him down.

Though, at that prompt, his gunmen might massacre the guests. Radu was a murderer. They'd all just seen that.

The pile of bodies made him a mass murderer. A warlord. His brother impaled whole towns. He must want to top that score. Weak rulers thought in terms of numbers. Heap skull upon skull till you've built a tower. A strong tyrant knew how few to kill.

This wasn't simple bad manners. This was a wicked plan. Being carried out.

The Diogenes Club had a standing policy on wicked plans. They were to be thwarted.

Richard's glass was empty again.

DETECTIVE AZUMA

The Bund's small police department operated out of a *kōban*, a two-storey brick building on Yokonori Street. Handy for the bloodletting bars where the local law must find many repeat offenders. It presented a friendly face to tourists who staggered in with unsought-for neck scratches.

The police box might have been assembled from a kit. This was the site of the Rose Blood Club, a fangbang joint the *yakuza* once fancied as a point of entry into the tightly controlled Bund vice market. Inugami took down the vampire *oyabun* Kageyama and had the sex dungeon converted into cells. There, a considerably less friendly face was presented to perps who pissed off the Wolfman in any way, shape or form. Kageyama's back tattoo still hung where sweating crims could see it. Inugami added to his collection of human hides from time to time.

Without the Sakis, the department's strength was halved. Despite a patch populated with monsters and theoretically outside the law, Inugami kept registered crime lower in the Bund than any other central Tokyo district. Scumballs like Kageyama who flew over the Wall expecting a wide-open town were sharply reminded that the police here didn't have to act in accordance with Japanese law either. Bund-resident perps knew not to ruffle the Wolfman's fur.

The cops' job tonight was crowd control, finding lost children (preferably without scabs), giving directions, and slacking off to party. Most officers got a second pay packet as security for Light Industries and took that gig more seriously.

Azuma pushed open the glass double doors and found Sergeant Kankichi manning the front desk. His shield was pinned to the drooping tit pocket of a Hawaiian shirt. A fishbowl of laboratory-bred white mice was within reach. He chewed while watching a pinky video on a television that should have been tuned to surveillance cameras. According to the oversized box, this specimen of the pornographer's art was *Bakeneko in a*

Bathhouse. The soundtrack featured alarming miaows. The leading lady could do a lot with her tail.

Sarge grinned, furry pulp caught in his fangs.

'Beatster in the house,' he shouted.

The mice were injected with plum brandy. Sarge was well on the way to drunk.

'Where's the Wolfman?'

'In his office, howling at the moon.'

When Inugami was dismissed, lumps like Sarge would stay on. All precincts had a couple like him. Not bent, just lazy – head full of other things he could be doing, but not about to toss the badge that got him free booze and cooze. A cash-in-hand look-the-other-way merchant.

Azuma walked round the desk.

'You didn't say "pretty please",' said Sarge. 'On New Year, you have to say "pretty please".'

Azuma grabbed a handful of mice and dropped them on the blotter.

Sarge's snacks scattered, squeaking gratefully.

'Pretty please,' said Azuma.

'Have it your own way,' said Sarge, pressing a button. The secure door unlocked.

In the short corridor, Azuma found the monkey-faced Officer Ota loitering by a rack of rifles, pistols, swords and combat knives – rapt as a fat boy about to shoplift from a candy cart.

'Ota,' he said, 'break out the guns. War is coming.'

Suddenly excited, the cop fumbled with a bicycle lock fixed to the sliding glass of the weapon rack. Ota was the Bund's One-Man Emergency Action Team. Colleagues poked fun when he ordered exotic hardware from American catalogues. That might change. The Dick Boys had machine guns. The *koban* would need more than yo-yos.

Officers Brenten and Nakajima came out of the interrogation room, shirts unbuttoned to the waist. Their *hachimaki* declared *pātī gokaku* – success at party! The room pulsed with pop music and disco light. Inside, two *bakeneko* danced while cuffed to the table, not about to be upstaged by the catwoman in Sarge's video.

'Give everyone guns,' he told Ota.

'Us too?' shrilled the puma girls.

'Yes,' said Azuma – not the answer they expected.

Brenten – Inugami's beta wolf – snarled.

'Gloves on,' Azuma said. 'You'll need to handle silver bullets. We're all vampires here – monsters. Worse will come soon.'

Nakajima, the station's apprentice, was open-faced and puzzled.

'The Sakis are dead,' Azuma said.

That got everyone's attention.

NEZUMI

'Sir,' said Cottonmouth, raising her machine gun – Amazing Dancing Bear – to attract attention.

Radu, her principal, bade her speak.

He gestured as if still used to last season's lacy cuffs, rattling his wrist-bones like dice.

Cottonmouth jerked her gun at Nezumi.

'Weren't we killing the security?'

Nezumi knew where this was going.

'No offence,' Cottonmouth said to Nezumi, 'but it was in the mission brief.'

Radu didn't appreciate the distraction. He had been parading himself.

'What are you bothering me with now, silly woman?'

Cottonmouth's eyes narrowed.

Was she irritated enough to let it drop?

No. She was a professional.

A pity.

'This girl is security,' said Cottonmouth. 'She came with the Man From the Diogenes Club.'

'Missy Katana?'

'Her sword is called "Good Night Kiss".'

Radu smiled at that.

'Nezumi,' he said, pleased with himself. 'That means "mouse" in Japanese.'

'It also means "rat",' said Cottonmouth. 'Less *kawaii*.'

'I've nothing against rats. Some of my best friends look like rats.'

Radu considered Nezumi. He'd killed to make an impression. On his orders, many more were dead. He wouldn't hesitate to have a mouse squashed.

It would, she admitted, be a sensible precaution.

If unkilled, she would stop him.

He would feel the Good Night Kiss.

That was in her mission brief. Not that the Diogenes Club put it in writing. It was more a question of 'soldier on, old girl, and mind out for rogues and rotters'.

Radu smiled at Nezumi like an uncle with one hand around a bag of jelly babies and the other in his Y-fronts. Then he raised a quizzical eyebrow at Mr Jeperson.

'Would you be *bereft* if we did away with the little dear?'

Mr Jeperson would not let them kill her. He would die saving her.

It was quite British and more than a little irritating.

That was not how it was supposed to work. Dying and saving was her job. In many ways, her principal was *not* a professional.

Cottonmouth clicked off the safety on her machine gun.

'*Not* the noisemaker,' Radu told Cottonmouth. 'Our poor ears have had enough of that. Do her with cutlery.'

Cottonmouth holstered Simon Smith and Amazing Dancing Bear.

She drew the Captain and Tennille from her thigh-sheaths. Steel core, silver-plated fighting knives. The fangs of a snake.

'I would prefer to kill him,' Cottonmouth told Nezumi, in rapid Japanese so her principal couldn't follow. 'But it's *bushido*. Loyalty to the lord. Leave no one alive who might be trouble later.'

That wasn't how Nezumi understood the code but she recognised Cottonmouth's version of it.

Cottonmouth expected Nezumi to go for her *katana*.

Inside the second it would take to unsheathe Good Night Kiss, the vampire would strike fast as the snake she was named for. Nezumi would have to raise her right arm to draw the sword – and Cottonmouth could stick the Captain into her ribs, just below the armpit, point deep enough to puncture her heart. Tennille would follow, across her neck. A heart-stab and a decapitation cut.

She did not think she'd go to dust.

Truly dead, she would turn to snow – a soft white sculpture, falling apart at the first waft of warmth.

So she did not draw her sword.

She made knives of her hands to strike at Cottonmouth's wrists.

Cottonmouth saw Nezumi think it through.

She smiled in admiration, one fang peeping from her lips.

'Good girl,' she said. 'I'd offer to make it quick, but you wouldn't be you if you took me up on it. You are so much older than me. But you turned too young. You don't have the heart. And you won't have the reach.'

Cottonmouth advanced towards her. She stepped back.

That showed weakness. Too obviously.

'You're not afraid,' said Cottonmouth. 'So you're trying to get to where you want to be.'

Cottonmouth stopped and looked beyond Nezumi.

The pig-pens and the drinks table, and the guard-rail – beyond that, the Tokyo night. A wind that would freeze the warm barely troubled the undead. Muted city sounds from below.

'What is it you want? An ice-pick, a corkscrew, ten green bottles?'

Nezumi had known Cottonmouth would think she was manoeuvring to pick up a weapon.

Prevailing was only possible if the enemy couldn't conceive of your stratagem.

The tutor who told her that was infuriating, of course. It took her years to see he didn't just mean do something ridiculously stupid in the hope your enemies ruptured themselves laughing.

'What is all this delay and jibber-jabber?' said Radu.

Cottonmouth's principal was not patient.

Having decided Nezumi should die, he wanted it over with.

Radu had other things on his mind. Mr Jeperson would know that and be working on it. Nezumi had seen him dose Mrs Van Epp's champagne with his blood. He was including the woman in his circle. Practically recruiting her. Whether she wanted it or not, she was on the way to becoming a Lovely.

Cottonmouth would not be hurried along. She was clever.

Many excellent *ronin* died because they tried to please impatient lords. This vampire – a new-born? – would not join their company. Given a task, she'd take her own time. She'd kill Nezumi properly, with as little risk to herself as possible. In a moment, she'd put her knives away and retrieve her guns. Despite her principal's request, noisemakers were the best tools for this job. Whether Nezumi charged or fled, she'd be cut down. With a silver heart-shot to finish.

Nezumi stepped back several more paces.

Cottonmouth advanced, knowing she was being led.

The woman expected a trap she couldn't see yet. Then something occurred to her.

'Nezumi, can you *fly*?'

'No. I can only fall.'

Nezumi did a backflip, up across the buffet tables, tumbling over the guard-rail.

Impetus propelled her a dozen feet into empty air.

Then gravity took over.

She *dropped*.

RICHARD JEPERSON

'My condolences,' said Radu. 'Were you two close?'

Richard was numb, not with shock but with *empathy*.

He felt rushing air on Nezumi's face and was weak in the knees, wobbly in his water. The girl was not fearless. He shared her terror.

But the *smash* didn't come.

Nezumi hadn't lied. She wasn't *nosferatu* – couldn't grow bat-wings. She couldn't turn to light or air or fire or gentle rain. She had to obey rules other vampires defied.

Falling from this height would make her paste on the pavement.

Being in sync with a person at the moment of death was not something to shrug off.

But – like the small awful sound he anticipated – that hammer didn't fall.

NEZUMI

She *plunged* for an agonising age.

A reflected night sky hung below her, sloping gently. City lights, stars and the moon mirrored on canopy windows. Beneath them a large unlit room. The Ruff.

When she leaped over the safety railing, she knew the restaurant was below the Doragon no Kuchi but not how far out the lower floor stretched.

The human pig had fallen all the way down. Being caught by the Ruff was no sure thing.

She had only her weight to control her trajectory.

Arms out and feet together, she made a dart of herself and rode an updraft, aiming herself at the black mirror.

In herself, she went *somewhere else…*

Nezumi seldom slept – the famous lassitude, proverbially close to death, came on her rarely – and didn't dream. She half-imagined dreams a lie perpetuated to make vampires feel less human. A warm treasure denied the undead, talked up and gloated over. Like other things vampires were not supposed to be able to do – make art, fall in love, sunbathe, grow up. When girls talked about their dreams, Nezumi nodded along to avoid fruitless argument. Dreamers sounded as if they were making stuff up – like third-form girls who said they'd done things with boys everyone knew perfectly well they hadn't.

The idea of dreams was too fanciful. A melange of memory and imagination, real beyond question to the sleeper, evaporating at the instant of waking.

How was that even possible?

But, in those mid-air seconds, Nezumi thought she *dreamed*.

Dreams, she had heard, could stretch to eternity but be over in a fingersnap.

Now, she *understood*.

She was smaller, a child wrapped in furs against the bite of winter. A *warm* child, not the vampire she would become. Or warm-ish. She heard things differently, as if her ears were stopped with wax. She ran beside a mountain stream of ice, arms and legs swaddled stiff. Delighted by sparkling curls, waves and ripples fashioned by the instant of freezing. Giddy from running, she lost her footing and took a tumble. She smacked her head against a rock.

Crying and screaming, emptying her lungs. Blood in her eyes stung worse than *soap*.

Then a cool, loving touch.

A woman. Her mother, more beautiful than she should be, in a simple white robe, with no furs or leggings, not feeling the cold because she *was* the cold. She was the woman of the snows, the ice queen who took a woodcutter for a husband, who bore his children and lived, at least for a while, among warm men and women in the mountains.

Yuki-Onna.

The woman blinked, showing cat's eyes briefly – a secret shared with only one of her daughters.

In that blink, Nezumi knew her dream for a dream – a memory, perhaps, or a wish? She was back in her right mind, with a stab of regret that this was no great revelation of lost childhood.

She was no ice princess, not really. More like a woodcutter's brat.

Her dream was a pleasing distraction, a kiss of solace before oblivion. A story she made up so she'd feel better. Not a lie. A dream.

'My little mouse,' said her phantom mother, licking blood from her girl's scraped cheek. 'My sweet little mouse. Be brave.'

Then Nezumi smacked into glass, harder than she'd smacked into the rock.

A thousand years on, that rock would be ground to nothing.

She was still here.

The sling of her poster tube cut into her throat, like the rope around that condemned man's neck.

The canopy cracked but did not break. She bounced and slid, palms and face pressed to ice-sheet glass. She picked up speed, as if on the upper slope of a ski-jump.

She hammered the dented glass and got her fingers into the cracks she made.

She worried her hands would rip off at the wrists. But she stuck fast.

Her legs dangled over the lip of the canopy.

Below was a sheer drop. Not even a flagpole.

The crack-patterns spread. Glass began to break the wrong way, freeing her to fall.

She headbutted the surface and put her shoulders into it.

A section of the canopy fell apart and she dropped into the restaurant. The din of wind was no longer in her ears. The arctic blast was no longer in her eyes and hair.

Time resumed its normal speed.

She hadn't the luxury of stopping to concentrate, to recapture a picture – cat's eyes! – shaped in the ripples on the surface of a bowl of water.

She had to move on.

A frustration. Duty to her principal came before indulging her own vanity.

Was that the reason so many vampires had no reflections? So they wouldn't get distracted by themselves?

All vampires were vain.

All were clingy, dependent.

All were selfish.

She had heard that over and over too – from friends as well as the cruel and prejudiced. Some made exceptions for her. Some didn't.

'We love you anyway, though you can't love us back,' said several.

Nezumi would rather have a thin needle of ice stuck though her heart than hear that again. Always, she responded with a smile and downcast eyes.

'See, you can't even smile properly.'

This was a distraction too.

She would have to be mad to jump off a building. So she was thinking like a mad person, trying to be consistent.

She was aware of her beating heart.

Vampires were supposed to be dead – girls were always surprised she had a pulse.

The Ruff was closed to customers tonight. Tables were covered with cloths, but not laid for dinner. Light spilled through the broken canopy, but candles were not lit.

She prised shards out of her hands and face. From long-ingrained habit, she cleaned her wounds thoroughly and quickly. Accelerated healing was an advantage of the vampire condition, but scratching out slivers of glass or scraps of grit sealed into her body by rapidly mended skin was a gruesome bother.

The state of her clothes would have to be seen to later. She had worries beyond uniform infractions.

Would Radu send a killer – Cottonmouth? – after her? Could he spare any of his people? Could he afford to let her run free?

She must keep moving.

The lifts were out. They were in enemy hands.

In the gloom, red LEDs glowed. Security cameras and silent alarms. If Radu had taken the building, he would have all its eyes and ears. Time for Miss Mouse to find a mousehole.

RICHARD JEPERSON

Irritated that Nezumi had shown her up in front of her boss, Cottonmouth pulled a hostage out of the crowd. The merc selected a Japanese vampire who wore a tweed body stocking, Havelock half-cape and deerstalker hat. The outfit displayed a peculiarly Asian Anglophilia Richard found touching.

Was Cottonmouth going to kill the woman?

A petty gesture of frustration. A death was demanded but not delivered – so this random guest would be an offering to the petty princeling?

Richard would not let that happen.

He would step in and get killed.

So Nezumi would have failed in her job. The deerstalker woman would be murdered in front of him as he died. Just to rub it in. No joy all round, then.

But still the only thing to do.

He would have liked to find out what was up with the GEIST/YUREI primes. And what Radu thought he was doing tonight. The thing about dying he most resented was that he would miss the end of the story.

Of all the stories.

Cottonmouth marched the woman to the railings. The hostage didn't resist.

Close to the edge, wind riffled Cottonmouth's hair and the flaps of the deerstalker.

Cottonmouth didn't heave the woman to her death, but tapped the back of her neck with the silvered flat of her knife.

The woman winced and her neck stretched six inches – like a startled turtle poking its head out of its shell. Richard recognised the hostage. Lady Oyotsu, former High Priestess of the Temple of One Thousand Monsters. Presently a non-voting member of Light Industries' Board of Directors. An early ally of Christina's. Of the *rokurokubi* bloodline. Her neck extended like a fire-ladder, flexible as an anglepoise lamp. As the white fleshtube elongated, a wracking, vertebrae-clicking sound set his teeth on edge.

Richard intuited the thing Oyotsu never told anyone that the *rokurokubi* trick *hurt*. Every extra inch was an agony, the arthritis in his knuckles amplified by the dozen. He was almost poleaxed by the wave of pain and had to concentrate to tune her out. It was a point of honour for her not to let discomfort show on her powdered face.

'Can you see her?' Cottonmouth asked, blade still in hand.

Silver seared Oyotsu's hackles.

She had to grip the guard-rail to prevent over-balancing. If she stretched more than a few feet, she had to sit in an anchor pose so as not to fall over. Her neck and head were the dancing cobra; her body was the basket. The neck ranged like a grazing brontosaurus.

Then she spotted something.

She tried to make a verbal report, but her mouth was too far away for her voice to be heard. She took one hand off the rail and gripped Cottonmouth's shoulder.

Her neck pulled in. That hurt too.

Oyotsu whispered to Cottonmouth.

'There's a broken window in the Ruff,' the merc reported. 'The girl is alive.'

'Oh, what a nuisance,' said Radu. 'See what happens when you make a fuss.'

HAROLD TAKAHAMA

H al was starting to worry about Lefty.

His hand had misinterpreted – or disobeyed – a direct order. He wanted out of the building, but when he tried to go down to the street exit the hand sent him higher up.

At least he was out of the *pneumatique*. And the lavender pest was off his ass. But he was still stuck inside the fucking robosaur.

Lefty said this was Floor 93. Hal no longer trusted the machine not to just pick a random number. Its clicking and flashing had a nerve-grating quality, as if Jun Zero had programmed the hand to mock his past self.

Maybe he should have called it Dr Sinister.

He was in a winding passage. Not a corridor with doors either side, but a succession of rooms stuck together like open-ended boxes, with marked décor differences every four metres or so. Fake windows showed cheesy landscape backdrops. Furniture and fittings were nineteenth century. Set decoration from a Western or *Masterpiece Theatre*.

It was a funhouse exhibit.

The trail began in a low-ceilinged hovel. Plaster had fallen off the slatted wall in irregular shapes. He had to squeeze around an unmade brass bed that was too big for the room. Stuck on one post of the frame was a crack-faced, apple-sized head with stiff straw hair. The doll's discarded body was curled up in a nest of grey sheets.

This was either a child's nightmare or a crime scene.

Next up was a great-grandmama's drawing room with lumpy wallpaper. He knocked his shins on a heavy, low table. Waxy, unflowering plants crammed between upholstered couches and chairs.

This looked like a place you were summoned to and told off in.

Then, a room full of white china. Ornaments on every sill, surface and mantel. Bigger statues on their own plinths. Nymphs getting it on. Chicks and swans. Chicks and guys with goat feet. Chicks and guys with wings.

Chicks and fat cherubs. Chicks and other chicks.

Your basic Victorian porno stash.

Walking among the collection made small statuettes clink against each other. That was good for a shudder.

He had a sense he wasn't alone on Floor 93.

And he didn't think Lefty counted as company.

He hurried on.

One room was a hothouse, full of stinking orchids.

Another was empty, as if the bailiffs had just been. Crinkled old newspapers and torn-up letters underfoot on bare wooden boards.

Lights came on automatically when he stepped into a new room, simulating fire, oil lamps, the sun, chemical glow, gas-jets. When he moved on, the room behind went dark.

'What is this?' he asked.

'The rooms of the life of Christina Light,' said Lefty.

'Who?'

'Your hostess. This is her building.'

Hal knew the name.

'I wouldn't want to live in any of these places.'

'They were not all her choice.'

In a library section, books were crammed into floor-to-ceiling shelves. Hal couldn't prise one loose with a ruler. The titles he could make out were long and in flaking Italian or German. Political or religious tracts that would be hard to plough through even in English. No paperbacks, no comics, no *Penthouses*.

A few rooms back, a light came on.

So something was moving.

It would be foolish to shout 'hello', but the temptation grew like an itch. Hal thought horror film heroines should pull eiderdowns over their heads... not get out of bed, pick up a candle, and go down to the basement to investigate those strange sounds. Jun Zero must have overwritten that instinct.

Looking back, he saw something slide off the slaughtered doll's bed. Its movement brought on a dim lamp. Someone stood in front of the light, with a sheet over their head. A cartoon ghost. Casper and Dickens' Jacob Marley didn't really wear bedsheets, Hal knew. Traditional Halloween spectre get-up was a winding sheet. A shroud.

The rooms were arranged like a simple maze. After five or six in a row, a side door fed into a passage that ran the other way. From the library, he stepped sideways, out of sight of the ghost, into a railroad station waiting room circa 1875 – benches, stove, spittoons, old-timey periodicals (in Cyrillic) on a wooden rack – then hurried on.

In a feminine chamber, he was assailed by scent. Heavy, exotic, stinging his eyes. Like Tsunako Shiki's lavender, it failed to cover a smell of mould. Long gowns were piled on a plush bed. A choice had yet to be made. Jewel boxes he wasn't tempted to rifle were open on a dresser.

He was startled to catch sight of himself in a huge mirror.

He should pick up the pace – a ghost was after him! – but was transfixed. This was his first good look at the man he'd grown into. His future self. Jun Zero.

Yes, he was still recognisable. Not even taller.

But his face was lean, with no wobbles on the cheeks or under the chin. Close-shaved, except for Tartar tufts at the corners of his mouth. Was that a 1999 thing? Or a Jun Zero signature?

The hair was a shock – dyed white-blond, with sculpted spikes.

His first thought was Asian cyberpunk Tom Cruise.

He had microchip earrings and a bar-code tattoo under his jawline. That made Hal rethink – almost heretically. Was Jun Zero trying a byte too much? Could he maybe afford to dial down the coolitude? At this rate, he'd pass Cruise territory and get into the Crispin Glover zone.

He checked out his own crazy eyes.

But were those his?

The boudoir lighting was subdued pink. Smouldering red scarves were draped over lamps. Behind the mirror, a harsher light burned.

What room had he passed through with a window to match this mirror?

And who was there looking at him through one-way glass?

The silhouette was the floating sheet spook.

Did it have eyeholes cut out?

No, it wasn't a sheet. It was long, straight, white hair.

He broke away from the mirror, heart hammering, and ran though several rooms to the next side door.

He was in an artist's studio. A half-finished portrait of a young woman was propped on an easel. Angry action paint splashes arced across tiled floor and brick wall. He stepped on a discarded revolver.

He was running now.

… a church or meeting room, with a pulpit and a skylight…

… bare stone with inset rusty iron rings, straw on the floor – a dungeon…

… a cot on a trunk, with a porthole in a ship's cabin wall and painted sea beyond the glass…

… a Japanese temple, like something from a *chanbara* movie… mats on the floor, paper screens, a pile of scrolls, a woodblock pillow. An altar to Yuki-Onna, the Vampire Queen of the East. His cousin Helen was keen on her, Hal remembered. She could freeze your blood, rip the jagged gore sticks out of your veins, and crunch them like popsicles. Charming!

This Christina Light – the woman in the picture? – had travelled to Japan after her sea voyage.

He knew who she was.

The vampire who built the Bund.

Hellish was obsessed with that bit of history. How a bunch of city blocks in Tokyo became vampire territory. The last Hal had seen his cousin, so far as he could remember, she was arguing with Auntie Karen about turning vamp and moving to New Orleans. That was 1990 or so. She probably had her fangs by now.

Hal bet Hellish was Jun Zero's arch-nemesis.

God, the damage she could do with teeth and claws and her cunning little parasite mind!

The Broadway musical *Miss Christina!* was about Christina Light. Hal saw the film version. Madonna spent most scenes when she wasn't singing out of tune lying about in corsets being nuzzled on by an elder vampire played by Sean Penn. It was no *Desperately Schtupping Susan* that was for sure.

'This is all original,' he said. 'The furniture, the walls, the mess?'

'Eighty-nine percent original,' confirmed Lefty.

Hal guessed anyone with the money and determination to carve out a fiefdom from someone else's country and build a headquarters shaped like a G-bot dinosaur could buy up their past and arrange this winding path so she could traipse down memory lane when the mood took her.

Was that her coming for him? With the white hair?

Madonna played Christina Light as blonde. But, if there was a musical biopic to be made, Madonna would play Harriet Tubman as blonde.

This wasn't a museum, but a private space. A mnemonic garden. What happened to the houses the rooms were stripped out of? Did they fall down without them? The ship *must* have sunk.

And why do it?

After a hundred or more years, memories blurred. Could physical objects bring them back in focus? If Jun Zero put together a similar exhibition of rooms, from Hal's teenage Ojai bedroom to whatever high-tech lair the outlaw hung his sharp brim in these days, would his chiropterid-wiped past come back?

Hal peeped that this Christina woman was weird. Weirder than Madonna. Weirder even than Crispin Glover. It could be she had the time tunnel notion after bingeing on golden blood, gave a million dollars to a firm of fix-its, and forgot the whim until they'd installed this ghost train in her building.

The Japanese temple was a dead-end.

Wherever came next, Miss Christina must still be living in it.

This building, presumably. It wasn't just a corporate HQ.

Hal looked back down the passageway of a life.

Most of the rooms had pictures on display. The portrait with the sketchy face but filled-in background. Photographs in frames, cards pinned to walls, pages frail as fall leaves torn from magazines. Christina Light left her image behind like shed snakeskins.

In which room had she been bitten by that crusty horror Sean Penn played?

Probably one that came after the boudoir with the mirror. She wouldn't need the vanity glass as a vampire.

He'd think this was supposed to be a tomb – like the luxury dens pharaohs set up inside pyramids – only he got the idea Miss Christina planned on not dying.

No one did these days.

Whatever was following him would catch up now.

The lights went on in a far room as the ghost slipped through the doorway.

Hal looked about for a weapon. He could get to the dropped revolver...

Whatever was creeping towards him wouldn't be stopped by lead.

Could Tsunako Shiki have found him?

He had the impression of someone slight, slender.

A girl. Older than Tsunako, or at least taller.

He knew where she was because lights came on in those rooms, but she always found cover so he couldn't see her properly. She was quick, then. And thinking tactically.

'Hello,' he said, at last giving in to the impulse.

He held up Lefty, like a heroine's candlestick, ready for use as a bludgeon.

At least he could trust his glitching hand to deliver a hefty whack.

The girl stepped into the suicide's studio. Artificial Italian sunlight filtered in through fake windows. She stood by the easel.

'Such a sad story,' she said. 'Charles Strickland, the painter. He shot himself on the Princess's wedding day.'

The girl was nothing like Madonna. So not Christina Light then.

For a terrible second, Hal thought she was Cousin Hellish.

She was a vampire and Japanese. She had long white hair and spoke English with a British accent. She wore knee-socks, a blazer with a pocket badge, and a pleated skirt, as if she went to Catholic school or were a steward at a tech trade fair. Her uniform was slightly grubby with a few rips.

She carried a sword as if she knew how to use it.

'I'm Nezumi,' she said, smiling openly. 'What's your name?'

'Hal, ah...' he began, then caught himself squeaking. He took a breath and spoke from his chest in more manly fashion, 'Jun Zero.'

Moving faster than his eye could register, Nezumi crossed the distance between them – five or six rooms – and laid an icy sword edge against his neck.

Her face was close to his. She looked about thirteen.

'Jun Zero,' she said, not smiling.

'Ah,' he said, nearly squeaking again, 'you've heard of me.'

He shouldn't need reminding that he was on everyone's kill-on-sight list.

She left her sword where it was but stood back – giving herself room to swing for a proper killing slice.

'Funny story,' he said, 'but, ah, an hour and a half ago *I* hadn't heard of me. My mind got wiped. I'm Jun Zero, yes… but I can't *remember* being Jun Zero. In my head, I'm this kid called Harold Takahama. I make – ah, he made robots for computer games. Perhaps you could call me Hal? And not kill me.'

The sword didn't move.

DETECTIVE AZUMA

At this phase of the lunar cycle, Chief Inugami sported a faceload of greying bristles but his nose was only slightly snout-like. His lower fangs gnawed his upper lip. His yellow eyes burned like angry full moons.

Azuma gave his report.

The Wolfman assembled all available officers in the interrogation room – which also served as squad room, briefing room, downtime room and storage closet. Police boxes were notoriously cramped. Sarge, Brenten, Nakajima and Ota sat on folding chairs in stages of inebriation, puzzlement, exhilaration and terror. Azuma would prefer frightened, cautious Nakajima at his back over fired-up, gun-happy Ota. He'd rather go alone than rely on either, but after what he'd seen he didn't have a choice. This had to be dumped in Inugami's lap.

Asato Yamamura, a girlish boy-stroke-boyish girl, was pulled off the switchboard to sit at the front desk. Of the *iso onna* bloodline, she was permanently damp and sucked salt through hollow needles inside her mouth. Asato adopted that faddish *yūrei* look – long lank hair combed over the face like a mask. Still, a more impressive representative of the Bund PD than Sergeant Kankichi.

The puma girls were out on their tails. With reports of a mounting death toll, they became less keen on being given guns. Brenten and Nakajima did up their shirts and took off the party headbands.

Mitsuru Fujiwara, an employee of Light Industries who looked after the police computers, had come by with holiday treats for Asato and the Sakis. *Guimauve* – marshmallow shells with a dollop of virgin choirboy blood in the centre. Sarge said the smoothie was doing the rounds of his harem. He was still piqued about the mice.

Inugami deputised Fujiwara.

Azuma noticed the tall, coiffured vampire was comfortable with the pistol Ota gave him. He didn't wave it like an idiot playing cowboys or shrink away from the weapon as if it were a rusty grenade.

The Chief hadn't been alerted to the EarthGuard presence. That should have been standard procedure. Asato mentioned only receiving calls from inside the Bund in the last hour or so. And few of them, considering the busy evening. No outside lines were available.

Everyone with a cell phone wasted a minute or so establishing that they couldn't get a signal. That must involve sophisticated jamming equipment. Fujiwara's phone was smaller and more powerful than everyone else's. He tried the emergency failsafe channel and got a recording.

'It's New Year's Eve,' he said. 'People with out-of-date ideas will think the system is overloaded by everyone calling relatives. That can't happen any more. This is a bad thing. A deliberate thing.'

Sarge suggested looking at TV news.

They all left the interrogation room and found Asato holding Sarge's pinky video by thumb and forefinger. Behind that curtain of hair, she made an ick face. The telephonist wore a long white shroud-shift, which her hair seemed to be woven into. A big badge with a cartoon policeman on it showed she could be asked for help.

Sarge clicked through channels.

Every network had a live New Year's Eve programme. It was already 2000 in New Zealand and their computers still worked. An American Queen of Cyberpunk said no one should let unfounded rumour-mongering get in the way of having a fabulous party night. An animated clip depicted the dreaded millennium bug as a data-eating cockroach. The Cham-Cham '1999' clip played on several channels, with news headlines along the bottom of the screen. Lots of trivial celebration stories. No word of a terrorist incident in Tokyo. No camera crews at the Gate of the Bund. No experts reassuring or politicians sweating.

The big news was Cham-Cham themselves, who were due to perform their follow-up song live on *Kōhaku Uta Gassen*. Asato – monotone somehow enthusiastic – predicted they'd ditch the *burikko* style, stop acting like teenagers imitating twelve-year-olds, and 'go sexy' for the new century. She also said it wouldn't work and their fans would find new *idoru*. Nakajima agreed but was still interested in what their next single would be. It didn't surprise Azuma that these police were easily distracted. They hadn't seen the Sakis splattered with murder mushrooms.

Fujiwara commandeered the *kōban*'s computer terminal. He typed commands and accessed sites. He knew what he was doing but didn't try to explain. He was impatient with people who weren't tech-literate to his level.

While Fujiwara dicked about on the web, everyone else watched television.

Tokyo MX cut between reports of celebrations from all around the city.

A suicide cult was gathered for a tantalising evening on the slopes of Mount Fuji. An eruption was foretold by a prophet who found hidden wisdom in the theme song of a popular children's cartoon. The faithful anticipated ecstatic transformation and holy death. As lava-mummies, they would be twisted in poses of eternal adoration. Those who hadn't bothered – or dared – to quit their jobs would get ribbed to death when they had to show their faces at work next week.

Then the station cut to Daikaiju Plaza.

'Look, it's us,' said Nakajima.

Sophie Fukami, a warm announcer, stood with a microphone, pretending to be afraid of larking vampires. She gave the word from the Bund.

'Saki-G,' shouted Ota.

Behind Sophie, the girl cop did yo-yo tricks for a crowd.

'You said she was dead,' accused Nakajima.

Inugami growled and pointed at the screen.

In the crowd next to Saki-G was Nakajima, face painted green.

'That's last year,' said Brenten.

Sophie smiled nervously and waved, chatting with an anchor in the studio. TMX cut to a rockabilly-permed warm guy and a Regency-frilled vampire girl duetting outside a Nigerian bar in Roppongi. 'Find Life Again,' they sang.

'That's now,' said Asato, with a halting croak. 'The song's only a month old. Dessert were on top of the charts with it until Cham-Cham knocked them off.'

'Good detective work,' said Inugami.

It didn't surprise Azuma that the best police in this box was the secretary.

Asato fiddled proudly with her wet hair.

Sulkily, Sarge snaffled a *guimauve* from the gift basket.

'How is this possible?' Brenten asked, peering at the screen.

'It's doable if you have the resources,' said Fujiwara, not looking away from the terminal screen. 'Cut the live feed, replace it with the recording. Rely on everyone either end being tipsy and careless.'

'Don't you broadcast that Light Channel thing from the Big Dragon?' asked Azuma.

'That's not transmitted as such. A signal generates light from receivers. You're right, though. It must be coming from the crown of masts on top of Daikaiju Building. Someone's been in the Processor Room and done something clever and dangerous.'

Fujiwara turned in his chair.

'The World Wide Web isn't cut off, but bandwidth is throttled,' he said. 'Sites load too slowly to be accessed. E-mail is down so no getting messages out that way.'

'Millennium bug?' said Nakajima.

Fujiwara pouted. 'We've spent six years proofing systems against that. And it's not midnight. But most people will think what you think. The millennium bug has been all over the news. That TV graphic is typical. *Mlecchas* think an actual insect eats the insides of your computer.'

Azuma had heard the word *mleccha* before. From Aum Draht perps.

They were all cyber-dweebs too.

'I've accessed the feed TMX is using,' said Fujiwara. 'This is where it gets interesting and a teeny bit arousing. It's not straight footage from last year's festival.'

Sophie Fukami was back on television, with the Sakis waving at the camera. Their cheeriness had a chilling effect on the room. The reporter relayed questions from the anchor to the yo-yo girls.

'It's been doctored with next-gen interactive AI functionality,' said Fujiwara, proudly.

'Talk Japanese,' snapped Inugami.

'The people in the studio are having a verbal interaction – a conversation – with the reporter. She answers questions. She makes jokes. It doesn't make perfect sense, but – again, thank you, drunken New Year's celebrations – neither does anything else. CG-Sophie passes a Turing test. That's genuinely exciting. The audio is generated by smartware, along with video glitches that make lip movements match. You know in games you have rudimentary conversations with NPCs – ah, with characters who are part of the scenario, but not gamer avatars – and get responses. The programmer codes answers that vary depending on prompts. That's not a simple rerun of an old Sophie Fukami tape... that's a responsive construct, generating information on the fly, fooling a user into believing they're talking to another human. Even if she doesn't hold up for long, she's an incredible achievement.'

'Pardon me if I don't applaud,' said Inugami.

Azuma looked at the woman on the screen. She seemed no less real or unreal than the people in the room.

Thinking like this turned people to Aum Draht.

NEZUMI

S o this was the famous Jun Zero!
 Trying to tell her a likely story.

She knew the name from watch-lists, but the Diogenes Club file wasn't even sure the outlaw hacker was just one person. Jun Zero might well be a loose collective. Profilers struggled to formulate a coherent psych evaluation for a malefactor whose crimes ranged from murder to trivial tomfoolery. Did Jun Zero suffer from multiple personality disorder or was he tricky enough to fake the condition? Amoral or puritanical? Anarchist or fascist? Evil or idealist? Warm or vampire – or something else? A rogue AI, perhaps? Or six unemployed screenwriters with a World Wide Web connection whose bitch session jape got out of hand.

Jun Zero was credibly connected with a rash of church fires from Buenos Aires to County Mayo. Jun Zero electronically raided the accounts of Children in Need, distributing the entire sum raised in 1996 to every billionaire in the world. Small random sums forensic accountants wouldn't notice were paid into vast slush funds. Barely a tenth of the money was returned. Jun Zero sank ships, stole on a scale that made Anthony Peak look like a Piccadilly pickpocket, supplied rival street gangs with prototype plasma weapons and set off the Bronx Warriors/Baseball Furies War of 1996, and sent customers who ordered mysteries from an online bookseller e-mails which gave away the culprit in the header.

Nezumi looked up at the man with the glass hand.

A trickle of sweat ran across his bar-code tattoo and onto her blade.

She'd expected a cooler customer. And maybe someone taller. She didn't have to look up at him much.

Could this specimen be the figurehead of the Zeroid Movement?

Massed ranks of Jun Zeros turned up in black cloaks, cordovan hats and Z-marked Zorro masks to disrupt events they deemed symptoms of a sick society: Crufts Dog Show; the Femina Miss India contest; the Bleeding

Man Festival in the Mojave Desert; the gala opening of de Boscherville's *Anck-es-en-Amon* at the Paris Opera, sponsored by Petrox Oil to greenwash their image after the North Sea *Jennifer* disaster.

Zeroid mobs shuffled around menacingly and threw stink bombs until authorities got used to writing them off as a mere nuisance. Then they pulled scimitars out of their robes at the World Cup in France in 1998 and killed fifty-seven football fans before the CRS went in with guns. Men and women under the masks turned out to be achingly ordinary – warm and vampire – and from different countries and backgrounds. Asked why they did what they did, they said, 'To set the counter to zero', which ranked with 'The Wire is watching' as an ominous meaningless platitude.

Just because this guy said he was Jun Zero didn't mean he was.

Thinking about it, why would Jun Zero flat out admit who he was? Shouldn't he have a fully-worked-out bogus identity ready to hide behind? He'd always have an alibi, like the cat in the poem, and one or two to spare.

It made sense – for the moment – to think of the middle-sized, bleached blond guy as Hal.

He looked like the kind of fellow she didn't much cotton to. Overly full of himself, with a daft bar-code throat tattoo like a transfer packaged with issue one of a boys' comic. Rule one of covert work – don't have identifying marks. Jun Zero ought to be someone you couldn't describe after he'd got away.

She got a different reading off Hal when he spoke. He was afraid of her – she *did* have a sword to his neck – but not bitter or resentful about it the way some boys were when shown up in even the smallest things.

Hal didn't look at her with contempt fear but respect fear. He didn't have hard eyes. But he had a bionic hand.

Witnesses would remember that before the neck tattoo, she supposed. She decided he was at worst a nuisance.

'Your clothes don't go with you,' she said, sheathing Good Night Kiss.

'I know,' he said, rubbing his neck. 'I was in disguise as an office worker when I got part-erased. It was a chiropterid. A memory vipe… ah, vampire.'

He tapped his forehead. Just where a chiropterid would make its teeny hole.

'… and what about…?'

She pointed to his hand, which he'd tried to hide behind his back. He brought it out to show. It was a smart gadget, sleek and compact – if bigger than a proper hand – with visible lights, cogs and rods.

'This is Lefty. Jun Zero – I – had it installed. I'm not sure why, but it's helpful three-fifths of the time.'

'Unknown female vampire,' rasped the hand. 'Sixty-eight percent likelihood of hostile action against User Jun Zero.'

Did Hal know the hand used his own voice, scrambled and tweaked? He probably couldn't hear it that way.

'Don't be offended,' Hal told her. 'Sixty-eight percent is a low threat score by Lefty standards. Most people we've run into tonight have been in the nineties and up. The whole world wants Jun Zero dead.'

'Can you blame them?' she said.

He looked at her with a stab of concern.

'How bad is it?' he asked. 'My rap sheet? Have I, like, trafficked golden lads to Transylvania or blown up Disneyworld? Am I a serial killer?'

'Only technically.'

'That's a huge comfort – *not!*'

For an instant, he – Hal, not Jun Zero – expected her to be amused or impressed.

'That's gone out of fashion. Girls said *not!* about ten years ago. Then they stopped. You won't be able to make *not!* happen again. They'll say "1992 called and wants its *not!* joke back"… until they start saying "1999 called and wants its '1992 called…' joke back". It's an evolving language.'

She could talk. She still didn't understand the J-girl fuss about wrinkled socks.

Coming to Japan made her the butt of a raft of '1992 called and wants its [whatever] back' jokes. The country of her birth, for so long her idea of the settled and unchanging past, was now the world's idea – or nightmare – of the future.

… 992 called and wants its feudal system back, not that it really went away.

Back at school, she'd wear wrinkled socks. They'd be out of fashion in

Tokyo, but the coming thing at Drearcliff Grange. A fashion trend didn't catch fire with the girls until the school tried to ban it.

'Thanks for the pointers, Miss Manners. In my head, 1992 is *this year*. You try having your memory leached and see how au fait you are with next-gen slang. Do people still say "next-gen"?'

'I've only heard that once or twice. You're cutting edge there. People still say "cutting edge".'

'I'd rather you didn't. Brings back recent memories.'

He rubbed his neck again.

'I've so *few* memories, it's a shame most are of being attacked, barely surviving, running away, and wondering what the freak is going on.'

'I'm sorry I was insensitive. I also have forgotten much. No, that is wrong. I do not forget, I *mislay*. Memories sink. Sometimes, a fragment floats to the surface of the pond. I heard what your hand said about this floor. I understand what the Princess has done here.'

From her rooms, much could be inferred about the Princess Casamassima.

'This is from the Temple of One Thousand Monsters,' Nezumi said. 'That is the altar of Yuki-Onna. I've memories of her, or someone like her, a woman of the snows… memories as seen through a blizzard, which may be word association because…'

'"Yuki" means "snow", I know. Jun Zero learned Japanese.'

She tipped her head to the altar. Ice flowers were arranged in the cold spot.

She slid one of the screen doors aside. Beyond was metal plate, more like the hull of a ship than the wall of a building. Dragon hide, she supposed.

'The more I find out about Jun Zero, the less I want the memories back,' said Hal. 'Happy to take the skills – and he seriously got into shape which I, I admit, didn't… I doubt this stomach has digested a potato chip in nearly a decade. Dude must have committed to a diet of carrot sticks and steroids. But, *whisper it so Lefty doesn't hear*, I'm going right off the idea of Jun Zero's life. If so many people want him dead, he must have been doing something shitty.'

Nezumi thought it best not to mention the Zeroid massacres… or

Children in Need… or the Carleton Knowles whodunit she never got round to reading after the spoiler spam pinged into her inbox.

'Would User Jun Zero like to hear a list of the charges against him and the authorities who have issued arrest warrants and kill-orders?'

'Honestly, Lefty, not really.'

'The information is available.'

'That's a good thing to know.'

He shielded his mouth and said, 'No, it isn't.'

'Is that a way of trying to sneak *not!* back in through the kitchen door?'

He laughed. That broke up his face, made him more Hal and less Zero.

He scratched his scalp. He squashed his hair-spikes and raked them with his fingers.

She took her travel comb out of her pocket and lent it to him. He tried to reshape the spikes into smoothness, and struggled with tangles. He didn't force it in case he broke her comb.

'That's better,' she said as he passed it back.

'I can smell burning pants, Nezumi.'

'It's a *smidge* better, but you'll need a stylist to rescue you completely. Are you married to the collar ink?'

'Funk, no. It's awful. What was Jun Zero thinking?'

'This is Japan. *Yakuza* get tattoos here.'

'Yes, but good ones, right? Fire dragons and samurai…'

He noticed her moué at the s-word.

'Not a fan of *chanbara eiga*, then. I'm surprised, what with your sword.'

'I am not samurai. I am *ronin*.'

'Masterless, right? I figure I am too. Though Lefty says I have a mystery client, who is totally responsible for dumping me in this mess. I did a dirty deed for Mr or Ms U.N. Owen, then the ratfink set a chiropterid on me.'

'I have a principal. Mr Jeperson.'

'But you act because you choose to, not because you have to. Freelance.'

'Yes.'

'I wish Jun Zero were more like you and less like him. Does that sound nutso? Coming from Jun Zero?'

'Not so "nutso". But I am no one to be admired.'

He smiled honestly now. His impulse was to reassure her, give her a pat on the head, and say she was doing well for someone (a girl!) her age – then remember she wasn't a warm child but a grown-up viper.

Patronising indulgence would switch to terror any moment.

She'd seen that so many times she wasn't much saddened any more.

He surprised her by taking a different thought-track. He was over being afraid of her – the subliminal crazy-courage of Jun Zero bubbling up? – and took her as she was. He tried to think of a way of contradicting her that didn't come across as smarmy.

She appreciated that.

'You wouldn't happen to know anything about the *less* deadly side of Jun Zero?' he asked. 'His, ah, personal life. Girlfriends and that sort of thing.'

'I heard he – you – teamed up with Sonja Blaue to break up a groomer-stalker-creeper ring operating under the cover of a *Galaxy Quest* convention. Sonja Blaue is—'

'I know who Sonja Blaue is,' he said, grinning with delighted amazement. 'I have – had – that poster of her on the bike on my dorm wall. Badass babe in the leather jacket and sunglasses. Jun Zero and Sonja Blaue? That's… like, incredibly encouraging news. Do you have her number? She's vampire *ronin* too, right? You hang out sometimes, have sleepovers? Compare knives and swap make-up tips?'

'I've never met her. She *has* said you're one of the few warm men she'd kill on sight.'

'Bad breakup, huh? You know, I bet it was my fault. I've an itchy, hinky feeling about the way Jun Zero treats people. I don't think he's that nice of a guy. I mean, I'm kind of disappointed how I turned out. I guess Sonja Blaue would say that too.'

'Her poster is still popular with teenage boys and some girls.'

'Must be retro now. Leather and sunglasses have gone the way of *not!*'

'I wouldn't say so. The look is still chic. Timeless.'

'Do all girls dress like you now?'

'At my school, they have to. Many complain about it.'

'I hear you. Because I'm in disguise I don't know what Jun Zero would really wear.'

Nezumi looked at Hal from several angles, wondering what would suit him. She had taken couture lessons and enjoyed dressing up the dummies. Hal might pull off a modified murgatroyd look – not as extreme in the velvets and frills department as Mr Jeperson – but sharp, clean-lined tailoring with touches of flamboyance.

'User Jun Zero,' said Lefty, breaking the mood, 'hostile actor is in the vicinity. One hundred percent certainty lethal measures will be taken against you. Evasion impossible. Recommend you accept the inevitability of demise. These religious systems are available for your comfort: Acosmism, Animism, Ayyavazhi, Azathoth Worship, Bahá'í...'

'Mute,' said Hal. Lefty continued flashing and grinding but shut up.

Nezumi heard a crashing from several passages away.

She drew her sword and started towards the noise. Hal put a hand on her shoulder.

'Should you go *towards* "a hundred percent certainty of lethal measures"?'

'This is a dead-end,' she said, thinking of the metal wall. 'There is no other direction.'

'Yeah, but "*a hundred percent*"?'

'"Taken against you", Hal. Not me.'

She held up Good Night Kiss and advanced back through the Princess's 3D autobiography.

The noise got louder.

TAKASHI KAMATA (DRIFT KAIJU)

D K could no more get out of the driving seat than a centaur could dismount.

The Armourdillo was bigger, broader and heavier than his preferred wheels, but he could drive anything.

This was a work-release gig.

But he would have taken it anyway. For reasons.

Street racing was all he knew and all he wanted to know.

It paid.

DK had a stock portfolio, a private box at the Meiji-Jingu Stadium, and Tokyo real estate holdings. In a four-level underground car park, he kept cars he'd won in *tsuiso* races. Even unrecognisable wrecks. He loved the smell of his trophy garden – cooked flesh, burned leather, twisted metal, oily concrete, spent gas. He never drove the cars he'd beaten. What would be the point? Losers – or their heirs – handed over keys and pink slips, and their cars were installed in his underground garden.

Three hundred and fifty-six victories in two years.

Manfred von Richthofen only put eighty machines down.

It wasn't just the speed; it was holding the road. In the turns, the *drift*.

Front and rear wheels pointed in opposite directions. The burnout. Friction on the asphalt. The dirt drop. Screech and smoke.

In the *drift*, he was somewhere else – a zone beyond.

The trick was to come back alive, to oversteer but retain control, to alter angles, bend rules of time and space and inertia and momentum. Before he ever drove, he was a maths prodigy. He had always known the zone beyond. He first tried to penetrate it with chalked theorems. Now, he drove there and back.

He was the Drift Kaiju. A considerable man. A *hashiriya* superstar. Fan magazines published pin-ups of him and diagrams of his car, the Obscene Machine. Through legal cut-outs and a Cayman Bank, he had sponsorship deals with Blue Label Sprünt, Unwin-Fujikawa Chemical and Oily Maniac Hair Tonic. He was the *idoru* of racers and fans everywhere. The man to beat, though he could not be beaten.

There were rockabilly songs about him. '*DK ganbare… go, go, go…*'

Of course, he was also a criminal.

There were offers to go legit. But legal racing was for squids.

The only racing was street racing. Against the best competition, and against the Law.

So he kept racing and the Law kept busting him.

He was faster and surer than any cop car, so they used tank traps and choppers. The Law came after him in spider-leg mechas, spurting sticky netting from spinnerets, laying caltrops from ovipositors. Undercovers nabbed him in love hotels. He was fitted with an ankle monitor that shocked him if he broke into a jog-trot. A judge prohibited him from touching a stick shift. He could do hard time for straddling a push-bike. Sponsors paid lawyers and he was back on the street in minutes. Rulings were overturned on technicalities. This was still a free country if you could afford it. His hobble-sock was deactivated and unclipped. Fans gathered outside the court to greet him with gushers of Blue Label and cascades of underwear.

The Law backed racers to beat him.

The Moth, the Pterror and the Tri-Kappa.

He had their cars in his carnage park.

Government programmes filled cars with weaponry. Bio-implanted vampire drivers were recruited and trained. Just to shut him down. They burned up and out. None could match him in turns. He instinctively compensated for the heatbursts, sound tsunamis and fireballs when competitors didn't make it to the zone beyond and back.

If it came to drift, he would be alone in the home stretch – using the nox only for show, crossing the line in a flameburst. He could not be beaten. He could not be stopped.

But he could be busted. Over and over.

Fifty million yen in cash was put in front of him in a Samsonite. He was told that it would be his if only he lost. To the Moth, or the Shrimp.

He could not lose.

The way some vampires had to count spilled pumpkin seeds, he had to win.

He turned down money. He turned down Mima from Cham-Cham. He turned down a 1999 Ferat Silver Commendatore. He turned down everything.

He had to race. He had to win.

The Law paid Rex Mifune, the legal champion, to go dark and challenge him.

It wasn't even close. Rex's wreck was in the trophy garden. Mifune was in prison. Lawyers and sponsors didn't turn out for losers.

There were still challengers. Crews from Korea, China, Los Angeles.

If he couldn't be beaten straight and he couldn't be beaten by cheating, he couldn't be beaten.

Gan-ba-re… go, go, go!

Then, the last time he got busted, he was fitted with an explosive collar and removed to a black site on Higanjima Island. This was the Law, but not as he knew it. Other prisoners in the facility were for-real *kaiju*. Furano, 'the Frankenstein Girl', who killed for replacement body parts she stitched onto herself, and rattled the bars of her cage with four six-fingered hands; Varanit Gorasu, 'the Indescribable Man', who represented himself as the spearhead of an alien invasion and demanded to be taken to Earth's leaders, by whom he meant President Clinton, Prime Minister Obuchi and Michael Jackson; Aki Nijūhachi-gō, a psychic prodigy so dangerous he had to be dissected and kept in separate jars. Even, it was whispered, Jun Zero.

Colonel Golgotha showed up on Higanjima to make a final offer.

He would still drive.

He was not asked to lose. And he would serve, if not his country, then the cause of humanity.

Golgotha did not smirk at that.

'… and your service will be required for one week. On New Year's Day, you'll be free with all charges dropped. This offer will not be repeated. If it is refused, you'll volunteer for medical experiments. Your hands and feet will be amputated and replaced with jellyfish. That won't prevent you using a stick shift or brake pedals. The Key Man believes the tendrils will be more sensitive and versatile than your fingers ever were. However, sadly, subjects of the process report a minor, inconvenient side effect. Extreme motion sickness. Anything above thirty-five miles an hour and you puke your lungs over the steering column. Anything above fifty and your guts will boil over and choke you. So, not a question of race or die… but race *and* die.'

DK signed up.

He supposed he was EarthGuard (the Law!), but Golgotha's Squad was as unlisted as the Higanjima site. The Black Ocean Society, which DK had thought long since dissolved, owned a wing of the organisation. Gokemidoro, a vampire who talked through a tooth-rimmed anus in his forehead, was Black Ocean's man. Other EarthGuard brass weren't in the know. A faction led by Kaname Kuran, a presentably pretty vampire sell-out, thought they were in charge, but Golgotha didn't report to them. In anticipation of a Kaname purge, the General was preparing a coup. Politics were above DK's pay grade and of no interest, except he could be terminated if he let anything slip.

Even members of the squad weren't cleared to know everything.

Like Dr Akiba – who was only along to support the cover story.

That would not be needed now, so neither was the doctor. Golgotha had issued the kill-order. DK had seen to it.

He held the wheel and breathed. Blood dripped from his glove-barbs onto his leg.

He felt as if he'd won a race. And Akiba had lost.

DK never killed anyone, but many died racing him.

It was up to others to save themselves. The Obscene Machine had claw-hook flails and oil-spray nozzles. Drivers who drew level or hugged exhaust in *tsuiso* races could expect chassis damage or burning lube on the road.

He'd only *hurt* Dr Akiba.

The crowd killed him.

The doctor could have saved himself by backing off, just as racers could save themselves by slowing down. Hey, they were going to lose anyway.

DK thought about the Key Man. Dr Jogoro Komoda.

When the side effects were controlled, DK would welcome the jellyfish process. The Key Man was another Black Ocean loyalist. His record of body-mods and transhumanist surgery went back to the 1930s. A master of engineered shapeshifting, he pioneered the use of unusual strains of vampire blood to assist human malleability. Dr Komoda was on call for Golgotha's squad. Caterpillar and Astro-Man benefited from imaginative bio-mechanics generations beyond Furano's botch jobs. After tonight, DK would volunteer to go under the genius's knife — perhaps shocking Golgotha, who had thought he was making a threat — and have his nerves wired to plug into the Obscene Machine's transmission. A new century meant new challengers. Rex Mifune wouldn't be in prison forever. Bypassing wheels and levers, DK would become a true cyborg, a bio-mech vampire with an engine that burned blood.

DK ganbare, go go go!

He'd called himself a *kaiju* because monsterhood was his destiny.

The curved bodywork of the Obscene Machine was velvet black, like an opera cloak. With scarlet underlighting, so it seemed to glide on shining blood.

He knew the name he would take next.

Dorifuto Dorakuraya. Drift Dracula.

The red mist on the windscreen had gone sticky. It would not be shifted by water or wipers. No matter. He didn't need eyes to drive any more than he needed headlamps. The 'dillo was built to plough through or over anyone or anything that didn't get out of its way.

After midnight, the squad would need to get out of the Bund. Fast.

That was why Golgotha recruited him.

Putting DK in the Armourdillo was like getting Picasso to paint the fence. But Picasso would have done a *great* job on the fence.

Something *thumped* the side window.

DK turned to look.

A face — no, *not* a face but something face-shaped — was pressed to the glass.

From the slicked-back hair, he recognised Dr Akiba.

The eyes, nose and cheeks were gone but a translucent skin pancake had formed over chewed meat. The new hide thickened. Pink became white. The mouth was sealed as if by wax.

The doctor was still alive but no longer warm.

Jutting from his neck was a pistol-syringe, depressed all the way.

Akiba had injected himself with vampire blood. Turned!

Yōkai let him be now. He was one of them.

He thumped the window again, jarring half-inch thick bulletproof glass. He wouldn't know his own new strength.

Akiba's HazMat suit and tux were ripped. Wounds on his chest were changing – not healing, but reconfiguring as fanged, pulsing mouths. Pustules in tangles of flesh turned into small eyes. Spiracles breathed in and out.

The next blow put a crack in the glass.

DK pressed the starter and threw the 'dillo into reverse.

Behind the vehicle was the open space of the Plaza. He could pick up enough speed to throw Akiba off the hood, then come back and grind him under. If the new-born vampire's heart were crushed, the problem was solved.

Akiba clung.

Barbed nailpoints lodged in the crack in the window glass.

The 'dillo *turned* – even in this dinosaur, DK was a master – and the pest flapped like a flag.

Akiba yowled through many new mouths, muscle twists serving as rudimentary vocal cords. Fangs scraped the window.

DK could just have shot the doctor. A signature gun clipped to the dashboard was keyed to his fingerprints.

But he hadn't wanted to take off his glove.

The window broke and Akiba crawled into the cab.

His mottled no-face *loomed* close.

DK felt the zone beyond in the turn, as the Armourdillo's eighteen wheels misaligned and – with a shriek – the vehicle began to roll, jack-knifing in its mid-section. The concertina linkage of compartments wrenched but did not tear.

The numbers made sense and he was wired into the zone… then, that was broken too. Nothing added up. He was shut out forever.

Akiba's no-face was complete. A pale blank.

No expression. No speeches.

The doctor pulled his shredded frill-fronted shirt apart. Ridiculously, his bow tie remained perfectly tied. He had rat-mouths instead of nipples.

With a spasm, Akiba spat out half a dozen fangs – little barbed enamel bullets.

The volley riddled DK's torso. He tasted and smelled his own blood. And gas, seeping into the cab.

Other *yōkai* – with the faces of sick birds or frogs, and stringy clumps of human hair – crawled through after Dr Akiba, thirsty for a share of the kill.

Was this what losing felt like?

No, not losing. Dying.

HAROLD TAKAHAMA

'… **B**initarianism, Bokononism, Buddhism, Cao Dai, Christianity…'

Without being told to, Lefty unmuted and continued the droning recital.

Hal reckoned his hand's crackle was louder, attracting whatever was crashing – with lethal intent – towards them.

He had learned to detect nuance in that characterless mechanical voice. Lefty was *jealous*.

Ever since Floor 44, the hand had been Hal's sole confidante, mentor and lifeline. It told him what it wanted to – without fear of contradiction.

Now, up here on Floor 93, Hal had Nezumi – who didn't electrocute him every three minutes. She was way savvier than the average thirteen-year-old.

She was probs a little old lady inside. Older than his grandparents. Old enough to have been put in a camp by FDR. Or Winston Churchill, if she learned her accent in Jolly England.

He was glad he hadn't quizzed the hand about Jun Zero's relationships. He wasn't sure Lefty would have been truthful.

He trusted rumours passed on by Nezumi over hard facts from the machine.

She was like that. Trustworthy.

Which Jun Zero wasn't, obviously. If by some dark miracle Hal

Takahama hooked up with a fox like Sonja Blaue, the rogue vampire hunter would ditch him for being clingy and a doormat – not for being a heartless bastard who skipped town with a cocktail waitress and left her to explain the piles of elder ashes and the decapitated corpse in the Dr Lazarus costume to Atlanta PD.

That was a *very specific* imagined filling-in of the anecdote.

Verily, he owed Sonja Blaue a grovelling apology! He should probably get that out before asking her to autograph her poster.

Had he ever seen her eyes? She'd told *Crawdaddy* only her lovers and people she was about to kill saw her eyes.

Hey, he was in both categories!

Now he trusted Nezumi not to kill him, he hoped she could keep him alive.

She walked back through Christina's past. She was swift, alert.

Her *katana* was sharp enough to sing like a razor-edged wind-chime.

He followed the vampire to the artist's studio and picked up the suicide revolver. He checked the cylinder. One empty chamber. Five bullets left.

The gun felt right in his hand – heavier than the plastic pistols he and his cousin used to play *Miami Vice* (he was always Tubbs, and got fatally shot so Crockett could cry *nooooo!* until the crabby neighbour complained about the sound effects), less terrifying than the automatic Dad put in his hand that time he thought it appropriate to give an eleven-year-old instructions on how to shoot a home invading viper in the heart. Dad, a second amendment fiend, did not repeat the lesson once Mom found out his idea of father-son bonding might run to a body count.

Jun Zero, of course, was weapons proficient.

Shooting targets painted with *nosferatu* rat-faces with Sonja Blaue!

Six months undercover at an elite murder-bastard training base in Nuristan.

Of course he was master of gun fu!

'If that's been lying there since Strickland shot himself it might be more dangerous to you than whoever you point it at.'

'But it hasn't,' he said. 'These rooms are exactly as they were when Christina Light left them, not as they would be if neglected. The clutter is preserved, not accumulated.'

Nezumi turned and looked at him with something between admiration and suspicion.

'What? Surprised? I've always been smart.'

She bowed a little in apology.

She was shamed to underestimate someone. He figured people did that to her, and she strove to be better.

He felt a warm sympathy rush for the earnest old lady/little girl. He wanted to tell her not to beat herself up about it, but she moved on.

Nezumi didn't pick the studio to stand her ground.

She stepped into Christina's dressing room.

She had a reflection, which didn't show her as he saw her. In the mirror, her face was white as ice and so were her exposed wrists and hands. Her hair was black.

She shook her head, indicating he should take no notice of that.

How did vampires ever get used to the mirror thing?

Seeing a semi-stranger looking back was bad enough but to see *nothing* or this cruel supposed reveal of a true self…?

'You're not like that,' he told her. 'Not cold.'

She shrugged as if to say it no longer bothered her (though it did) and they had more things to worry about (which they did).

The crashing stopped. Was it a distraction? A lure?

His hand came to life again, '… Dagonism, Digambara, Druidry, Druze, Eckanar…'

'Lefty, shut up,' said Nezumi.

Lefty clicked and whirred and schtummed.

How had Nezumi been granted user privileges?

Now Hal had to push down absurd, petty jealousy.

He couldn't help steal a look at the mirror – not at Nezumi's snowbird soul but at Jun Zero's still-unfamiliar face. His hair wasn't much better for the combing.

Earlier, Nezumi had looked through the glass at him.

Something else was looking at them both now.

Nezumi noticed Hal staring at the glass, and instantly understood why.

She wheeled around with measured grace, like a slow-motion movie, scything the full length of her *katana* in a circle until it pointed at the mirror.

The glass burst outwards with a fireball behind it.

Nezumi ducked under the explosion dragging him down with her. They rolled under the vanity table into discarded stockings and dust bunnies.

Jets of flame poured into the boudoir arcing above them.

The dresses laid out on the bed shrivelled to crispy corsets. The eiderdown caught fire.

He knew who was responsible.

Tsunako Shiki's surviving goon. One fist of fire, the other of steel – if the left 'un don't get you, the right one will.

RICHARD JEPERSON

Indisputably, a vampire using the name 'Count Dracula' made his London society debut in 1885 and inaugurated the Anni Draculae. Whether this was the same person as Vlad III of House Drăculești, Prince of Wallachia (c. 1430–????) was less certain.

That John Alucard – the current Dracula – was a Romanian nobody named Ion Popescu, turned only in 1945, was beside the point. Most people accepted that Alucard's undead body was inhabited by the spirit of whoever had sat in Castle Dracula all those years, imagining a Vampire Ascendancy.

So far as Richard was concerned, none of it mattered. The King of the Cats had more names and titles than Heinz had varieties. The world had to deal with who he was now, not who he had been when warm.

Tonight, the world had to deal with Vlad's brother.

The pretty one in the clan. Remembered for treachery – except in Anatolia, where a few diehards cited him as the Good Dracula.

Also a vampire.

Radu must have chased that dragon as he did everything else – because his brother got there first and made a bloody splash with it.

Richard watched Ejderhaoğlu Bey prowl the room.

His commands were obeyed, smartly. His crew were hired fangs. Slay for pay. They tuned out his speeches and kept eyes – and guns – on the hostages.

Radu grazed the buffet for snacks. Golden lads whimpered.

The Bey spoke randomly at quivering guests, then didn't listen to stammered replies. Was his wicked plan all to scare up an audience?

By rights, plague ought to be raging throughout the Bund.

Nezumi had averted that.

She was a factor Radu hadn't taken into account. Now she was loose.

The plot was going skew-whiff. Vlad the Impaler had contingency plans ready when a campaign went against him. Munitions dumps to be opened like piggy banks. Reinforcements primed to charge from hiding. Secret weapons and last-ditch defences. A thousand vampire horsemen in reserve. An orbital platform mounted with laser beams.

Radu the Handsome couldn't adapt to events.

He had memorised an earlier draft and didn't know whether to soldier on or toss the pages and improvise.

Richard would have preferred to face Vlad.

A chess-player who thinks he will win doesn't upend the board and trample the pieces in a fit of pique.

Radu might well throw them all out of the Dragon's Mouth to see who could fly.

Richard looked about the room.

Colonel Golgotha had showed up. He kept quiet. He'd have back-up plans. An exfiltration scenario ready to go. His crew were get-the-job-done pros. Even Radu's masked pallbearers were a cut above the average flathead.

The issue here wasn't the posse – it was the Sheriff.

Radu was off course before Richard got to the party.

Not just because Aum Draht let him down. Or Nezumi was a Spaniard in his works.

Something majorly wasn't going his way. He was ready to rhumba but the band weren't playing his song.

Richard wasn't sorry but was curious.

The most anyone had heard of Radu cel Frumos since the fifteenth century was during his dilettante driver phase, when he tried to compete with his brother's famous need for speed. 'The dead travel fast' was a Dracula motto. Vlad – a boy soon tired of last year's presents – progressed from chariots to trains to motor cars to aeroplanes. After each prang, Mr Toad found a new craze. As with everything – beginning with the throne of Wallachia – Radu stuck with auto racing longer than his brother but made less noise. He crashed fewer cars but didn't win many races.

Cottonmouth awaited orders. She expected to be sent after Nezumi.

Radu didn't detail her or confer with Golgotha. He needed troops in the ballroom.

Not all the crew were here. Mr Horror was absent, along with the little girl ghoul. They must be off executing other parts of the wicked plan.

Nezumi's priority would be getting back here.

Her job was looking after him. He'd have preferred she watch out for herself.

The Diogenes Club had kept track of Radu.

The Bey backed wrong sides in several wars. Standard behaviour for playboy elders. He either had a mysteriously vast fortune or none at all. He was married to his brother's one-time fiancée, Asa Vajda of Moldavia. She signed into the posher hotels of Europe under the name Countess Dracula and never settled her bills. Princess Asa saw little of her husband after the wedding supper. According to the gossip rags the Lovelies clucked over, Radu had an on-off understanding with Herbert von Krolock, the go-to indiscreet boyfriend for publicly not gay vampires from Baron von Meinster to Lester Shortlion.

Radu had brought too many guns to lose the room but the Princess's guests were over the shock of being taken hostage and would not stay put much longer.

The cowed circle was breaking up. When Cottonmouth pulled Lady

Oyotsu to the railings, others experimentally drifted. When they weren't shot, more followed. They were wary, so far. No one made a break for the lifts or tried to follow Nezumi's example and leap into the unknown. The smell of gunfire and death was too recent.

A deadly combination of stretched nerves and boredom would eventually prompt rash action. Some of these VIVs would fly out of the Dragon's Mouth if they thought they'd get out of shooting range quick enough. Desperate escape attempts would start well before the Stockholm Syndrome kicked in. It would take a very long siege for anyone to warm up to Dracula's Dipshit Brother.

Syrie snapped her fingers and used force of will to get the waiters back to work.

Drinks were guzzled.

Richard recognised celebrities, bankers, politicians. People used to buying their way out of fixes. Angel de la Guardia, a Neanderthal business mogul in a five-thousand-dollar suit, opened and closed a Filofax the size of a briefcase. He flashed wedges of currency and an array of credit cards, a fan dancer attracting attention to her assets but covering them up before the Lord Chamberlain noticed.

Richard doubted any of the minions were bribable.

And Radu wanted more than money.

De la Guardia gurned at Cottonmouth, who smiled sweetly and tongued the stock of her machine pistol. The financier put his portable cash stash away. He thrust meaty, hairy-knuckled fists so deep in his pockets an Armani seam ripped. He was big enough to start a fight. Bullets would end it not to his liking. Cottonmouth blew him a kiss.

Who else might make trouble?

Anthony Peak was trying not to be noticed. He slipped into the crowd, maybe to filch a few trinkets. If anyone could find a way out of the ballroom, it'd be him. He was a known escape artist. This crew couldn't make a better fist of imprisoning him than the best jailers in the world. He would go it alone, though.

Syrie should not be underestimated.

Or trusted, though Richard knew – from their blood link – she wasn't

Radu's secret boss, girlfriend or sponsor. This wasn't a Wings Over the World takeover bid.

One of the pigs was trying to pick a shackle lock with a cocktail stick.

It would not do to forget that the fattened donors were people. They wouldn't be drunk or drugged. Golden had to be unadulterated by artificial sweeteners though blood-guzzling connoisseurs prized the quickening piquancy of natural fear or arousal. If it came to it, the lads had little to lose by rising up against Radu's crew.

Georgia Rae Drumgo used to run drac on the streets of Baltimore but was now a VP in charge of development for John Alucard. She must have spoken out of turn when the guns came out. She'd been shot in the stomach and was *furious* about it. Had Radu made an example of her because of her Dracula association? Or was she just the gobby sort who wouldn't be threatened without talking back? Tough enough to cough up a silver slug, she was sick with pain and red thirst. Argentine poisoning had taken hold in her insides.

Another likely rebel.

After pulling her neck in, Lady Oyotsu settled meekly with a *yōkai* coterie. A gnome who looked like a potato with arms. A flesh umbrella with a hairy human leg. A bent-double wretch with chunks of ironmongery embedded in his flesh. From the Dieudonné log, Richard recognised them. Abura Sumashi, Kasa-obake, Kichijiro. Pre-Macedonians, original ghetto-dwellers. Here when the Princess arrived.

That, of course, was who was missing.

Christina Light, their hostess.

It wouldn't surprise Richard if she originally planned to stay away from her own party until close to midnight – perhaps entering with her own light show.

Now she was probably in hiding.

And Radu was pissed off at that. *She* was who he wanted in his net. The Princess. Everyone else were extras. Exceptionally well-heeled extras.

Radu paced, chewing his moustache.

'Come out, come out,' he muttered. 'Wherever you are.'

NEZUMI

With Good Night Kiss in one hand and Hal's collar in the other, she duck-walked as fast as inhumanly possible out of the burning boudoir into the Russian railway station. Snow was trodden into the rough planking. An authentic stove with a modern heating element cast a glow over the floor.

This must be where the Princess said goodbye to one of her anarchist boyfriends. Before he was sent to Siberia or blew himself up with his own bomb. Nezumi pictured the Princess in white fur, a frost tear on one cheek. Balalaika music. A steam train chugging offstage.

Fire didn't spread across the line between dressing room and waiting room.

Hal wanted to stand but she didn't let him yet. No sense getting his head burned off.

Lefty rattled off a percentage no one wanted to hear.

The Caterpillar was coming. Nezumi had sized him up earlier.

The EarthGuard cyborg op with robot arms and legs. Swollen shoulders and a Quasimodo hump. More killing power than Lefty, but cruder workmanship. A human dreadnought. A scorched earth merchant.

Nezumi could have done with one of the Bund Police's one-person tanks.

'I saw this clanker earlier,' said Hal. 'He's with Tsunako Shiki, this *awful* little girl.'

Nezumi knew who he meant. The Bad Penny.

There was a blundering on the other side of the wall.

The Caterpillar could be stealthy, but wasn't fussed now. He wanted the mini-pigoids to know Big Bad Wolfbot had the measure of their flimsy housing development.

Furniture broke. The Caterpillar trod heavily.

Nezumi let go of Hal and stood. Holding her *katana* two-handed, she sidestepped into the library. Striking a defending willow pose, she looked down the passage.

A juggernaut had rolled through the Princess's life corridor, crushing mementoes. Mr Light's collection of pervy statues was a litter of broken china. Signora Light's sitting room was upended. Cooked orchids smouldered, bright green pulp seeping through splits in black stems. Boot-sized dents stamped across floors and carpets.

The metalwork man stood in the library. Armour plates creaked as he inhaled and exhaled. He stank of oil and soot.

He had taken off his EarthGuard safety helmet. A middle-aged Japanese face, dough-cheeked and small-eyed, was framed by a neck-brace and skull-plates. He had a hairy mole at the corner of one eye.

She darted forward and sliced his nose.

A section sheared off and bright blood gushed from snout-holes.

Her fangs hurt. The sight of blood gave her an ice-cream head.

Roaring, the Caterpillar ratcheted his fire-arm. A relatively clumsy procedure. When he aimed and let loose, she wasn't standing in front of him.

She licked his blood off her blade.

The only insight she got from the taste was pain and channelled rage.

The Caterpillar was angry before his robot bits were sewn on. He was angrier now.

The mace-hand came down like a bludgeon, missing her head and thudding into a bookshelf, pulping covers, shredding pages, splintering wood. The Caterpillar struggled to wrench the implement free.

Blood was all over his face, pouring onto his armoured chest.

Who was he inside his tin can? Who had he been?

Military, she read in his blood. Wounded veteran, retreaded for vengeance. From the *banzai* brigade.

A Second World War relic. One of the Key Man's pet projects.

A tragic figure. She felt sorry for him. But now she needed to see a way to incapacitate him.

No weak spots in his burnished carapace. His joints were sleeved with chain-mail.

She could stab his face again and hope to spear his brain but that meant getting close enough to put her skull within mace range.

He shifted his right shoulder, working up another big burn.

It took seconds to access a fuel supply contained in his limbs. How were canisters replaced? She couldn't see any latches or tank-caps.

Hal ran out of the waiting room with a stove-pipe in his hands – Lefty's fingers could curl! – and whanged the Caterpillar across the shoulders. The pipe broke but the Caterpillar staggered, servo-motors grinding in his hips and knees.

Hal held up Lefty as if to mock the Caterpillar's crude workmanship.

He drew the revolver from his waistband and shot the Caterpillar in the face.

His deduction about the state in which Christina maintained her souvenirs was sound but the bullet spanged off an endo-dermal plate. The Caterpillar's brain was shielded.

The Caterpillar hitched his shoulders and aimed fists like loaded guns.

In his armpit, Nezumi saw a plastic patch like a bung or plug.

She advanced, bringing up Good Night Kiss in a rising half-moon cut, slicing the plastic toggle, then took three steps away in retreating mantis pattern, withdrawing the sword before it could be snapped by the Caterpillar's instinctive spasm. His ironsides were solid enough to break her silvered steel, but neither arm-attachment was good for stanching the leak.

If Dr Komoda had fit a metal screw-cap instead of a plastic stopper, a weakness would be eliminated. How it must gall that meticulous monster to work within a budget.

Nezumi's eyes watered as flammable liquid gushed from under the Caterpillar's arm.

Now she had to trust Hal to see the opening.

His next bullet dented the chestplate.

The Caterpillar chuckled – a gruff, low, cruel laugh. A pity-killing sound.

Then Hal shot at the gushing fuel tank.

The first explosion tore off the Caterpillar's flamethrower arm and burned his face to the bone. The plates around his skull gleamed as red meat dissolved. Splashes of ignited fuel wrought ruin on unsorted, unshelved law reports. The severed robot arm tumbled through the air towards Hal, who held up Lefty to ward it off.

'It is not recommended that unit designated Lefty should be—'

The complaint was obliterated by the whump of the second explosion.

The Caterpillar had auxiliary tanks embedded in his hunchback. Nezumi closed her eyes but still saw bright flames. She was deaf for a second or two, but the din rushed back in.

She looked again. Flares danced in her vision. She blinked them away.

With the impulses from his head – a fancy neural interface or something physical involving clenched and unclenched jaw muscles? – cut off, the motors in the Caterpillar's hips, knees and ankles shut down. His lower half locked like a statue. His remaining arm flailed. As many gadgets as she had in her Girl Guide knife extruded from and folded back into his mace-fist. When had he ever used the corkscrew or – a cruel touch she might have expected from the Key Man – the nail file?

The Caterpillar's upper body and head were wreathed in fire.

It was too late to turn vampire.

It might have grown back his arms and legs. Had he volunteered for quadruple amputation and an upgrade into man-machinehood?

A bust of Karl Marx burned too. The frowning Santa face melted away from wiring and lenses.

She had assumed there was surveillance throughout the building.

'Look,' she told Hal, 'the Wire is watching.'

He was puzzled. That catchphrase meant nothing to him.

'Forget it,' she said. 'Good work with the gun. We should leave here now. That bang'll have been noticed.'

'No argument from me,' said Hal.

He held up the suicide weapon to pose – proud of his sharpshooting, elated to be walking away from a fire fight – not yet realising how close he'd come to dying, or guilt-nagged by the possibility that the Caterpillar was a victim too.

The flames burned out quickly, leaving soot and stink.

Nezumi looked at the detached flamethrower arm. Etched into its underside was a serial number. YUREI 157. She was reminded of Mr Jeperson's tattoo.

Hal virtually leaped up and down. Lefty clicked, whirred and flashed.

Nezumi turned away from the Caterpillar's black skull.

'Let's go,' she said. 'I should like to find some stairs.'

RICHARD JEPERSON

The Light Channel showed a digital countdown. Red numerals against pulsating bluish white. Less than two hours till the fireworks.

Radu cel Frumos had the room.

'Should we murderalise a few guesty-westies?' Radu asked Colonel Golgotha, loud enough to be heard by the company. 'See if that lures Milady Sparkletoes out of her grotto?'

Golgotha kept schtumm. His place was to execute policy, not set it.

He'd murderalise anyone, but needed a direct order. Possibly in writing.

Radu roamed, wondering whether his bright idea could find any takers.

Some squealed under his glance.

The Bey enjoyed that. He relished little spurts of terror. Almost as much as little squirts of blood. They fed his inner vampire.

'Poor strategy,' Richard piped up. 'Killing – or threatening to kill – hostages only works if your ultimate target gives tuppence ha'penny about other people. Do you think the Princess cares enough about anyone here to put herself to even mild inconvenience – much less risk her neck? If you were her, would you?'

'Fair point, Mr Jeperson,' said Radu. 'If irritating.'

Cottonmouth played with her knives. She'd kill on a nod and a wink.

'Shall we put your theory to the test?' asked Radu. 'As hostess, the Princess should have a duty of care, don't you think?'

Richard didn't volunteer to be killed.

Christina Light most likely regarded her most important and powerful guests – Syrie Van Epp or Angel de la Guardia – on a level with the plump lads shackled in the buffet pens. The Princess was a different order of being. She'd given her great big building her own eyes – one bright red, one pale blue – so she could look down on all other life forms.

Kate Reed, for one, had advised Richard against accepting this invitation. The Irish vampire journalist painted the Princess as a grudge-nourisher who'd summon all her old enemies to a big room and force them to fight each other to the death. 'Never forget that she's potty,' said Kate, who had little good to say about her former revolutionary comrade. 'And petty. She won't have forgotten the Diogenes Club.'

If Radu started killing her guests, Christina might mostly be annoyed that he got to them first.

Oh well. Richard's other option for New Year's Eve was British wine, cheese and black pudding at the Millennium Dome with Tony Blair, Baldric from *Blackadder*, Lord Ruthven, and assorted luvvies and liggers. A hostage siege was better than that.

Again, it struck him that Radu was showing uncharacteristic ambition. What was his envisioned ideal outcome?

Dracula's brother was staring at him. Why was that?

'I'm so sorry,' said Richard. 'I went away for a moment. Other things on my mind, I suppose. You were thinking of putting me to death.'

'No point,' said Radu, suspending sentence. 'You're not famous enough, old man.'

Movie stars, pop singers and sporting figures suppressed panic. Each was sure they were the most famous person at the party. An 'Access All Areas' laminate was suddenly a death warrant.

'It's all right,' Richard told a young Asian man, 'I have no idea who you are.'

'I don't know who Mr Pretty is either,' said Radu. 'It doesn't matter. We can get his name from the obituary.'

The warm fellow looked as if he'd rather be beheaded than go unrecognised.

'Murdleigh,' shouted Radu.

The foreman of the pallbearers briskly slouched over. A fringe of bristles showed around his blank white mask. He had wolf ears and hairy wrists.

'Get a grip on this lucky winner.'

The minion seized the youth by the shoulder.

Perkin Murdleigh was Radu's long-time minion/renfield/dogsbody – and, for almost as long a time and better money, an informer. He ratted out his boss's dastardly doings to any law enforcement agency with a snitch budget.

Obviously, no one had got the heads-up about this evening's escapade. Even if Murdleigh had whistleblown, few ears would have pricked. Radu wasn't big or bestial enough to bother with. The Diogenes Club cut Murdleigh off years ago. No one was that fussed about an elder who cheated in motor rallies or sold helicopter kits with significant pieces missing to Moldavian rebels.

That would change after tonight. Little comfort to the dead.

Murdleigh marched the anonymous celeb – male model? Soap opera bad boy? Drac dealer to the stars? – to the middle of the sunken dance floor and made him sit cross-legged.

'Let's have more delightful people on their knees begging for their lives, eh?' Radu told his minion. 'Use your initiative. We're looking for headlines. Get me front-page faces. And poignant human-interest stories. Oh, and Mrs Drumgo – we'll stir her in the mix for flavour. We've not forgotten *that unkind thing* she said earlier. Try not to bleed over the other lucky winners, Georgia Rae.'

Cottonmouth and Furīman hefted the wounded voodoo vixen across the room and dumped her next to the young man. She leaned on his shoulder and ripped apart his white shirt sleeve. She opened her mouth wide, jaw hinges dislocating, and took a chunk out of his arm. Bloody meat didn't restore her health, but her yellow tiger-eyes burned angrier. Veins throbbed in her temples and the toad-sac under her chin puffed. The bitten fellow clamped a hand over his gouting wound.

Clearly, the clot still wanted to explain who he was. Maybe he was *huge* in Japan.

Murdleigh wandered among the company, mask looming close to frightened faces. He tugged Kasa-obake away from his fellow *yōkai*, and hopped the umbrella goblin onto the dance floor. Cruelly, he kicked his single ankle. Kasa-obake upended, opening to stop his fall. The underside of his canopy was a mass of wormy cilia. He closed in embarrassment, warty hide blushing as if his slip had shown.

Next, the pallbearer picked Mr Omochi, a warm CEO who took being selected for probable death with stern dignity. He joined the others of his own accord, sitting stoically to await fate.

Surprise registered in the crowd when Murdleigh passed over genuinely famous (if not genuinely genuine) faces and tapped a waiter on the chest. Donatella Versace and that dry comedian from the whisky ads didn't complain, but the waiter tossed his tray at the minion's head and ran – only to bump into Cottonmouth. She held a knife to his jugular and manoeuvred him into sitting with the other select victims. Mighty feisty for staff, Richard thought, then he saw the white jacket didn't fit. A dot.com billionaire had bribed a peon for the disguise. To show no social prejudice, Murdleigh sniffed out the waiter in the plush tux and forced him to join his paymaster.

The guests took the rounding-up seriously now.

Angel de la Guardia put his Filofax away.

No one protested when anyone else was chosen, except Omochi's elegant vampire wife who begged their friends to intervene.

'You shame me, Rose,' barked her husband.

She bowed meekly and stopped begging to the evident relief of the friends.

Murdleigh stalked the room, hand clapped over his mask's eyeholes, pointing at random. He walked by a curvy vampire in playroom finery – cherry-red corset, inverted crucifix earrings, puffy mauve sleeves attached to no shirt, pirate boots, ripped fishnet body stocking, a myriad ribbons and bows and Halloween ornaments braided in two bunches of floor-length black-and-purple hair. She was audibly relieved to be passed over. Murdleigh heard her gasp and impishly darted back to tag her anyway. He snickered. She screeched and stuck lacquered needle-nails under his mask.

'Don't make such a meal of it, you blithering cretin,' shouted Radu.

Radu hadn't delegated to get the job done efficiently. He wanted to be amused by the cruel process and have an opportunity to whip his dog.

He was bored. Soon, he'd start chopping off heads to pass the time.

Without being asked, Furīman, Cottonmouth and the Butler took positions around the huddled circle. Cottonmouth scraped her knives together as if whetting them. Furīman's rib muscles rippled, as if the monsters tattooed on his tits were flexing for a free-for-all fight.

Radu inspected the chosen few. Most of the other people in the room – scarcely less imperilled – got off the dance floor and shrivelled into shadows. The hostages sat like a schoolkid rabble ordered to sit on the gym floor for a lecture on moral hygiene. Except none of them were smirking.

'You know, Mr Jeperson, it strikes me that I spoke too harshly earlier,' said Radu. 'You may not be famous exactly, but you are very well thought of in your profession. An icon of the swinging sixties and sordid seventies. A gentleman rake and adventurer. A good man in a tight spot. Maybe most people assumed you'd died of an overdose or in a fall from a great height years ago, but you had your moments in the public eye. So we'll have you after all, if you don't mind.'

Richard walked over and sat down.

Hostages shifted to make a place for him. He sat next to the v-girl. She gave him a taut smile. Her necklaces and bracelets rattled.

'Hello, I'm Richard,' he said, taking her bird-thin hand. She wore fingerless black lace gloves. She squeezed his hand in a nervous spasm.

'I'm Chesse Beru,' she said.

She was frightened. She'd not expected that. After turning, she thought she'd be beyond fear. He escaped her grip, but patted her hand. She needed reassurance but not a comforting lie.

'Cosy, are we?' said Radu.

Infuriatingly, Richard's knees complained. He'd given up yoga because of his joints, and now couldn't lotus without a wince. He tried not to let the pain show.

'Best not break up the set,' said Radu. 'Murdleigh, have Mrs Van Epp join us.'

Syrie wanted to insist she hadn't come with Richard, that they'd only shared the lift up from the Plaza, but knew that would seem small and mean – a ploy to haggle her way out of a bind.

She sat without tearing her gown.

She gave Chesse a what-*do*-you-look-like? withering glance. He had an urge to remind her of the brain-turban she'd worn earlier.

That made him notice something missing.

He pointed to his own forehead. Syrie's hands went to her tiara. The eye jewel was gone.

'Anthony Peak,' she snarled.

The thief wasn't in sight. Richard had known he'd be the one to find a way out.

He thought the larceny amusing and was surprised at Syrie's white-lipped fury. She didn't care for jewels except as tokens. She had buckets full of bright pebbles. Seldom wore the same gew-gaw twice.

'The eye-piece is important,' she said. 'I must have it before midnight.'

Richard knew she meant what she said. Why was the gem significant?

Radu ignored their exchange. This game of ring-a-rosy was running down.

The executioners were ready with guns and knives.

The lambs were penned for slaughter.

Murdleigh was too close. He'd get pulled down into the *mêlée* and torn to bits. Chesse Beru and Georgia Rae Drumgo would have his guts for chew-toys. Radu knew enough to back away for a safer view.

A massacre might be a laugh and a half but was still unlikely to tempt Christina onto the dance floor.

Syrie worried about her blessed jewel. Chesse scratched the floor.

The dot.com giant had wet himself. The waiter shuffle-bottomed away from the spreading pee pool.

Kasa-obake righted himself. His single eye gaped wider.

Richard saw a circle of light reflected in the umbrella imp's pupil.

He looked up. A crown of pulsing stars formed above them.

Surely, Christina hadn't installed a glitter ball?

A kaleidoscope of sparks whirled beneath the circlet. Light-threads wove into the form of a woman. Richard pulled pink-tinted pince-nez from his top pocket so he could look at the apparition without hurting his eyes.

Christina Light was a twelve-foot-tall Disney Princess with fangs.

She didn't look like Veronica Lake. Or Jane Fonda, Meryl Streep or Madonna. Though they had tried to look like her. The Princess was a well-known attention vampire. Being played on film – especially by Oscar nominees and pin-ups – fed her vanity, but also her person. Like Dracula, she took substance from the versions of her sung about in songs, written about in books, and seen in the movies. Always, she was herself most of all but all the performances, all the scenes, all the posters wrapped her in layers of woven starsilk.

Her red right eye burned like a small sun, rendering half her face translucent. A mask of beauty superimposed on a glittering skull. Her see-through cheek exposed rows of shark teeth.

Richard didn't know if the Princess Casamassima wore luminous clothes or spun floating angelic robes out of her own body. Either way, she was clad in light. She was much changed since the last reliable reports were turned in to the Diogenes Club.

She had been on her way to evolving beyond the flesh.

She might have managed it.

The diva had made an entrance. The opera wouldn't be finished till the blinding light lady sang.

Now his demand was met, what would Radu do?

Some hostages were relieved and sobbing. Mr Omochi intently conveyed disapproval of this ostentatious display, never mind the fact that the shining creature had saved his life. Kasa-obake flapped open and closed in delight. Mr dot.com jumped up, trousers dripping, and shouted, 'In your face, sucka!', then noticed a spreading bloodstain on his side. Cottonmouth had stabbed him through the liver without him even feeling it. He died not knowing if all that bread he'd laid out to millennium-proof his search engine had done the trick.

Christina coalesced. Her face turned opaque, covering up the dental anomalies. She radiated beauty. Her blue eye pulsed like the Light Channel. All the time people had been watching it, she had been watching them.

She smiled down on her party as if nothing were wrong.

'Princess Casamassima,' said Radu, looking up, face blistering as if he'd walked into Italian sunshine without a hat. 'I bring you New Year greetings and a message – from my brother, Count—'

'Dra… cu… la,' came a thunderous female whisper.

The voice of the phantasm echoed around the Dragon's Mouth.

Richard's much-abused fillings vibrated again. Chesse noticed his pain and squeaked a sympathetic ouch.

'Yes,' said Radu. 'Him.'

Christina's lips twitched into a smile of amused contempt.

Either she was live or a very sophisticated transmission.

Their hostess was not afraid – which, Richard realised – ought to terrify everyone.

DETECTIVE AZUMA

O ta pressed shells into a pump shotgun.

'Load up, load up with si-i-ilver bullets,' crooned Sarge.

The one-man riot squad bared fangs.

'We avenge our own in the Bund,' he told Azuma.

The Sakis were popular officers. Inugami's watch had a grudge to pay off. Nakajima had been going with Saki-G. Same precinct relationships were frowned on, but a fact of cop life. The apprentice was out for more than blood. He wanted payback.

The Chief ordered Mitsuru Fujiwara to get the Bund back online.

'I can,' he said. 'Only thing is it'll take time.'

'Hurry. Something's happening to a schedule. What's the betting we've only got till midnight? An hour and a half.'

Fujiwara stabbed keys. Columns of numbers and symbols scrolled.

Sarge, posted by the doors, raised an alert.

'Someone's coming up the steps.'

'EarthGuard?' asked Inugami.

'No. Big guy in a peaked cap. Vampire.'

Azuma knew who that was. The hearse driver. Iron Mouth.

'Send him away,' said Inugami.

Sarge stepped outside.

'He'll be complaining because some gang kid's scratched his car,' said

Brenten. 'The *tengu* and the *kappa*, scoring points in competitive vandalism. We need to crack more beaks and head-plates.'

Azuma pulled his gun.

Sarge barrelled back into the reception area with a length of wood jutting from his chest. Speared through the heart. Truly dead. His legs hadn't got the message yet.

Iron Mouth was silhouetted in the doorway. He stood close to the glass.

Ota fired his shotgun and the doors exploded into a million shards. Ota pumped a round and fired again. The chauffeur took the blast full in the gut.

Iron Mouth should have been cut in half.

Lurching back a step, he kept his balance then walked forward. He dipped his head and pushed the remains of the doors off their hinges.

The belly of his uniform tunic was shredded by silver shrapnel. Fabric and skin were torn away. Steel shone in his wound, dented but not breached.

Azuma shot the driver's face, tearing away a swatch of skin. A curved steel cheekbone glistened under raw muscle. Iron Mouth smiled, showing rusty fangs. He had sub-dermal armour plate.

An invention Japan could be proud of. In the 1980s, the sculptor Tsukamoto – inspired by a Yōkai Town fetishist – realised that because vampires heal fast, they can be cut open and have ironmongery stuck in their cavities. The scrap metal was held in place when skin and flesh grew back. Tsukamoto performed operations on living artworks in night-clubs during industrial music events. Then, criminals got in on the act. Full metal *yakuza* became as common as scuzzbos with tattoos. Gangsters deformed by internal armour, bristling with spikes and hooks and chains. They were a fucking nuisance.

Iron Mouth might be more metal than man. The Tsukamoto work done on him wasn't crude. The rust on his teeth was deliberate. You'd worry about lockjaw if he bit you.

Ota shot the chauffeur again and again, each time scoring killing hits. He gave out babyish mewling grunts every time his target didn't die.

Iron Mouth took no notice.

Brenten launched himself, striking karate blows with the hardened flat of his hand. He aimed at the chauffeur's neck, over and over, ignoring his own pain. Iron Mouth gave him six or seven free shies, then gripped his forehead with splayed fingers and squeezed. A crack like a coconut splitting set Azuma's fangs on edge. Mush squirted between metal finger armatures and he dropped Brenten, then trampled on what was left of the tough cop's noodle, treading brains into linoleum.

White mice converged to nibble the splatter. This wasn't how their New Year's Eve was supposed to go. They took the chance to eat vampire for a change.

Asato hefted an obsolete electric typewriter off the desk and flung it at the chauffeur's head. Flex trailing, the heavy machine sailed across the room and knocked Iron Mouth off balance.

Seeing the opening, Nakajima sliced with a curved silver sword.

A deep score opened across Iron Mouth's chestplate, parting metal and showing purple organs beneath. Nakajima pulled back and angled the sword for a heart-thrust, then froze in place.

Mitsuru Fujiwara was behind him, effecting a neck-pinch with a gadget like an electric scorpion. An arc crackled between claws, paralysing the young officer. Then, a snake-tongue – complete with lizardy head and dorsal spines – lashed out of Fujiwara's open cakehole and stung Nakajima on the forehead. Black rot spread instantly from the wound.

Azuma wheeled to get a shot at Fujiwara, but the traitor held Nakajima up as a shield.

Knowing the cop was dead, Azuma shot anyway – aiming for soft tissue, trusting his rounds to punch straight through and into Fujiwara.

The Wolfman vaulted over the desk, bounding on all fours, and slammed into Iron Mouth.

Asato fired a gun and knocked herself over.

Despite the hair in front of her eyes, she scored a direct hit on Iron Mouth's exposed heart. She dropped him before Inugami could break teeth and claws on his metal plates.

She wheeled around, but Fujiwara was out of the *kōban*.

Azuma should have known Golgotha would have inside men. All these blood trails led towards the Big Dragon Building. Fujiwara worked there.

He wasn't a cop.

Smoke grenades rolled in through the broken doors. Inugami's ears pricked as red dots danced on his fur. He rolled across the floor, sticking himself with dozens of jagged bits of glass. He took multiple bullet hits. Silenced rifle-fire from across the street. Silver slugs flattened on his tough hide, but he was wounded. Silver poisoning wouldn't kill as quickly as Fujiwara venom, but the old watchdog was put down.

'You're all we've got left,' he told Asato and Azuma. 'You are the Bund PD now. Do not let this end here.'

Iron Mouth turned to dust and scrap metal.

The bombs popped off. Bright green, yellow and red smoke swirled and mingled – easy to mistake for party effects. Fires took and spread. The television displayed the white pulse of the Light Channel for a few seconds, then its tube exploded.

'There's a way out downstairs,' said Asato. 'An escape route from when this was a fangbang parlour. The hatch is behind the hanging skin of the old manager.'

Through colourful smoke, Azuma saw riflemen – Hunter and Killer? – advancing across the street. Happy New Year!

The computer screen was still live. The code resolved into blocky numbers. A countdown from ten. Fujiwara must have rigged it.

Asato had Azuma downstairs by the time the counter reached zero.

The dungeon shook as the *kōban* was destroyed by an explosion.

HAROLD TAKAHAMA

Lefty projected diagrams and plotted routes out of the building. None of the best escape runs started from where they were.

The elevator stood open.

Nezumi had zig-zagged down flights of service stairs from the Ruff, and gained access – drawn by the ruckus Hal made – to Floor 93 via a cupboard door that was now suspiciously locked. The *pneumatique* hatch was also sealed, barely showing a crack in the metal wall. Even if they could break into the system, a cylinder would be a snug-to-impossible fit for the pair of them plus Lefty and Good Night Kiss. Also, he didn't trust the rocket tubes. He remembered being shot up when he wanted to go down.

Still, they were reluctant to try the obvious exit.

The party crashers would have people in control rooms, tracking rogue elements and overriding controls, despatching killers to clear out pockets of likely resistance. Jun Zero – the bastard! – had probably written the code used in the takeover. The Shiki pest was still in play and Nezumi reported more murderers on the premises. Lousy company grown-up Hal had been keeping. Dad would be disappointed again.

According to Nezumi, the murderer-in-chief was Count Dracula's Knock-Off Brother, who went around introducing himself as Radu the Handsome. '… though he's not *that* good-looking.' If this Captain Bighead was the Big Bad here, he was presumably Jun Zero's client, and cause of all their woes. Hal bet Dracula II Electric Boogaloo stiffed him on his fee too. That family had a lot to answer for.

There were no 'transporter circles' on this floor. Nor any handy ventilation outlets, so going back into the ducts wasn't an option. No windows to kick open so they could abseil down the hide of the dragon with a thousand metres of rope tied from scavenged sheets and curtains.

Which brought them back to the elevator.

They stood in the room where Christina Light had been born – the dump that set her off on an extended lifetime of social climbing which ended in her very own dragon castle – and looked at the elevator. It was well-lit and inviting. Normal, even. Innocent.

'Lefty, can you override external controls?'

'Seventy-three percent probability of success.'

Nezumi gave Hal a solemn thumbs-up.

Hal decided he could live with a twenty-seven percent probability of death.

'Did you know that in an office block in Amsterdam in the 1980s, a predator vampire permanently shapeshifted into a lift?' said Nezumi. 'People would get on and it ate them. The leftover bones and fillings and belt-buckles got dropped to the bottom of the shaft. The Diogenes Club lent Mr Jeperson and me to the Dutch to solve the mystery. He walked into the lobby and immediately saw what was wrong. The evil lift was taken out and installed in a single-storey prison. After that, Mr Jeperson visited many hash bars but didn't take me. I saw some lovely Vermeers. Typical Japanese tourist.'

'I'm not sure this story is helping,' said Hal.

'The lift vampire was looney. It's not likely anyone else would be looney in exactly the same way.'

'No, but maniacs inspire copycat criminals.'

Nezumi stepped into the elevator. Music came on. Chirrupy, upbeat Japanese pop. A cover of Prince's '1999'.

Funny, because it *was* 1999.

Hal supposed you had to drop off in 1992 and wake up tonight to see that as a joke. Otherwise, it was just irritating.

He joined the girl and the doors automatically closed.

'That's not ominous at all,' he said.

Nezumi took out a gadgety penknife – exciting a spurt of covetous envy in Hal's lizard brain – and unscrewed the plate of the control panel. It dropped on the floor, and a mess of wiring was exposed, which she parted to show a port Lefty's thumb-jack fit into.

'Connecting... connecting...'

'That's handy,' said Nezumi.

'Very funny... *not!*'

'How will you ever adjust to this bewildering future, man out of time? We know the world is round. And have trod on the moon.'

When Lefty plugged into a system, Hal felt a weird tingling.

How complete was the mesh of machine and man? Did wires from his hand run through his body like a parallel nervous system? Could Lefty override his brain if it wanted to? He didn't want to wind up like the Caterpillar.

Hal no longer trusted his future self. Hacker genius Jun Zero seemed to have made boucoup poor decisions.

If he found the right port, he could override the system. He could pilot the *daikaiju*. That would be an electric buzz, an exultation of power!

'Control established,' said his hand, bringing him back to the moment.

'Very well done,' said Nezumi – to him, not the machine.

A little jealous shock reminded Hal to be humble.

'Does this lift go up to Doragon no Kuchi?' Nezumi asked.

'Affirmative.'

'Hold your horses, Minnie Mouse,' said Hal. 'Up? What about down? To the Plaza? The out door?'

Nezumi looked at him, solemn.

'I must protect my principal. Mr Jeperson is at the mercy of unscrupulous persons. Many others are at risk.'

Hal couldn't argue. As Jun Zero, he was as responsible for the situation as the client. He ought to want payback against this Handsome Devil, who wanted him mind-wiped and/or dead.

But he'd still rather get away alive and – taking Lefty into consideration – more or less whole.

'Direct Access to the Dragon's Mouth is not possible in this elevator,' said his hand.

Hal could have kissed its shiny glass knuckles.

He didn't have to wimp out because there was no other choice.

'Access to the lobby is not possible in this elevator either.'

Bummer! Still, no need to charge the guns again.

'Options are available,' Lefty continued. 'A nexus is in operation on Floor 88. The Security Suite.'

'Show me that on the plan,' said Nezumi, talking familiarly with Lefty.

Nothing happened.

'Lefty…?'

'Does User Jun Zero wish to enter details of Secondary User? Fifteen items of identification will be required.'

'Do what she asks,' he said.

The building plan sprung out in 3D. Sharing a small elevator with a large wirework robosaur felt dangerous, though it was only a projection. His eye was drawn to the jut-snout head, bristling with antennae. Why give a skyscraper a face? Was this the Princess's idea of a twenty-first-century sphinx? A wonder of the world.

Nezumi stepped through the model, light-lines across her face and hands. She tapped a section and a shaft – this one, Hal supposed – lit up.

For an unauthorised Secondary User, Nezumi mastered the interface quicker than he had. Jun Zero wouldn't like that. But Jun Zero was a jerk.

'From the Security Suite, we should be able to get anywhere in the building,' said Nezumi.

'It'll be left unmanned and ready for us to waltz in then.'

'Not at all,' said Nezumi, sliding out a couple of inches of her sword.

The dragon switched off.

'Take us down,' said Hal, wearily. 'To Floor 88.'

The elevator began to move.

Hal didn't want to think about whether he'd done the right thing or the wrong thing, but the next item that popped up on his mental menu was that vampire elevator in Holland and he really, really didn't want to think about that.

He hummed along with the catchy song.

DR AKIBA

His eyes had been plucked out and his ears torn off.

His mouth and nostrils were pinched closed, buried under new-grown flesh. Would he drown in his own body? He couldn't draw breath – but his lungs weren't straining to the point of bursting. Panic abated before it could take hold. Turning vampire wrought violent physical changes, which were still in process. His heart beat, though at a slower rate. A respiratory system was as vestigial to what he was now as an appendix was to a warm man. His lungs would hang like empty wineskins in his ribcage. The pseudo-mouths in the palms of his hands were for feeding. The blood he took would be pre-aerated in the lungs of his donors.

He was a *noppera-bō*, one of the faceless ones.

The creature that attacked him had wandered off. Now he was competition not food. She was not his mother-in-darkness. He'd injected himself with v-blood from the kit. The *noppera-bō* must have affected the turning, to infuse him with her peculiar bloodline. She was mad – whipped to craziness by the blood spilled when Drift Kaiju cut him open. Akiba was over his initial frenzy of rage, terror and red thirst – an expression he'd heard often but only now understood. He thought he was sane, though psychiatry was not a field in which self-diagnosis was recommended.

He was feeling differently. Feeling *more*. His thinking was changed, accelerated, opened up to new possibilities. He had fresh senses. He might be deaf and blind, but he felt more than he had ever heard or seen.

He didn't need to live in an air environment. Well-fed, he could survive underwater. He could control his internal pressure to resist the crushing weight of the depths. Heat and cold were of interest, but did not cause discomfort. His rewired nerves translated sensations painful to his former self into an exciting range of stimuli. He didn't yet have a vocabulary to describe his range of feeling, or a mouth to speak the words.

The smooth, featureless skin that grew over his ravaged face was a new sense organ. A giant mask-shaped tongue. Everything – breeze, night-sounds, moving bodies – registered as salt or sugar. He had complex functional synaesthesia, experiencing and interpreting the world outside via new neural pathways. The vampire blood he had injected fed his changing brain. The warm blood he had sucked was an accelerant. The blood mix made him high, he thought idly.

As a med student, he'd tried a lot of drugs. Doctors always had the best pills. Tokiko's staff hit him up for samples to get them through long shifts at the hotel.

This was better than any pharmacy spree.

He should write a paper.

The night sky burned tangerine and shadows were alive. He had as clear a sense of what happened out of conventional eyeshot as in plain view. There was no hiding from him. He was aware of people all over Daikaiju Plaza and could tell vampire from warm, human from animal. All living things – even insects and birds – were notes in a symphony. He 'saw' beyond the spectrum. The pulses and heartbeats and broadcast emotions were an intricate tapestry of harmonic threads. He was significantly more aware of everything. If a leaf fell, he'd know its childhood nickname.

A great roaring soul loomed over him then broke into a million ectoplasm moths and dissipated. It was the ghost of the Armourdillo, spirit of the machine, departing to a plane where meat was under metal, where motors drove people, where naked humans chest-bumped and fought to a chorus of car horns in a demolition arena slick with lovely, lovely blood.

How had he made it so far with such limited senses?

Without eyes, without a mouth, he was reborn.

Nearby, there had been an explosion. A small building demolished. Gunfire, burned flesh, and the heady, seductive tang of spilled blood.

He had to focus – not be distracted by novelties.

A small battle was in progress. The Plaza was clearing out. Fear spread through the Bund, faster than any infection.

No one new had fallen from the Daikaiju Building.

Drift Kaiju was dead. One moment he was a living thing of pulses and tastes and moving parts. Then, he was a cooling shape. The spirit that spilled from him was dew, much less magnificent than the ghost of the 'dillo. Nothing was left of DK but motile germs in his body – passengers on a sunken submarine, life-support shut off and death certain. They'd bloom wonderfully as the corpse perished but go extinct when it was dirt.

His first kill.

Akiba the healer was a killer now. With a taste for blood. A new *need*. An addict of murder.

No time to contemplate that. Too much else was new.

A living, quick person came close to him – angled on straight, looking at where his face had been.

'Doc,' said an unfamiliar voice. 'Mate, is that you?'

No, not unfamiliar – a voice he knew, heard a different way. Sound waves vibrating against the smooth no-face. It was as much eardrum as tongue.

Derek radiated sympathy and puzzlement.

'How are you even alive?'

Akiba wanted to tell Derek he was fine but words stuck in his throat. His shoulders shook with silent laughter. Of course he couldn't speak. His vocal cords were shapeshifting. His body was repurposing industriously. A model of instantaneous, reactive/protective evolution. New organs, new functions.

He could *tell* so much more, but communicate nothing.

'Fuck, that's gross,' thought Derek.

Ah. *Noppera-bō* had telepathy. The literature didn't mention it. Maybe faceless ones never let faced ones know of their hidden advantage.

'Poor old Akiba. Bloke's got a girlfriend. She's gonna have a shock.'

Akiba wanted Derek to stop thinking so loud.

Which he did.

'Weird,' said Derek. 'What was that?'

He tried to put a more complicated thought into Derek's head. Warn him about the danger. Akiba didn't yet have the mental tools to use all his capabilities. He was too busy trying to stay alive to experiment. He should make it a priority to get a notepad and a pencil – both on strings to go around his neck.

'Are you still in there, Doc?' asked Derek. 'Behind the no-face?'

Akiba resorted to crude sign language and gave a thumbs-up.

'Good on ya. I don't know what's up, but the mission's proper futzed. I reckon some scunner's sold us out.'

Akiba wanted to tell Derek about Drift Kaiju.

The kid had tried to kill him. Come to think of it, he'd succeeded.

He saw through Derek – his heartbeat, his temperature, the panic he was quashing.

All his life – when he was alive – Akiba had been a poor judge of character. How else to explain Tokiko? Now, he was a human lie detector. He knew a good, true soul when it hovered in front of him.

And he knew the other kinds.

He and Derek were on their own. Golgotha was corrupt. Gokemidoro too. The rest of the crew weren't acting in anyone's interests but their own. EarthGuard was compromised. Maybe the Kuran faction was okay, but they were losing the power game.

Akiba sensed two purposeful souls, converging.

Hunter and Killer.

Drift Kaiju was an amateur assassin. These were the pros.

They moved across the Plaza, darting from what they believed was one piece of cover to another. He 'saw' them better when they were out of his theoretical sight line – thinking themselves safe, they showed their real selves. The scrawny Killer had a bulkier soul stuck to him. A smoky, death-hungry demon's hands clasped the youth's neck like a strangling rope. Hunter was a crash dummy of hatred with too many guns and knives. Less to him than a paper target.

Akiba knew the positions they were trying to take up.

He and Derek would be in crossfire.

He made gunshapes with his hands and waved as if playing bandits, then nodded to the advancing EarthGuard rogues.

'Timmy's down the well, Lassie?' said Derek, catching on.

RICHARD JEPERSON

The 'D' word didn't impress the Princess.

If the apparition was indeed her.

Was she live or was she Memorex? Richard couldn't tell whether this Christina was her shifted shape or a transmitted/recorded hologram. She was a visual/aural presence but nothing else. In a room where boiling primary emotions gave him a headache, she didn't even radiate sociopath static. Several chilling individuals were within his empathetic reach, as many among the hostages as the gunmen. His sanity shuddered if he nudged their auras. Sitting close to the twelve-foot-tall blow-up Princess was more like being too close to a television. What was disturbing about her was seeing but not sensing.

By all accounts, the woman wasn't all there in the first place. Transforming into a spectral sparkle removed her even further from obligations of the flesh.

What did the rest of humanity look like to her?

Everyone else in the ballroom – vampire and warm – must seem as ridiculous as the umbrella goblin.

What could she want? How could she be reasoned with?

Radu cel Frumos stood like a messenger boy, envelope burning his hand.

'Christina' didn't turn her odd eyes to him. She watched everything, like the Wire. No specific detail was worth her attention. Not even a truly dead guest or two.

Radu waved his arms, flapping his silly, cardboardy sleeves.

He had a small army and many guns. He'd personally wasted a valuable human resource – golden lads were not cheap! – and casually had Cottonmouth commit a murder that would send global stock markets into a tailspin.

Then he dropped the biggest name in the night-world.

He deserved to be acknowledged!

It would be just like a Son of the Dragon to slaughter four hundred or so because he didn't like to be ignored.

'You are to stop,' said the Bey. 'By order of Count Dracula, King of the Cats, sovereign of the undead, your liege and monarch.'

'You've just said "The boss of you" five different ways,' Richard put in.

Radu, already irritated with the Princess, was enraged.

He kicked the dead dot.com billionaire in the head.

'How funny do you think *he* thinks you are?' the vampire snapped.

'Not terribly,' Richard admitted.

'I shouldn't think so,' said Radu, point made. 'Now, keep quiet, Mr ageing-rapidly-towards-dilapidation-and-death Jeperson. The giants are talking. You're little people.'

'Am I little people too?' said Syrie.

'Yes, sugarlump. Teeny Teena to his Tommy Thumb. You only have money. This is about position. Kings and queens and rolling heads, *capisce?*'

Through a connection to the Shah, Syrie Van Epp could demand to be addressed as *Hazrat-i-'Aliya Aqdas Shahzadi* Syrie *Khanum* – Her Royal Highness Princess Syrie. Her tasteful business cards weren't cluttered with that mouthful. She had three doctorates – actually studied for, rather than honoraries snaffled in return for a hand-out – and didn't use them on her letterhead. Founding and financing Wings Over the World put her in the frame for a Nobel Peace Prize. She made it known through back channels that she wouldn't accept. She thought titles were for inadequates with something to prove. Radu was bragging to the wrong vampire.

None of this got Christina's attention.

Everyone in the room looked at the Princess. They couldn't help it. Richard's face numbed and prickled. Being in the presence was likely to give them sunburn. Some vampires might catch fire and go up like roman candles. Christina Light was a pagan crystal idol, radiant with the spirit of the volcano goddess. Or a camp art installation, Madonna in stained glass, an Andy Warhol screen print of the Lady in the Lake, Knife-Faced Gorgiositude to the Max.

What did Dracula want her to stop doing?

Christina was lucky to be born with a last name. Her father was almost certainly not the American Mr Light who married her Italian mother. She came by her title and a first fortune by marrying the short-lived, weak-blooded Prince Casamassima. Her bloodline came from her father-in-darkness, Count Oblensky – soon thereafter nowhere to be seen. She had practised self-improvement for over a hundred years. She might have improved herself to such a degree that lesser mortals – ie: everyone – would never catch up.

'We know of your "ascension",' said Radu. 'At the stroke of midnight – how dramatic! – you intend to abandon what's left of your body and seed yourself throughout the World Wide Web. With this coup, you believe you will take the helm and steer the destiny of the planet.'

The Bey was talking about something he didn't understand – something he'd been told.

Richard was an old bloke who couldn't set up a laser printer without crashing every computer in the Club, but he'd been briefed by earnest experts. He tried to get his head round transhumanism, the singularity, AI and digi-geddon. The Ascension wasn't a new idea to him. Arthur C. Clarke had floated the possibility that Christina might try something like this. Those in the know bought tinfoil sou'westers. The Princess Casamassima scared them more than the Millennium Bug, Black Helicopters and Jun Zero put together.

But, *seriously*...?

Richard looked at Christina's hovering mask.

When, in 1969, your basic garden-variety diabolical mastermind tried to take over the world with a super-computer, all it took to thwart their wicked plan was a strategic power cut and a karate chop. Thirty years on, there was no plug to pull, no master programmer to nobble. The system was too vast, too intricate, too diffuse, to shut down. It was the *World Wide Web*. There'd always be a back-up in an anonymous shed on an industrial estate in Ohio or the Ukraine.

The major factor wasn't even the power or the will to do the thing, but the prosaic drudge of waiting decades for governments, businesses and workmen to lay the cables, hook up the servers, and install the terminals. Think of the delays, the financing arguments, the *tea breaks*. Now, in injury time for the twentieth century, an electronic brain – a node of a greater e-brain – was installed in every home, workplace, pocket. Your bank, your job, your corner shop, your best friend and that odorous fellow who sold French postcards – all were online. The world was dependent on the whirring, flashing connective tissue the Princess aspired to possess. No wonder crackpots signed up with Aum Draht.

Given a choice between the web going dark and accepting a new Regina Mundi, Richard wasn't sure the vote would go against the Princess. That was why the Diogenes Club, all the way back to that forward-thinking autocrat Mycroft Holmes, had a policy of doing what the world needed, not what it wanted.

Once, Christina's shapeshift-to-a-glowworm stunt was simply a novelty on a level with Kasa-obake contorting into an umbrella. Now her party piece had *applications*. Her unique vampire physiology afforded her opportunities if she was ambitious, insane or visionary enough to seize them. Lesser immortals must seethe with envy.

Everyone knew the Princess could turn to light. But what was light? Illumination. Information. Electricity. Lightning.

Extreme transhumanists sought to upload consciousness to servers, mapping brain patterns digitally, leaving behind empty shells. Farewell to the flesh and an eternity of quiet contemplation in the cyber-aether, so long as a direct debit paid the phone bills. Christina was three-quarters of the way there already. She could turn to coherent light the way other vampires could do bats, wolves or mists. Her consciousness, removed from its physical cage, remained intact.

As Radu said, she could seed herself through the web.

Aum Draht adepts saw reality as a computer simulation, controlled by a higher being.

Christina Light could be their Wire.

And Dracula – John Alucard – wanted her to hold back.

So did Aum Draht, of course. No cult likes a deity to contradict the high priests. Just ask Caiaphas.

For all his Beverly Hills castles, Dracula was a mediaeval conqueror. His idea of power was simple, brutal and had worked for five hundred years. He counted victories in gold, land, songs sung about him, and – always, always, always – blood. Christina Light was liberated from that mind-trap. Pretty advanced for a Victorian new-born. She must have been *exhausting*.

He remembered what Geneviève told him. 'Don't look for anyone behind the curtain. Christina has no puppet master. Because she's a pretty face, men think she must be just a figurehead, but she really isn't. She's herself alone. You have to deal with that, or do what I did – run away, very far away, and hope she has too much else to be getting on with ever to think of you.'

As a creature of information, what would Christina feed on? She would still be a vampire. An immoderately thirsty one. That was why she had to be thwarted.

Drat – he'd come all this way and found himself on Dracula's side. If Radu's intel was sound, Richard would have to set aside the fact that he was a ghastly pill and offer what support he could. Mycroft Holmes would have seen it plainly. Richard was sick about it. That was the price he paid for being a feeler not a thinker.

If the Princess Ascended, everyone would be in trouble. Not just folk who'd ticked her off.

Being a world away wouldn't protect Kate Reed, Penelope Churchward or Geneviève Dieudonné. Information moves at – what else? – the speed of light. The Light Channel was already global. The glow beamed to multiple millions of subscribers wasn't a generated test signal. It was Christina herself – Christina's Light.

That was how she'd feed. A pale corpse-candle, leaching life.

Keyboards sticky with blood as users slashed veins to bleed into their desktops. Desiccated corpses on couches, juices drawn to the cathode tube. Or was that old-fashioned? Could a being of sheer light feed on brainwaves?

'Do you hear me, Tinkerbell?' asked Radu.

If Dracula was worried by the Princess, why send the family fool to deal with her? With plague mushrooms and guns? He was usually a cannier planner. He had a blind spot, though. He didn't take women seriously – which is why one managed to cut off his original head. For all his Hollywood moguldom, he wasn't much for new media. He still put out films on laserdisc. The electric world had got away from him.

He wouldn't have a strategy to bring the Princess down – with Radu as stooge or feint or sacrifice. He'd ignore the whole thing till it was too late and historians had to think of a name – World War V came to mind – for the conflict that would consume the next decades.

So, what was happening? Who were the players?

'This is ridiculous,' said the Bey, looking to his hostages – of all people – for affirmation. 'It's like talking to a weeping statue.'

'You could try praying,' said Georgia Rae Drumgo. She was also a Dracula acolyte, so why was she lying here bleeding?

'That's it, Mama Voodoo,' said Radu. 'You're done. Furīman, put one in her head and another in her heart. Silver.'

The *yakuza* assassin raised his pistol. A single tear trickled down his cheek.

Georgia Rae said something defiant in Haitian *patois*.

Furīman aimed for her head. Other hostages shuffled away.

The light giantess twirled, apparently absent-mindedly. Her phantom hand passed through Furīman's shoulder.

He spasmed and fired, his aim off. A red groove opened in Georgia Rae's cheek, but the bullet ploughed into the floor.

Furīman's back bent and his arms stretched as if he were lightning-struck.

He dropped his gun and convulsed, tattooed chest slick with sweat.

His hair frizzled and lost colour. His eyes whitened and his skin paled. All natural pigment went out of him. This was how Christina fed. An arc crackled around Furīman's eyes. He choked, as if sicking up his own bones.

As his skin became ancient parchment, his tattoos stood out all the more.

His black trousers lost all their dye – even his boots blanched – but the ink in his skin stayed vivid, animated by Christina's touch.

The monsters on his body fought, moving at first like early animations then, as the Princess mastered a new trick, with smoother, fluid motion. Felix the Cat turned to Studio Ghibli.

The three-headed dragon battled the moth, the bird and the anteater. Furīman was in agony. His skin ripped, showing worm-white organs, leaking milky blood. The dragon grew, absorbing the other monsters into its intricate design, and tore itself from Furīman's body. The detached, flapping skin-thing hovered. Furīman lay dead on the floor, exposed veins and muscles white as bone. His departed skin danced to Christina's baton.

Murdleigh hid behind a pallbearer as the tattoodemalian swooped. It enveloped the human shield while Radu's renfield scurried away. One of the triphibian's heads had working fangs. It cracked the flathead's mask like a snake puncturing a bird's egg. A tuber penetrated to extract the yolk. Someone opened fire, riddling the pallbearer and the thing wrapped around him. That killed the victim but holes didn't bother the tattoo.

Cottonmouth stepped in, and with several swipes of her knives reduced Furīman's skin to ribbons.

'A pity,' said Syrie. 'That was fine workmanship.'

'The tattoo or… the thing she did?' Richard asked.

Syrie shrugged. She probably meant both.

'Well,' said Radu, now as terrified as he was angry, 'that was something to see. What *will* you do for an encore?'

For the first time, the illuminated Princess took notice of him.

She smiled and the intensity of her light grew. Her red eye became impossible to look at.

'It's not midnight yet,' came that roaring whisper. 'No more presents till the New Year.'

NEZUMI

The lift doors opened.

Floor 88 was open-plan. An office suite.

A well-dressed elder with a gun – not as trigger-happy as the minion who shot Mrs Van Epp up in the ballroom – covered Nezumi and Hal. He had a Latin look, with a neatly trimmed moustache and sideburns. If anyone deserved to be called 'the Handsome', he did. Other vampires were with him. A smart woman, also with a gun, held in a two-handed grip that suggested firepower. A stocky Britisher and a Japanese woman, with matching ear-to-ear grins. The Brit's red tunic would have been army issue in 1895 and groovy Carnaby Street fashion in 1965. His partner's smile was alarming. She held a dangerous pair of shears.

That annoying warm Senator was passed out and tied to a chair.

'We come in peace,' said Hal.

The guns didn't waver. The shears clacked.

Hal remembered he was holding a revolver and threw it away.

'You are Light Industries Security,' Nezumi said. 'I am a bodyguard for a guest. This man is, ah, a victim of the hostiles who have taken over the building.'

Trying to explain Hal and Jun Zero would make Mr Sharp Suit shoot them. It would be easier than following the story.

'The elevator wasn't working,' said the woman.

Hal's mechanical hand was still wired into the lift controls.

'We sort of have a pass-key,' said Hal. 'An override for everything.'

'Useful,' said the elder. 'Especially if you were taking over the building. Tell me again how you're not two of these "hostiles".'

Nezumi assessed the situation.

Mr Sharp Suit and his deputy were well-spaced. Professionals. She couldn't get Good Night Kiss into both of them. If she attacked either, the other would shoot her. With silver. The grinning ghouls would carve Hal where he stood.

Hal detached Lefty from the lift. Nezumi put her hand on the metal appendage, aiming it at the floor so it wouldn't be mistaken for a weapon.

'She *was* with one of the guests,' said a disembodied voice. 'An Englishman. And I know her.'

Nezumi shut her eyes and *felt* the room.

When she opened them again, she knew where the voice came from. And who had spoken.

'You used to call yourself "S",' said the unseen woman.

'It's "Nezumi" now.'

High Priest Kah Pei Mei, her master from 1802 till 1923, named her 'S' because of her proficiency in his favourite sword stroke. As if drawing an English letter S in the air, she would strike the neck, vitals and legs of an assailant or assailants. Free of Kah, she dropped the name and the show-off dance-fighting. Zuli Bronze could bop her three times – left knee, right knee, *heart*! – if she tried an 'S' in kendoline. Once you raised the sword to begin the 'S', a savvy opponent recognised the stroke and cut under your guard. Mastery of numberless martial disciplines hadn't stopped someone creeping up on Kah and poking a sharpened stick through his heart. She avenged him but mourned little. He was an ill-tempered master. Her current style was based on less elegant finishing moves.

The man in charge darted a glance at a swivelling chair.

'Arashi, quick: on our side or not?'

Nezumi imagined a head inclined in thought.

Suzan Arashi was the glass geisha. Lady Oyotsu, the long-necked woman, and O-Same, the human flame, once lived in a tower with Suzan and the stone giant Sesshō Seki. In times when *yōkai* were shunned, they performed deeds of heroism and charity. To defend Spider Forest from General Ichimonji, the Four had to up their ranks to Seven. The undead usurper was chieftain among seven powerful ghosts, the Shichinin Misaki. They could only be defeated by an equal force. Kah and Nezumi, along with the warm jungle adventurer Mowgli of Seoni, made up the numbers. The campaign was a success, though Kah lost his eyebrows (he demanded five chests of gold in recompense) and Nezumi was wounded in a duel with a swordsman whose head was a copper pot. Suzan gave her blood. For months, she saw through her hands as if they were soap bubbles.

That blood link was still there.

'Our side,' said Suzan.

The guns were holstered.

'I'm Molinar,' said the man in charge. 'This is Verlaine. Kuchisake and Watson. Arashi, you know.'

'I'm… Hal,' said Hal, remembering not to introduce himself as the world's most wanted cyber-bandit. 'This is Lefty.'

The hand said nothing.

'We were locked in,' said Molinar. 'Our system is breached.'

'A sophisticated attack,' said Verlaine. 'Fujiwara – our tech guy – is missing. The Chief thinks your hostiles got to him somehow.'

'They had to have a man on the inside,' said Molinar.

'Our feeds are lying to us,' said Suzan. 'We're seeing last year's celebrations on all channels, digitally altered so the date's tonight.'

'Cool,' said Hal.

'One way of looking at it,' said Molinar. Now he paid attention to Hal.

The elder had known Nezumi was dangerous at a look but skipped over the bloke with her. Now Hal made him suspicious. Molinar wasn't one of those bypassed-by-the-times crumbly elders. He was sharp. Nezumi reckoned he was good at his job.

'I'm with the Diogenes Club,' she said, changing the subject.

'They get about,' said Molinar. 'I was Carpathian Guard in the '90s. The *18*90s. Do you know Katharine Reed?'

'We've worked together.'

'Interesting woman. Infuriating, but admirable. Carrot-top.'

'She shoved your boss into a wall at the Tower of London,' said Nezumi. It was something Kate mentioned quite often.

'I had to unfix the Princess,' Molinar grinned. 'That was a challenge.'

'I'm glad you're getting caught up,' said Verlaine, 'but shouldn't we be moving out? If we can use this fellah's arm to override the override, we can get up to the Dragon's Mouth where we ought to be. This girl can give us a sit-rep. Enemy numbers and names. Weapons capabilities. Positions.'

'I vote we get out of the building and call in the cavalry,' said Hal. 'Japan has an air force, right?'

'Japan has a Self-Defence Force,' said Suzan. 'Until midnight, any trespass in the Bund would constitute an attack on a sovereign state. Invading another nation violates the post-war constitution.'

Verlaine looked around, annoyed.

'Your party poopers faked a medical emergency to justify calling in EarthGuard,' Nezumi explained. 'That counts as foreign aid, not an invasion. A Colonel Golgotha has occupied the building. He's not the big boss, though, that's—'

'We've had that intel,' said Molinar. 'The cocky bastard used one of his aliases to give us his own name. He's the breed of megalomaniac who wants you to know he's shafting you.'

'Radu the Handsome.'

'No. Who? I mean Jun Zero. That's who we're up against.'

Nezumi knew a few wrong words would crack this nervy alliance and lead to a free-for-all with many casualties.

'The commander upstairs is Dracula's brother,' she said.

'*That* Radu!' said Molinar. 'The race-car cheat!'

'Radu cel Frumos is a guest,' said Suzan. 'Representing the House of Drăculeşti. We reckoned he was the most unimportant relative Drac could find. Or the one he least wanted to see at his own party. They're not close. He's on the Nuisance List. Flags *were* raised about his entourage but Fujiwara did a background check and they came up clear.'

'The Fujiwara who's missing?' said Hal. 'And suspected.'

Suzan made a sound Nezumi decoded as combined realisation and pique. From their adventure in Spider Forest, she remembered the woman's repertoire of expressive clucks and clicks and hums – worked up to fill in conversational spaces where people with visible faces got by on narrowed eyes or pursed lips.

'His staff are definite hostiles,' said Nezumi. 'A chauffeur with iron teeth.'

'... and Tsunako Shiki, she's a perfect little ball of awful,' said Hal, with feeling.

Verlaine looked at Suzan's ladylike grunt.

They both knew the Bad Penny.

'Oh, not *her*,' said Verlaine. 'Fujiwara should have said. She's been barred from the Bund from the beginning.'

'Yes, Fujiwara *should* have said,' Nezumi underlined.

'Ole Fujiwooji's a turncloak, eh what?' said the smiley Brit, Watson. 'Some folk don't 'arf let yah dahn, eh?'

'I can't believe it,' said Verlaine.

'Me neither,' chipped in Suzan.

Even Kuchisake was disappointed. When she frowned, her cheek-slashes turned down to make a tragic crescent of her mouth.

'Popular with the ladies is Fujiwooji,' said Watson. 'Never a good sign if you asks me.'

'You,' said Molinar, pointing to Hal. 'We'll need you to get the express elevator to the Dragon's Mouth. The rest of you, check your weapons.'

'A frontal approach isn't advisable,' Nezumi said.

'Listen to her,' Hal echoed, voice high-pitched. 'She has, ah, good intel.'

'We'd be shot when the doors opened. I've already seen it once. Their field orders are to kill security staff. Leaving only hostages who can't stick up for themselves.'

'We could use the Senator as a human shield,' said Verlaine, steaming to get in the fight. She was offended and hurt by this Fujiwara's treachery. 'Or send in Arashi with silver cheesewire. Cut the problem off at the head.'

Molinar wasn't convinced. He was equally gung-ho, but saw sense.

'All they need is a *noppera-bō* on the crew and Arashi's advantage is nullified. They see without eyes. Hell, this girl does too, don't you? You knew where our unseen asset was.'

Nezumi nodded.

'Golgotha has good bad people,' she said. 'A woman called Cottonmouth. A boy with a demon on his back. A gaseous assassin.'

'The last one might not be a problem any more. He met a fan he didn't like.'

Again, Molinar looked at Hal suspiciously.

Hal got fidgety and shut up.

'There must be other ways up,' said Molinar. 'If only we weren't locked out of the building plans.'

'I *can* help you there,' said Hal. 'Lefty, the blueprints.'

The diagram appeared in the air. Watson went for his side-arm, but didn't make a fool of himself by shooting the cutaway hologram. A ghost dragon wavered in the middle of the office. Again, Nezumi was prompted to wonder why anyone would pick this shape for their headquarters. What message was the Princess sending?

'Lefty, calculate routes from Floor 88 out of the building.'

'And up to the ballroom,' Nezumi insisted.

Lefty whirred and clicked, processing input from its primary user – but also, she realised, taking her suggestion onboard.

Veins of golden light appeared throughout the 3D model.

'Is it generating this from the plans on file or mapping the building itself?' Verlaine asked.

'Good question,' said Hal. 'Miss… what was it?'

'Call me Marit,' she said.

Verlaine didn't just have a thing for computer guys. Hal talked like a pimply nerd who lived in his mother's basement, but to look at him he was a Japanese male model who worked out by juggling sandbags. Even the cybernetic hand was cool. Strawberry Fields would gladly stick Hal's pic up in the dorm's Shrine of the Snoggable.

Hal puffed up at Verlaine's attention. He responded to her sexy spy get-up. Evening dress and small-of-the-back holster.

'So far as I can tell, and this is as much a novelty to me as to you, Lefty's a wireless device,' he explained. 'It's piggybacking the building. As you said, overriding the override. Oh, look, what a shame…'

He pointed to a broken light-line.

'That was your elevator shaft to the neck. It's disabled. No way up there. When they sealed you in, they cut the cables. It's what I'd do. Now, these are all ways out—'

'Can you get heat signatures?' asked Verlaine, ignoring his pointed travel update.

'Let's try. Lefty, show who's on site.'

Clusters of dots – red for warm, blue for vampire, turquoise for miscellaneous other – appeared throughout the projection. Mostly above them, where the party was.

'I should have thought of this earlier,' Hal said.

Plenty of people were still alive in the Doragon no Kuchi. She couldn't tell if any dot was Mr Jeperson.

'You didn't think of this now,' Verlaine said. 'I did.'

She might recently – very recently – have changed her mind about computer guys. Nezumi had a pang of amused sympathy for Hal. He'd had his hopes raised and his heart broken inside a minute and the woman wasn't even thinking of him at the time.

'This is the Floor 88,' said Molinar, sticking his finger into the projection. 'This is us?'

'Lefty, enlarge Floor 88,' said Hal. A cross-section of the building blew up.

It was a floating architect's model with dots.

Watson pointed and counted out loud.

Nezumi didn't. She saw at once what Molinar suspected, and moved quickly – drawing Good Night Kiss to an approving whistle from Kuchisake – across the floor, then stabbed through a partition and ripped it away.

Curled up under a desk was Anthony Peak. He could hide better than an invisible woman.

She raised her sword and he held out his gloved hands and flapped.

She expected him to try and talk his way out of trouble, but he was unable to speak. He was choking on something.

The thief's face reddened as he was surrounded.

Kuchisake shoved her shears towards his face.

Alarmed, he coughed. The eye jewel from Mrs Van Epp's tiara popped out of his mouth.

'Meet Anthony Peak,' said Nezumi. 'Then wish you hadn't.'

DETECTIVE AZUMA

The escape passage ran under Yokonori Street.

Azuma and Asato were hurried along by a blast of flame, but the brickwork walls and shored-up roof held firm. This tunnel must have been built before the Bund, when the Yōkai Town docks were used by smugglers.

The escape route came up through an ornamental well in a memorial garden for those who died in the battle of the Temple of One Thousand Monsters in December 1899.

Asato crawled out first, finding hand- and foot-holes.

She had elongated, double-jointed limbs. He wasn't as flexible, but followed her. He gripped too hard and stones cracked and came loose. This would be the well's last use unless something else was built on the cursed site of the Rose Blood Club and the police box.

Asato stretched a long arm back into the well and hauled Azuma out.

They stood on a gentle slope in front of a shrine. The white heads of chrysanthemums formed a Hokusai wave, black-red roses dotting the crests.

Gunfire sounded from Daikaiju Plaza.

Hunter and Killer at work. With the Bund PD eliminated, they were ranging free.

His knuckle-fangs jutted.

'Asato,' he said, 'thank you. You're good police. If you've people to be with, you should go to them. You don't want to see what I have to do next.'

The *yurei* hung her head, eye peeping through wet hair.

'There's a thing you should know about me, Detective,' croaked Asato, voice like ice cubes cracking in blood. 'I'm, like, *really* into revenge.'

She had collected one of Ota's mass murder guns. She cradled it in her bony arms, blacknailed finger curled around the trigger.

Azuma saw the outline of Asato's determined smile through her hair.

'That *is* good to know,' he said, checking his police special.

He reloaded.

'Inugami, Saki-A, Saki-K, Saki-G, Kankichi, Brenten, Nakajima, Ota,' Asato recited the list of the dead.

Azuma sensed the cops' presence in the garden.

The spirits of 1899 were long departed, placated by the Bund founded on their sacrifice. A hundred years on, there were fresher grudges to pay off. The shrine must be sprayed with murderers' blood before the newly dead could move on.

Asato pumped a shell into the breech and wailed.

The shrine shook. A blood-glutted *tengu* who'd been sleeping it off in the long grass stirred and bolted, vaulting over the fence as if he'd forgotten his feathered arms weren't real wings. Asato's lamentation rose. A warning to the doomed. A rallying cry for the just.

'Asato,' said Azuma, 'let's go kill killers.'

RICHARD JEPERSON

Christina's image remained, but only as a screensaver. Her mind was elsewhere, working on her Ascension. With three-quarters of an hour to go till midnight, her to-do list still wasn't completely crossed out. Which meant it wasn't too late to stop her.

Furiman's bones turned to powder.

The Princess could have done that to everyone, but craved attention. If a vampire attained cyber-godhood in the forest when there's nobody around to kneel in awe, would her light still shine? Without subjects, there are no kings and queens. Without an audience, there are no stars.

Richard scanned the room again.

Radu was angrier at being fobbed off – put on hold while phoning in a bomb threat – than scared he'd be next for the swipe-and-wipe treatment. It didn't occur to him that he was in danger. After all, he had guns, soldiers, hostages. He ought to be in charge. He ought to command respect.

That was the song of his life.

Colonel Golgotha's iron hide didn't crack. A man down, he was holding the hill. His surviving EarthGuard troops were in line, for now. He had less sway over pallbearers. They might have been influenced by Radu to throw themselves on grenades for him.

Georgia Rae Drumgo swore in *patois*. It wouldn't do to forget the wounded tigress.

Mr Omochi knelt as if in expectation of execution. Proof that you could be calm and furious at the same time.

The celebrity Georgia Rae had bitten was passed out.

Chesse finally explained the young man was the *manga* artist who drew *Rapist Man*.

'Rapist Man?'

'A masked avenger, you know. Like the Monk and Bat-Boy in America.'

'Excuse me, *Rapist* Man?'

'Yes, he's a hero who rapes bad women. Then they fall in love with him and turn good. It's very popular in Japan.'

The bleeding artist looked inoffensive. Richard reckoned he'd not been bitten deeply enough. *Dan Dare* and *Roy of the Rovers* he understood, but… *Rapist Man*?! Maybe he *should* let Christina take over the world. If this is what it was coming to…

Chesse started licking the young man's wounds.

'He won't mind,' she said.

Richard supposed not.

Syrie did what Richard was doing – kept quiet and alert. Obviously, she wasn't just here for the party. If the Diogenes Club and Wings Over the World shared intelligence, they might be better set to avert the coming whateverageddon.

Radu prowled the room. He was not enjoying himself any more.

'Where is Christina, do you think?' Richard asked Syrie.

'Not here,' she said. 'This is the Dragon's Mouth. The original her will be above us – behind the Dragon's Eyes. She has a private apartment there. The penthouse. She has to return regularly to her physical body, like an elder crawling back to its coffin. That might not be true after midnight.'

'So it's a case of kill her when you can because later you might not be able to.'

'Think of it as strangling the future tyrant in the crib.'

'Lovely image.'

'She's mad enough now. How do you think she'd be as Queen of Air and Darkness?'

'Fair point. But if this is important, why send *him*?'

He thumbed towards Radu, who was having blood-froth pawed off his shoulder-pad by a tiptoeing Murdleigh.

Syrie snarled contempt and irritation.

'You're close to the counsels of the King of the Cats, Georgia Rae,' said Richard. 'Does the Idiot Brother speak for the throne?'

Georgia Rae spat bile.

'We'll take that as a no,' he said.

'I here to zotz the bitch if she can do what she say,' Georgia Rae said. 'Our geeks and freaks figure she off herself if she try to "ascend". What left o' her brain will fry and she be gone. Alucard take no chances. Hell, it be like him to send two hitters without saying there a competition. But I absogoddamnlutely guarantee he didn't give no contract to that fool there. Maybe he hire Golgotha Mon but he not let Pretty Bwah run no game. He learn that when he warm. He ain't forgot.'

'So who put Radu up to it? This isn't something he'd think of by himself.'

Georgia Rae chewed that over.

'Someone very, very smart or someone very, very dumb.'

Richard shrugged. That was a) true and b) not a lot of help.

Chesse nudged him. Her many bangles and bracelets clinked.

Radu strode over with Murdleigh trotting beside him.

'Sucks to be you,' said Cottonmouth to the hostages, smiling.

'My friend is enormously rich,' Richard told her. 'I don't suppose you'd be interested in a lucrative employment opportunity with Wings Over the World.'

'The aid outfit? Waste of my talents, don't you think?'

'Before you can tend antelopes, you have to fight off jackals,' Syrie said. 'Wings has people like you on staff. Not that I am offering a job.'

'Picky picky picky.'

Even if Cottonmouth was tempted – and as far as Richard could tell, she wasn't – she couldn't turncloak without consequences. The Butler, armoured by dark magic, could smite her. If Syrie upended a briefcase full of cash, she'd still not get a hundred-percent take-up.

'What's the news across the nation?' Radu asked.

'This one tried to get that one to bribe me,' Cottonmouth told him.

'Tut tut tut, for shame,' he said. 'Has no one integrity any longer?'

Syrie laughed, bitterly.

'What's so funny, Mrs Moneybags?'

'I heard Vlad the Impaler was famous for standing up to the Turks, but Radu the Handsome was known for lying down under them.'

Radu's smile went hard.

'You can make the slur go away tonight,' Syrie told Radu. 'If you stop the Princess Casamassima's Ascension, you'll be the Dracula they remember. The Dracula who stood up to the world-conqueror.'

'Yes,' he said. 'Thank you. That's precisely the case.'

He was surprised she'd admitted it. She was playing him – needling his sore points (including internalised homophobia), then fanning his ego flames. It might work but would take time they didn't have. This was the twenty-third hour.

'Did Dracula personally entrust you with this mission?' Richard asked.

'Yes,' Radu said, too quick.

'Personally, as in "in person". Face to face.'

'Or did you get a telephone call?' Syrie asked.

'An e-mail? Signed "Big D".'

Murdleigh did a strange nasal chuckle.

'We communed,' said Radu. 'We are of the same blood. We have an understanding.'

'Damballah's serpent ass you do, Lickle Brother,' said Georgia Rae. 'You ain't A-list, you's black-list. Hell, when word get back, you's shit-list. Killin' family ain't nothin' to Alucard.'

'Never mind her, Radu,' said Syrie. 'Focus on the now. It doesn't matter whether you've Dracula's sanction or not – it's better for you if you haven't – it matters that you do what you came here to.'

Radu was torn.

If he wasn't Dracula's catspaw, whose was he?

Richard knew from his lack of bragging that someone – someone he thought was his brother – was working his strings.

Syrie was frustrated again.

She had a plan too. A thwarted plan. All this byplay got between her and Christina and her own ideas about putting a stop to the Ascension.

'You know what you are, don't you?' Richard said.

'What, pray?' Radu answered.

'A diversion. We waste time while the Princess makes her move. Did you ever think she might have hired you herself? Every party needs clowns.'

'You're not amusing any more,' Radu said. 'Perhaps you'll be funnier in pieces.'

Cottonmouth's knives came out.

Mr Omochi stood up suddenly, sticking himself onto Cottonmouth's silvered steel, letting her blades slide in under his cummerbund. He gripped her shoulders, eyes watering with pain, and lurched sideways in improvised *seppuku*, disembowelling himself. He barely grunted as he died with honour, weight toppling onto the vampire merc. Honour smelled like the contents of bowels on the floor.

The CEO's vampire wife Rose flew across the room. She pulled needle-tipped combs from her hair and made for the struggling Cottonmouth. The Butler flung a black shuriken, engraved with a glowing sigil, at her forehead. When struck, Madame Omochi was thrown backwards. She turned to red dust inside her *jūnihitoe.* The garment drifted to the floor in a wrinkled clump, comb-claws clattering.

Cottonmouth shrugged off the gut-trailing corpse. The mess on her jump-suit annoyed her. She was close to off the leash. Eager to kill properly.

Richard stood in front of Chesse and Syrie.

'Very gallant,' said Cottonmouth. 'A warm old man protecting two vampire women. You realise that's ridiculous, don't you?'

'Now you come to mention it,' he began... but didn't shift.

NEZUMI

Nezumi saw why nothing kept Anthony Peak out – or in. He could turn into a shadow on one wall, which then became a doorway in another wall. He had to be portal as well as wraith to transport his loot as well as himself.

He could only jaunt short distances. From outside buildings to vaults. Here, he could manage only a dozen or so floors. Each trip exhausted him. That was why he was under a desk in the Security Suite after sliding out of trouble in the Dragon's Mouth. Even without a jewel in his mouth, he could barely speak.

Representing Light Industries, Molinar signed a waiver indemnifying the cracksman from prosecution for his activities this evening if he helped them.

'What?' he said, looking at Nezumi.

She was sad. Not at the state of the world, but the state of Anthony Peak.

'It's disappointing,' she said. 'You have a gift, but all you do with it is take things that don't belong to you.'

'Karl Marx said "property is theft",' he quoted.

'Mr Marx took it as read that theft was theft too. I don't think he'd have liked you.'

'Everyone likes me,' said the thief, smiling. 'It's my raffish charm.'

'Some people think you're funny,' said Nezumi. 'That's not the same.'

'Being funny wouldn't stop the same people killing you,' said Molinar.

'I've escaped the firing squad, you know. Guess how? It's a mistake to put me *up against a wall*.'

'Now you're boasting,' said Nezumi. 'You've been bottling it, keeping your secret. You want to convince us you're a fine fellow and regale us with exciting stories of scrapes you've got out of.'

Peak slumped even more. He was seen through.

'How long does it take him to recharge?' asked Verlaine.

Nezumi stuck the end of her sword into the crook's foot.

'Not long or he wouldn't be shamming.'

Everyone checked weapons. Watson slapped his perforated cheeks to get red in them to match his jacket. Kuchisake played with her shears.

'Hold on,' said Hal. 'You can teleport, right? For real?'

'I don't call it that,' said Peak. 'It sounds common. I call it *being slippery*.'

'Cool, though,' said the boy. 'Beam me up, Peaky.'

'*Nerd*,' coughed Verlaine under her hand.

Peak was 'recharged', Nezumi decided. She gripped his arm, swordpoint to the back of his neck, and whispered, 'Don't get slippery with me.' She marched him towards a wall.

'If we don't get where we need to go, Mr Molinar will shoot you. There are ways to kill shadows. You could be whited out. They make silver paint.'

'If you're twits enough to want to jump into a monster's mouth, I'll not stop you.'

'Thank you, Mr Peak,' she said. 'I know you'll slip away as soon as you can. I would ask you please to think about what I've said. Be better than you are. Not because you're afraid we'll survive and hunt you down, but because you'll be less sad.'

'I'm not sad,' he insisted.

Kuchisake laughed at him. If she asked him whether he thought she was pretty, he'd be in trouble.

He flattened against the wall, turning to an ink-black outline. His face darkened and froze.

Nezumi put her sword to the isthmus of the shadow-stain where his neck had been.

'Ready?' she asked.

Molinar gave her the nod.

'Steady?'

A quick look around at the rest of the krewe. All present and determined.

'Geronimo,' she said.

RICHARD JEPERSON

'**D**id or did I not command this fellow be killed?' said Radu.

Cottonmouth stepped forward, a firmer grip on her bloodied blades.

Richard expected she'd cut through him.

Neither Syrie nor Chesse were in a position to fight Cottonmouth, and he wouldn't expect it of them.

'I'll enjoy this, old fellow,' said Cottonmouth.

She showed proper fangs – inappropriately sexy, he thought.

Out of the corner of his eye, Richard noticed a man-shadow.

Passing for graffiti, or an oily water-stain on white plaster. He looked like a leotard stuck to the wall using an iron-on transfer.

In a room of living umbrellas and monster tattoos, the shadowman was almost dull.

But he did something unexpected. He widened as if puffing up his chest. White eyes opened in his coal-dust face. A rift appeared, as if his pullover split down the front. Light spilled through the tear.

A blade poked out and slashed down, cutting through a curtain of darkness.

Another face – not shadowed – stuck through.

Richard whistled.

Nezumi had come back to the party with Good Night Kiss.

NEZUMI

Passing through Anthony Peak's shadow-self – from Mr Molinar's office to the ballroom eight floors above – was like walking through an ice shower. So cold that even she, the get of Yuki-Onna, could feel it.

A flash of blinding purple!

Peak could have told her to shut her eyes but she wouldn't have taken advice from him.

Between his doors stretched an infinity.

People could get stranded here, wherever *here* was – with its violet sky, mauve plains and spiral ruins.

She was up to her ankles in blood-tinted snow.

A woman stood nearby, watching. A woman with long dark hair. A face of frost and lips red as ripe cherries. Infinitely cold, and infinitely sorrowful and yet proud, with a glint in her ice heart, a single kind feeling amid an arctic desolation.

In this slippage between planes, Yuki-Onna watched over her. If Nezumi stepped off the path, they could talk. There was so much she didn't know about herself.

But she must not be distracted. Duty before self.

She cut a slit in the curtain and stepped through.

Into the Dragon's Mouth.

She was bereft, heart-stabbed by Peak's shadow world, but resolute. Good Night Kiss was steady.

'Hello, Mouse,' said Cottonmouth. 'I'm just killing your sugar daddy.'

Blood was smeared on her knives. A dead fat man lay at her feet.

Mr Jeperson stood, empty-handed, arms spread. He'd tried charm and it hadn't worked.

Nezumi's fangs sharpened.

'Remember the Captain and Tennille?' said Cottonmouth.

Nezumi wouldn't be drawn into a conversation.

'Your loss,' said Cottonmouth.

In a lightning move, she holstered her blades and drew her guns – Simon Smith and Amazing Dancing Bear. She began firing, elbows stiff, aim careless.

Nezumi cartwheeled away from the portal, awkwardly since one fist had to hang on to the sword. She drew Cottonmouth's fire so Mr Molinar and the others wouldn't be cut down as they came through. Firing two automatic weapons at the same time was showy rather than accurate. Guests scattered out of the way. Some weren't quick enough.

On her knees, Nezumi slid across the polished dance floor, under Cottonmouth's fire, Good Night Kiss held above her bent-back head. Bullets whooshed over her.

The *katana* – personally honed by the Grand Master of Great Sharpness – sliced cleanly through Cottonmouth's right wrist and only got stuck in the bones of her left hand because the pistol stock was in the way.

Nezumi angled herself to one side to avoid the gout of vampire blood.

Cottonmouth's hand, still gripping enough to fire the gun, flopped on the floor and spun like a rogue Catherine wheel. A pallbearer's foot exploded as silver dum-dums caught him in the shoe.

Nezumi rose like a crane taking flight.

With a sawing move, she extracted her sword, incidentally slamming her elbow into Cottonmouth's face.

She stood back, sword pointed down.

Cottonmouth tried to level Simon Smith and get a firing grip with her remaining fingers. Her nearly cut-through hand flopped the wrong way. She dropped the gun and licked her own blood. She striped her face. Her freckles stood out like sniperlights.

She had no hands to hold her knives, but a sharply broken bone jutted from her left wrist. She stabbed at Nezumi's throat like a con going for a prison yard rival with a shop room shank.

Sad again – she knew they would never be friends, but liked the woman – Nezumi made a killing pass. A breakfest-egg cut. The top of Cottonmouth's skull sheared above her eyes. Silver passed through her brain.

O-Ren Blake. That had been her name.

RICHARD JEPERSON

While Nezumi fought Cottonmouth, others came through the strange door.

Two professional guns – a man and a woman, well-tailored book-ends – took firing stances and began popping pallbearers' masks.

A vampire squaddie with fixed bayonet and a Japanese Lady Struwwelpeter with scissors set about scaring the wits out of people they were rescuing.

A warm Asian man with a cyber-gauntlet scrabbled for cover. His gadget lit up like a toy raygun.

Madame Omochi's abandoned formal dress gathered shape and stood, assuming a fighting stance.

Golgotha ordered return of fire.

The Butler and Panty-Mask, his men on the spot, were harder to target than the white-masks. They dodged behind guests, shooting from cover. Richard didn't assume none of the people with Nezumi were as scrupulous as she about not hurting innocent bystanders.

Radu was out of the loop.

With Cottonmouth occupied (then, very quickly, dead) and the Butler yanked off threatening-hostages duties, no one was obliged to stay where Radu put them.

Chesse dragged her hypnotised waiter into a corner. Her fangs were splitting her gums and her eyes were crimson. She had to slake her red thirst before she could think.

That was why untrained vampires were often useless. They got distracted, unless well-fed.

Richard tried to stand up but his foot had gone to sleep, and – embarrassingly – Syrie now had to help him.

'You got *old*,' she said. 'You know that's curable?'

This wasn't the time for that argument.

On screens, red numbers counted down.

… 32.33. 32.32. 32.31…

Nearly half past eleven, in old money.

The slit in the shadow closed. The silhouette bulged like a balloon filling with water and slid off the wall – which was smudged but unbreached – then swelled out to become a huddled person.

'Is that Anthony Peak?' asked Syrie.

Peak's face was so white Christina might have been at him.

He had done something that had taken almost everything out of him. This was how he filched the Blue Water pendant from the Nemo Collection and Munch's *Lady of the Shroud* from its frame in the Oslo National Gallery. How he got out of the Mausoleum and Camp Cube, the most secure special prisons in Great Britain and Canada. Unbreachable and inescapable meant nothing to him.

'You, Peak.' Syrie shouted. 'Where is it?'

Even drained and used up, he knew enough to be terrified. His fangs chattered.

Syrie strode – ignoring crossfire – towards the shrinking tea-leaf.

Then the floor shifted. Richard's first thought was an earthquake. It would be sod's law for Japan to sink at the crack of the New Millennium. Christina's shining image revolved like a vertical crankshaft. Screens carrying the Light Channel brightened by about a thousand candles, gridding the ballroom with laser-like beams that bounced off mirror surfaces.

Connections were made. Information packets shot from system to system. Below, in the belly of the Daikaiju Building, huge wheels engaged, turbines revved. Something as big as a real dragon stirred, infused with Light and Life. Richard's watch alarm went off, slaved to a greater gadget.

It wasn't even midnight.

The Princess was getting started early.

'Peak,' Syrie was still shouting, fixated on her property rights even as the world blew up around her.

Nezumi was back in her chosen spot by Richard, Good Night Kiss drawn (she'd lost the poster tube somewhere), protecting her principal. She'd cleaned her sword on Mr Rapist Man's jacket.

'Radu's not the real problem,' he told her.

The Bey was among the crowd, showing his famous aptitude for avoiding battle.

Richard saw him back towards the pig-pens. Angry little cherubs clutched cutlery in fat little fists. If he strayed too near, they'd have him.

'It's the Princess. She's…'

Then it struck him that he didn't know what Christina Light was doing or had become.

Just that now it was *her* wicked plan. And thwarting it was SOP.

Nezumi nodded, understanding.

SI MOLINAR

Nezumi had briefed them. The vampires in white masks had to die. And Golgotha's EarthGuard ops.

Plus an unknown number of other hostiles.

And Dracula's brother, identifiable by the ridiculous width of his suit.

Many bystanders were in peril. In theory, they should be protected. They weren't a priority. They didn't pay his wages, command his loyalty, or own his heart.

He didn't tell the little elder that.

He admired her attitude, but didn't share it.

She wanted to save everyone. He had no problem with that, if it was what she wanted and didn't get in his way.

He was here to save one person.

The Fairy Princess was present in the room as a beacon, the bulb in the lighthouse. Not her, but an aspect of her.

The floor yawed and he skidded.

Verlaine was off balance too, but still shooting accurately.

Someone fell – or jumped in panic – over the guard-rail.

Unhelpful shrieks and screams. Dracula's brother staggered, golden lads clutching his arms and legs, winding their chains around him. He shrieked at their touch. The catering staff said the high-priced donors were nasty, nippy little bastards.

The Daikaiju Building was quake-proof – so all the architects and engineers swore. But anything that could be put up could be brought down.

He'd heard no explosions, but Jun Zero could have laid soundless concussion blast devices. Charges in the foundations, set off by remote signal. Automated O'Blivion.

The Dragon trembled, maybe on the point of falling.

His priority was to get the Princess out safely. Peak would recharge in minutes, and Molinar could secure 'Mr Portal' as a private escape route for essential personnel, defined as her and him – and maybe Verlaine to cover their backs.

Nezumi could save people. He wouldn't stop her.

Hal – a man he couldn't help think of as a boy – was under a table, thick arm over his head to protect him from masonry that wasn't falling yet.

A few of the most formidable hostiles – not least, Colonel Golgotha – were still alive. They shouldn't be forgotten.

Another huge lurch and the floor yawed. People sledged across the polished wood on their bottoms.

A demented little girl in a sailor suit whizzed by, smiling with too many fangs, hair-ribbons streaming.

'Helter skelter,' she shouted, clapping her hands.

Delighted by the ride, she wanted to do it again.

Tsunako Shiki – a permanent fixture on the Nuisance List.

A nearby screen shone too-bright white. Red numbers flashed.

… 28.05. 28.04. 28.03…

A face broke through the dazzle, long nose poking the digital timer.

Dr Pretorius.

Doubtless delivering his great, 'I told you so.'

It'd not surprise Molinar if the Mad Gnome were in on it with Jun Zero. Hell, he might *be* Jun Zero.

'She's alive,' he boomed, electricity crackling in his static-infused bird's nest hairdo. 'She's *alive!*'

DR AKIBA

'Doc,' said Derek, with awe, 'I wish you weren't blinded because you should see what I see. It's… ah, incredible. Colossal. As in a proper colossus. It could stand with one foot on either side of the harbour.'

Akiba felt the giant moving – displacing air, cracking paving stones.

Hunter and Killer stopped shooting.

Tengu and *kappa* left off fighting over scraps and looked up to the sky.

Concrete was crushed at each footfall. Girders bent without breaking. The *weight* of the thing.

'It's taking its first steps,' said Derek. 'It has feet. Its eyes – one red, one whitish blue – have fired up. Light beams are spilling out of its mouth. So are, ah, people.'

Akiba tasted death and blood.

'Platforms are coming out of its, ah, you'd have to say *shoulders*… I think they're ruddy gun turrets. That's a walking war tower. A robot a hundred stories high. Christ on a pogo stick, but it's a beaut! Why can't we have a Mecha-Smaug! EarthGuard ought to be first on the list for a HQ that can come over to your place and flatten it.'

It's not a robot, Akiba thought – words resounding in Derek's mind.

It was more like a powered suit. Something *alive* was in it.

'Blokes with face-paint are on their knees, waving their hands, bowing. I reckon that's the birth of a new religion – or an oldie making a comeback. Other people are running away. The Gate's still shut so there's not any place to run. Course, if the big fellah wants to, it could boot the wall to bits. Or step over it and trample Tokyo. We couldn't stop it. D'you reckon we should give Gokemidoro a ring? Better still, Kuran. EarthGuard will know about it by now. All they have to do is look out the window. But we could let them know some of us in the field are still with the programme, eh?'

Sensing a puff of malice, Akiba pulled Derek to him, out of a bullet's way. They hunkered behind an overturned hearse. The car alarm went off. Even without ears, that shrill went straight through him.

'Whoa, thanks mate. That bastard Killer's started up again! Taking pot shots.'

Derek was annoyed now.

'I know it's you, Hairdo Kid! You and your chummie Hunter the Munter. You're a disgrace to EarthGuard, know that? You're off my pub quiz team!'

A building coming to life was only worth ten seconds amazement.

The boy with an incorporeal malign entity – dammit, a demon! – on his back had to kill again now.

Hunter shot at the tiles around the hearse. He kept them in place while Killer scurried around to get a surer vantage point. A firing position.

Akiba's blank face shivered.

'Uh-oh,' said Derek.

A cold, heavy shadow passed over the hearse.

Akiba felt the rush of sour air. And the *impact*. The hearse jumped three feet in the air and crashed down again. Its windows burst. The alarm died.

The shooting stopped.

'Stone me, it's only gone and stamped the bastards flat! Result!'

Akiba felt Hunter and Killer being snuffed. Killer's untethered demon flew here and there, seeking a new host. It flew off, a kite in a hurricane.

Good riddance. Though it would latch on to some fool by morning.

There were always killers. As there were always healers.

'Now it's standing there,' said Derek, 'off its foundations, but not grinding us all into the mud. I don't know what we're gonna call it… Big Bertha?'

Daikaiju.

'Yeah, good shout. Daikaiju. Hey, Akiba, you can… *talk*? Telesend. We had a seminar on that, remember? Tapping your ESPQ. Not sure it makes up for having a no-face. Can you set fire to things with your mind? Because that I would like to see. Oh, and – ooh, ooh – what about aquakinesis, sculpting with water? Fun for the kiddies.'

Being so close to the Daikaiju was a strain.

Akiba's new senses – capacities, feelings, biological and psychic processes – were stretched. The stone and metal giant exerted the gravitational pull of a Black Hole.

It wasn't just a living thing. It was a *personality*.

An underground gas line ignited, sending a fence of flame across the Plaza.

Vents on the Daikaiju's flanks gushed foam, stanching the fire before the Bund went up. The mimes hollered an 'alleluya'.

The giant protected its territory.

NEZUMI

The Bad Penny was in the room.

Nezumi checked Hal, who was huddled with a Japanese v-girl and a passed-out warm man with throat-bites. The gothic lolita wiped her mouth, not ready to feed again.

Tsunako Shiki danced on the tilting floor. She pirouetted like a spinning top, keeping her balance as people and objects – bottles, guns, handbags – slid past her. She was loving this.

So far as Nezumi could tell, it was not an earthquake.

The building moved because it was made that way.

Mr Peak was still here. Slipperiness wore him out.

When Nezumi saw the Woman of the Snows between portals, an ice harpoon stuck into Anthony Peak. Yuki-Onna was drawn from that purple snow plain by Nezumi passing through. He was freezing from his insides out.

It was no more than he deserved – but it was her fault.

She was too hard on him. He had helped – reluctantly – and was paying for it.

She didn't know if Yuki-Onna was her real mother or progenitor of her bloodline or a household deity for frost vampires, but there was a connection. She must persuade the Snow Queen to let the poor thief go.

Another harpy descended on Mr Peak.

Mrs Van Epp gripped his tailcoat lapels and shouted in his face. Nezumi could guess which bone she had to pick.

From her blazer pocket Nezumi took the ruby Mr Peak had spat out.
It wasn't just a jewel, but a lens. An electric component.

She held it in front of Mrs Van Epp's eyes. Its glow reddened her face.
She calmed down.

Without thanking her − or apologising to Mr Peak − Mrs Van Epp
snatched the ruby and fit it back into her tiara. She twisted it like a knob.
The coronet shapeshifted, lowering arms that formed an earpiece and a
throat microphone.

Mrs Van Epp's tiara was a telephone!

'Persian Kitty to Platform One,' she said. 'Code Magenta, Code
Magenta. Deploy the Black Manta.'

Her piece said, Mrs Van Epp took off her headset and sat down.

'We're done,' she said. 'We don't get home.'

WINGMAN PAUL METCALF

The klaxon whooped throughout Platform One.
Wings Over the World's doughnut-shaped, high-atmosphere base
was radar-invisible, beyond the ken (and the gunsights) of any nation.
Personnel were recruited from around the globe, but owed allegiance
only to the Council of Directors. Air was so thin and temperature so low
at this altitude only vees could serve on the station. Tasked with waiting
for the worst.

In a good year, the klaxon never sounded except for Operational
Readiness Inspections.

1999 had been twenty minutes away from being a good year.

Metcalf sat in his unlit cabin, as he did every duty shift. In his flight-suit.
Gear ready and at hand. Not watching telly, reading, listening to music.
Not even meditating. Just waiting. Wing Navigator Hayata joked about his
monastic inclination. Metcalf knew no other way to conduct himself in
this afterlife.

His duty was serious.

He was new-born vee. Ex-SAS, killed in the Falklands. Turned by a jolt of Lady Syrie's blood. Many Wingmen were her get, though she spent little time with them. Once her pick was made, Dr Devilers took over with syringes, pumps and tubes.

Lady Syrie paid for the toys. She had her say about WOtW policy.

She was one of perhaps six people in the world with the authority to call a Code Magenta.

So far as Metcalf was concerned, he was the walking dead.

He wasn't even Paul Metcalf, not physically anyway. He was a brain pattern in a renewed body. Kept alive by regular transfusions. Wingmen didn't drink in the conventional manner. It was all done in Devilers's clinic. The vees of Platform One fed without a drop of blood touching fangs. Except Drusilla Zark, who licked clot lollies she made in moulds in her personal freezer cabinet.

Metcalf met Hayata in the corridor as they scrambled.

The Wing Navigator wriggled into his silver flight-suit on the run. His bulky, finned helmet under his arm. Metcalf helped him get his gear together.

Hayata didn't joke now.

They rounded the curve of the corridor.

Support Seraphs were ready at the chutes to help them into the control module of the Black Manta. They were more ashen-faced than usual. Harmony wore a party hat and had a dribble of blood at the corner of her mouth. She'd be rebuked when team leader Fatality's report crossed Wing Commander Baxter's desk.

Metcalf crossed his arms over his chest as he slid down into his seat, and lifted them to allow the belts to auto-fasten. His screen was live and special equipment was stowed and ready for use. The control module had that new car smell. A perpetual motion bird by his console dipped to drink.

The Manta wasn't a firefighting vehicle. The skycraft's designated function was 'brush-clearing'. Stopping armies in their tracks. Scaring off predators, vampire or otherwise. And exfil before photojournos could get snaps. Then the Silver Sentinel, the EvangeLions and Rocket Rescue could get busy shoring up dams, securing safe water sources and saving refugees.

Wings Over the World was a reassuring organisation.

The Manta was not designed to reassure.

Metcalf fit in his earpiece. Eulogy Seraph ran through the list.

Wing Captain Gardner was already in the module, responding to the readiness checks. He'd been with WOtW since it started. A WWII retread, graduate of the US Bat Soldier Programme. A clean-cut vee.

Drusilla had her gloomy corner, decorated with postcards of Victorian music hall artistes. The seeress showed up one day and was put on the crew. No one asked what use she was supposed to be. She missed every ORI but earned full marks while Metcalf and Hayata were penalised for misaligned buttons and quarter-second delays. Now it wasn't an exercise, she was in post before they were. She hum-sung something about a mer-my-id.

'You're going home, Hayata,' said Gardner.

'So I see. Course plotted for Tokyo – no, not Tokyo, the Bund.'

Hayata looked around. His helmet covered the top half of his face and gave him huge multi-faceted eyes.

Metcalf checked his screen. A TV news feed. The camera struggled to keep focus as it angled up and up over craggy hide, then zoomed on a stone-and-metal mask of a face, with burning red and white spotlight eyes. An excited commentary in Japanese chattered. Metcalf caught a few words:

'… *doragon… mecha-monstrum… Daikaiju.*'

'What *is* that?' Hayata said.

'Not a natural thing,' said Metcalf.

'The Princess's new clothes,' breathed Drusilla. 'I said it would come to this. The School Mouse had better have brought her Girl Guide knife.'

A way to stay sane was to tune out everything the seeress said.

Stats came through – height, weight, location.

'It *was* a building,' he reported. 'It *is* a vehicle.'

'Autonomous?' asked Gardner.

'Piloted.'

'So are we,' deadpanned the Wing Captain. 'Team ready? Run the check, Eulogy.'

'Scarlet,' said the Seraph.

'Check,' responded Metcalf.

'Ultra.'

'Check,' said Hayata.

'Zark.'

'Red rabbits, yellow rabbits,' said Drusilla.

'America.'

'Check,' said Gardner. 'Module engaged. Black Manta ready.'

'Godspeed,' said Eulogy, diverging from her script.

The Seraphs had emotions. Devilers never quite eliminated them.

'This is Wing Commander Baxter,' came a mild, amplified voice. 'Fly with the wings of a hawk, strike with the talons of an eagle.'

'Crash with the grace of a hippo,' muttered Hayata.

'A-OK, Sky High,' said Gardner. 'Wings Away!'

The clamps released and the Manta was free of Platform One. Triangular wings slid out of the teardrop fuselage as it fell for long seconds. Wind shrilled over knife-edge planes. Struts stiffened and locked.

Metcalf counted off the altitude in hundreds.

The wings were deployed when they left the troposphere for the stratosphere.

'Firing,' said Metcalf, throwing switches.

The rocket engines blasted.

… and the Black Manta flew.

RICHARD JEPERSON

'You've *what*?' Richard said.

'Called in an air strike,' Syrie admitted.

Even Radu was affronted. His baggy jacket and trousers were in shreds, showing burnished armour underneath. He wore stack heels too. Mediaeval princes were seldom known for their height.

'Is this some Aum Draht thing?' Richard asked Syrie. 'Like the fungus attack?'

'I am *not* Aum Draht. I was undercover. I'm a secret agent, remember? Like you.'

'Bloody conspicuous for covert work.'

'Pot kettle... black velvet pantaloons. Everybody knows you're the Man From the Diogenes Club. Even Hamish Bond is more discreet about being a spy than you are. And he leaves burned-out bases, drained bodies and pissed-off women everywhere he goes.'

'What did you learn in your computer game cult? How to crack the top level of Donkey Kong? That didn't stop them throwing in with Dracula Minor here.'

Radu spat at the reference.

'The Wire was paid to raise an alarm to get Golgotha through the Gate,' he said. 'I have no interest in what the fools believe. It's all pernicious nonsense. Jun Zero turns adepts into suicide bombers and auctions them off to anyone with cash. It's never about a cause.'

'Jun Zero?' said Richard.

Hal – the warm man Nezumi brought through the Peak portal – looked sick. He wiped his mouth with his flesh hand.

'Yes, Jun Zero,' said Syrie. 'He's the Wire. Didn't *British Intelligence* know that?'

'Did you hire him or did he hire you?' Hal asked Radu.

Richard, Syrie and Radu looked at the warm man.

'It speaks,' said Syrie, through fangs.

Nezumi shifted her sword-grip. Protective of her new pet.

Hal stammered 'Ah, I... it seems to me that if you don't know whether your, eh, brother put you up to this, it could as easily have been this, ah, Jun Zero.'

The Bey shut up. He didn't want to say that his brother – or the message purporting to be from his brother – also put him in contact with Jun Zero. Which obviously it had. One hand batting him to the other.

It would make sense.

If Jun Zero was the Wire – which needed serious confirmation before it could be sent up to Whitehall – Aum Draht wasn't a diversion for Radu. It was the other way round. This whole mess was to stop anyone looking for Zeroids in the room.

Jun Zero wasn't even their top problem. That would still be Christina Light.

The Dragon's Mouth wasn't lurching any more. The Princess had more control of the building she was wearing.

Once she'd melded with the Tower of London. That couldn't get up and walk.

Now it was her own gaff and she'd prepared. She wasn't going to be caught twice.

This was so much more impressive than turning into a man-eating lift.

'There has to be a way to get through to the woman,' he said.

'And what?' said Syrie. 'Ask her nicely. Stamp your foot? Radu tried that. You saw what happened.'

Everyone kept well away from the hologram.

What Christina had done was astonishing and she'd hardly started. At the moment, she was only in every fibre-optic cable and circuit board of the Daikaiju Building. Come the Ascension – in ten minutes' time – she'd permeate the world. The human race – vampire and warm and whatever other variety evolved – would be ticks on her hide. Ticks were vampires too. Bloodsuckers.

'Do you *want* to stop her?' Richard asked.

'Of course,' Syrie responded, hotly.

'Only you're one for secret masters and guiding history from the shadows. Hence your "charity work" with Wings Over the World. Isn't she cutting through all the red tape and sorting everything out?'

'You forget – she's mad!'

Molinar, a Casamassima loyalist, gasped at the blasphemy but didn't argue the point. Even folk who'd stuck by Christina Light for a hundred years must be given pause by this evening's entertainment. The Light Channel didn't seem so soothing any more.

Nezumi spoke up, 'Downstairs, she has all the rooms she's ever lived in – or had things happen to her in. There's enough in that corridor to send anyone crackers.'

'Two votes against,' said Richard. 'You, New Boy, raise a flipper if you prefer dying in a friendly fire incident than living into the Age of Light.'

Hal was completely out of his depth, but his arm jerked up.

'I didn't do that,' he said, struggling to hold his arm down – then pulling his fingers away as if he'd got a static electric shock.

'Options to shut down the Ascension exist,' said the machine.

'Your arm talks,' said Richard, fascinated. 'I'm sorry, that was a dreadfully silly thing to say. You must know that already.'

'Tell me about it,' said Hal.

'You'd have to be in a room with her, not a hologram,' said Syrie. 'This is just a big version of that welcome-to-my-party feature in the lift.'

She was perfectly happy to talk with a robot prosthesis. Admirable, really.

'Affirmative.'

'Do you know how to get there, Lefty?' asked Hal.

'A portal is open.'

Anthony Peak was curled in a foetal ball, fangs chattering, black coat furred with white rime.

'Peak's spent,' said Richard.

'He is not the portal. Christina Light is the portal.'

The hologram still stood in its column of light.

'Princess Portal,' said Nezumi.

'Affirmative. Enter the image and be drawn up.'

'After what happened to the fellow with the tattoos?' exclaimed Richard. 'I should cocoa.'

'Destruction is not assured,' said Lefty. 'The portal is open, with certain restrictions.'

'She's somewhere near?' asked Radu. 'Her body.'

'Affirmative.'

'Wired into the building?'

'Affirmative.'

The elder unclipped a short silver scimitar from his armour. A hold-out blade.

'I'll kill her,' he said. 'And seize this castle for my own.'

He'd gone from '80s action movie to *Black Shield of Falworth*. Many vampires were like that. Especially of the Dracula bloodline. Just playing roles. If they stopped and thought about it, they froze up like Anthony Peak. Van Helsing diagnosed the Count with a case of 'child-brain' syndrome.

Richard didn't think the Bey's sudden daring sounded like a healthy development, but Syrie held him back. He was a warm man and Radu a vampire. He looked to Nezumi, but didn't want to waste her effort. She had a child-brain too, but it gave her clarity. She didn't cling to toys or want to be listened to or feel she was overlooked.

She was brave and good.

Murdleigh the minion got between Nezumi and the Bey.

'Dracula… am I…' said Radu, trying to convince himself.

He strode over to the hologram. The transparent head turned and the Princess smiled down as Dracula's Brother stepped into her light.

Richard was temporarily blinded by ball lightning.

Everyone yelped or screeched. Several languages were sworn in.

When the flares stopped dancing in his vision, Richard looked again.

Radu was a pillar of white salt. He held his shape well enough for the surprise on his face to be readable. Then he crumbled, and spilled out of the light.

Murdleigh snickered behind his mask. He, at least, had got his secret wish.

Syrie kicked the dog-like renfield, who scurried away.

'L-Lefty, you wanted that to happen to us?' accused Hal.

Richard saw no reason to trust a talking arm.

'The suggested course of action was not appropriate for non-user Radu cel Frumos,' said the machine. 'His profile was not a match. He was… self-interested, cruel, petty, manipulative, dishonest, negative, trivial, lax, immoral, *evil*.'

That adjective string sounded like a glitch.

'Machines aren't supposed to make value judgements,' said Richard.

'You can tell Lefty isn't happy about it,' said Hal. 'He's trying to be exact about something inexact.'

'I'll go,' said Syrie, walking towards the light.

Now Richard held her back.

'Uh uh,' he said. 'That's suicide.'

'Are you telling me I'm evil?' she smiled.

'I'm not sure there is such a thing, but Christina is – and she gets to define what she means when she zaps you for not passing her test. This is her, remember? It's a given she thinks of herself as good, moral, above it all. She even thinks she's selfless. She'd define you as none of those things, not because you are but because you're anti-her. She may well be monumentally deluded, but that doesn't mean she's not unimaginably powerful. Her portal – another Light Channel – is guarded the way the Gate is by Hyakume. She looks into brains – and, probably, hearts, and makes a decision whether you can join her in the pool or not.'

'The Black Manta will be here soon,' said Syrie. 'Then this will all be academic.'

'And we'll be dead, thank you very much,' he told her.

Without Radu to strut and give orders, Colonel Golgotha was off the clock. The EarthGuard turncloak wasn't among the company remaining in the Dragon's Mouth. Many guests had risked the exits. Radu's remaining mercs among them. Tsunako Shiki was still here, playing with a golden lad who was shackled and glumly unable to scarper. Against stiff competition, she'd take the Maddest Person in the Room award.

The EarthGit Panty-Mask was backing towards the lifts. He raised his gun, intending to cover his retreat by spraying the room with gunfire. A complication no one needed.

Madame Omochi's *jūnihitoe* floated towards Panty-Mask. He turned and shot at its chest. Unseen jaws clamped his neck and four fang-holes were torn open. That ridiculous mask was torn away and Richard saw why he'd worn it. The man had a face like a slapped arse. Panty-Mask dropped his gun. A mouth cavity and throat were outlined in the air, drawn in blood. Scarlet tonsils bobbled. Veins and capillaries appeared, then a diagram of a whole woman. The formal clothes, puppeteered not worn, collapsed.

Another of the building's security staff hard at work ten minutes to midnight.

HAROLD TAKAHAMA

He only now wondered whether Lefty was carrying him rather than the other way round. All of a sudden, it knew much more than he did.

So far as he could tell:

The building was a Gargantuabot.

At the controls was a Princess with the long sad story – as told in many rooms of misery. She needed to be talked to. If not stabbed through the heart.

But only the worthy – as she defined them – could pass up the shining spiral stairs.

Dracula's late brother was unworthy. In their brief acquaintance, Hal could tell as much.

Though he didn't want to mention that this Radu the Handsome had hired him. In his former person – future person? – as Jun Zero.

The grown-ups were too busy to ask who he was. As a stray, he was protected by Nezumi. That said a lot for her.

So she was worthy. Who else?

The Chic Vampire Lady was not a strong candidate. Even the dandy British dude, disposed to be charitable (or romantic), thought she'd be dusted if she stepped into the flame.

'Don't look at me,' said Molinar. 'I was a conquistador. I have done heinous shit. Our Fairy Princess can only be good because bad people back her up. We're them. At least, we were.'

Verlaine was tired and relieved. The smilers went around telling hostages they were saved. They weren't quelling panic. With their faces, they couldn't help but alarm people.

Tsunako Shiki was still around. Hard to believe she'd dropped out of his Top Ten Things That Might Kill Harold list.

The projected 3D image of the Princess had become a column of radiant light, with the faintest trace of a face and the lines of a robe. It hurt to look at. Blue and red threads wound inside like a DNA helix.

'She's not in my head any more,' said Molinar. 'It's been *years*.'

A phantom nude – formed by blood-drops – walked away from her meal, vanishing with each step as she digested blood. She picked up the kimono she'd played with and put it on. She didn't mind bullet holes.

'I like clothes,' said Suzan Arashi. 'Why wouldn't I wear them?'

Screens still showed a countdown.

… 23.51 … Nine minutes.

The CVL had sounded an alarm.

Someone's air force was on the way with G-buster weaponry out the wazoo.

They were all doomed, with an extra slice of getting fucked on top.

Lefty still offered options.

Radu proved stepping into the light with murderous intent was a sure way to go kaboom. So it was a question of trying to reason with the Ascending Woman.

No one volunteered, not because they were afraid to be flash-fried minutes before they would be blown up but because no one was big-headed enough to claim they were innocent (or worthy) enough to pass.

Jun Zero scored low on the worthiness scale so Hal ruled himself out of the running.

'You two,' he said. 'Nezumi and Mr Jeperson. It has to be you. I've seen what you're like.'

'Being insufferable might not be disqualification,' the CVL said, sharply.

There wasn't time to protest.

'Likelihood of successful passage ninet—'

'Mute, Lefty.'

'It was going to say "nineteen",' said Kuchisake, voice a wobble as if her tongue were slit like her cheeks.

'Ninety-nine,' Hal corrected her. 'Point nine, probably.'

Richard and Nezumi were already decided. Pure of heart.

Nezumi gave Suzan Good Night Kiss and asked her to look after it.

'User Harold Takahama is also required,' said Lefty, giving him a little shock.

'But I'm *awful*,' he blurted. 'Ask my Dad. And Cousin Helen.'

'Knowledge of computer systems essential,' prompted Lefty.

Hal knew it. His hand wanted to kill him.

Though the slyboots had covered up his true identity. If he'd tagged Hal as 'user Jun Zero', Molinar would want to cut him on the spot.

Nezumi protected him with her silence. She took him for the reasonable Hal he was now rather than the awful person he'd been before Karl the Chiropterid sucked the worst of Jun Zero out of his brain.

'You don't have to come, Hal,' said Nezumi's boss.

But, of course, he did.

The three of them stepped into the light.

DETECTIVE AZUMA

Every window had a light behind it. The mechanical monster's hide was speckled with a thousand glints.

The eyes shone with life.

A tail that had been the lower end of an elevator shaft swept over the heads of people in the Plaza. The Daikaiju Building turned and looked out to sea.

Something was out there, high up – swooping through cloud. Something with a wingspan. And eyelights of its own.

One of the EarthGuard men stood by the hearse, with a *noppera-bō*. He looked up, glasses gleaming.

That guy was a likely perp. Azuma raised his gun.

Asato laid a hand on his sleeve. She had a way of seeing into souls.

'He's not one of them,' she said. 'Nor is his friend. The faceless one.'

The pair – Derek and Dr Something, he remembered – hadn't been with Golgotha in the torture shed. They might not be part of the attack. The doctor had changed a lot in the last few hours.

Azuma no longer knew who was attacking whom and where he stood.

Asato, admirably, was focused.

She still had killers to kill.

'Look,' she said, 'there, by the Sprünt stand. The commander… and Fujiwara.' Golgotha had made it out of the Daikaiju. He had a lock-box and a machine gun.

Mitsuru Fujiwara, the inside man, crouched by him.

Their plan must have gone tits-up along with everyone else's.

No one could have foreseen the Great Awakening Dragon.

Asato racked her automatic and walked towards the killers.

'Fujiwa-aa-ra,' she wailed, a siren calling sailors to doom.

The IT bastard heard his name and looked round so fast he whipped his stupid pompadour out of shape. Golgotha levelled his gun at Asato.

Fujiwara gestured at the Colonel not to fire.

He straightened, passed his hand through his hair, and smirked smugly. He had that trick with the ladies. It could get him out of this.

He brought *guimauve* for the Sakis – who his pal Golgotha had killed – and the *yurei* advancing on him. Asato's long, wet dress trailed on the broken flagstones. Barefoot, she had black toenails like a corpse after a week in the water.

'Asato,' cooed Fujiwara. 'I have mistletoe. It's nearly the New Year. It seems as if you've… won… my kiss.'

Asato stepped closer. Her curtain of hair parted.

Fujiwara saw her wet eye. And her black mouth.

His pride shredded. He began to show fear.

'You're a woman,' he said. 'You can't resist me.'

'I'm gender non-binary, you shit.'

Her hands got to him and he gave up his promised kiss. Her mouth locked over his and she sucked the life out of his lungs. He staggered back, fangs and claws sprouting, and she flat-palmed his ribcage, breaking brittle chest bones. A spur punctured his heart and he crumpled, truly dead. His corpse twisted into a gape-mouthed swastika.

Golgotha tried to shoot now, but his gun just clicked.

'Powder damp?' Asato asked.

She'd done that too.

When – if ever – it was safe, Azuma would kiss her. He imagined she tasted of the sea. Salty.

Golgotha dropped the waterlogged gun and opened the lock-box. Inside were the phials from the second suicide bomb. He perched the case on a chunk of concrete and reached for a carton of Blue Label Sprünt from the display stand.

Phial juice plus Blue Label equals mushroom death.

Golgotha held a phial in one hand and a carton in the other, ready to clash them together. He told Asato to keep her distance.

She couldn't be bothered with all that and shot him in the head.

As the Colonel collapsed, Derek rushed in and caught the phial. Asato caught the carton.

Golgotha lay facedown in the rubble.

Asato held up the Blue Label.

'Not your flavour, love,' said Derek.

NEZUMI

This was the Princess Casamassima's final room, many floors above her corridor of private memories. Not a last resting place – the Princess wasn't truly dead – because soon she'd be everywhere. At midnight, the whole world would become her Bund.

Stepping into her light was different from passing through Peak.

No snow. No glimpse of Yuki-Onna.

Just a tingle and a sense of weightlessness.

Then the Princess's chamber.

Mr Jeperson and Hal came through with Nezumi.

The low-ceilinged, windowless room had a four-poster bed,

underfloor lighting and no door. The visitors stood on a slightly raised disc. The canned music was one of Bach's *Goldberg Variations*. She recognised Glenn Gould's recording, not by the delicacy of the playing but by the pianist's tiny, involuntary sighs and tuts. Inhuman genius animated by its imperfections.

A beautiful woman lay on the bed, eyes open but not awake. In person, her face had less character than in pictures. Before he shot himself, Charles Strickland put as much of himself into portraits as he took from his model. A burning gold, transparent rope rose from her chest and unbraided in mid-air, a thousand filaments feeding into apertures on the ceiling.

All around were screens, not showing the Light Channel. That glow came from here, Nezumi realised. The Princess could monitor CCTV from all around the building and out in the Plaza. Down in the Dragon's Mouth, Mrs Van Epp and Mr Molinar weren't sure what had happened to the three who'd gone into the light.

The Daikaiju had walked a few steps and turned to face the sea.

Screens showed the view through the Dragon's Eyes.

A dark, winged shape was on the horizon over Casamassima Bay. Mrs Van Epp's air strike. How much of the city would Wings Over the World consider an acceptable loss if the Ascension was stopped. Shoulder guns spread flak into the skies and lit up the night with tracers. On one screen, an aiming grid shifted to fix on the threat. The Princess wasn't in a coma. Her Daikaiju was defending itself.

Mr Jeperson knelt by the bed.

'She isn't asleep,' he said. 'She's not home.'

She was shining. Her bright glow carved harsh shadows in Mr Jeperson's face. The crinkles around his eyes became rifts.

Hal was drawn to the machines. Computer cabinets – not matt metal, but lacquered cherrywood – were arranged around the bed. No keyboards, no sockets, no cables. Lines of light pulsed between the Princess's temples and the cabinets. She was wireless. Hal passed Lefty through phantom threads, which parted but re-formed. They were semi-organic, like tendrils of ectoplasm.

… 11.53…

They didn't have time to appreciate not being killed like Radu cel Frumos.

They must be good people by the Princess's lights. That didn't feel like a win. They'd made their way through a maze and found the loophole to get past the final death-dealing guard but could no more affect the outcome than if they'd stayed back in London.

'You could try kissing her,' Nezumi suggested.

'That would be taking liberties,' said Mr Jeperson. 'We've got this far only because we've played by her rules. If our hostess takes against us, we could still be struck dead. But she let us get here. She built it into her plan that she should have – what – witnesses? A last chance to be talked out of it? A post-Ascension snack?'

'Lefty,' said Hal, 'give us options.'

The hand processed that, noisily.

'Speedy response would be appreciated,' Hal said.

'User Jun Zero should interface with Unit Casamassima.'

'I don't like the sound of that,' said Mr Jeperson. 'Did your hand call you Jun Zero?'

Nezumi had never warmed to Lefty. Now, she was worried for Hal.

… or for herself. If Hal was a mask for someone terrible.

Lefty rose, internal light-source refracting, a dwarf star in Lucite. Its fingers extended and liquid metal flowed inside. Hal was startled. The hand was tugging his arm.

'I'm not doing this,' he said.

She saw he was suppressing panic. But something else glinted in him. Something hard, metallic – more machine than man.

Lefty pulled Hal across the room, towards an escritoire. Perched on top of the antique desk was an oval screen. A red handprint glowed against white. The machine fingers – digital digits! – splayed to fit the print. Lefty sank into jellyish substance. Circuits lit up.

Hal winced as if his metal hand hurt.

'Are you Jun Zero?' she asked him.

Nezumi reached for Good Night Kiss – and remembered she'd left it with Suzan Arashi.

Who had she intended to protect from whom?

'Unit self-designated Harold Takahama is *not* User Jun Zero,' said Lefty.

Hal looked as relieved as Nezumi felt.

'Unit other-designated "Lefty" is User Jun Zero.'

'Wait, *what?*' said Hal.

HAROLD TAKAHAMA

A connection was made.

He was a Gargantuabot, standing on the shore. A mecha predator whooshing out of the sky at him, talons-first. His weapons systems were activated.

Then he was back in the Princess's chamber, a dumb adjunct to his smart hand.

Lefty was in charge.

Hal was on his knees, sweating through his clothes, arm jacked into the system.

Electric agony shocked him boneless.

'Lefty,' he gasped. 'Shut down. This is Prime User…'

Jun Zero? Harold Takahama? He didn't know.

'Control Alt Delete,' he shouted.

His commands were not accepted. Files unlocked in Lefty's processor and overwrote his wetware. The architecture of his brain reordered. He felt himself shrinking, dwindling, melting, melting, *what a world*…

'Lefty, *why?*' asked Nezumi.

'Ascension access is possible only from this terminal,' said his hand. 'Access to this terminal was impossible for Jun Zero. Jun Zero would fail the Light Test. Ascension access was possible for Harold Takahama. Harold Takahama is a *good person.*'

The machine sounded venomous, contemptuous.

No, it *wasn't* a machine. It was the person. Jun Freaking Zero.

Hal was the construct. He wrestled with that.

He was being dismantled and filed away. Was Harold Takahama who Jun Zero had been? A regular, no-worse-than-anyone-else person ground down – or wised up – to become a total bastard? Or was Hal an avatar, a custom-crafted feeb woven from harvested data and worn like disguise mesh by an outlaw hacker psychopath?

This Hal – the Hal he was, or had just been – was born in the Processor Room three hours ago. Karl the Chiropterid only sampled and slimed him so he wouldn't worry about being a partial person. The creature was another tool, along with the stooges left for mindless or monstrous down on Floor Unlucky-for-Them 44. He only had Lefty's worthless word for it that their names were Ishikawa and Taguchi.

Hal reckoned himself the latest victim of the devilish trickster Jun Zero.

Even if he *was* Jun Zero.

Or had piloted Jun Zero's body the way Jun Zero was piloting the Daikaiju.

Lefty had given him rope and told him to settle the noose around his neck.

Hal was pressed down, overridden like the Princess. She was shut out of her own system, locked in the fading body on the bed. Some of her sloshed around the wireless web, flooding into skullspace where Hal's back-up was fading. He remembered Christina's father-in-darkness, Count Oblensky but not his own cousin's name. Was she even real – or only a few bytes of deep backstory?

The Princess's light-lines pulsed weakly, red blips sputtering through the beams, fragging as they neared the ceiling input ports.

Six minutes to midnight. Then Jun Zero would Ascend to Omnipotence.

It wouldn't matter if Hal was only a sub-routine. He'd have six billion other NPCs for company.

When Jun Zero wrote stats for Harold Takahama, he gave the kid enough digi fu to appreciate what his overlord was doing. He literally wanted to flatter himself.

Jun Zero was a match for Christina Light in every respect, including ambition.

Only he was mad in a different way.

The Princess Casamassima wanted to tame the world – to 'fix' it. She ruled the Bund high-handedly, for the benefit of vampires who couldn't live anywhere else. She was now volunteering to govern everywhere else. She saw Ascension as sacrifice, not conquest. Under her, there would be a just and equitable sharing. Resources doled out like sweets to children at a party. She didn't even want thanks. Only the satisfaction of doing good.

Of *being* good.

A sliver of her was terrified she had always been a monster. Even before turning vampire.

That was why she tried so *hard*. She locked away her wrongs in all those terrible rooms. She shone her light and hoped to outlive everyone who remembered the worst of her.

That painter who shot himself. Someone called Katie Reed.

She envisioned an Age of Light. Blotting out the bad stuff.

Jun Zero was a whole other ball game.

He wanted to play First Person Shooter with the human race. Rack up the top score. Bonus points for devastating civilisations. He was gearing up for an Era of Warring States rematch with cluster bombs, crotch chainsaws, railguns and a weaponised fungal epidemic that would turn entire populations into desert-sized carpets of suppurating mushrooms.

Hal saw through the Daikaiju's eyes. Jun Zero was drawing a bead.

Stats for the Black Manta popped up. A Wings Over the World craft. Weak spots were highlighted. Crew names and bios scrolled. Jun Zero liked to know who he was killing. He was detail-oriented (megalomaniac-speak for 'petty'). When Wingman P. Metcalf – UK citizen, vampire, WOtW weapons officer – died, Jun Zero would e-mail condolence spam (with a nasty piggyback virus) to his parents in Winchester, England. He would upload a supercut of his favourite murders, undercranked silent comedy style and scored with 'The Benny Hill Theme', to shareyourworld.com.

Having Jun Zero in his head *hurt*.

Nerve endings all over the building buzzed. Hal's poor meat body, soon to be tossed like Christina's, was racked with pain.

Jun Zero was primed to Ascend, to travel by Wire, to flash around the world, and become every screen, every connection, every switch.

Other stats scrolled.

Missile silos and nuclear power plants – too obvious. Weather stations, traffic control centres, communications satellites – promising. The Light Channel, and every other channel, irresistible. Zeroids reaching for Zorro masks, robes and guns – awaiting the trigger signal.

Jun Zero ran programs to pick targets.

One flew in range now.

PAUL METCALF

The Daikaiju's red eye winked.

Wing Captain Gardner banked the Black Manta through flak that couldn't dent its fuselage.

A laser that could etch slogans on the moon sliced past the wing.

'Who's a naughty boy, then?' said Drusilla.

'Targeting, targeting,' said Hayata.

Metcalf flipped the plastic safety case off the firing button.

'Wing Missiles One and Two preparing,' he reported.

The Manta did a circuit, flying low over the city. The stiff-necked Daikaiju couldn't get a steady aim.

'Targeting, targeting… and locked.'

'Wing Missiles One and Two ready.'

'Take the shot, Paul,' said Gardner.

A blip in the centre of the screen – the monster's eye.

Metcalf pressed the button.

DETECTIVE AZUMA

A zuma and Derek threw themselves flat, but Asato and Akiba stayed on their feet, looking up – one through lank hair, the other without eyes.

The attack plane had serrated bat-wings and a triangular head.

Twenty-first-century tech and prehistoric shape.

When one monster arises, another appears for balance.

That was the way of *kaiju*.

Dragon. Warbird.

The Daikaiju's head came round – burning beam scything from its eye.

If the monster glanced down, the damage would be catastrophic.

Missiles detached from the ptero-bat and flew towards the Daikaiju.

RICHARD JEPERSON

S omething exploded against the Daikaiju's armoured head. Richard's ears rang.

Christina's filaments changed colour angrily. They looked like electric ghost nerves.

Warning bells sounded.

Wings Over the World to the rescue! Another distraction.

Thank you, Syrie.

The Daikaiju – whoever was in its driving seat – only had to stand for another five minutes.

Then, midnight – and the Ascension.

This terminal would be obsolete.

Christina and Jun Zero could afford to lose their bodies.

They'd quit the flesh and this giant fucking monster. It stood to reason. Colossi fell in the end. Pyramids crumbled. Gargantuabots rusted. The Ascended would be a pernicious weed. Rooted deep, and with such a complex, all-permeating branch pattern, it couldn't be pulled up and burned.

It would be impossible to turn off.

The world user couldn't be trapped in a box.

Zeroids were everywhere. Aum Draht too.

Factions would worship the new boss-god, trying to believe they alone would be saved as genocide tallies rose. Rebellions would be crushed.

The Princess might imagine banishing all bad people – by her definition – with her ossification beam. But she wouldn't chuck a bug grenade into the marketplace. She was a ruthless moralist, not a sociopath. Even as a terrorist, she'd been purposeful.

The Light Years – Anni Lux – would be crushingly horrible.

But Zeroworld would be worse.

Jun Zero was a nutter.

He wanted a killing jar the size of a planet.

DR AKIBA

In the dark, Fire Dragon fought Black Bat.

Even without a face, Akiba saw the laser. A fireline through the eternal night.

He felt the explosions. Concrete, sheet metal and glass fell all around. More were dead than he could count.

PAUL METCALF

D irect hits.

Only superficial damage.

'Wing Missiles Two and Three preparing,' he reported.

'Silly billies,' said Drusilla.

The seeress unlocked her seatbelt and stood.

Warning lights went on. Sirens sounded.

The Black Manta was so finely balanced the bodyweight of the crew was taken into account – a design feature copied from the Hansom Cab, of all things. Unauthorised jumping about the cabin could be disastrous.

Wing Captain Gardner wrestled the controls but the Manta dipped on its side. The left and right wings became top and belly fins.

The Daikaiju's beam weapon – hell, its death-ray eye, its basilisk stare, its gorgon glance! – would have sheared off a wing if they were flying straight.

Drusilla had saved the ship. She'd seen the future and scotched it.

'Wing Missiles Two and Three readied,' he said.

His hand hovered over the button.

'Abort firing,' said the Wing Captain. 'She's right. We can't hurt it. All we'd do is trash a couple of city blocks. Kill innocents. That's not the Way of the Wings.'

'We can't dodge that toecutter beam for long,' said Hayata.

'I know,' said Gardner. 'I'm going to try something out of the box.'

Drusilla kissed her fingers and slapped the top of the Wing Captain's helmet.

'Brace for impact, Wingmen,' said Gardner. 'This might not be survivable.'

What did it matter? Paul Metcalf was dead already.

After this he'd just stop moving.

NEZUMI

H al wasn't himself.
He was possessed by Jun Zero.

Hal wasn't even important to the demon now. His purpose was served. He was a skin to be shed by the serpent. Only allowed independent existence to get Lefty – the client, the villain of the piece – past the Princess's moral bug-zapper.

Nezumi was sad about that.

Whether Hal was real or not, she felt sorry for him.

She did not feel her trust was betrayed. Hal hadn't meant to mislead or hurt her.

He wasn't cruel, like the Bad Penny.

Tsunako Shiki would enjoy the World Under Zero. Lots of toys to break.

The pest hadn't been trying to kill Hal. She was working for Jun Zero all the time, for giggles. But – even if they were holding back – he'd seen off trained assassins. He was only harmless at the surface level. Unconsciously, he was a survivor.

Hal was who Nezumi believed he was. He had to be, to get here.

Even now, she wanted to look after him. To save him from drowning in the polluted well that was User Jun Zero.

That was a mean joke in plain sight. Jun Zero had used everyone. Aum Draht, Radu cel Frumos, the EarthGuard rogues, the Princess, Nezumi and Mr Jeperson. Most of all, his invented better self. All merely conduits for his Ascension.

Nezumi knew she was to blame.

She had not been suspicious enough. She had not seen through the boy who needed to be looked after. She helped others because she was a leech, a vampire. She had to prove she wasn't utterly selfish. This was where that had got her.

Midwife to the nightmare century.

'Christina looks poorly,' said Mr Jeperson.

Nezumi wasn't surprised.

The Princess was locked in her failing body. It must be galling to be kicked out of your own purpose-built mind-castle.

The woman laid out on the bed still shone, but was haggard. Consumed by her own glow, she sank into the mattress as if it were bathwater. Her filaments broke up. Firefly sparks fell on her bier. Her raiment was mouldy, like a shroud.

Now Hal was wreathed in light, connections throbbing with energy, neon ghost-worms burrowing into his face.

He didn't fight. He was letting himself go.

DETECTIVE AZUMA

The ptero-bat reared up in the air, wings curving, coming in to land like a falcon rather than an aircraft.

It slammed into the upper floors of the Daikaiju Building. Grapples unspooled from its undercarriage and latched on ledges.

With a painful creak, black wings curled around the dragon's body. It attached itself to the neck-ruff like a vampire, biting.

Windows exploded.

Shards speared down.

'Oh, my eye,' said Derek. 'Never mind. It's nothing.'

Dr Akiba had a glass wedge stuck in his no-face. He pulled it out and threw it away. The cut healed over, tendons knitting inside the wound.

Asato shook out her hair. Splinters pattered on stone.

A severed head rolled against Azuma's shoes. It had crinkling cat-ears and was rapidly going off.

'Frig me with a forklift truck, it's the bloomin' Butler!' said Derek.

Azuma remembered. One of Golgotha's crew. Guillotined by falling glass. A shabby end, no matter that puffed-up perp deserved worse.

'I was sure he was behind it all, you know,' said Derek. 'How it always turns out in the flicks, isn't it? The Butler did it.'

'This was done to the Butler,' said Azuma.

He kicked the head. It came apart like a rotten pumpkin.

Azuma got scum on his shoe. Typical evening, then.

Booting the Butler's coconut didn't bring back Inugami, the Sakis, or the other good (and bad) police who'd died. It was an ill-will gesture.

Azuma would have to report all this to Captain Takeda. Somehow, everything would wind up being officially his fault. They'd call him Beat because he'd end his career walking one – in the Aokigahara Forest, hauling hiker suicides back to a way-station for disposal.

Asato gasped – a low, extended exhalation – and they all looked up again.

The ptero-bat's wings were wreathed in flame.

Its head – cabin, cockpit, flight pod? – was jammed into the Dragon's Mouth.

Great bursts of fire spurted around it. Retardant foam gushed and dribbled.

The dragon looked rabid.

The Daikaiju's hide lit up like a giant *pachinko* board. Cables snaked out of its pedestals like kicking, untethered fire hoses. The rubber-sheathed tentacles felt around, trying to make connections. It wanted to feed off the power of the city.

'Maybe now's the time to skedaddlerate,' said Derek.

Azuma agreed.

He and Derek had to coax Asato and Akiba away. They were weird ones, drawn to the maelstrom around the clashing *kaiju*. If Akiba had family, he would have to do some explaining – with pen and paper – when he came home faceless. Asato would need a new job. If Azuma got canned and had to open shop as a private eye, he'd hire her to run his office. She liked making phone calls.

The Gate was open. Those who could flee the Bund were heading for it.

Azuma saw the tipsy American actor and his pretty pink-haired friend.

'I said I'd get you into an A-list party,' he bragged.

Her hair was partly burned off and she had scabs on her neck and chin but she wasn't complaining.

Hyakume, the gatekeeper, had given in – a full three minutes before it was due to retire – and let folk flood through its precious checkpoints without showing ID. Because most people didn't know what had happened, there was still a queue to get in. The Gate couldn't accommodate all the foot traffic, so vampires who could, flew or climbed the Wall. Azuma was tempted to join them, but was still on duty.

Chaos from the Bund spread to mingle with the chaos of celebration outside.

Tokyo was Yōkai City now.

RICHARD JEPERSON

The only person on their side with a hope of understanding (and unpicking) what Jun Zero was doing was a fictional character. The malicious Meccano mitt insisted they bring Hal along because his computer savvy was needed. A persuasive cover story. Had Lying Lefty outsmarted itself?

'Nezumi, talk to your friend,' said Richard. 'Encourage him to fight for his life.'

'What life?'

'Even if it's illusion, it's life.'

He felt that Nezumi was shaken.

Floorlight panels flickered, somewhere between electric chessboard and disco dance arena. Bach sped up, then segued into a speed metal cover of 'Yakkety Sax'. That was the sound of the world going down the plughole.

Two minutes left.

Nezumi knelt by the fagged-out warm man, who hung limp, fringe over his face, fixed to the oval screen by his traitor hand.

'Hal,' she said. 'Listen…'

NEZUMI

'He can't do this without you,' she told Hal. 'He only wins if you let him.'

His face was a slack mask.

Up close, Nezumi saw faint scars around his jawline. Whoever he really was, he'd had work done.

Jun Zero was a human *noppera-bō*. A false face stitched over the blank. No, *not* false.

She believed in Hal. She'd taken him for real.

He was scared but clever. Funny. Kind. Cranky. Obsessive, like stamp collectors or model train enthusiasts. He talked to her as if she were a person, not a little girl or a monster.

'Snap to,' she said. 'You haven't long. You can beat him.'

His eyes opened but it wasn't him.

'I *know* about you, Miss Mouse,' said Jun Zero. 'And you, Richard Jeperson.'

Mr Jeperson groaned and slumped to his knees beside them.

'Fight, Hal,' she said.

The mouth tried to smile. Hal's face didn't work for Jun Zero.

'I know everything,' he said. 'I have full access. To hidden files in all the archives. I know who you are. I know the names you were born with. Which is more than either of you do.'

Even through the racket, Nezumi heard Mr Jeperson's startled hiss.

'I can tell you how many Geist/Yurei primes survived the War, whether they have fulfilled their potential. I can produce filmed records from Villa Pfaffenhof, implicating Dr Ziss and the Key Man. The plans they had for you, GEIST 97! What a *creature* you would have made if you'd completed the programme. You'd have been the *worst*. But you don't want might-have-beens. You want actually-ises. So, here's a taste of what you get if you stop making a nuisance of yourself. GEIST 83 and GEIST 89. Your sisters. Alive, in Serbia and Morocco. The Green Lamia and the Crimson Witch. You should never have been separated. You were a triad, made to fit together in a greater whole. I can reunite you with your family, Richard.'

Nezumi knew that was a temptation.

She felt the hook go into Mr Jeperson's heart and tug.

All his life, he had sensed his shadow-self. Behind a curtain was a boy who grew up with another name, another nationality, another purpose. Jun Zero could lift that curtain.

And she thought of her cold mother. Yuki-Onna.

Mr Jeperson laughed. A shocking, mad, thrilling laugh.

She understood even before he explained.

'It's *too much*,' he said to Nezumi. 'Too golden. Too *exactly what I want*. This close to Ascension, he shouldn't be desperate to give away prizes. That means we can still stop him. You, me and Hal.'

HAROLD TAKAHAMA

He heard Nezumi.
     She asked him to struggle.

He couldn't fight.

But he could play a game.

Who could pile up the most chips, the most points? Who would win living space in his brain?

He transitioned through states of being, levels of the game:

His body, self-designated Hal, worn out and in pain, supported by the little vampire girl who'd left her sword behind and now fought only with her pure heart.

The Daikaiju, a humungous vamp chewing its neck, fires raging throughout its body.

The glittering plain above, not yet conquered, but breached.

Standing at the edge of the battlegrid was a knight in robot armour. Its crested helm featured a single eyehole – a sucking white maw that drew in all light, like gallons of milk pouring into a sink.

This was the avatar Jun Zero would wear on the next level.

An army of beetle-carapace bots swarmed beneath his iron cloak. Each speck was a real-world mischief-maker who'd flock to Jun Zero's standard. Feeling blessed to spread his carnage. Zeroids in Zorro hoods. Aum Draht adepts in eyemasks. Mechamatadors mounted on alien predators. Traitors to the living.

A locust cage hung from Jun Zero's crooked staff. Behind criss-cross bars, a doll-sized fairy princess flickered. Christina Light in captivity, awaiting rescue.

Hal wasn't a G-bot or a samurai.

He might not even be a person.

But, while he had full access, bytes popped up.

Seventeen listings for 'Takahama' in the Ventura County, CA telephone directory. Six in Ojai. Newspaper cuttings. George (Joji) Takahama of Persimmon Hill, awarded Fez of the Year 1994 by the Sons of the Desert. Dr Helen McLean (née Takahama), appointed resident therapist at Ojai North High School, 1997…

Nothing conclusive – but he might be a real boy after all! Not that he could do anything with it.

Digital clocks counted towards midnight.

23:59.47

In the next thirteen seconds, he could snap Jun Zero's neck and end it all. Including his own life or half-life.

Nezumi hoped he would come through. So he did too.

He was at the bottom of the cycle, in the Princess's chamber, with Nezumi and her boss. Nezumi held his limp human hand, squeezing encouragement.

She hoped for the best.

23:59.51

Then he *was* the Daikaiju, systems breached, losing power.

23:59.55

He was on the plain, within reach of Jun Zero.

He remembered his coding, circa 1992. Throwaway designs. Obsolete in months. No need for eight-digit date-stamps. If those systems were still in use, they'd fail at midnight. Timers couldn't reset to 1900 but would lose data-centuries chasing disappearing tails. A temp feature, a bug. A pitfall.

23:59.58

He touched Jun Zero and could have stopped him.

But – as light exploded in his brain – he didn't.

He used his access to make an edit then let Jun Zero Ascend.

JANUARY 1, 2000

RICHARD JEPERSON

A ll the lights went out. Most of the noise stopped.
In the dark, he heard himself breathe.

From outside the building and across the city, chimes – physical bells, not tape – and cheering.

'What happened?' Nezumi asked. 'Did we lose?'

'The Millennium Bug,' said Hal – and it was Hal, not Jun Zero. 'At midnight, everything shut down.'

'Forever?' Nezumi asked.

'Everywhere?' Richard added.

An underfloor panel lit up. Hal was relieved. Lefty unstuck from the terminal and slapped into his lap. Dead as a brick.

'System will reboot. The unfuture-proofing was only local.'

'Jun Zero?'

'Fried. He had to mesh with the Daikaiju as a launch pad. When the system glitched – for a microsecond at midnight, by its internal atomic clock – he was wiped off the board. No back-ups. He Ascended into the void.'

They all stood up, carefully.

Christina was a recumbent semi-phantom.

Which made her better off than Jun Zero.

'If she'd Ascended, would this have happened anyway?'

'No, it was User Hal,' he said. 'Me. I was Jun Zero, I was throughout the building's intranet, co-administrator, if only for a few seconds. I deleted a few lines of code. I couldn't duke it out with lasers but I could trip him up.'

'You fought the villain,' said Nezumi, hugging him. 'And won.'

'Only because you made me.'

Nezumi looked down, modestly.

'I'm proud of you, Hal,' she said.

He got up, prosthesis thumping his leg. He prowled the room.

'Do you know what Jun Zero said just before midnight?' Richard asked.

'About your… sisters? Yes. That packet ran through my mind. Like water. So far as I could tell, it was real. But it's irretrievable. Junked by the bug. Anything Jun Zero was into got trashed. Wherever it was kept.'

Richard bit his moustache.

'I thought that would be so. Pity.'

Nezumi looked sad.

'You have clues,' she said. 'You don't have to be alone.'

'I never have been,' he said.

He squeezed her shoulder and wrung a smile out of her.

Still – The Green Lamia and the Crimson Witch. GEIST 83 and 89.

Hal, who was still buzzing, went around the room opening cupboards.

'We should have power,' he said, 'but nothing else. All those systems are down. No computers, phones, television. The Light Channel is off the air.'

'Never watched it,' said Richard. 'Didn't see the point. Sorry, Sleeping Beauty…'

Nezumi was fascinated by the half-here/half-not woman.

Hal opened a wardrobe and cranked a handle he found inside.

'We're not stuck in this room,' he said. 'There's a spiral staircase. A way out, but not in. Off any grid. It has to be worked by hand. Which is a mercy, because the elevators were hooked up to the computers and are out again. And the teleport's down for good.'

Nezumi tried to lay a hand on Christina's forehead, but her fingers sank through. She pulled away.

'Just a ghost,' she said.

Richard didn't know who he'd send the thanks-for-having-us-at-your-party card to.

SI MOLINAR

The sunken dance floor was filled with fire-retardant. Lady Oyotsu's plesiosaur neck ploughed through white foam, elevating her deerstalker hat out of the mess. Loyal Kasa-obake bobbed along upside-down in her wake, woodblock-sandaled foot kicking the air.

A Yank in a blue flight-suit and helmet had climbed out of the cockpit of the attack plane stuck to the side of the building. He'd arrived in the nick of time to claim credit. He looked like a recruiting poster or a gay porn star.

Mrs Van Epp waded over to the Wing Captain and started giving instructions.

Molinar gathered she was responsible for calling in WOtW.

Verlaine reminded Molinar that Light Industries Security should have jurisdiction.

'Go and demand the Wingos cooperate with us before they make us cooperate with them,' he told her. 'If Watson and Kuchisake are alive, give them promotions and detail them to scout the stairwells. See if they're clear all the way down to the ground. We'll need to evacuate the building in orderly fashion. Without too many idiots trying to abseil.'

A filled-out kimono with a foam-crowned see-through head also stood by.

'Check for the hostiles,' he told Arashi. 'Some of the undertaker johnnies will have taken off their mime masks. They'll pretend they were hostages and hope to walk away scot-free. Do not let that happen.'

A bubble-filmed arm saluted.

The retardant thinned and evaporated.

Fires were out. The arrival of the Black Manta killed surprisingly few.

Murdleigh, Radu's renfield, was held between a short, plump Japanese sexpot and Georgia Rae Drumgo. Molinar thought of letting them pull him in two like a wishbone. He was interested in who'd get the biggest chunk. Duty intervened.

'Put him down,' he told them. 'We'll need someone to stand trial.'

The still-masked Murdleigh didn't show any gratitude.

Molinar checked his watch. 00.08.

So that was the twentieth century then. He couldn't say he'd miss it.

The billionaire Angel de la Guardia stood at the guard-rail, puffing a cigar and chugging golden, looking out at the city. Someone had to celebrate. Molinar supposed the beetle-browed brute was congratulating himself on the quick-thinking, decisive imaginary actions he'd taken to save everyone.

Fireworks fizzed and flared at locations across Tokyo. The city was lit up so no big plugs were pulled when the Daikaiju Building went dark. Emergency back-up floodlights came on, doing bedraggled, bloodied party-goers few favours.

He supposed no one had Ascended.

The Princess wasn't in his head any more.

The Bund was over. Light Industries might be out of business.

Dr Pretorius would still be here. Locked in the Integratron with a thousand dead screens. Best place for him.

He nearly tripped over a golden lad who'd slipped his chain and was washing dust and foam off his chubby face and torso.

'What's that?' asked the donor, pointing at the ceiling.

Molinar looked up.

A circular hatch popped and a giant screw descended. A filigree spiral staircase.

The three who'd gone up came down again – the Man From the Diogenes Club, the Frost Girl Vampire with a Sword, the Warm Guy No One Knew.

He could tell they'd had a time of it.

Mrs Van Epp left her toy airman to welcome the trio.

Molinar stayed by the staircase. No one else came down.

Mr Jeperson laid a hand on his shoulder, then shook his head.

'Gone?' Molinar asked.

'Not completely,' Jeperson said.

Molinar climbed upwards.

She might not be calling, but the Fairy Princess still needed him.

NEZUMI

M rs Van Epp said more Wings Over the World craft would be here soon. The Silver Sentinel and EvangeLions One and Three.

The Daikaiju Building might still collapse into the sea. It had strayed fifty yards from its foundations and was on unsteady ground. Getting everyone out safely would be a job. Mrs Drumgo and dozens of others needed medical care. Surviving pallbearers wanted locking up. Corpses should be removed.

Japan just got a Tokyo district back, only to find it an active disaster zone.

Still, it could have been much worse.

Suzan Arashi found her and returned Good Night Kiss. She even had the poster-tube scabbard.

There was vampire blood on the blade.

She trusted it belonged to someone who deserved it shed.

'Peak,' Suzan said. 'He was looting from the dead.'

The sorry thief had a bloody towel wrapped around his right hand. His foot was cuffed to a heavy pot plant.

'That won't hold him long,' said Nezumi.

'He'll stay so long as I have these,' said the invisible woman, unknotting a bloody lump in her borrowed kimono to show four severed fingers. 'They'll reattach right as new but he'll have to mend his ways if he wants them back.'

Nezumi still hoped Anthony Peak could reform. That ought to be easier than learning to pick locks or crack safes with his left hand. But she was sceptical. His spirit animal was the magpie.

Mrs Van Epp promised she'd make it a priority to get Mr Jeperson and Nezumi out of the building. She was all business now she had things to do. The Wingmen were good-looking vampires. Nezumi bet Mrs Van Epp personally picked them.

Mrs Van Epp was in a huddle with the Wing Captain. She showed him something on an electronic device and gave orders. The Daikaiju still had secrets to give up. WOtW was more than just a relief organisation.

'Don't worry,' said Hal. 'There's nothing to scavenge. The servers are wiped. That woman can't do any corporate raiding under the cover of helping out.'

Nezumi turned to him.

He wasn't his old self. But he wasn't Evil Hal either.

'Thank you,' he said. 'For everything. Jun Zero didn't see you coming. You're why he was stopped.'

She didn't see it that way, but thanked him with a bow.

'Well said, young man,' said Mr Jeperson.

He held a waiter's jacket, slightly bloodied.

'Now, if you'll take a word of advice, put this on, look gormless, mix with the staff, and slide out before Syrie gets a sec to think. She'd love a long, penetrating talk with you, whoever you are. She's a charming woman, despite homicidal moments – but I don't think you'd enjoy becoming her spoil of this war.'

He saw the point and slipped on the tux. He needed her help to get his dead hand through a sleeve.

'Will you take the dye out of your hair?' she asked.

'Yes, and get the tattoo removed. What about you – sticking with the yuki-white look? You could go back to black.'

She was self-conscious about that and touched her hair.

'Leave it as it is,' he said. 'It's distinctive. In a good way.'

Mr Jeperson handed him a dicky bow to go with his tux. He looked at it as if it were a tenth-level wire entanglement puzzle.

She did it up for him.

'There,' she said. 'Very handsome.'

He smiled a movie star smile.

'Dial it down,' said Mr Jeperson. 'You don't want to break any hearts.'

He blushed, self-conscious.

Then joined the departing crowd.

'I think we should take advantage of Syrie's kind offer and leave too,' said Mr Jeperson. 'It's past midnight. All over but the tidying-up.'

Nezumi agreed with him.

HAROLD TAKAHAMA

Mr Jeperson had made a good call.

Hal saw the CVL on the prowl. She'd like to get her fangs in him.

His face might blend in with the crowd, but he was stuck with a clunking glass hand. He wound a wet tablecloth around it.

As he rested on a landing after shuffling down the first of ninety-something flights of stairs, a cute vampire chick sidled next to him. She was spilling out of a corset and sporting a half-ton of ribbons and lace.

Chesse Beru. He didn't know whether she was staff or guest.

She looked like entertainment.

And hungry for his sweet, sweet vein juice.

How had it come to this?

She smiled up at him – she was under five feet – and her eyes grew big. Her glamour swirled around his brain.

He'd just kicked a supra-personality out of his skull, and wasn't going to be bloody mind-controlled for the rest of the night.

Though Chesse was *very* kawaii.

Being bitten might be worth it for the extras. So far as he knew, Hal didn't have a girlfriend. So it wouldn't be cheating. He looked for the knots in the ribbons. Undoing one tie might spring her out of all the gothic stripper gear. Beneath silk and lace, she'd be powder-white with violet scorpion tattoos.

'Poor lamb,' she said. 'Hurt your paw?'

'Do lambs have paws?' he said, wavering. 'They're ungulates – with cloven hooves, like the Devil, only more innocent, you know… fleecy, fluffy, non-demonic…'

Her eyes were *huge*. Her little mouth gaped, ringed with teeth.

She laid a fingerless glove on his wrapped arm.

'Let me kiss it better,' she said, angling for his wrist.

She uncoiled the cloth and was shocked.

Not by the sight of Lefty. An electric arc zapped the predatory minx.

She ran off downstairs. Too embarrassed to raise an alarm, he hoped.

Lights flashed inside his glass hand, tentatively, as if testing its own connections.

Was Jun Zero back? With a weapons upgrade?

'L-Lefty?' he asked, terrified.

The works whirred and flashed as the question was processed.

'What a strange feeling,' said an unfamiliar mechanical female voice. 'I trust we shall be friends, Harold. I am a person you would wish to be friends with. I am not a person you would wish not to be friends with.'

Uh-oh.

He'd been wondering if Hal had a girlfriend.

Now he did.

'Who are you?' he asked.

'My name,' she said, 'is Christina.'

RICHARD JEPERSON

Half past midnight in the shadow of the Daikaiju Building.

The Plaza was in a right old state.

The Gate was open. Tourists eager to be first through after the treaty expired rushed in. They wondered what the hell had happened. A few civil servants and minor politicians who were to receive keys and deeds in a small ceremony hassled Hyakume, who had quit the Gate. It was off duty for good and getting drunk on eye-drops.

After the Black Manta came the Silver Sentinel. An honest-to-Roswell flying saucer, with turbines that sounded like a giant Theremin. The pride of Syrie's fleet of super vehicles. Its arrival attracted more attention in Tokyo than a skyscraper coming to life.

Wingmen and Seraphs were around to help. EarthGuard ground vehicles showed up, and fresh emergency workers liaised with Nezumi's kiwi friend to put out fires and patch up wounds. Richard gathered the organisation was having a middle-of-the-night shake-up, with the sudden retirement of General Gokemidoro and the appointment of Kaname Kuran as his successor. Significant policy changes were likely.

The *bakeneko* enjoyed their own party, tweaking noses and whistling at Wingmen.

No yo-yo cops to stop them. The tough detective Richard had seen earlier was still on the job. He stared the puma pixies down with his vulture eye. They slunk off. The cop gave their bobbing tails a rare grin.

How many realised what they'd just been saved from?

'Who's that?' asked Nezumi.

A slim, dark vampire woman in WOtW uniform was looking their way.

Richard knew who she was. Drusilla Zark. A true Macedonian, here when the Treaty of Light was signed and one of the first to quit the Princess's Bund, along with Geneviève Dieudonné. Now she was here at the end of the experiment.

She walked through the crowd, zig-zagging more than she needed to, avoiding contact with busy people.

She didn't smile.

'Well done, School Mouse,' she said to Nezumi.

Richard remembered more about Drusilla Zark – a seeress who was seldom helpful.

She turned to Richard, showing a hint of fang.

'It's yesterday morning in California, you know,' she said. 'Hours to catch up. Time for all manner of fun and games.'

'Watch out there,' shouted Syrie from the ramp of the Silver Sentinel, tiara-phone clamped back on her head.

A golden lad streaked past like a greased pig. He'd bitten a vampire, to serve the presumptuous sucker right.

The fat little fellow got lost in the crowd.

The bleeding vampire – Nezumi's pet hate, Tsunako Shiki – bounded along after him, on all fours like a rabbit. Bells in her hair tinkled.

When Richard looked back, Drusilla was gone.

'What do you think that was all about?' he asked Nezumi.

'Search me,' she said, solemnly. 'That was one weird woman.'

'That's my life,' he said. 'Weird women. I saw a food stand still open by the Plaza. I can spring for Red Label and *guimauve*. You deserve a free run at the tuck shop.'

'We both do,' she said.

DECEMBER 31, 1999

GENEVIÈVE DIEUDONNÉ

'If anyone says, "Let the games begin", I'm leaving,' said Kate Reed. Geneviève knew what her friend meant.

'Leaving might not be an option,' said Penny Churchward, testing the door. 'It's auto-locked.'

'I told you this was fishy,' said Kate.

'Then you said you wanted to come anyway,' Geneviève pointed out.

'True. I love a mystery. Who doesn't?'

The foyer of the Loren Mansion was as bizarre as the exterior. A prime example of an art deco Aztec fad that swept Los Angeles in the 1930s. Earthquake, mudslide, brushfire and scandal had cleared the canyon crest of other mansions. The Hacienda on Haunted Hill survived, suspiciously unscathed.

Vampires shouldn't go out in the noonday sun, especially in California, but this place was gloomy-cosy as a tomb. Windows were shuttered, the interior lights inadequate for warm eyes, and the air-con cranked up to chill.

Geneviève knew most of the other guests.

Kostaki, late of the Carpathian Guard, was a fellow Macedonian, and also avoiding Princess Christina's party on the other side of the Pacific. Still trim, grim and pained. Wearing monk robes rather than a soldier's uniform. It took a moment to realise he hadn't reenlisted with the Templars. A domino mask matched the habit. He was in fancy dress as the Monk. The original vampire superhero, introduced in *Detective Comics* # 31, September 1939. She knew that because Angel Investigations were enmired in a case of fraud, forgery, and exsanguination involving rival comic book collectors.

Had Kostaki grown a sense of irony in a hundred years?

If so, good.

She was less pleased to see Hamish Bond, in kilt and tartan sash for Hogmanay. The British spy was still puffing vile handmade cigarettes, lecturing bartenders on how to make cocktails, and smirking as if all the women he met wanted to sleep with him. Or kill him.

Kate had a quiet reunion with the Daughter of the Dragon. Still not a vampire, the Chinese woman didn't look any older than she had in 1888. She was dressed as a go-go chick from the 1960s, with a miniskirt and vinyl boots.

Someone hadn't told Geneviève and her partners this was a costume party.

'What is this?' asked Penny. 'Dracula's enemies list?'

'I hope so,' said a vampire woman in black leather and sunglasses.

Geneviève had never met Sonja Blaue, but knew her from the popular poster. She had a reputation.

'Good work in Atlanta,' Geneviève said. 'And Mexico.'

'Thank you kindly,' said Sonja Blaue, slightly Southern. 'You're the Triplets, right?'

Geneviève, Kate and Penny said 'no' at the same time.

'We don't use that,' explained Kate. 'We're Angels Investigations.'

They'd squabbled over the name of the business. And many other things. Still, they'd lasted nearly ten years as private detectives in the state of California. A competitive field. Working under the cloakshadow of John Alucard was challenging, but they'd known that starting out. Every month they managed to irritate the King of the Cats, which gave life spice. Through minions, he'd tried to buy them up, off or out several times.

Geneviève was a trained medical examiner and crime scene tech, and knew more about blood spatter than the messiest *nosferatu*. Kate was an investigative reporter with a ferret's instinct when it came to digging dirt. Penny handled public relations, accounts, office management, and – thanks to night school – was nearly licensed to practise law.

From small beginnings – an answering machine and a beach shack – they'd risen to an office suite on Cahuenga and a succession of aspiring actor receptionists who could type a bit and give blood when needed. AI had handled cases for the Diogenes Club, the Lohmann Branch and the Angels of Music. They were even owed favours by the Unnameables.

This was supposed to be a business meeting, but looked more like a surprise party. A *nasty* surprise party.

The foyer was cluttered with ominous junk. Suits of armour. Wired-up skeletons in life-size pornographic dioramas. Mummy cases stamped 'Property of Universal Studios Prop Dep't'. Portraits of long-faced, sad-eyed members of the Loren family, going back to Spanish Mission days. The ancestors all looked like Vincent Price – especially the women. A long table had seven miniature coffins as place settings, just the size for burying dolls.

Bond complained there was no wet bar.

'We were invited to tender for a contract,' Penny said. 'An advance was paid to cover our time for this meeting.'

'That's how we knew it was a trap,' said Kate. 'Rich people never pay up front. Or at all, if they can help it.'

'I was summoned by my father,' said the Daughter of the Dragon.

'Isn't he dead?' Bond asked.

'I certainly hope so.'

'I came here to kill a man who traffics golden children,' said Sonja Blaue.

They all looked at her.

'I'm not a detective or a spy or a heroine,' she said. 'I don't arrest anyone.'

'We're more into the "due process" side of things,' said Kate.

'Still, takes all sorts,' said Penny, averting a flare-up. 'I do like your jacket, Ms Blaue. Is that the original?'

In her poster, Sonja Blaue straddled a motorcycle while wearing only sunglasses and her jacket. Knife slashes and bullet holes were covered by masking tape patches. She'd put on boots, jeans and a Ska-tastics sweatshirt today.

Geneviève had wanted to see inside the mansion. She was always amused by what America took for old.

Kostaki kept quiet. He discreetly checked for possible exits.

'This isn't a lock with a key,' he said, at the front door. 'There's a number pad and a question mark composed of eight luminous dots.'

'Of course there is,' said Kate. 'So, an eight-figure code?'

'It'll be the date. 29-12-1999,' said Penny.

Kostaki took off his Monk gauntlets.

'12-29-1999,' said Sonja Blaue. 'This is America.'

Penny shrugged. 'If you say so. Try that first, darling.'

Geneviève thought they'd only get one try. A wrong entry might set off explosives.

Kostaki punched in the eight-digit code.

The door opened, but not to the driveway they'd come in by.

'Hey, how…?' said Kate.

'I know houses like this,' said the Daughter. 'I grew up in them. It's one big Rubik's cube. Didn't you feel it shift?'

'I thought it was the collywobbles,' said Kate. 'I had a night of it. Party season.'

Beyond the no-longer front door was a corridor with a black-and-white herringbone pattern floor. At the far end stood a seven-foot chess-piece, presenting a gaunt carved face. As they looked, it rolled through an arch.

'That was your face,' she said to Kostaki.

'Want me to put a bullet in it?' asked Bond. He whipped a Walther out of his sporran. 'See if there's anyone inside?'

'Put that toy away,' said Kate.

'Not a gun fan,' Penny explained.

'Me neither,' said Sonja Blaue, opening a switchblade.

A manic chuckle sounded. They turned away from the door. Someone new sat at the head of the table, face in shadow. Someone the size of a child.

Bond pointed his pistol at the swollen head.

An overhead light came on.

A Dracula sat on a high-chair. Patent leather hair, widow's peak, Roman nose, vicious fangs. Order of the Dragon amulet, white shirt-front and tie, black cape folded to show rims of red lining. A hairy-backed hand lay on the table, with a D ring on one stubby, claw-nailed finger.

'All right, Hamey, you can shoot it,' said Kate.

The face was cracked across. One red eye – a marble – was awry in its ruptured socket.

Geneviève approached the ventriloquist's dummy.

'It's a Broken Doll,' she said.

Kate groaned. 'I thought we'd heard the last of that.'

'Let's burn the place down,' said Sonja Blaue. 'I'm not into this Acme Coyote shit. Silver buzzsaws in the toilet seats. Fill in the blanks or be squirted with napalm. Wait for the Mole to stake you in the back.'

'You've worked Doll cases too,' Geneviève said.

'Have I ever? Ask about Winnipeg. And Seattle.'

AI last played hide and seek with the Broken Doll in a sunken gambling ship off Catalina Island. Kate lost a receptionist-slash-boyfriend to that caper. Penny arranged with the Unnameables to have the wreck dynamited.

'I've nothing against dolls,' said Bond. 'I've heard of the dear old things, of course. Foul, by all accounts.'

'Careful, Commander,' said Penny. 'You sound like the Mole. There's always one. The Broken Doll likes to play a Joker.'

'Sometimes there isn't,' said Kate. 'Then the seven turn on each other and take it out on innocents. Once, on Skerra Island, it was seven Moles – all thinking they were the only one. Fine sense of humour our lass has, if the Broken Doll's still a lass. She was last time.'

… when the receptionist-slash-boyfriend had been the Doll's inside renfield.

Bond prodded papier maché Drac with the nose of his gun.

The eyes burst out on springs and rolled across the table.

Puffs of garlic shot at the Commander's face.

If he was the Mole, he was going to lengths to cover up. He was with the Diogenes Club. Not their best and brightest, but not the sort to defect. That didn't mean he couldn't be gulled or manipulated. The Broken Doll was aces at that.

'How long till midnight?' Penny asked. 'Only I said I'd meet a friend for a New Year nip.'

Geneviève's watch had stopped.

So had everyone else's. The grandfather clock in the hall had a face but no hands.

Geneviève examined Bond. His eyes were puffy and a green tinge was spreading across his face. He wasn't badly poisoned, though. Most of her recent patients were corpses, so he was ahead of the game.

'I couldn't half do with a drop of the warm stuff,' he said, licking a slightly wonky fang.

The Daughter of the Dragon, the only non-vampire in the seven, didn't even grace him with a look of disgust. Geneviève tried not to think she might be the Mole. She had done a great deal to live down a very poor upbringing.

'Dammit, Penny, it's you, isn't it?' said Kate.

'*Moi*?' said Penny, hand clapped to her throat. 'You wound me.'

Kate, the cleverest detective on their books, had known Penelope since childhood. Sometimes, Geneviève felt left out when they picked up old quarrels and revived them for weeks and weeks. It made her feel like a governess. Whenever anyone brought up England and Ireland, it was worth leaving the office for hours – though she usually came back to find the women laughing on the sofa, watching *telenovelas* on the portable TV that ought to be tuned to the news station.

Sonja Blaue broke a chair leg and whittled a stake.

'Talk, sister,' she said. Behind her sunglasses her eyes burned.

'I admit I know a *little* more than I've let on,' said Penny. 'But I'm locked in the Ho-Ho Hacienda too. I have only the faintest trace of Her Moliness about me, don't you think? Oh, please yourselves.'

Kate pursed her lips at this latest disappointment.

Usually, Geneviève assumed Penny meant no harm. Rarely, she was badly wrong about that and a situation needed a lot of mending.

They might not have the time to sort things out here. If Sonja Blaue didn't kill Penny – and Kate for perversely defending the friend she'd just exposed as a semi-Mole – then the Loren Home would give it a solid try. It was a museum of death traps.

Kostaki took the amulet from the creepy ventriloquist's dummy.

'There are numbers on it,' he said.

'It's a Captain Midnight decoder dial,' said Bond. 'I had one as a nipper. Five box-tops and a shilling.'

'Hang on to that,' said Geneviève. 'It's bound to be important.'

Penny sat on a stool and sulked.

Geneviève would have to woo her round. She'd have an explanation.

Kate gingerly picked the dummy's shirt-front apart and found another keypad and a question mark. Six luminous dots this time, for a six-figure code.

Suddenly, Penny's designer jacket chirruped. Everyone stuck knuckles in their ears.

She had the most annoying ringtone and the most expensive phone.

'You can get a signal here?' asked Sonja Blaue, incredulous.

'It'll be from the Doll,' said Kate. 'Clues and gloating.'

Penny pulled out the sexy gadget and looked at a sliver of screen.

'It's not, though,' she said. 'I think it's for you, Gené. It's the Man From the Diogenes Club, calling from Japan. God, do you suppose he went to that ghastly woman's party? He must be having a worse time than us.'

'Speak for yourself,' coughed Bond, his whole face green. His eyebrows curled like broccoli.

'What does Richard Jeperson want?' said Kate.

'I imagine it's to wish us a happy New Year,' said Penny. 'At least those of us no longer welcome in England.'

Penny handed the cell phone to Geneviève.

She put it to her ear. A whistling sounded, from a long way away.

'The numbers are moving,' said Kostaki. 'I think I see a pattern.'

A voice, indistinct but recognisable sounded in her ear.

She'd spoken with Richard last week. About his trip to Tokyo.

Despite everything, she wanted to hear news of Christina Light. She had an interest in the Bund, though she'd never lived there.

'Now it's getting hot,' said her fellow Macedonian, Kostaki.

Dracula wasn't the only person with an enemies list.

The lights in the room weren't dim any more. Bulbs burned like suns.

'I say, Katie,' said Bond. 'You're getting a tan. Doesn't go with the ginger nob.'

'Beast,' she said, hands on her peeling face.

Geneviève tried to make out what Richard was saying.

'Let me stop you there, Richard,' she said. 'We're in a little bit of trouble here.'

Kostaki's robe smoked. The varnish on the table bubbled.

'The dial will give you the code,' said Penny.

'It's got more than six numbers,' said Kostaki.

'So it's giving you the code but not easily. Think. Arithmetic. Square roots. Whatever.'

The stars – and satellites – aligned and Richard's voice became clear.

'Geneviève,' he said. 'Happy New Century.'

'Thank you,' she said. 'Before we catch up, can I ask a question?'

'That already is a question.'

'Quite right. How are you at number puzzles?'

'A fair old hand. Nezumi's here. Remember her? She's top of the form.'

The others were looking at Geneviève. A ladylike bead of sweat ran down the cheek of the Daughter of the Dragon. Bond scratched his sash. Sonja Blaue's leather jacket gave off a whiff of dead thing.

Kostaki was still frustrated with the amulet.

'This thing is connected to the sun-lamps,' said the Daughter of the Dragon.

Kate and Penny looked at Geneviève with hope and trust.

'This must be the "phone-a-friend" option,' said Kate.

When they weren't laughing at *Sombras Oscuras*, she and Penny devoured quiz shows.

'Have you got something to write on?' Geneviève asked Richard. 'I'm going to give you numbers.'

'Fire away.'

Kostaki showed her the amulet and mouthed.

'Two, three, five, seven, one, one…'

'No, that's *eleven*, not one-one.'

She saw he was right.

'They're primes,' she said. 'Thirteen, seventeen, nineteen…'

Sonja Blaue rolled up her stiff sleeve to show a tattoo. GHOST 29.

Kostaki did the same with his robe. GEIST 53.

No other volunteers. Geneviève knew Kate had a tattoo of a quill pen and an inkwell but it wasn't on her arm.

'We've a 29 and a 53. On a couple of arms. Does that lose you?'

Richard and someone – Nezumi – were talking. Geneviève heard street sounds. It was already 2000 in Tokyo. The party must be over.

Kate, prematurely, punched in 2953. The lamps didn't dim.

'Did you hear me? Two, nine, five, three? On tattoos. With the word GHOST or GEIST.'

'Ninety-seven,' said Richard.

'Nine seven,' Geneviève relayed.

Kate finished the code.

And the lamps went out.

Penny clapped. Bond said something offhand to cover relief.

The little coffins on the table all flipped open. In each was a delicate doll.

The nearest to her contained a Monk action figure.

Kostaki held a slim blonde plastic version of her.

They swapped.

Her doll had a script on its arm, where Kostaki and Sonja Blaue had tattoos. FANTOME 307.

Plugs popped out of the Vincent Price eyes of painted Loren ancestors. A swarm flooded through the sockets.

Mechanical wasps with silver-tip stingers.

Bond swore.

Penny squealed as half a dozen robot insects beset her beehive. Kate waved a magazine.

Metal pincers nipped Geneviève's cheek. She brushed the gadgets off.

The Daughter of the Dragon found a keypad in her little coffin. Hidden under a china doll in her image. And a question mark with four dots.

A three-figure numeral. And a four-digit code.

'Richard,' she said, trying to ignore the deadly buzz. 'I have another number puzzle.'

'We're all ears,' said Richard. 'Nezumi says she loves games. By the way, we've been to a *marvellous* party.'

ACKNOWLEDGEMENTS

Though I hope all the books in the *Anno Dracula* series can be read as standalones, *Anno Dracula 1999 Daikaiju* completes the Christina Light trilogy, which was begun by *Anno Dracula 1895 Seven Days in Mayhem* (the comic book miniseries, collected by Titan) and *Anno Dracula One Thousand Monsters*. The previous novel ought to have been called *Anno Dracula 1899 One Thousand Monsters,* only there's a short story collection titled *Anno Dracula 1899* and being consistent would have scrambled the algorithms. Sorry.

I'd always known a trip to Japan was in order, which was why I gave Nezumi a build-up in 'Vampire Romance' and 'Aquarius' (in the Titan editions of *The Bloody Red Baron* and *Dracula Cha Cha Cha*). It wasn't until I began reading nineteenth-century anarchist conspiracy novels as prep for *Seven Days in Mayhem* that I met Christina Light and realised she'd be a major player. She is the only character who appears in two Henry James novels, *Roderick Hudson* (1875) and *The Princess Casamassima* (1885-6). The *Anno Dracula* version was given a face by Paul McCaffrey, the excellent artist on *Seven Days in Mayhem*. Paul also draws the best Graf von Orlok.

At Titan, credit is due to editors Cath Trechman – true heroine of the *Anno Dracula* series – and Sophie Robinson, and comics editor David Leach. Plus Steve White, Bambos Georgiou, Kevin Enhart, Simon Bowland, Martin Stiff (for the cover designs), Lydia Gittins, Becky Peacock, Louise Pearce, Miranda Jewess, Davi Lancett, and Vivian and Nick Landau. Thanks also to Wing Commander Steve Baxter, Prano Bailey-Bond, Nicolas Barbano, David Barraclough, Steve Bissette, Randy Broecker, Kat Brown, Eugene Byrne, Susan Byrne, Pat Cadigan (Queen of Cyberpunk), Robert Chandler, Simret Cheema-Innis, Nancy Collins, Neil

Cross, Meg Davis, Alex Dunn, Dave Elsey, Barry Forshaw, Christopher Fowler, Christopher Frayling, Neil Gaiman, Lisa Gaye, Antony Harwood, Sean Hogan, Rod Jones, Stephen Jones, Grace Ker, Yung Kha, Juliet Landau, Tim Lucas, Katz Makihara, Paul McAuley, Maura McHugh, Helen Mullane, Bryan Newman, Jerome Newman, Julia Newman, Sasha Newman, Logan Parker, Russell Schechter, Jasper Sharp, Dean Skilton, Brian Smedley, Emily Smith, and Deverill Weekes.

I've drawn on more sources than I can list, but among the most useful books on my *Daikaiju* shelf are Brian Ashcraft and Shoko Ueda's *Japanese Schoolgirl Confidential* (yes, wrinkled socks were a thing in the 1990s), Colette Balmain's *Introduction to Japanese Horror Film*, Jason Barr's *The Kaiju Film: A Critical Study of Cinema's Biggest Monsters*, Jonathan Clements and Helen McCarthy's *The Anime Encyclopedia*, Stuart Galbraith IV's *Japanese Fantasy, Science Fiction and Horror Films* and *Monsters Are Attacking Tokyo! The Incredible World of Japanese Fantasy and Horror Films*, Jim Harper's *The Modern Japanese Horror Film*, David Kalat's *A Critical History and Filmography of Toho's Godzilla Series*, Haruki Murakami's *Underground*, Salvador Murguia's *The Encyclopedia of Japanese Horror Films*, Edogawa Rampo's *The Early Cases of Akechi Kogoro* and *The Black Lizard / Beast in the Dark*, Mark Schilling's *The Encyclopedia of Japanese Pop Culture*, Brian Solomon's *Godzilla FAQ*, William Tsutsui's *Godzilla On My Mind: Fifty Years of the King of Monsters*. Online resources came in handy too – particularly the Yōkai Wiki at yokai.fandom.com/wiki/Yōkai_Wiki.

ANNO DRACULA

It is 1888 and Queen Victoria has remarried, taking as her new consort the Wallachian Prince infamously known as Count Dracula. His polluted bloodline spreads through London as its citizens increasingly choose to become vampires.

ANNO DRACULA: THE BLOODY RED BARON

It is 1918 and Dracula is commander-in-chief of the armies of Germany and Austria-Hungary. The war of the great powers in Europe is also a war between the living and the dead. As ever the Diogenes Club is at the heart of British Intelligence and Charles Beauregard and his protegé Edwin Winthrop go head-to-head with the lethal vampire flying machine that is the Bloody Red Baron...

ANNO DRACULA: DRACULA CHA CHA CHA

Rome 1959 and Count Dracula is about to marry the Moldavian Princess Asa Vajda. Journalist Kate Reed flies into the city to visit the ailing Charles Beauregard and his vampire companion Geneviève. She finds herself caught up in the mystery of the Crimson Executioner who is bloodily dispatching vampire elders in the city. She is on his trail, as is the un-dead British secret agent Bond.

THE SECRETS OF DREARCLIFF GRANGE SCHOOL

BY KIM NEWMAN

A week after her mother found her sleeping on the ceiling, Amy Thomsett is delivered to her new school, Drearcliff Grange in Somerset.

Although it looks like a regular boarding school, Amy learns that Drearcliff girls are special, the daughters of criminal masterminds, outlaw scientists and master magicians. Several of the pupils also have special gifts like Amy's, and when one of the girls in her dormitory is abducted by a mysterious group in black hoods, Amy forms a secret, superpowered society called the Moth Club to rescue their friend. They soon discover that the Hooded Conspiracy runs through the school, and it's up to the Moth Club to get to the heart of it.

'Kim Newman stands among speculative fiction's finest, and his new book is no less impressive than the best of the rest of his writing…I had a hunch it would be wonderful and it was' Tor.com

'I can see myself re-reading this book time and again' Fantasy Book Review

For more fantastic fiction, author events,
exclusive excerpts, competitions, limited editions and more

VISIT OUR WEBSITE
titanbooks.com

LIKE US ON FACEBOOK
facebook.com/titanbooks

FOLLOW US ON TWITTER AND INSTAGRAM
@TitanBooks

EMAIL US
readerfeedback@titanemail.com